Emile Zola, born in Paris in 1840, was employed by the publishers Hachette before beginning his career as a writer with *Contes à Ninon* (1864). In 1871, *La Fortune des Rougon* launched the great series of twenty novels *Les Rougon-Macquart*, depicting the life of a family under the Second Empire. Zola's interest in painting is enshrined in *Edouard Manet* (1880), and his work as a photographer reveals his close links with the Impressionists. Towards the end of his life his famous open letter *J'accuse*, indicting the persecutors of Dreyfus, caused an upheaval in French politics. He died in 1902.

By the same author

The English titles of those of Zola's works which are available from
Granada Publishing in paperback and/or hardback editions are indicated
in parentheses.

EMILE ZOLA

The Beast in Man

Translated from the French by Alec Brown

PANTHER
Granada Publishing

Panther Books
Granada Publishing Ltd
8 Grafton Street, London W1X 3LA

Published by Panther Books 1985

First published in Great Britain by
Elek Books Ltd 1956

This translation © 1956 by Elek Books Ltd

ISBN 0-586-06652-7

Printed and bound in Great Britain by
Collins, Glasgow

Set in Ehrhardt

Introduction

Zola's *Bête Humaine* is for me a 'best-loved' novel, and making an English version of it has proved not merely an intellectual exercise, but also emotionally absorbing, even terrifying. For that reason I should perhaps explain both how and why I so love and esteem this book – for I count it one of world literature's masterpieces (and I have read most of them in their original tongues).

I first loved *La Bête Humaine* in adolescence. I then lived a highly spiritual, a thinker's disembodied intellectual life, and of jealousy had known only one episode, heart-racking indeed, but an illness mainly spiritual.[1] Consequently, certain vital colours of Zola's novel being concerned with that profounder jealousy whose impulses lie on the far side of real sexual knowledge, my first love for Zola's work was inevitably for the shadowy black-and-white drawing by which alone I then apprehended the story.

In such faint reproduction the plot of a novel is stripped bare of what seems superfluous. It is thus reduced to something like one of Lamb's tales from Shakespeare, so different from the blood-curdling reality from which they are distilled.

But even on that level the pattern of *La Bête Humaine* is fascinating. Seven people, inter-connected in their lives by pairs, are all drawn into the supreme crime by the most convincing logic of action: they are all murderers. By unrestrained sexual debauch, Judge Grandmorin has driven little Louisette Misard to her death. He has also debauched the book's heroine, Severine. He has then married her off to Roubaud, who, when he learns the truth . . . But no, I must not tell the story here. Sufficient to say that there are seven horribly plausible murders[2] in an amazing network of concentrated action, occupying little more than one year, dovetailed together with the most convincing motivation. In addition, there is the brilliant picture of the prime mover of

[1] Any disturbance of balance is surely illness.
[2] The story of one murder and the proposal of another make this work a pendant to Dostoevsky's *Crime and Punishment*.

the Ministry of Justice shielding the guilty and acquiescing in the bill of murder also being footed by completely innocent Cabuche, whose only sin was to love twice with calfish innocence.

We have here a canvas as compact with motive as any Ibsen play. The springs are all fully wound when the curtain goes up. They are all fully unwound when at last it comes crashing down. It is plot construction at its very highest, while in the background, never obtrusive, but always displayed with masterly suggestiveness, are the two great backcloths, which in this black and white version also stand out vividly: aspects of the life of the Western Railway Company and the vision of the decadent last convulsive efforts of France's Third Empire.

By reason of these backcloths alone, *La Bête Humaine* has reason to be counted among the world's great masterpieces. We with so many judicial murders on our conscience cannot remain unmoved by the picture of M. Denizet with his logic and 'proofs'. What a temptation it must have been to the arch-propagandist in Zola to over-do either of these pet political themes! Yet instead he offers a dazzling example of restraint. Neither time when Camy-Lamotte withholds the crucial piece of documentary evidence does Zola show him as doing so solely for political reasons. It is the magic momentary touch of Severine Roubaud's dainty fingers, plus a guess what delights she afforded that practised old libertine Grandmorin, or, when she is dead, the mere evocation of her sexual appeal that stirs to regretful desire and thus to mercy the senile blood of the ageing arbiter of justice.

The wonder of the design is enhanced by the self-control which Zola maintains, despite his innate love for harsh daubs of pure colour. He shows indeed such a remarkable sense of sheer architecture that one is almost inclined here to embrace his pet, stubborn and rather silly belief in hereditary forces. Lover of garishness though he was, in his best work he always produced the stark lines of masses of granite;[3] his basic form redeems the surface of limestones.

---

[3] Zola's father had a grand architectural mind. He came to France as an engineer from the North Yugoslav littoral, where he was born amid colossal naturally ordered masses of limestone and miracles of the handling of stones, such as, for instance, the cupola of Shibenik Cathedral. The father had landscape vision too, and today Marseilles regrets not having taken up his plan for the position of the port, and France brings to completion hydro-electric works in the mountains which he began.

We come to the novel's other backcloth, the poetry of the Western Railway Company of France, 85 years ago (twenty years before Zola wrote of it), when its engines still used such Heath Robinsonish devices as the Furness lubricator, by which oil in a container on the upper side of each single outside cylinder is drawn through a small valve in the cylinder wall which during the exhaust stroke opens about 1/16″, closing automatically again on compression. On *Lison*, which Jacques Lantier drove with such artistry, the valve-gear (apparently that devised by the Belgian engineer Walschaert),[4] happened to be peculiarly susceptible to fine adjustment, though – as Lantier was never tired of lamenting – *Lison* was 'heavy on oil'. (Of course, the Furness lubricator was partly responsible for that.)

But though enjoying this might seem to require an engineer's mind, Zola so vigorously refrains from specialist detail that anyone can understand the lyricism of Jacques' love for *Lison*. Zola depicts this sublimation of sexual love with astonishing delicacy. Never once does he over-step the borderline of fine taste. Just before his description of the parts of *Lison*'s body becomes too blatant, he sharply brings it all down again to humdrum engineering terms. It is inspired objectivity[5] and there are five great passages of this sort: that which introduces us to the theme, the drive through the snowstorm, Lantier taking his once beloved locomotive out of the Batignolles locomotive yard, Lantier putting *Lison* away one night at Le Havre, the destruction of *Lison* by Flora – and, of course, also the death ride on insensitively-valved Locomotive 608, a sister engine of *Lison* unfortunately utterly devoid of her soul.

All this brilliant plot and décor are however merely the groundwork on which with frenzied savagery Zola piles a crude impasto of colour. But it is never clumsy, for turgidity, violence and madness are the very essence of the emotions which Zola is here concerned to illuminate. I doubt if anybody has ever equalled the revelation of jealousy he gives us in this book. Tolstoy in his *Kreutzer Sonata* is a mere toddler, Daudet in his *Sapho* too pure. For jealousy springs not only from pique at neglect by the rival interest. When openly sexual,

[4] It was a form of radial gear.
[5] It would be absurd to think of such writing as either realism or the intellectually 'constructed' 'naturalism' of a writer addicted to card-indexes.

it springs in a more absolute manner from the mere thwarting of coital love, and it is a gloomy fact that at its highest point naked coital love becomes not only grossly sentimental, but also grossly possessive. When either men or women enter that unreal world they inevitably draw near this madness of excessive, obsessional possession which can all too easily logically culminate in murder. In short, they are out of their minds. Their individualism has grown till it denies all social being, by which it becomes evil and self-destructive, for man by his nature is a social animal.[6]

La Bête Humaine is indeed a fine pamphlet against that endemic disease of western civilization – romantic love as the basis of marriage.

It is here that Zola's real genius shows. In the mere complex of plot, in the political satire or poetry of the machine, there is virtuosity of craftsmanship; greatness, yet not genius. But the power both to know – and to know one's knowledge,[7] plus also the strength to lay it all bare within the framework of a plausible, invented story of this consummate form, exemplifies the supreme power of creation. Emile Zola is here so vital that not only does the underlying motivation of action emerge unscathed by the didacticism which he throws in, but even his own convictions are amended by his own truth.

This is one of the novel's highest points. In a thrilling story, Zola reveals man the social animal pitted against man the absolute individual, and demonstrates that the community too, whenever it tries to be absolute, is corrupt, fallible and unjust. Man the social animal like man the individual has in himself the instincts of right living and fairness, but if even to further these he carries his powers to their limit, becoming absolute, he is but man the beast again, the denial of the higher, social creature.

To conclude, there is a curious pointer to the folly of regarding Zola as merely a craftsman building up his novels from rationally accumulated details. One of the two misprints which have crept through all editions of *La Bête Humaine* up to the latest reprint (1956) shows him unable to be subservient even to the simplest of the facts

---

[6] The hermit is no exception proving the rule, for he is not a true individual at all, but less than one, being merely the inversion of man the social entity.

[7] How revealing the poverty of our language regarding levels of knowing!

recorded in his notebooks.[8] In the last chapter he actually did not make up his mind whether the final events took place in June or July, and hovered between the two months! The same night is on subsequent pages a 'warm June night' and a 'sultry July night'. Yet if ever any timing of action were fixed, this should be, for the date is clearly enough conditioned by that of the declaration of the Franco-Prussian War, through which Zola had lived, and about which he was about to write one of his grandest works (*La Débâcle*)! Even in small detail the man of vision and insight is more powerful than the man of many notebooks!

Tarrant Gunville,
April 1956

ALEC BROWN

---

[8] Both errors of course are corrected in this translation. The first was a curious substitution, in the tool-shed where Jacques and Severine first make love, of benches (bancs) for the sacs (bags) of which they make their lovers' couch. But this might have been an undetected printer's error. The other mistake must be Zola's own!

1

Entering the room, Roubaud put down the pound loaf, the pâté and the bottle of white wine. Phew! Before going on duty that morning, 'Ma' Victoire must have packed a frightful lot of slack on her fire, it was simply stifling in the room. So the assistant station-master opened a window and leant his elbows on the sill, looking out.

It was a tall block in which the Western Railway Company housed some of its staff, the end building on the right of Amsterdam Close. In the angle of the attic roof, which here made a bay, this fifth-floor window overlooked that vast cutting of the St Lazare station, which bites into Europe Square, a sharp recession of the horizon, on this particular afternoon still vaster by reason of a mild and moist mid-February sky, with grey sunshine.

On the far side, dusted with sunlight, the houses of Rome Street etherealized, their outlines blurring, fugitive. To the left the enormous smoke-dim glazed roof over the main line platforms gaped wide, as if to invite the prying eye – the Post Office building and the foot-warmer house cut them off from the smaller roofing over the Argenteuil, Versailles and Circle lines, while on the right, beyond the starred iron-work of the Europe bridge which dissected the whole cutting into two parts, the tracks reappeared to lead away towards the Batignolles tunnel in the background, and the three double-tracks which shot out from under the bridge immediately underneath the window ramified into a broad fan of countless twigs of gleaming metal, finally vanishing beneath the roofing. Bare of crops, the gardens of the three pointsmen's boxes just outside the tunnel lay exposed to the eye. In the tangled, hazy confusion of coaches and engines which cluttered the tracks one blotch of red from a large signal stained the pallid daylight.

For a while this tangled scene engaged Roubaud's interest. Dreamily, he compared it with his own station at Havre. Every time that something brought him to Paris for the day and he made 'Ma' Victoire's apartment his *pied-à-terre*, his profession thus preoccupied

him. For instance, under the main line roofing the arrival of the
Mantes train had just brought life to the platforms. He also followed
the movements of a small tender-locomotive with three low-coupled
wheels shunting coaches into sidings. There was also another, a
powerful express loco, emitting dense black smoke, which was rising
very straight and very slowly in the motionless air. It was however the
3.25 Caen train, already packed with passengers and awaiting its
engine, which really drew his attention. He could not actually see the
locomotive, which for the moment was halted on the far side of
Europe Bridge. He could only hear it demanding the all clear with
short pips of its whistle, like any human being overcome with
impatience. Somebody then shouted orders, and with a short blast the
engine signified that it had understood. But before it moved, there
was a moment of silence, then the steam cocks were opened and
the vapour hissed on the ground in deafening jets. Next, he saw the
immense puffs of white vapour belly and eddy up from under the
bridge, belching like so much downy snow out between the girders.
The whole of one corner of the station world turned white with it,
while the smoke accumulating above the other locomotive spread its
black veil. From the background came a prolonged whistling, more
cries of command. The reverberation of rolling metal was suddenly
muffled, the clouds rent, and behind it all Roubaud caught sight
simultaneously of a Versailles train on the up line and an Auteuil train
on the down, crossing each other.

Just as he was about to withdraw from the window, hearing
somebody pronounce his name now made Roubaud lean out. Down
below him, on the fourth-floor balcony, he saw a young man of about
thirty. It was Henri Dauvergne, leading guard, who lived there, with
his father, assistant station-master in charge of the main lines, and his
two fair-headed sisters, Sophie and Claire, twenty and eighteen
respectively, charming girls, keeping house for their two menfolk on
6,000 francs in a state of never-ceasing jollity. At this very moment,
there was the elder one billowing with laughter while the younger
sang, and a cage-full of birds from the Caribbean vied with her in
their trills.

'What a surprise, Roubaud,' cried Dauvergne, 'seeing you in Paris!
Ah, but of course, you've run up about your little brush with the
Under-prefect, I suppose?'

Propped again on his elbows, the Havre assistant station-master explained that he had indeed had to catch the 6.40 that very morning, orders from the management head bringing him to Paris, on the carpet. He had been damn lucky not to get the sack outright!

'And how's the wife?' Henri Dauvergne enquired.

The wife, he said, had been glad to come with him, at the moment she was still out shopping. He was expecting her back at any moment now. 'Ma' always left them the key when they came up to town. They liked to lunch there quietly, on their own, while the old dear was still tied down below, at her salutary post. Yes, he ran on to explain, on this occasion they had wanted to finish their business first, so they had had a roll at Mantes, and he was expecting his wife for lunch. But it was already after three, and he was dying with hunger.

Just to round off the conversation, Henri put one more question. 'Spending the night in Paris?'

Oh no, they were both going back that evening to Havre, he said, catching the six-thirty express. Yes, bit of a day off. They only disturbed you to have you on the carpet. Then it was back to the mill at once.

For an instant the two railwaymen exchanged glances and meaningful nods. But they could no longer hear each other, a demented piano had suddenly burst into full sonority, it must be Dauvergne's sisters hitting the ivories together. They were laughing at the top of their voices, and their cage birds were all excitement too. The gaiety suddenly communicated itself to young Dauvergne, and with a wave of his hand, he disappeared indoors, leaving the assistant station-master gaping for an instant down at that balcony from which such youthful high spirits came. A moment later, raising his eyes, he saw that the Caen loco had closed its cocks and the signals were directing it to its train. The last wisps of white vapour were swiftly swallowed up in the vast belchings of black smoke which were fouling the sky. Then Roubaud too withdrew inside.

He turned away from the cuckoo-clock with a gesture of exasperation. 'Three twenty!' What the hell could be making Severine so late? Get that girl into a shop and you could never get her out again. To mask the famishment which was turning his stomach, he had the idea of laying the table. He knew his way about the spacious two-windowed room which served as kitchen, dining-room and bedroom

13

in one, with its walnut furniture, its bed draped with a red cotton counterpane, its sideboard and dresser, its round table and its Normandy wardrobe. From the dresser he took napkins, plates, knives and forks, and two glasses. They were all sparklingly clean. He became like a child playing with a doll's set in the happiness he found in arranging the things on the white linen. For Roubaud loved his little wife dearly, and he grinned broadly to himself as he thought of the lovely cheerful laugh she would greet him with the moment she opened the door. He had put out the pâté on a plate and stood the bottle of white wine beside it, then was suddenly all alarm, his eyes searching everywhere, till all at once he realized the forgotten little packages were still in his pockets, and he drew out the tin of sardines and the piece of gruyère cheese.

The half-hour struck. Roubaud strode up and down, swinging round at the least sound, his eye on the stairs. Waiting like that, with nothing he could do, he suddenly halted as he passed the mirror and quizzed himself. Though he was on the brink of forty, there was no hint of ageing in him, unless it was that the flaming auburn of his crisp hair had rather faded. His full, sun-gold beard was still bushy enough. Indeed, with strength which in spite of his modest height was outstanding, he was rather satisfied by his own appearance – the somewhat flat, low-browed face on a thick-set neck pleased him, he approved of his own florid, rotund countenance and the large and lively eyes which glinted in it. Since he had married a wife fifteen years his junior, these frequent fleeting check-ups in looking-glasses proved most reassuring.

There was the sound of footsteps, and he ran to take the door off its latch and peep out. But it was only the woman next door who sold papers in the station returning home. He withdrew again, and turned his attention to a box of shells on the sideboard. It was a very familiar box, that, a present which Severine had made 'Ma' Victoire, for 'Ma' had been her wet-nurse. And that trifle was enough to send the whole story of his marriage flashing through his mind. It would soon be three whole years now. Born at Plassans, in the *Midi*, son of a carter, he had left the army with his sergeant's stripes, to spend a longish time as general porter at Mantes, then stepping up to chief porter at Barentin. It was there that he first got to know his wife, when she used to come from Doinville to catch the train together

14

with Miss Berthe, daughter of M. Grandmorin the Assize Judge. Severine was only the younger daughter of a gardener who died in service with the Grandmorins, but the Judge made himself both her god-father and her guardian, and he spoiled her terribly, made her his daughter's companion, sending them both together to the same Rouen boarding-school. Severine had had such native distinction that for a long time Roubaud contented himself with desiring her from a distance, with all the passion a refined working man can work up for a delicate piece of jewellery which he covets. It was indeed the only romance he had ever known. He would have married her even if she had not a penny to her name, just for the pleasure of having her, but when at last he did pluck up courage, the reality surpassed his wildest dreams, for when Judge Grandmorin gave away Severine, it was together with a nest-egg of ten thousand francs, and then, being in retirement, and on the board of the Western Railway Company, he had made Roubaud his protégé, so that immediately after his marriage he found himself no less than Assistant Station-Master at Havre!

As a matter of fact, to help him, Roubaud must also have had a fine record as a good employee, being reliable, punctual, obliging, perhaps none too bright, but on the other hand very straight, that is to say, possessor of excellent traits sufficient in themselves to explain the ready response there had been to his application and the rapidity of his promotion. But he himself preferred to think it all due to his wife. He simply adored her.

However, when at last he had got the sardine tin open, Roubaud definitely lost patience. They had agreed to meet at three. Where on earth could Severine be? She was not going to tell him that buying a pair of boots and some slips took a whole day. And when he now caught sight of himself again in the glass, it was to see his forehead above his bristling eyebrows cleft by a deep furrow. In Paris not only all sorts of dangers but also all sorts of deceits and peccadilloes came to his imagination. The blood rushed to his cheeks, and he gripped his ex-porter's fists as if he were again pushing a luggage waggon, turned back into an unreasoning monster of sinew. He was indeed all at once in such a flood of blind rage that he could have made mince-meat of her.

Then the door swung open, and there she was, all freshness and

15

delight. 'It's me . . .' she cried. 'Darling! You must really have thought I was lost!'

In the fresh blossoming of twenty-five years, she seemed both tall and slender and very supple, yet, being small-boned, she was well fleshed. At first glance she was not at all pretty, her features being long, her mouth rather prominent, with large, prominent teeth, but when one looked more closely, it was at once to be captivated by her charm and the unusual widely-set blue eyes under opulent masses of jet-black hair.

And now, as her husband just went on staring at her with that worried, fugitive look she knew so well lingering on his face – and did not answer – she added: 'Oh! what a rush it has been . . . Just think, there wasn't a single bus, so as I didn't want to spend on a taxi, I just ran . . . See how hot I am!'

'Now come off it,' he said, roughly, 'you're not telling me you've come straight from the *Bon Marché*.'

But without hesitation, and with the sweetness of a child, she collapsed against his chest and pressed her pretty, dimpled little hand on his lips.

'Naughty, naughty,' she cried. 'Shh! You know how I love you.'

Her whole person breathed such sincerity, he felt her still so frank, so upright, that he could do nothing else than crush her fiercely to him. His suspicions always evaporated like that. And she fitted in with his reaction, loving him to pet her like that. He smothered her with kisses, which however she did not return. Here indeed was really the origin of his inward unrest – in this passivity of hers, she was like a big child, all affection which was almost filial, totally ignorant of the real fire of love.

'And so you've stripped the *Bon Marché*, eh?' he teased her.

'But of course, I was going to tell you . . . Only do let's eat first. How ravenous I am! . . . Ah, but just a moment, I have a little present for you. Darling, say: *my ickle present*.'

She had thrust one hand into her pocket, where she was holding something which she did not produce. She laughed up close into his face.

'Quick, say: *my ickle present*!'

Complaisant husband, he laughed foolishly, and submitted. 'My ickle present,' he said.

16

What she had just bought him was a large clasp knife to replace one he had lost and had for the past fortnight been bemoaning. He uttered a cry of delight, finding this lovely new toy superb with its ivory handle and gleaming blade. He would make immediate use of it, he cried, while she, delighted by his pleasure, laughingly made him give her a penny – 'so that their love should never be severed.'

'And now let's eat, let's eat!' she cried. 'No, no, darling, please don't shut it up yet, I am so hot.'

She had joined him by the window, and now lingered there, leaning on his shoulders, surveying the huge bowl of the station. For the moment there was no smoke to obscure the view, and the coppery disc of the sun was going down in pure mist behind the houses of Rome Street. Beneath them a shunting engine was bringing up the ready formed Mantes train, due to leave at four twenty-five. It pushed the coaches in the length of the platform, under the roofing, then was uncoupled. In the background, under the hangar of the Circle lines, the bumping of buffers indicated the last-minute addition of further coaches. And in the centre of the tracks was a heavy slow-train engine, its driver and fireman black with the dust of their trip. The engine was stationary, as if weary and out of breath, only a slight sound of steam escaping from a valve. It was awaiting the signal, to make its way to the Batignolles engine yard. There came a click from a signal and the red light went out. The engine pulled slowly out.

'High-spirited, those Dauvergne girls, aren't they,' said Roubaud, as he left the window. 'Hear them strumming their old pianner? I saw Henri Dauvergne just now, he said give you his respects.'

'Luncheon is served, sir, luncheon is served,' cried Severine. She flung herself on the sardines, wolfing them. Those rolls they had eaten at Mantes were certainly a long way off! It always went to her head when she came to Paris. She was always thrilled with the delight of window-shopping and her *Bon Marché* purchases would make her quite feverish. At one go, every spring, she blued all she had saved during the preceding winter. She liked to buy everything at Paris, making out that she saved the cost of her ticket that way. She babbled on now, without missing a single mouthful, either. Rather abashed and blushing, at last she ended by blurting out how much she had spent – more than three hundred francs!

'Damn it, you spread yourself pretty well, don't you, for the wife of

17

an assistant station-master!' grumbled Roubaud, playfully. 'But surely you said all you needed was six slips and a pair of boots?'

'But darling, there were such bargains going . . . There was a length of silk with such lovely stripes, and such a choice little dream of a bonnet, and petticoats ready made up with embroidered flounces, and all for a mere song, I should have paid double at Havre . . . They are going to send the things, then you'll see!'

He decided to laugh it off, she was so lovely in her delight, with that air of penitent embarrassment. Besides, it was all so dandy, this picnic lunch ensconced in this cosy room where they were alone, far better than any restaurant. And Severine, who as a rule drank only water, let herself go and tipped down her glass of wine without noticing it. The tin of sardines was emptied and with the lovely new knife they tackled the pâté. It was a delight, it cut so well.

'But you, darling, I quite forgot – how did you get on, my pet?' she cried suddenly. 'You make me do all the talking, not a word from you how that awful *prefect* business went.'

In detail, he proceeded to relate how the managing director had dealt with him. A proper dressing-down, it had been. But he spoke up for himself, he told the absolute truth, how that little squirt of an assistant prefect had insisted on taking a dog into a first-class compartment when there was a second-class coach reserved for sporting gentry and their animals. Yes, he told them all about the dispute which developed and every word that had been said. But in the end, the big chief had said he was quite right to insist on respect for the regulations, but the bad thing was what he himself admitted saying. He had said: *'You won't always be the bosses!'* And he was already under suspicion of being a republican.

The fact was, the debates which had marked the opening of the 1869 session of the Assembly and lurking apprehension of the results of the forthcoming general election had together served to put the administration in a captious mood. The result was that he would definitely have been transferred as punishment, had it not been for the strong support of Judge Grandmorin. Even so, he had had to sign the letter of apology which Judge Grandmorin had suggested and indeed had himself drafted.

Severine interrupted. 'There!' she cried. 'Was I not right to tell you

18

to write to him and go to see him this morning before you went to take your medicine? I was sure he would get us out of the hole.'

'Yes, M. Grandmorin's very fond indeed of you,' said Roubaud, 'and he has a lot of influence in the Company, too ... But at the same time you at least ought to see that the fact that I do my job properly does mean something. Yes, I can tell you straight, m'dear, they didn't spare the praise, they said that even if I was rather lacking in initiative, I could always be relied on, I was a faithful servant of the Company, in a word, I was a sticker, and they praised me for it. Though, my sweetie, if you had not been my wife and Judge Grandmorin had not taken my side out of affection for you, I'll admit I was beaten, they would have sent me to do penance at some poky little place back of beyond.'

Staring hard into space, and as if talking to herself, she murmured: 'You're right there, darling, M. Grandmorin is a man with a lot of influence.'

There was a silence. Lost in thought, she stared wide-eyed into the distance, and for the first time left her plate untouched. No doubt she was recalling the days of her childhood, down in the country at Doinville Manor, four leagues distant from Rouen. She had never known her mother. When gardener Aubry, her father, died, she was nearly thirteen. It was then that the judge, already a widower, had taken her in as companion for his daughter Berthe, living with his sister Madame Bonnehon, widow of a manufacturer. The manor-house, indeed, was now hers, and she had looked after the two girls. Six months after Severine's marriage, Berthe, the senior by two years, herself became the wife of one de Lachesnaye, a dry, sallow little fellow who was counsellor of the Rouen court. The year before, Judge Grandmorin had still been president of that court, having retired to that post in his own home country after a dazzling national career. Born in 1804, Deputy Public Prosecutor at Gigne after the 1830 revolution, then at Fontainebleau, then Paris, subsequently Prosecutor at Troyes and Director of Public Prosecutions in the Appeal Court of Rennes, he thus ended his career as first President of the Rouen courts. A millionaire, he had been a member of the Council of State since 1855, and on his retirement was promoted Commander of the Legion of Honour. Since the earliest she could remember, Severine knew him exactly as he still was – a rather squat, stout little man, who went white early, but with that glint of gold of one who had formerly been fair – his hair cropped short and brushed upwards, his face framed in a close-cropped beard without moustaches, his countenance itself square and rendered still more forbidding by hard blue eyes and a large nose. He had a brusque manner and made everybody about him shake.

Roubaud had to speak quite loud when for the second time he demanded: 'Well, whatever are you thinking about?'

She shuddered, a sudden shiver passed through her, as if taken by surprise and scared.

'Why, nothing, in particular,' she said.

'You're not eating,' he said, 'not hungry any more?'

'But of course . . . You'll see.'

Draining the glass of white wine he had poured her, she finished the slice of pâté on her plate. Then came an alarm: they had eaten up all their loaf and there was not a morsel to go with the cheese. There were cries of dismay, then they both laughed when after turning everything over they unearthed a hunk of stale bread right at the back of 'Ma's' dresser. Though the window was open, it was still warm in the room and the young woman, having the stove at her back, could scarcely be said to have cooled down. Indeed, she was pinker than before and the rather unexpected turn this talkative lunch in 'Ma' Victoire's overheated room had taken had rather agitated her. At the same time, thinking of 'Ma' brought Roubaud right back to Grandmorin, for was not 'Ma' herself another who owed the judge a great deal. Seduced as a girl, but her child dead, this wet-nurse of Séverine's whose own mother had died to give her life, later becoming the wife of a locomotive fireman of the Western Railway Company, 'Ma' had lived poorly in Paris on her sewing (her husband eating all they earned), when a meeting with the girl she had suckled renewed old ties so that in the end she too became a protégée of the judge, and now he had got her a job in the sanitary service, attendant in the first-class *ladies*. There could not have been a better job for her. The Company paid her a bare 100 francs a year, but she made nearly 1,400 more on the tips, and there was this room thrown in, heating inclusive. In short, 'Ma' was nicely off, and, as Roubaud figured it out, if only, instead of wenching hard at both ends of his run, the husband, a fellow named Pecqueux, had brought home his full

20

fireman's wages (which counting bonuses came to 2,800), they would have had more than 4,000, twice what he himself had at Havre as assistant station-master!

'I don't say,' he declared, 'but some women would not much like looking after public lavatories, yet a job's a job, you know.'

They had at last taken the edge off their hunger, and were only nibbling languidly, slicing off little pieces of cheese, just to spin out the feast. Their tongues also slowed down.

'By the way,' he said suddenly, 'I meant to ask you – whatever made you decline M. Grandmorin's invitation to spend two or three days at Doinville?'

Freed by the satisfaction of digestion, his mind had just been running through the call they had made that morning, near the station, at that house in Rocher Street. He had seen himself back in that large but perhaps forbidding study and again heard the judge telling them that tomorrow he was going down to Doinville. And then, as if in response to a sudden impulse, he had suggested instead taking today's six thirty evening express together with them, and taking on his god-daughter down to stay with his sister, who had long since been asking after her. But Roubaud's young wife had insisted that for more than one reason she was unable to accept.

'I must say,' Roubaud continued, 'for my part I could see no harm in your taking a trip down there, you could have stayed on till Friday, I would have managed all right. Surely, placed as we are, it's to our advantage to keep in with M. Grandmorin and Madame Bonnehon. It wasn't exactly tactful, declining their kindness, especially since your refusal really seemed to hurt him. Which is why I kept on trying to persuade you to say *yes*, till you tugged my coat like you did. Then of course, I piped up like you, but without making head or tail of it . . . Why didn't you want to go?'

Severine looked this way and that and made an impatient gesture. 'Now, could I leave you all by yourself?' she demanded.

'That was no reason . . . After all, in the three years we've been married you've already been there twice and spent a week each time. There was no earthly reason why you shouldn't go a third time.'

The young woman's discomfiture increased. She turned her eyes away from him.

'If you want the truth,' she said, 'I just didn't want to go. You are surely not going to force me to do things I just don't want to do?'

Roubaud spread his arms wide, in a gesture which assured her that of course he would never force her to do anything. But, all the same, he did go on to say he thought there was something she was hiding from him . . . 'Was it because last time Madame Bonnehon wasn't all that nice to you?' he asked.

Oh, no! Madame Bonnehon had always been most hospitable. Madame Bonnehon was so kind a lady. Tall, powerfully-built, with her lovely fair hair, Madame Bonnehon was moreover still beautiful, though she was fifty-five. Since she was widowed – indeed, since before, while her husband was still alive – it was whispered of her that her heart was often engaged. But at Doinville everybody worshipped her. She had turned the manor into a great social centre. All Rouen society went there, especially the bench. Indeed, it was among the judicial profession that Madame Bonnehon had so many of her men friends.

'Then, my dear,' Roubaud persisted, 'it was the Lachesnayes who turned you the cold shoulder, now, wasn't it?'

There was no question, since her marriage to M. de Lachesnaye, Berthe had never been quite the same to Severine. She was rarely well-disposed, poor Berthe, and so unprepossessing, with that red nose of hers. Rouen ladies always made much of how distinguished she was. But what was to be expected, with a husband like hers, ugly, hard, miserly, apparently specially made to vent his bile on his wife and make her spiteful. Yet, in spite of all that, Berthe had always been very nice to her old friend, and Severine had nothing she could reproach her with.

'Then it's M. Grandmorin himself somehow put your nose out of joint down at Doinville?'

'M. Grandmorin put my nose out of joint? What a ridiculous idea!' Severine cried, and went on, with tense little phrases – one hardly saw M. Grandmorin. In the park he had a little summer-house of his own. It opened on to a little lane nobody used. Nobody knew M. Grandmorin's goings and comings. Why, even his sister never even knew exactly when he arrived there. He would take a cab at Barentin and drive out to Doinville by night. He might spend several days in his summer-house, without a soul knowing. Oh no, M. Grandmorin was the last one to be in anybody's way, down there.

'I only spoke,' said Roubaud, 'because you yourself have told me a score of times that when you were a girl the judge used to put you in a blue funk.'

'Oh come, a blue funk, darling, you always exaggerate so . . . Oh yes, I know he hardly ever laughed. That's true. He would stare so hard at you with those big eyes that you looked down at the ground at once. I have seen people so upset they could not utter a word, he impressed them so with the name he had for severity and wisdom . . . But me he never scolded, I always felt he had rather a weakness for me . . .'

Once again her voice grew faint, and her eyes were lost in the distance.

'I remember . . . when I was quite a kid and used to play with my friends on the walks, if he came along, they would all hide, even his own daughter, Berthe, she was always in terror she'd done wrong. But I used to face him, calm as you please. When as he passed by he saw me with a smile on my face and my little snout cocked up in the air he used to give my cheek a pat . . . Later, when I was sixteen, whenever Berthe wanted to get something out of him, it was always me she got to ask him. I spoke out, I never looked the other way, I could feel his keen eyes piercing me through and through, but I never cared, I was always so sure he would grant whatever it was I asked . . . Oh yes, it all comes back to me, it all comes back. Why, there's not a clearing in that park, not a ride, not a room in the manor I cannot recall if I close my eyes.'

She was silent now, her eyelids closed. Over her flushed and swollen cheeks seemed to pass some hidden thrill of former events, events which perhaps she did not mention. And so she remained for several moments, her lips twitching slightly, as if some distressing nervous tic was plucking at the corners of her mouth.

'No doubt about it, he has been kind to you,' resumed Roubaud, who had just lit a pipe. 'Not only did he give you the education of a lady, but he was also very decent with that little bit of money you've got, and he rounded off the sum too, when you married me . . . Without counting that he's sure to leave you something, he said so to my face one day.'

'Yes,' murmured Severine, 'the house at Maufras Cross, that property the railway has cut in two. Sometimes we used to spend a week there . . . Oh, not that I really count on it, the Lachesnayes are bound to see to it he leaves me nothing at all. Indeed, I would really rather he didn't leave me anything at all!'

These last words she uttered with such sudden force that she astonished him. He took his pipe from his mouth and stared open-eyed at her.

'Aren't you a queer one!' he murmured. 'Everybody says M. Grandmorin has millions, what would the harm be if he included his god-daughter in his will? Nobody would be in the least surprised, and it would certainly suit us all right.'

And then an idea which flashed into his mind suddenly made him laugh.

'Or are you afraid they'll think you are his daughter?' he asked. 'Because, you know, for all his seeming a bit of an icicle, there's a deal of spicy tittle-tattle about him. People do say that even while his wife was among the living he had a go with all the maids. Why, I believe the old rogue is capable of putting any woman on her back even at his age . . . By Jove, just think, if you were his child!'

But Severine had leapt angrily to her feet, her cheeks burning, real terror in the uneasy blue eyes beneath the heavy mass of her black hair.

'His child? His child? . . . Please don't joke about such things, do you hear me? Do you think it possible? Am I a bit like him? And that's enough of it, let's talk about something else. I don't want to go to Doinville because I don't, because I would rather go back to our little home together.'

He nodded forcibly, to calm her with a gesture. All right then, if that got her on the raw. He smiled. He had never before seen her so worked up. Must be that white wine. Anxious to be forgiven, he took up his new knife again and wiped it well, with a lot of lavish praise, and then, just to show how razor-sharp it was, he started trimming his nails with it.

'Quarter past four already,' murmured Severine, standing by the cuckoo-clock. 'And I've still some errands to do . . . We must think of our train.'

But, before putting the room a bit straight, she went to the window,

24

to lean out again, as if to finish calming down. Then Roubaud left his knife, left his pipe, and also got up from the table, to go up to her and take her gently in his arms, from behind. He held her thus embraced, put his chin on her shoulder, and leant his cheek against hers. Gazing out, neither stirred.

Beneath them the little shunting engines kept up their ceaseless to and fro, one could hear them only just moving, husbanding their power, their wheels muted, their whistles all discretion. One now went right away under Europe Bridge, taking a Trouville train off to the marshalling yard sidings. Away on the far side of the bridge it brushed closely by an engine come alone from the sheds all fresh and debonair, copper and steelwork gleaming, ready for the trip. This engine now halted, and gave two short blasts of its whistle to the signalman, who almost immediately sent it on to its train, which was ready waiting at one of the main-line platforms – it was the four twenty-five Dieppe train. A flood of passengers were pressing forward. Severine and her husband could catch the rumble of luggage barrows and the clatter as one by one the men thrust the foot-warmers into the carriages. Now the engine and tender had bumped the leading luggage waggon and the foreman shunter could be seen screwing up the coupling. Towards the Batignolles the sky had grown more sombre. Like a cloak of ash the dusk seemed to descend on the fanned-out tracks, absorbing the house fronts, while throughout this whole process of blotting out could be heard the ceaseless coming and going of suburban and Circle trains. Beyond the gloomy tenting of the vast station roofing far away over darkened Paris, floated the tattered, lurid tufts of engine smoke.

'No, no, let me be,' murmured Severine.

Gradually, excited by the warmth of that young body which he thus held enlaced in his arms, he had without a word taken her in a new grip, which fondled her more intimately. The very odour of her person went to his head, till, suddenly arching her loins to shake him off, she ended by driving him quite mad. With one jerk he had her away from the window, which with his elbows he managed to push to. His mouth had found hers, his lips crushed hers, and he carried her towards the bed.

'No, no!' she cried. 'We are not at home here. Please, no, not in this room.'

She felt a little dizzy, the food and wine had gone to her head, still buzzing from her fevered rush through Paris. The over-heated room, the remains of their meal on the table, all the unexpectedness of this trip which was turning into an intimate little party – all this had fired her blood, quickened her with animal desire. But in spite of this, she now refused him, resisted, arched her back against the foot of the bed, in a rebellion of terror which she herself could not have explained.

'No, no, I don't want to,' she repeated.

But he was flushed and held her firmly in his big, harsh hands. He was quivering from head to foot, he could have crushed her in his grip.

'Silly,' he said, 'who will know? We can soon straighten the bed after.'

At home, at Havre, she meekly enough always let him do what he wanted after the midday meal, days when he was on night duty. It did not seem to afford her any pleasure, but she always exhibited a cheerful softness, affectionate recognition of the pleasure it evidently gave him, and what now made him mad was feeling her suddenly as he had never known her, ardent herself, all vibrant with bodily desire. Her ebony hair cast a shadow in her calm periwinkle eyes, and her powerful lips were blood-red in the soft oval of her face. This was a woman he did not know at all. Why on earth did she refuse him?

'But why ever not?' he cried. 'We have time.'

Then, most inexplicably troubled, torn by forces she herself did not seem to distinguish quite clearly, as if she had not even known herself before this moment, she uttered a cry of real pain, which made him hold back.

'No, no, please, please leave me be!' she pleaded. 'I can't tell you why, it chokes me, the mere thought of it, just now . . . It would be all wrong.'

They had both sunk now to the edge of the bed and went on sitting there. He brought his hand down over his face as if to remove something that smarted. Seeing him thus cooled down again, she was all sweetness and in her anxiety to show him that all the same she did love him very dearly, she bent to implant a kiss on his cheek. For a moment they just sat there like that without a word spoken, getting back to normal. He took her left hand and began to toy with an old

26

gold ring – a snake with a tiny ruby as head – which she wore on her ring finger. Ever since he had known her she had worn that ring.

'My little snake,' she murmured, automatically, as if in a dream, for she thought he was examining the ring and felt she absolutely had to say something. 'How funny, it was at Maufras Cross that he gave me that, for my sixteenth birthday.'

Roubaud looked up in utter astonishment.

'Who do you mean?' he demanded. 'M. Grandmorin?'

When her husband's eyes fastened on hers, Severine started violently back into wakefulness. She felt the air chill on her cheeks. She would have answered him, but could find nothing to say. A sort of paralysis took possession of her and choked her.

'But you always told me it was a ring your mother left you,' he said.

There was still time to take back those words she had let fall in a state of utter forgetfulness. All she needed to do was to laugh and pretend to be such a silly. Instead, she turned stubborn, no longer mistress of herself, thoughtless.

'But darling,' she murmured, 'I never told you my mother left it me.'

Roubaud's eyes quizzed her sharply and the colour left his cheeks too.

'What? You never told me your mother left you it? But you've told me that a score of times ... There's nothing wrong about the judge giving you a ring, he's given you lots else besides that. ... But why on earth hide it from me, why lie about it, with all that talk about your mother?'

'But I've never mentioned mother, darling, you're mixing things up,' she said.

That stubbornness was really stupid, she could see she was digging a pit for herself, that he could see through her. She would have liked to take it back and eat her own words, but it was now too late. She felt her face losing control and the confession coming out despite herself. The cold of her cheeks had spread to her whole countenance, her lips were twitching nervously. At the same time, he became terrifying, suddenly all red, as if his blood was going to burst his veins. He had seized her by the wrists, thrust his face close to hers to drink in every trait and try to make out from the dismay in her eyes, from her inability to face him, whatever it was she would not tell him.

27

'Good God!' he stammered, at last. 'Good God!'

She took fright, lowering her face, to hide it under her forearm, forestalling the blow of his fist. One insignificant, petty little fact, forgetting the lie about this ring, had now in so few words given him the necessary clue. He only needed an instant to figure it out. Suddenly, he flung her across the bed and struck out at her with both fists, not caring where the blows fell. In three years he had not even given her a single slap. Now, blind, drunk, out of control like any animal, or rather, like a man with enormous fists who had once pushed luggage waggons, he proceeded to beat her.

'You bloody little tart!' he cried. 'You've slept with him . . . slept with him . . . slept with him!'

As he repeated the words he worked himself into a fury, bringing his fists down every time he uttered the words, as if to pound them into her very flesh.

'An old man's droppings, that's what you are! You bloody little tart! . . . You've slept with him . . . slept with him!'

He was so angry that his voice choked till all he could produce was a whistle. Finally, he could not speak at all. It was only then that he realized that the body which had gone limp under his blows was still saying *no*. She could think of no better defence, merely denied it, solely in order not to be killed. It was however that protest, that stubborn lie, which finally maddened him.

'Confess,' he cried, 'you did sleep with him.'

'No! No!'

He had taken her up again, held her, preventing her from falling face downwards on the bed, like any poor creature hiding. He made her look at him.

'Confess,' he repeated, 'you did sleep with him.'

But by going quite limp she escaped from him and tried to run to the door. However, leaping after her, fist in the air, he dominated her again, then with a single infuriated blow, beside the table, he knocked her down, flung himself down beside her, grabbed at her hair and by it held her head to the floor. For a moment they stayed thus, facing each other, motionless. The terrible silence which followed was flooded by the exuberant singing and laughter of the Dauvergne girls. The piano down below was luckily going mad and concealing the

28

sound of the Roubauds' struggle. Claire was shrilling children's catches while Sophie pounded out an accompaniment.

'Confess! You slept with him!'

She no longer dared say no, so she said nothing.

'Confess you slept with him, God damn you,' he cried, 'or I'll knife you!'

And he would indeed have killed her, she could see murder plain on his face. As she fell she had caught sight of the knife. It lay open on the table. Now again she caught the flash of the blade, and had the impression he was reaching out. Fear overcame her, she let everything go, capitulated, just to end it all.

'All right then, yes, it's true. Now let me go.'

After that, it was frightful. The admission which he had so savagely exacted was a direct body blow, so out of the question, so monstrous. He thought he would never have imagined such infamy. He seized her head in his hands and banged it against the table leg. She struggled to get free, but he dragged her across the room by the hair, heaving chairs out of the way, and every time she made an effort to get up he sent her flying to the floor again with another blow of his fist. Throughout, he breathed hoarsely, grinding his teeth, wild with lunatic fury. He pushed back the table so violently that it nearly knocked the stove over. Hair and blood stuck to one of the corners of the dresser. And when they paused to take breath, aghast and swollen with the horror of it, weary alike of striking and being struck, they had come back to the bed. She was still on the floor, grovelling, he was crouching over her, still holding her down by the shoulders. They breathed hoarsely, while down below, the music never ceased, laughter billowed up, ringing laughter, youthful laughter.

'Ah, you little tart, so you did sleep with him! . . . Say it again, say it again, I tell you, you did sleep with that old bastard. . . . And how old were you, I wonder? When you were quite small? – When you were quite small, eh?'

All at once, she burst into tears, and the sobs prevented any answer.

'Good God, will you answer me!' he shouted . . . 'Out with it, you weren't ten, when you gave that old bastard his bit of fun, eh? So that's the reason for his charity, is it, it was just for his dirty little pleasures, out with it, God damn you, or you'll get some more!'

She sobbed away, unable to utter a word, so he raised his hand and with another blow knocked her half senseless. And, as he did not get any answer to the question he kept on repeating, he smacked her like that three times more.

'At what age, come on, you whore, out with it!' he cried.

Why struggle? She lost all sense of shame. With those coarse labourer's fingers he was capable of tearing out her heart. And on went the questionnaire, with Severine telling everything, so obliterated by shame and fear that the few words she gasped jerkily were almost inaudible. Roubaud was maddened with pain. The scenes she recalled gnawed at him with monstrous jealousy. Yet he could not hear enough of it, forced her to go back over details, exacted the most intimate facts. His ear close to that miserable creature's lips, he tortured himself with the confession thus dragged out of her under the constant menace of the fist upraised, ready to strike again and again, if ever she faltered.

Thus all that past life at Doinville was revived at last, all her childhood, all her youth. Did he do it somewhere among the rocks in the big park? Or was it in a dark corner of a passage in the old château? Had Grandmorin already had her in view when he first kept her beside him and had her brought up with his daughter, after his gardener's death? At that time she had told him of, when the other little girls ran away at the old judge's appearance, but she could smile, her little snout in the air, waiting for him to give her a pat on the cheek as he passed by, all that must already have begun. And later, if she dared face up to him and talk to him and if she used to get whatever she wanted out of him, was that not because she felt herself the mistress, and he who was so worthy and stern with others bought her with his little skivvy-seducing tricks. Ugh! How filthy it was, that old man having her peck him with grand-daughterly kisses, keeping his eye on the little girl's growing-up, while he fingered her, going a little further every time, without even the patience to wait till she was properly the age for sex.

'Now out with it!' panted Roubaud. 'How old were you? . . . Tell me again, how old?'

'Sixteen and a half.'

'That's a lie!'

Dear God, whyever should she lie? She shrugged her shoulders in weary desperation.

'And where was it, the first time?'

'At Maufras Cross.'

He hesitated an instant, his lips quivering, a sallow light dulling his eyes.

'Now I want you to tell me exactly what he did the first time,' he said.

She did not speak. Then, as he waved his fist in the air, she stammered: 'You would not believe me.'

'No matter, tell me . . . He was incapable of really doing anything, is that the truth?'

She answered with a nod. That was just it. So he seized savagely on that first scene, wanted to know every detail, sank to the lowest words and most indecent enquiries. But now she did not unclench her teeth any more, she merely said *yes* or *no* with her head. Perhaps they would both feel better when she had confessed everything. But these details which she imagined might ease him merely made him suffer more. Normal relations, the complete act, would have haunted his mind less agonizingly. This perversity, however, made everything so dirty, thrust the poisoned shafts of his jealousy deeper in and twisted them about in the wound. Now all was over, life was finished for him, he would never escape the foul picture of this.

A sob broke from his throat. 'Oh Good God! . . . Oh, Good God! . . . it cannot be, no, no, this is too much, this cannot be so.'

Then, all at once, he gave her a fierce shaking. 'Good God, you little bitch, why ever did you marry me? Don't you see how dirty it was to deceive me so? There are thieves in prison who have less on their consciences . . . You despised me, didn't you, you never loved me? Out with it,' he cried, 'why did you marry me?'

She made a vague gesture. Did she really know? She had been happy, marrying him, happy in the hope she had completely finished with Grandmorin. There were so many things one did not exactly want to do, but did, because after all they were the most sensible. It was true, she had not loved him. And, though she took care not to tell him that, she would never have married him, had it not been for this thing in her past.

'It was Grandmorin thought of it, wasn't it?' Roubaud demanded. 'He wanted to get you off his hands. He found a poor fool. . . . Out with it, he wanted to fix you up with a husband, so he could go on

31

with you, didn't he? And you did go on with it, didn't you? Those two visits you paid there? That's why he wanted you to go and stay, isn't it?'

Again, she nodded assent.

'And that was why he invited you this morning, wasn't it? So all this filth was going to go on, was it, right to the end? And if I don't throttle you once and for all, you'll still be at it, eh?'

His contorted hands came forward to take her by the throat again. But this time, revolt broke out in her.

'No, no, look here,' she cried, 'that's not fair, because it was I who said I would not go there, and you wanted me to go, I had to get quite angry about it, not to go, don't forget ... You can see plainly I did not want to go. It's all over. Never, never again would I have let him touch me.'

He sensed that she was speaking the truth, but this now brought him no alleviation. The frightful pain, the iron which had pierced him through, the thought that what had taken place between that man and her could never again be mended! He suffered hell merely because he was powerless to make it all non-existent. But still he could not let her go. He brought his face up close to hers. He seemed mesmerized by her, drawn closer and closer to her flesh, as if in the minute network of tiny blood-vessels he was going to find imprinted all that she had confessed. And with obsession, like a man out of his mind, he kept muttering.

'At Maufras Cross,' he babbled, 'in that red room ... I know the room. The window opens on to the railway. The bed stands opposite. So it was there, in that room, was it? No wonder he should talk of leaving that house to you. You've certainly earned it. ... Well might he look after your pennies and give you a dowry. You were worth it to him ... A high court judge, a man of millions, so respected, so clever, standing so high! ... It fairly makes a man's head spin ... And how would you look if he were your father?'

With an effort, Severine got to her feet and with a strength surprising in such a poor, defeated little thing as she was, thrust him away from her. She was vehement in protest against that.

'No, no,' she cried, 'never that, anything else you like, but never that! Beat me, kill me ... But don't say that. That's not true!'

Roubaud had kept hold of one of her hands. 'Do you really know?'

32

he insisted. 'It's just because even you are not sure that you get so worked up about it.'

As she withdrew her hand, he suddenly felt the ring, a slender ruby-headed gold snake. He had forgotten it, on her finger. In a fit of rage, he tore it off and ground it into the floor with his heel. Then he strode the room from end to end, speechless, aghast. She sank to the edge of the bed and sat there, watching him with big, staring eyes. And the frightful silence seemed it would never end.

There was no abating of Roubaud's fury. The moment it did seem to have begun to wane, it would flare up again, like a sort of intoxication, wave on wave of it, increasing and carrying him away in fits of dizziness. He was no longer master of himself, fighting empty space, tossed by every gust of the hurricane of violence which lashed him, till he was reduced to the utter depths of all-absorbing need to assuage the howling beast deep within him. It was an immediate physical need, a starvation of a body which hungered for vengeance, a force contorting him and giving him no respite till he should satisfy his need.

Still striding up and down, he began to thump his temples with his fists, crying in agonized tones: 'Oh, whatever shall I do, whatever shall I do?' Since he had not killed this woman at once, now he could not kill her at all. His poltroonery in letting her live made him itch with rage. For this was indeed poltroonery, since merely because he still cared for her whore's skin, he had not strangled her. Yet as it was, he could not keep her. Was he then to turn her out, out into the street, and never see her again? And a new flood of agony overcame him, and when he realized that he would not even turn her out, he was overtaken by loathing and nausea. Then what was he going to do? And he knew that the only thing to do was to accept the foul situation and take this woman back to Havre with him, continue humdrum life with her, as if there had been nothing of all this. But no, no! Rather death, rather immediate death for them both, than that! And distress welled up so terribly in him that he cried out loud again in desperation: 'Oh, whatever am I going to do?'

All this time Severine's wide-open eyes had been following his movements from the bed, where she still sat. Out of the tranquil comradely affection she had always felt for him now arose a flood of pity and grief for the immense agony she saw he was in. Had his

33

insane rage surprised her less, she could have forgiven the harsh words and the blows. But this continued rage she could not grasp. Passive and docile herself by nature, having submitted when she was quite young to the lust of an old man who later allowed her, in her uncomplicated desire to get things decently settled, to get married, she simply could not comprehend such an explosion of jealousy as this of Roubaud's, moreover, all over long-past misdeeds which she herself regretted. Thus, being utterly devoid of viciousness, her body still not fully awakened, and despite it all, too, no more than half aware of herself, a gentle-natured girl who was even chaste, she watched her husband march up and down, jerking himself violently round each time he reached the wall, much as she would have watched a caged wolf or any other wild creature. Whatever was this fury in him? There were so many people with no such fury in them. What dismayed her was thus feeling the low brute in him which certain obscure mutterings had in these past three years occasionally made her suspect, suddenly let loose, rabid and ready to bite. Whatever was she to say to him to prevent further misfortune?

Every time he came her way, he came up to the bed and brushed close by her. And now she waited for him to come again, plucked up courage and murmured:

'Dearest, listen . . .'

But he did not hear her, he was already at the far end of the room, like a straw lashed by the gale.

'Whatever am I going to do?' he cried. 'Whatever am I going to do?'

At last she seized him firmly by the wrist and held him a few moments.

'Dearest, be sensible, as it was I who refused to go down there. . . . I should never have gone there again, never! It's you I love!'

What was more, she showed herself loving, she drew him to her, she raised her lips to him for a kiss. But falling beside her, he then thrust her back from him with a spasm of disgust.

'Ugh, you little bitch!' he cried. 'Now you would like to . . . Ah! . . . Just now, you did not want to, you did not want me . . . Now you'd do it, would you, just to get me back? If you can hold your man by that, you've got him, eh? . . . But it would burn my flesh, going with you would, I tell you, I feel it would burn my blood like poison.'

34

He shuddered. The idea of taking her, the imagining of their two bodies prone on the bed, had flashed through him like fire, and in the stormy night of his flesh, deep in the fouled lust which oozed blood in him, he suddenly felt the necessity for death.

'If going with you again is not going to kill me,' he cried, 'don't you see I must kill that dirty old scoundrel . . . I must kill him, I must kill him!'

His voice rose shrilly, he repeated the words, standing now, stretched to his full height, as if by bringing him a clear resolve, the very utterance of them soothed him. After that, without another word, he walked slowly to the table and looked down at that knife. The large, open blade of it gleamed. With mechanical movements he closed it and put the thing away in his pocket. Then, his hands swinging limp, his eyes in the distance, he stood there, lost in thought. The difficulties in the way of it now furrowed his brow with two deep lines. To find the way, he turned and opened the window, stood facing into the chill twilight air. Behind him, his wife rose to her feet, overcome again with fear, but, not daring to question him, merely trying to guess what was going on inside that bullet skull, she waited, and stood with him, looking out into the vast heavens.

With night beginning, the houses on the far side were now silhouetted black, the extensive field of the station turned to a gulf of violet-hued haze. Especially on the Batignolles side, the great hollow of the station seemed deep in ashy grey, which was already creeping round the girders of Europe Bridge, blotting them out. The other way, over Paris, a final flicker of daylight played whitish on the glass of the mainline hangars, while beneath the roofing the obscurity of night poured down and merged everything in a confused mass. There were tiny lights sparkling along the platforms, the gas jets were being lit, the Dieppe train's headlight glowed with one immense cone of whiteness. The train was packed with passengers, the doors already closed. All they were waiting for was the sign from the platform inspector. There were obstructions, the red signal light still barred their road, and a small engine chuffed up to remove some coaches which a bad piece of shunting work had left on the line. Across that chronic tangle of rails, weaving among files of motionless trucks held up on sidings, an unending stream of trains plunged away into the deepening shadows. A train for Argenteuil had just left, then another, for Saint-Germain, pulled out. One, very short, came in from Cherbourg. More and more signals, guards' whistles, locomotive whistles. From all quarters came lights, red, green, yellow, white. All seemed confusion at this hour neither day nor night. Surely everything must crash. Yet they all rolled by, face to face, yet never entangling, each with the same soft, insistent motion, in the imprecision of twilight. But at last the red signal light changed, the Dieppe train too uttered a whistle and moved out. Rare drops of rain now fell from the pallid sky. It was going to be a very damp night.

When Roubaud turned away from this scene, his features were as stocky and stubborn as if the falling night had impregnated them with its shadows. He had made up his mind, his plan was ready. In the fading light of day he gave a glance at the cuckoo-clock. 'Five twenty,' he said loudly. And was taken aback by his own discovery. An hour only, a bare hour, had passed, a single hour, for so much to have happened. He could have believed the two of them had been at each other's throats for weeks. 'Five twenty,' he repeated. 'There's time.'

Not daring to question him, Severine followed every movement with anxious eyes. She saw him rummage in the cupboard, find a sheet of paper, a tiny bottle of ink, a pen.

'Well, now you can write.'

'But . . . but what . . . to whom?'

'To him . . . Sit here.'

And when without even thinking she edged away from the chair, before she even knew what he was going to demand of her, he led her back so forcibly, to make her sit down at the table, that she acquiesced.

'Write,' he said. 'Write: "Take the 6.30 express this evening but keep out of sight till we get to Rouen."'

She had taken the pen, but her hand shook, her fear of all the unknown which those two simple lines opened up before her loomed large, till she found the courage to raise her eyes and look at him supplicatingly. 'Please, my dear, please, what do you mean to do? . . . Tell me, I beg you . . .'

But he only repeated, loudly, unbending: 'Get it down, come on!' He stared deep into her eyes, and in his now there was no anger, no harshness, only a terrible persistence, the weight of which, she felt, was crushing her and destroying her. He said slowly: 'You'll see all right what I am going to do . . . What's more, get this into your head,

36

what I'm going to do I am going to have you do with me ... That way, we shall still be together, you and me, with a real bond between us.'

He terrified her, once again she tried to withdraw.

'No, no, you must tell me now ... I must know ... I will not write till you tell me.'

Then words dried up in him, silently he took her hand, the fragile hand of a child, and with the continued grip of a vice, crushed it in his own iron fist, almost to the point of crushing the bones. Like that, by sheer pain he forced his will into her flesh. She uttered a piercing little cry then, inwardly broken, she was suddenly all submission. Her essential passive gentleness, her real innocence of heart, left her no choice but to obey, and be at once his instrument of love and instrument of death.

'Get it down, get it down!' he insisted.

And with that poor, painful hand, in great discomfort, she wrote the words which he dictated to her.

'That's fine, you're a decent girl after all,' he said, when the letter was in his hand. 'Now put things straight here, I'll come back for you.'

He was very calm. Peering in the glass, he retied his tie. He put on his hat. Then he left. She heard him double-lock the door, and take out the key. Night was deepening steadily. For a while she stayed seated, her ear open to all the sounds outside. In the nextdoor flat – the newspaper woman's – she now heard a continuous whimpering, no doubt a pet dog left alone. Down below the Dauvergnes' piano was silent at last. Instead, there was a merry clatter of pots and pans. The two young housewives busy together in their big kitchen, Claire was making a mutton stew, Sophie was washing a lettuce. Drained of all vitality, Severine listened to their laughter coming to her out of the frightful misery of this darkening night.

Just after a quarter past six the locomotive of the Havre express appeared from under Europe Bridge. It was sent on to take over its train. It was coupled on. So many lines were full that the train could not be brought in to any of the main line platforms, but stood out in the open, against a platform which ran on beyond the station proper, a sort of pier jutting into the darkness of the inky sky, where the chain of gas jets were merely tiny, smoky stars. A shower of rain had just ceased, leaving behind it a breath of chilly dampness permeating the immense gulf of the station, a world of mist which reached back to the faint gleam of the windows of Rome Street. It was all very vast and very mournful, a watery world with blood-red blotches of fiery light here and there, a space inhabited by a confusion of dense masses, locomotives, isolated waggons, files of made-up trains still slumbering in sidings. From the ultimate depths of this sea of shadows came multifarious sounds, giant breathing, fevered respiration, whistles of engines sudden and shrill, piercing the air like the shrieks of outraged women, and then far-off horses mournful against the confused murmur of the surrounding streets. She heard somebody shout ordering an additional coach. The motionless locomotive of the express suddenly shot jets of steam from its relief valves. The vapour shot up into the tenebrosity of the night, to be torn to shreds of cloud which scattered in white tears over the endless black crêpe of the heavens.

At six twenty, Roubaud and Severine appeared. As they passed the toilets near the waiting rooms, she had just taken Victoire her key. Roubaud was now urging her along, with the anxious air of a husband whose wife will dawdle, impatient, brusque, his hat tipped back, her veil tight drawn, her steps lagging, as if worn out. A throng of passengers were making their way down the platform. They merged with them, peering into the coaches as they passed, to find an empty first-class compartment. The platform grew animated, porters trundling their barrows along to the front luggage van, an inspector busy finding seats for a large family, the assistant station-master, signalling lamp in hand, giving an eye to couplings, to make sure they were firm and screwed up tight. At last, Roubaud found an empty compartment, and towards this he had just steered Severine, when M. Vandorpe the station-master passing by with his main-line deputy, Dauvergne, spotted him, the two of them sauntering, arms behind back, keeping an eye on the shunting on of the additional coach. There were mutual greetings and the assistant station-master and the guard had to pause to exchange a few words.

First, they talked of that business of the assistant prefect. That was now off the board, to everybody's satisfaction. Then they turned to a mishap that very morning, at Havre, news of which had come in by telegraph: a locomotive which went by the name of Lison, and on

Fridays and Saturdays pulled the six-thirty express, had broken a connecting-rod just as the train was entering the station. The repairs were going to keep Jacques Lantier, the driver, there for a couple of days, together with his mate Pecqueux – who happened to be 'Ma' Victoire's husband. And Lantier, so it seemed, was a native of the same part of the country as Roubaud.

Severine meanwhile waited by the door, loth to enter, while Roubaud, talking to his two colleagues, assumed an air of great high spirits, talking loudly and laughing boisterously. Then, with a great jolt, the train ran back some yards. It was the engine shunting the front coaches back on to the one which had been added (waggon 293) to provide a reserved coupé. Recognizing Severine through her veil, Dauvergne's son Henri, who was leading guard on this train, just managed to save her from a nasty bump from the heavy open door. With timely gesture, he swept her out of the way, then with a very charming smile apologized for his roughness, adding by way of explanation that the special reserved half-compartment was for one of the Company's directors, who had just asked for it, a mere half-hour before the train left. For no apparent reason, Severine gave a nervous, highly strung little laugh. Young Dauvergne, rather pleased with himself, hurried away, to resume his duties. He had always told himself that Roubaud's missus was just the girl for him to have a little affair with.

The clock showed six twenty-seven. Three minutes to go. Suddenly Roubaud, whose eye all the time he had been talking to the station-master had been on the waiting room doors, rejoined his wife. But their compartment, of course, had now moved, and they had some steps to go to get back to it. Turning his back on the station-master, Roubaud hustled his wife, and hoisted her roughly in with his fist while that submissive creature, tense with anxiety herself, automatically peered back. Yes, she made sure, there was the belated traveller, a man with no luggage, only a rug over his arm. The collar of his ample navy-blue travelling coat was raised and so broad, and the brim of his bowler hat pressed so low down over his eyes, that one could hardly see his face in the flickering gaslight, no more than a suspicion of white beard showed. Nevertheless, despite the traveller's manifest desire not to be seen, Vandorpe and the elder Dauvergne approached him at once and followed him. But he did not acknowledge their

39

presence till he had reached his reserved coupé, three coaches further on, and in great haste climbed in. Yes, it was Grandmorin. Shivering all over, Severine collapsed on to her seat, while her husband gripped her arm painfully, as if to demonstrate his possession. He was exultant, now that he was sure of completing the job.

Another minute, and the half hour struck. A newsvendor rushed up and down with evening papers. Passengers were still strolling up and down the platform, smoking cigarettes. Now they all scrambled in. From both ends of the train one could hear porters banging doors. And then Roubaud, who had just had the disagreeable surprise of seeing that in this compartment which he had thought was empty there was already a dark shape in one corner, apparently a woman in deep mourning, silent and motionless and when the door suddenly opened again and an inspector hustled in a further couple, a stout man and a stout woman, who collapsed on the seat, panting, he could not restrain an exclamation of real rage.

They were off. The rain had begun again, a very fine drizzle, filling the vast shadowy space of the station through which trains were still coming and going, only their lights visible now, in a chain of small moving windows. Green lights flashed up out of the darkness, lanterns flickered at ground level. Then there was nothing else, merely immense blackness, only the main line roofing visible, feebly lit by the gas. Everything had turned dark, even all sounds were muffled, only the roar and hiss of the engine to be heard, as it opened its cocks and emitted a turbulence of white vapour. The cloud of it rose, flocculent as the shroud of a ghost. Through it thrust billowing masses of black smoke, though where they came from, it was impossible to tell. These blotted out the sky anew, a cloud of soot floating away over the furnace-like glowing of Paris by night.

At last the assistant station-master raised his lantern, for the driver to ask for his signal. There were two pips of the whistle and then, in the far distance, near the signal box, the red light went out, to be replaced by white. Standing at the van door, the leading guard awaited the order to leave, then passed it on to the driver. The engine gave another whistle, this time a long one, the driver opened his regulator, and set the train in motion. They were pulling out. At first, the motion was almost imperceptible, then the express began to gather speed. It passed under Europe Bridge and plunged on towards

Batignolles tunnel. All one could see of it now were its three rear lights, a blood-red triangle of light. In the inky tremor of night, one could follow it but a few moments more. It had gathered speed now, nothing more would halt it, full speed ahead. It vanished into the darkness.

2

At Maufras Cross the house is situated diagonally in a garden plot which is cut in two by the railway, so close to the building that every train which passes shakes it. You only need to journey past it once to have it imprinted in your memory. Without knowing a thing about it, everybody who flits by at high speed sizes it all up in a flash, with its neglected appearance, its grey shutters always closed, green growth already creeping over them where the west winds breathe on them. It looks so utterly abandoned that it seems to make that out-of-the way corner a good three miles from the nearest habitation even more solitudinous.

The only other building is a railway crossing-keeper's cottage, where the road to Doinville, three miles distant, turns across the line. Low-pitched, the walls cracked, the tiles moss-grown, this dwelling huddles into the earth with a poverty-stricken, abandoned air, on all sides a vegetable garden, enclosed by a hedge, and including a well hoist as high as the actual cottage. The crossing is exactly midway between the stations of Malaunay and Barentin, just under two and a half miles from either place. But it is very rarely used and the poles which bar the road are beginning to rot and are scarcely ever raised except for carters from the Bécourt quarries, which are rather more than a mile and a half away, in Bécourt Woods. A place more withdrawn, more cut off from people, could not be imagined, for on the Malaunay side the long tunnel cuts off all the roads and the only link with Barentin is the badly kept path which runs beside the permanent-way. Hence strangers are rare.

This particular evening, when night fell, the weather being very hazy and mild, a passenger who had got off the train from Havre at Barentin went striding along the path towards Maufras Cross. The country there is undulating country, nothing but a series of hills and ravines, through which the railway track thrusts, alternately on embankments and through cuttings. On either side of the line these incessant irregularities of the land, endless steep rises and falls, hinder roads. This all goes to increase the sensation of intense loneliness. The land, poor, chalky, marginal stuff, is uncultivated. On the crests there are patches of woodland, while the narrow combes are traversed by willow-lined brooks. Some of the chalk ridges are quite bare, and here, one after another, one passes the sterile slopes, wrapped in silence and the desolation of death. And the sturdy, youthful foot-passenger accelerated his pace, as if anxious to escape even on so mild an evening from the depression of this desolate countryside.

In the crossing-keeper's garden a girl was drawing water from the well. She was a tall lass of eighteen, fair, powerfully built, thick-lipped, with large greenish eyes and a low forehead under a dense head of hair. She was far from pretty, and had the straight hips and sinewy arms of a man. The instant she sighted the young fellow coming along the path towards her, she put down her pail and ran to the garden gate.

'Well I never!' she cried. 'Jacques!'

He was at once all attention. He had just passed his twenty-sixth birthday, tall himself, very swarthy, but handsome, with regular features in an oval face, spoiled only by jaws which were too powerful. His thick-set hair was curly, like his moustache, which was so thick and black that it made his skin look even more pallid than it was. By his delicate skin and well-shaven cheeks one might have thought him a gentleman, were it not for the indelible signs of his calling, the engrained hands, the hands of an engineer, for all their delicacy and shapeliness.

'Good evening, Flora,' he bid her, then was silent, though his eyes – they were large and dark, only flecked with gold – his eyes seemed clouded by a smoky glow, which added vivacity. In sudden embarrassment, a lack of ease which was almost painful, his eyelids flickered and his glance avoided her. Indeed, his whole body seemed to obey an occult impulse to withdraw.

The girl did not stir, but her glance fixed unswervingly on him. She had not failed to notice that involuntary tremor, which he strove to master every time he approached a woman. It seemed to leave her very preoccupied and sad. When, anxious to conceal his shyness, he asked if her mother was home (though he knew very well she was ill and confined to her bed, unable to go out), her only response was a

43

nod. She stood aside so he could enter without touching her and without another word went back to the well, very proudly upright.

With his swift gait, Jacques Lantier crossed the little garden and entered the house. There, in the centre of the first room, a vast kitchen used as living-room, Aunt Phasie, as he had known her since he was a child, was alone in a wicker chair drawn up to the table, her legs wrapped in an old rug. She was a cousin of his father's, that is, herself a Lantier, and she had been his foster-mother. When – he was only six – his father and mother disappeared, flitting to Paris, and he was left alone at Plassans, where later he went to classes at the technical college, she had taken him to live with her. For this, he had always been most grateful to her, maintaining that it was her credit that he had got on as he had. And when after two years with the Orleans railway he became a first-class driver of the Western Railway Company, he came to seek out his foster-mother, who was now re-married, this time to a level-crossing keeper named Misard, to find herself consigned, with the two daughters of her first marriage, to this god-forsaken hole of Maufras Cross. Today, though scarcely forty-five, Aunt Phasie, who had once been such a fine woman, so big and strong, looked like sixty. She had grown thin and sallow, and was shaken by a persistent palsy.

But now, she uttered a cry of delight. 'Jacques, you! Not really! . . . Oh, my big boy, what a surprise!'

He kissed her on both cheeks and explained that he had suddenly got two days' forced holiday, for just as he reached Havre that morning his engine, Lison, had broken its tie-rod, and as the repair could not be finished in less than forty-eight hours, he was not due back on duty till tomorrow evening, when he had to take the six-forty express up to Paris. So he had wanted to come and give her a hug. He would spend the night there, he said, and not leave till the 7.26 tomorrow morning. He held her poor, enfeebled hands between his, telling her how her last letter had worried him.

She heaved a tremendous sigh. 'Yes, my dear boy, it can't go on like this, it really can't . . . How wonderful of you to guess how much I wanted to see you! Because I know how tied you are, I didn't dare ask you to come. But yet, here you are, and I'm so very, very happy!'

She broke off, to glance timorously out of the window. In the last vestiges of twilight her husband, always known just as Misard, was

44

visible on the far side of the track, in his hut, one of those match-board boxes set up every three or four miles, inter-connected by telegraph, to ensure safe train movements. While the wife – and later Flora – had been given the responsibility of working the crossing barriers, Misard had been made the crossing-keeper.

As if Misard might have overheard, Aunt Phasie shivered and then lowered her voice. 'I really believe he has been poisoning me,' she murmured.

This confidence rather made Jacques start. His eyes too turned to the window and once again they clouded over with that strange cloudiness, a faint pinkish haze which diminished the sharpness of their diamond-flecked blackness.

'No, no! Auntie Phasie,' he protested, in a low voice. 'What a wild idea! Why, he seems such a gentle, inoffensive little man.'

A Havre-bound train had just passed and Misard had left his look-out box to close the section behind it. While he was raising the lever, returning the signal to red, Jacques watched him. He was indeed a puny little man, with spare hair and beard, colourless, his cheeks hollow and poor-looking. In addition, he was taciturn and retiring, with not a trace of spite in him and he was also obsequiously deferential to anybody in authority. But now he had already withdrawn into his match-board cabin to enter the time of passing in the log-book and press the two electric buttons, one handing on the open road to the next man back, the other informing the next man forward that the train was on its way.

'All very well to talk, you don't know him,' said Aunt Phasie. 'I tell you, he must be giving me something foul . . . When I was so strong, I could have eaten him, now it's he, that little squirt of a man, who's eating me up.'

She became quite vehement, with a bitterness at once sullen and shrinking, now she could unbosom herself, overjoyed at last to have a responsive ear. What on earth had prompted her to re-marry a spiderish little man like that, penniless moreover, miserly into the bargain, and she five years his senior, with two daughters, one six at the time, the other already eighteen? Well, it would soon be ten years since she committed the folly, and there had not been an hour in all that time that she had not regretted it – this poverty-stricken existence, exiled in this chilly corner of the north, where she shivered all through with cold and it was deadly dull, never a single soul to talk to, not even a neighbouring housewife. And what was Misard? Only an elderly plate-layer, who now earned his twelve hundred francs a year as watchman. From the outset she herself had had fifty for the crossing work, which Flora now looked after, and there was their whole present and their future too, not another hope, only the certainty of existing till they rendered up their immortal souls in this hole, a thousand miles away from real living folk. What she said nothing of was the consolation she used to have before she fell ill, in the days when her husband was working on the track, leaving her at home alone to look after the crossing with her two girls. In those days she was known as a lovely piece of goods the length of the line from Rouen to Havre and all the track-inspectors used to visit her on their way past, and there was a good deal of fierce competition too, the plate-layer foreman of another section always hovering around, always on the *qui-vive*. The husband had never been a hindrance, he was obsequious to every man of them, slipping out of the house and slipping in again with a blind eye to all the goings on. But those distractions were finished, leaving her now, week in, week out, month in, month out, glued to her chair in this utter loneliness, feeling her body fading away little by little, hour by hour.

'I tell you,' she wound up, 'it's he getting me down all right, and little-'un though he is, he'll finish me too.'

A brusque jangle of the bell made her shoot another uneasy glance outside. This time it was the next post informing Misard of a Paris bound train. The needle of the section indicator, against the window, had tipped to show the direction of the train. Misard stopped the bell and went outside to announce the train with two toots on his horn. Simultaneously, Flora went down to close the barrier, then took her stand, the little flag extended in its leather sheath before her. The train, an express, was already audible, still beyond the bend, but approaching with a rumble which rapidly grew. Then it swept by in a burst of thunder, shaking the squat cottage and threatening to carry it away in a blast of air. Flora was already making her way back to her vegetables, while Misard, having sealed off the section behind the train, proceeded to open the opposite section, by lowering the lever which effaced the red signal. A new jangle of the bell, accompanied by an upward flicker of the other needle, had in fact just indicated that the train which had passed five minutes earlier had already passed the next post. He went inside, informed both posts, entered the time in his log-book, then again waited. It was a task which never varied and occupied him twelve hours at a stretch, living there, eating there, without reading as much as three lines of a newspaper, and apparently without having a single thought in his shallow brain-pan.

Jacques, who once had used to tease his foster-mother about the destruction she wrought among the track-inspectors, could not restrain a smile as he said: 'The man may well be a bit jealous, you know.'

But Phasie only shrugged her shoulders in self-commiseration, though even she could not prevent laughter lighting her washed-out eyes too for a moment.

'Come, my dear boy, what a thing to say!' she murmured. 'Him? Jealous? He never cared a damn once he saw it cost him nothing.' Then, after another one of those little shudders which shook her, she continued: 'Oh no, he never worries much about that. All he thinks about is money . . . You see, what started the quarrel between us was me refusing to give him those thousand francs father left me when he died last year. Then when it came to him threatening me about it, it did me harm, and I fell ill at once. . . . And I've never got better since that day. No, not since that very day!'

The young man thought he saw through this, and thinking a sick woman would be likely to have obsessions like this, he made another shot at dissuading her, but she tossed her head stubbornly, like any person whose mind is made up. Whereupon he ended by saying: 'All right then, what could be simpler – if you want to get over it, give him your thousand francs.'

These words brought his sick aunt dramatically to her feet, an astonishing effort. With new life, full of indignation, she cried: 'My thousand francs? Never! I would sooner die. Ah, and they're well hidden, too, they're well hidden, mark you that! You could turn this house inside-out, and I'd defy you to find them . . . And he's had a good try, I can tell you, the little rogue. I've heard him by night tapping away at the walls. And well he may look too! If I needed anything to keep me patient, the pleasure of seeing his nose grow longer would be enough! . . . We'll see who'll give in first, him or me. I don't care, I never touch a penny of his money, and if I were to

47

burst, he would never get mine, I'd rather they stayed under the ground.'

She sank back exhausted to her chair, when there came another blast on the watchman's horn. It was Misard, in the doorway of his look-out box, signalling a Havre train. But despite this stubbornness about the money in which she took refuge, Aunt Phasie's secret fear of her husband grew, the sort of fear which a giant feels for the insect which it feels is devouring it. Meanwhile the dull rumble of the train he had announced, the slow, which left Paris at 12.45 P.M., could be heard in the distance. They caught it as it emerged from the tunnel, suddenly breathing more fully in the countryside, then with the thunder of its wheels and the mass of its coaches it roared by with the irresistible force of a hurricane.

His eyes raised to the window, Jacques had watched the little oblongs of the lighted windows with passengers outlined flashing by. In an effort to distract Phasie from her black thoughts, 'Why, Mother,' he said, 'you complain that in this hole you never see as much as a cat – look! There's enough for you, surely!'

She was puzzled, did not grasp at once what he meant. 'Where?' she demanded. 'I don't see anybody ... Oh, you mean in those passing trains? A lot of use to me they are, strangers, all of them, and you can't talk to them.'

He went on teasing. 'But I'm not a stranger, and you often see me go by.'

'True,' she said slowly. 'There's you, of course. I know the time of your train, and I look out for you on your engine. Only you go so fast, so terribly fast! Yesterday, you waved, like this, I saw you! But I can never answer you ... Oh no, that's no way of seeing people.'

All the same, this notion of the flood of folk carried daily before her eyes by the up trains and the down breaking her vast silence and solitude, left her thoughtful, her eyes on the track, where night was now falling. While she was still able to get about, and took her stand at the barrier, flag in hand, such ideas never entered her head. But ever since she had had to spend her days glued to that chair, with nothing to think about but her sullen struggle with her husband, a tangle of ill-defined musings had certainly cluttered her mind, and she found it queer to live lost like that, in the heart of a desert, without a soul to confide in, while day and night men and women were continually swept past her in a tornado of trains steaming all out and shaking her house as they passed. There was no doubt about it, the whole world went past her, not only French folk, foreigners too, folk from the most distant of lands, for nowadays nobody was capable of staying at home and, as someone had observed, all the peoples would soon blend into one. That was what progress was, men were all brothers, swept on all together on their swift wheels, on, on, into cloud-cuckoo-land. She made an attempt to tot them up, by average, at so many per coach. No, there were too many, it was beyond her. Frequently she thought she distinguished faces, among them that of a gentleman with a fair beard, who must be an Englishman. He went to Paris every week. And that of a dark little lady, who passed every Wednesday and Saturday. But the lightning flashed them by, she could never even be certain she had seen them at all, all those many faces melted together into one, commingling, merging one into the other, all alike. The torrent swept on, taking all with it. And what saddened her was feeling that despite such an incessant traffic of faces, all so well-off, with so much money displayed, that human multitude so passionately breathing did not even know of her existence there, to such point in mortal danger that any evening now her husband might finish her off, yet those trains would still dash this way and that past her corpse without even being aware of the crime which had been done in the heart of that isolated little cottage.

All this time, Phasie's eyes had been on the window, and now she tried to say briefly what she sensed so indefinitely to state it at any length.

'You are right,' she said, 'it is a wonderful invention, there's no gainsaying it. It's quick, we are clever nowadays . . . But savage brutes are still savage brutes, and however much better machines men invent, there will still be savage brutes at the heart of them.'

Jacques nodded again, as if to indicate that he thought so too. For the past few seconds he had been watching Flora opening the crossing-bar to let through a quarry-worker's waggon with two enormous blocks of stone. The lane almost exclusively served the Bécourt quarries. Indeed, every night the barrier was padlocked and it was very rarely that Flora had to get up in the night for anyone else. Seeing her now chatting intimately with the quarry-man, a young, small, dark-haired fellow, he cried in surprise: 'What, is Cabuche ill

49

then, letting his cousin Louis take the tumbril? . . . Poor Cabuche, do you see much of him, Mother?'

She did not reply, merely raised her hands and sighed deeply. Quite a tragedy, that had all been, not calculated to improve Aunt Phasie's health. Her younger daughter, Louisette, who had gone to service with Madame Bonnehon, at Doinville, had taken refuge one night, beside herself, out of her mind and badly hurt, to die in her good friend Cabuche's cottage in the heart of the wood. Talk had sprung up that Judge Grandmorin had been responsible for trying to take her by force, but nobody had ever dared say anything. Even her mother, for all that she might have something to say about it, spoke of it most unwillingly. But at last she now said:

'No, he never comes in now, he's become very wild, has Cabuche. . . . Poor little Louisette, she was such a precious child, so white-skinned, so gentle! She was so fond of me, she would have looked after me, she would! Whereas Flora – heaven forbid, I'm not going to complain, but Flora's certainly a screw loose somewhere, all queer notions, sometimes you don't see her for hours on end, and she's that touchy and bad-tempered . . . It's all very, very sad.'

While he listened, Jacques had kept his eye on the quarry-man, who was now just crossing the railway tracks. The heavy wheels lodged against the rails and he had to crack his whip, while Flora shouted, to urge the horses over them.

'Damnation!' cried the young fellow, 'wouldn't do if a train did come along . . . There would be a mess up, a regular mess up there would be!'

'No, there's no danger really,' Aunt Phasie said quickly. 'Flora's queer sometimes, but she knows her job all right, she keeps her eyes peeled . . . Touch wood, these five years we've never had a single mishap. Earlier on, there was a man cut in two. But all we've had was a cow which once nearly derailed a train. Poor beastie, they found the body here and the head right away there, near the tunnel . . . But you can count on Flora without ever worrying.'

The quarry-man had passed, they could hear the wheels of the tumbril jolting in the ruts. Then Aunt Phasie came back to her permanent subject, that of health, both that of other folk and her own too.

'And how are you keeping these days, my dear boy?' she asked. 'Do you remember those attacks you used to have when you were a boy, that the doctor never could understand?'

Jacques' characteristic troubled hesitance came back to his eyes.

'I am very well nowadays, Mother,' he said.

'Really? All gone – those piercing headaches, behind the ears, and you used to have sudden bouts of fever and fits of shyness. Why, you used to hide yourself away like a little wild animal in its burrow.'

The more she ran on, the more disturbed he was, overcome by such misery that in the end he interrupted her. 'I do assure you,' he said, curtly, 'I am very well nowadays . . . It's all gone, every trace of it.'

'I'm so glad, my dear boy! . . . You having trouble would not make mine any better. Besides, you're at the age to be well and fit, there's nothing so precious as health. But how nice of you to come to see me, instead of going off somewhere to have a good time. You're going to have supper with us, aren't you, and you can sleep up in the attic, in the room next to Flora's.'

But here again the horn outside prevented him replying. Dusk had fallen, and when this time they looked out of the window, they could only faintly distinguish Misard, talking to another man. It had just struck six, and he was handing over to the night watchman. At last, after twelve continuous hours at his post with only the little table under the instrument panel, a stool and a stove, in that hut which got so hot that he had to have the door almost continuously open – he would be free.

'Sh! here he is, he'll be in at any moment,' murmured Aunt Phasie, again overtaken by her fear.

The train that was signalled now became audible, very heavy, very long, with ever growing rumble of wheels, and the young man, terribly upset to see his Aunt let herself get so low, and anxious to help her, was obliged to bend forward to catch what the sick woman said.

'Come, Mother,' he said, 'if he really has evil intentions, perhaps knowing I was putting my spoke in would stop him . . . You could do worse than entrust your thousand francs with me.'

But this was the last straw.

'Trust my francs to you? I would no more think of letting you have them than I would him!' she cried. 'I would sooner die!'

The train passed at that instant, with the violence of a sudden

51

storm, seeming to sweep everything before it. As the blast caught it, the house shuddered as if buffeted by a gale. Bound for Havre, the train was packed, for there were to be festivities on the morrow, a Sunday, *à propos* of the launching of a ship. Despite the speed one caught a clear glimpse through the lit-up windows of the crowded compartments, rows of heads packed one to another, in profile. One after another those rows came into sight, then vanished again. What a multitude of them! More and more of them, crowds, amid the rumble of the wheels, the hiss of the engine, the tinkling of the telegraph, the jangling of bells. It was like an immense body, a mammoth earth-hugging body, the head at Paris, the ribs all down the line, the limbs spreading wide at the junctions, the feet and hands at Havre and other terminal cities. On and on it went, endless, mechanical triumph that it was, hurtling into the future with mechanical directness, deliberately indifferent to the vestiges of the human lurking ever alert on either side of it, lust and crime everlasting.

It was Flora who entered the house the first. She lit the lamp, a tiny paraffin affair without any shade, and laid the table. Not a word was exchanged. She scarcely shot even a furtive glance at Jacques, who had gone to the window and stood, back to the room, staring out. A pot of cabbage soup was keeping hot on the stove. When at last Misard too came in she dished it out. He showed not the slightest surprise at finding the younger man there. Perhaps he had noticed his arrival, but incurious, he asked no questions. A handshake, two or three curt words, no more. Jacques had to recount the story of the broken connecting-rod on his own initiative, then he went on to tell how he had said to himself that he would run down to Maufras Cross and give his step-mamma a hug and spend the night there. All Misard did, and that meekly, was give a nod, as if yes, that was a good idea, and they sat down, to make a leisurely meal, for some time without another word spoken. Phasie, whose eyes had not left that pot of cabbage soup all day, accepted a plateful of it. But when, as Flora had forgotten it, Misard got up to pour her out her iron water – water from a decanter in which lay some iron nails, she did not touch it. A modest, timid little man with a nasty little cough, Misard seemed quite blind to the anxious looks with which his wife followed his slightest movement. When she asked for salt, which was not on the table, he told her she would be sorry one day for eating so much of it, that was what was making her ill. Then he got up and brought her a spoonful. She accepted it without mistrust, remarking that salt was a universal purifier. Then the remark was made, how mild it had been for the past few days, and they talked of a train derailed at Maromme. In the end Jacques was convinced his foster-mother was suffering from delusions, for he could see nothing wrong in that kindly little stump of a man with the misty eyes. They sat on at table more than an hour. Twice, at the sound of the horn, Flora vanished for a moment. Trains swept by, shaking the crockery on the table, but nobody took the slightest notice.

There was then yet another blast of the horn, and this time Flora, who had just cleared the table, did not return, but left her mother and the two men at table with a bottle of cider brandy. They stayed drinking another half hour, then, his fidgety eyes having suddenly fixed on a corner of the room, Misard took his cap and with a curt good night, went out. He always went poaching for fish in the neighbouring brooks and rivers, where there were splendid eels, and never went to bed without going the round of his deepwater lines.

As soon as he had gone out, Phasie shot her stepson a keen look.

'Well, now what do you say?' she demanded. 'I expect you saw his eye probing that corner? That's because he has now got the idea I may have hidden my little nest-egg behind the butter-crock . . . As if I didn't know him. Tonight, mark my words, he'll move that crock out, to see.'

But perspiration broke out on her and she had a sudden fit of shivering.

'See,' she said, 'there, it's back again, he's drugged me, my mouth is as bitter as if I'd swallowed old coppers. Yet, God's my witness, I never took anything from his hand. Makes you want to drown yourself . . . I've had enough for this evening. I had better go to bed. So good-bye, my dear boy, because if you're catching the seven twenty-six, that will be too early for me. But come again, won't you? And let us hope I may be spared.'

He had to assist her to her room, where she got into bed and fell asleep, worn out. Left to himself, for a moment Jacques could not make up his mind whether or not to stretch out himself at once on the hay awaiting him in the loft. But it still wanted ten minutes to eight, there was time yet for sleeping, so he too went out, leaving the little paraffin lamp alight in the empty, slumbering house, shaken from time to time by the brusque thunder of a train.

Outside, he was astonished to find how mild it had turned. It was surely going to rain again. A milky cloud now covered the whole sky, and the full moon, invisible itself above the bank of cloud, illuminated the whole vault of heaven with a lurid glow of indirect light. This brought out the whole countryside, the hills and slopes about him and the trees standing out black under that uniform dead light, like that of a nightlight. He went round the little kitchen garden, then decided to take a stroll towards Doinville, as that way the hill was less steep. But, the isolated house corner-on to the line on the far side of the track catching his eye, he passed through the side-gate, for the barrier was already finally closed for the night, and crossed the line. He knew the house quite well, for he saw it every time he drove his thundering engine past the spot. He could not say why, but it always haunted him, giving him an obscure feeling that it somehow affected his life. Every time he came that way he first felt a sort of fear it would no longer be there. He had never once seen either doors or windows open. All he had been able to learn about it was that it belonged to Grandmorin, President of the Rouen High Court, but this evening it so happened that he felt a compulsion to poke round it to get to know it better.

He stood for a long time at the wicket, drawing back, reaching up, trying to sum the house up. Cutting through the garden, the line had left only a small patch, now walled in, in front of the porch, whereas at the rear a fairly large plot of ground belonging to it was enclosed by a hedge. There was something most mournful about the unhappy place, lit as it now was by the red luminosity of this misty night, and with a gooseflesh shudder he was on the point of moving on when he noticed a gap in the hedge. The notion that it would be cowardly of him not to go in through that gap made him creep through. Then his heart thumped for suddenly, just as he was making his way along by a small ruined greenhouse, a shadowy shape stooping at the door of this pulled him up short.

'Goodness me, why it's you,' he cried, in surprise, when he saw it was Flora. 'What on earth are you doing here?'

She too started with astonishment. Then, calmly, she said:

'As you see, I'm getting some string . . . They've left a whole pile

54

of string here and it's rotting, no good to anyone. So as I often need a piece of string, I've come to collect it.'

She was, indeed, seated on the ground with a strong pair of scissors in her hand, busily untangling some lengths of string, cutting the knots whenever they were too stubborn.

'Doesn't the owner ever come now?' he asked.

'He come?' She burst out laughing. 'Since that business with Louisette,' she said, 'there's no fear of Mister Grandmorin showing his nose at Maufras Cross. That's why I can take his old string, see?'

He did not speak at once. It seemed to trouble him to be reminded of the tragic business she had referred to.

'I say Flora,' he said, at last. 'Do you mean, you think that Louisette was telling the truth, old Judge Grandmorin wanted to have her, and she got hurt struggling against him?'

Flora's own laughter stopped suddenly. In a burst of rage, she cried: 'Louisette never told a lie, nor would Cabuche tell lies . . . Cabuche is my friend, if you want to know!'

'Your latest sweetheart, perhaps.'

'Him my sweetheart? A nice sort of bitch you must think me! . . . No, no, Jacques my dear, I tell you, I haven't got any sweetheart, and I don't want any, either.'

She had raised her powerful head high, her dense fleece of fair hair falling in low waves down on her forehead. Her whole being, sturdy and lissom at once, was instinct with wild will-power. She was already becoming legendary throughout that countryside. There were tales of the accidents she had prevented – a cart heaved out of the way of a train just in time, a waggon coming down Barentin hill that she stopped, together with its maddened horse, galloping down on an express, all evidence of strength which astonished the local men and made them desire her, the more so since at first they thought her easy prey, for as soon as she finished work she would be off round the hedgerows, peering about for convenient nooks, lying about in hollows, staring up at the sky, silent and still. But after a first try none of them were ever at all anxious to have another go. Since she loved bathing for hours mother-naked in a nearby little river, some lads of her own age once banded together to peep, but Flora, without even bothering to pull on a slip, caught one of them and gave him such a drubbing that none of them ever tried the trick again. Finally the news had got round about her and a pointsman on the far side of the tunnel, where the Dieppe line branched off, a fellow named Ozil, unmarried, about thirty, a very decent chap, whom for a time she seemed to have encouraged but who when one evening he tried to take her – thinking she was willing – was nearly killed by a crack on the head from her stick. She was a combative virgin, was Flora, scornful of the male sex, all of which in the end had led folk to conclude that she could not be quite all there.

Hearing her announce that she wanted no sweethearts, Jacques went on teasing. 'So your match with Ozil is off, is it? I've been told you used to go off through the tunnel every day to meet him.'

She heaved her shoulders.

'My match with Ozil? I don't think! . . . I get fun out of the tunnel, that's what! One mile to lope through in the darkness, knowing you can get yourself cut in two by a train if you don't keep your weather-eye open, it's fine! You should hear how the trains roar through it! . . . But Ozil? Oh, I soon got sick of him. He isn't the man for me.'

'Oh, so there is another, is there?'

'I don't know,' she began, then suddenly cried, 'Bah! No! Of course not!'

At the same time, laughter again overcame her and she also felt sufficiently embarrassed to concentrate hard on a stubborn knot. Then, without looking up, as if very intent on her work, she went on: 'And what about yourself? Haven't you got one? No sweetheart?'

Now it was Jacques who was serious. He looked aside, his glance wavered, then fixed on something in the far distance. 'No!' he replied curtly, at last.

'As I thought,' she said, 'I've always been told you hated women. Besides, it isn't just yesterday I first set eyes on you. You never did have a nice word for any of us . . . Why though? Tell me that!'

He said nothing. She decided to leave the knot and look at him.

'Is it really true that the only thing you love is your old engine? It's a standing joke, you know. They say you've always got your hand on that, polishing it up, as if that was the only girl you had a hand to caress . . . It's because I'm a friend of yours I can say that to you.'

Now he too was taking notice of her in the pallid luminosity of the moon-lit haze, and he saw her again as she had been when small. Already then she was self-willed, with a real temper, but the moment he appeared she used to leap and fling her arms round his neck, in the throes of the first affection of an unsophisticated child. Later, often not having seen him for long periods, every time he came back he found her more grown up, though she greeted him still by that same accolade, increasingly embarrassing him with the fire in her large bright eyes. Now she was a fully-grown woman, a superb, desirable woman too. Moreover, she probably loved him in a distant way, out of the depths of her own childhood. His heart suddenly began to thud, for all at once he had the feeling that he was the man she was waiting for. At lightning speed his blood vessels suddenly swept a terrible disturbance to his brain. His first instinct was flight, because of the distress which had taken possession of him. Bodily desire had always maddened him. He saw red.

'Whatever do you think you're doing, standing there all this time?' she said, suddenly. 'Come on, sit you down here.'

He hesitated. Then, his legs suddenly flaccid, he was overcome by the need to attempt love once again, and he sank down next to her on the heap of string. He could not speak, his throat was dry. It was Flora now, proud, untalkative Flora, who, in her own astonishment, babbled on without ceasing.

'I tell you,' she said, 'Mother's mistake was ever to marry Misard. She will come to no good through it . . . Not that I care, one has enough worries of one's own, don't you think? Besides, Mother always sends me to bed the moment I try to say something. . . . So let her manage her own affairs! As for me, my life is outside. I dream about things, for later . . . I tell you, I saw you go by this morning on your engine, why, I was sitting behind those bushes down there, but you never have eyes for me . . . But some day, not now, I shall tell you the things I dream about, yes, later when we are really great friends.'

She had dropped her scissors. Still without saying a word, he took her two hands in his. In sheer delight, she let him have his way with them. But when he pressed them to his burning lips she started in virginal terror, the amazon in her awakened, she was all tense, bent forward, in combative mood at the first hint of the male's advance.

'No, no, let me be, none of that for me,' she cried . . . 'Behave yourself, so we can go on talking . . . That's all you think of, you men. I tell you, if I were but to repeat what Louisette told me the day she died, at Cabuche's . . . I already hated that dirty old judge, I'd seen

57

enough smutty goings-on here, he used to bring mere school-girls here . . . There's one I know, nobody would ever suspect, one whom he married off . . .'

But Jacques was not paying attention, and her words fell on a deaf 'ear. He had suddenly seized her in a fierce embrace and was crushing his lips on hers. She uttered a faint cry, a mere plea, a soft heartfelt supplication, a sudden avowal of the weakness she had so long hidden. But despite this, she still struggled, in spite of everything refusing him, the impulse to fight the strongest impulse of all in her. She longed for him, but at the same time such was her need to be conquered by force that she had to vie with him for her own self. Speechless, pressed to each other, they struggled on breathlessly, to see which should mount on the other. For a while it looked as if she must be the stronger, she nearly downed him, he was so agitated, but he suddenly seized her by the throat. Her bodice was torn in the struggle, her bosom sprang free, nipples tight swollen in the contest, her breasts white as milk in the translucid shadows. And then, there she lay on her back, conquered, yielding herself at last.

But in this very instant, breathless, he held himself back, and instead of taking her, he looked at her. Madness then seemed to come over him, a savage impulse which made him look all around him for a weapon – a stone, anything, to kill her with. His eyes lit on the pair of scissors glinting among the string. In one leap he had them and would have thrust them into that naked bosom between the two white breasts with their pink nipples, had an intense chill not suddenly sobered him. Then he cast the scissors away and took to his heels, aghast, while she lay there, her eyes closed, thinking he had now refused her because she had first resisted him.

Through that mournful night Jacques fled, racing up the hill by a footpath, to pitch down on the other side into a narrow gully. Some pebbles he dislodged suddenly frightened him and he turned off sharp to the left through a thicket, doubled again to the right and came out on to a bare patch of ground. He shot down the steep edge of this, to find himself up against the hedge along the railroad. A train was just coming, thundering and belching sparks, but he was so agitated that he did not at once grasp what it was, then realized, of course, it was all that eternal multitude of humanity passing by, and he crouched there in his misery. He turned back, climbing, then plunged downhill again. Time after time he came back to the railway track, deep in cuttings through the downland, or reared on vast embankments which blotted out the sky. This deserted countryside, all chopped up into its little hills, became a maze from which there seemed no escape. His madness moved in circles amid the miserable desolation of that waste ground. For some time he had rushed furiously up one slope after the other and down again, when before him he suddenly saw the gaping black jaw of the tunnel. Into this gulf plunged an up train roaring, whistling shrilly, and behind it, once the earth had swallowed it up, it left a prolonged tremor which shook the very ground.

His legs now aching, Jacques flung himself down beside the permanent-way, crouched in the grass, his face buried in it, and burst into convulsive sobs. Oh God, had it after all come back to him, that loathsome complaint of which he had believed himself cured? Aghast at himself, he only now realized that he had been seized with the overpowering urge to kill Flora. *Kill a woman! Kill a woman!* It throbbed in his ears, ringing from out the deep past, out of his adolescence, but now it had become reinforced with all the augmenting, maddening fever of sexual desire. Just as other men, when puberty awakened in them, dreamed of possessing a girl, he was obsessed with the idea of killing one. For, incapable of deceiving himself, he had no doubt what he had snatched up those scissors for – to plunge them into the flesh the instant he saw it revealed, girl's flesh, girl's bosom, girl's hidden white, warm flesh. Nor was this in the least because she had resisted him. No, it was for sheer bodily satisfaction he wanted to do it, because he lusted after doing it, with such lust that had he now not held fast to the very grass he could have gone running breathless back there to stab Flora's throat. Her throat? Oh God, the throat of Flora whom he had seen grow up! Nature's child whom only now he had suddenly sensed as passionately loving him. Convulsive, his fingers thrust into the soil, while in a rattle of frightful anguish the sobs tore at his breast.

Nevertheless, he compelled himself to calm down. He longed to understand. What exactly was it made him different from other men? As a boy at Plassans in the south he had often enough asked himself that question. True, his mother, Gervaise, had had him very young, at fifteen and a half, but then he was not her first, he was her second.

59

She had been scarcely fourteen when she gave birth to her first, Claude. Besides, neither of his two brothers, neither Claude the eldest, nor Etienne, younger than himself, seemed to have suffered from having so childlike a mother or a mere schoolboy as father – handsome Lantier, whose stony heart must have cost Gervaise so many tears. But perhaps his brothers too had their trouble, but concealed it – especially the elder, who was eating out his heart to be a painter, so frantic with his artistic urge that people said that for all his brilliance he was half a lunatic. The whole tribe of them lacked balance. Many were definitely queer, in one way or another.

There were moments when Jacques was very conscious of that hereditary weakness of his. Not that his health was really bad, though anxiety and shame of those attacks had at one time made him very thin. But deep in himself, that was the trouble, he was conscious of sudden losses of balance, as if something in him snapped, or as if there were holes by which his personality oozed out of him, leaving him lost in a sort of haze in which everything was distorted. He was no longer his own master, he was the slave of his flesh, of the maddened beast in him. Yet he did not drink, would not even take a nip of brandy, for he had noticed that the least drop of alcohol made him wild. He had thus come to the conclusion that he was paying the bill for others, for fathers and grandfathers who had soaked themselves, for generations of drunkards of which he was the impure blood heritage, with slow poisoning and something savage in him by which he was to be classed together with wolves in dark forests which devoured women.

He had raised himself on one elbow, pondering and gazing at the dark entrance of the tunnel. Then a fresh sob ran from his loins to the back of his head and he fell back on the ground, grovelling and crying out in his pain. Flora! Flora of all girls he had wanted to kill! It came back to him in all its poignancy and horror as if those scissors had really been thrust into his own flesh. No hair-splitting could soothe him: he had intended to kill her, and were she again beside him, her bodice undone, her bosom naked, he would kill her.

The memory was clear as day, he was barely sixteen when this ill first took possession of him. It was one evening, when he was playing with a young girl, the daughter of a relation of his, two years his junior. She had fallen down. In a flash he saw her legs revealed to the thigh, and he had flung himself at her. The following year he recalled honing a knife to thrust into another girl's throat. That was a fair-haired little thing whom he saw pass his door every morning. She was very plump-bosomed and very pink, and he had actually selected the spot, a mole directly under her ear. Then came others and yet others, a succession of nightmares, so many women whose flesh he had touched, to be possessed with that sudden lust for murder, women he happened to jostle in the street, women he did not even know, but whom chance meetings brought close to him, one in particular, recently married, who had sat near him at a variety show and laughed loudly. In order not to slit her belly open he had been obliged to run away in the middle of an act. Since he had not even known these women in any way, what could be the fury he felt against them? For on every occasion that attack was like a sudden onslaught of a blind fury, an ever new thirst for vengeance of some unknown hurt done him long, long ago, but which he never could recall precisely. Did it mean that this was all of such very ancient origin, springing from some evil that womenkind had done to men, born of rancour accumulated in the male through the generations since a first act of deception deep in prehistoric caves? For in those fits he also felt a need to give battle, to master the female, to conquer her, a perverse need to sling her dead body on his back as if an animal killed for food, snatched from all other males, in lust for eternal killing. His skull strained with the effort of his thought, yet he could never answer himself, he knew that he knew too little, his brain too obtuse in this agony of the male compelled to acts where volition played no part and root causes had vanished.

Again a train flashed by with its lights and was engulfed, its explosion of thunder extinguished in the depths of the tunnel, and as if that anonymous crowd of passengers, in all their wild hurry indifferent to him, might have heard his thoughts, Jacques started up, suppressing his sobs, and assumed the pose of a man entirely innocent. How many a time, during one of his fits, had he not at the least sound had that sharp sensation of being guilty. It was only on his locomotive that he could be calm, happy, detached from the world. When Lison bore him rushing onward amid the thunder of her wheels, his hand on the steam regulator, his mind entirely absorbed in the track ahead, his eye concerned solely to distinguish signals,

61

thought in him ceased, only then, as he drank deep of the pure air which roared past him, did he know peace. And this was why he loved his locomotive so passionately, as if she were indeed a mistress who satisfied his desires and of whom he could expect nothing but happiness.

When he passed out of the *School of Arts and Crafts*, and despite his scholastic success decided on being an engine-driver, it was for the sake of the segregation, the obfuscation which it offered him. He had no particular other ambition, and now after four years as leading driver had reached a salary of 2,800 francs, which, together with bonuses for firing and greasing, had him topping the four thousand mark, and he had not the faintest thought of anything beyond. He saw his friends of the third and second grade, the general run of the Western Railway Company men, the workers taken on as improvers and trainees, almost all of them marrying working-class girls, feature-less women of whom one sometimes caught a glimpse as one was setting out on a journey, when they brought along little food baskets for their men, while ambitious mates of his, particularly those with good education, expected to become at least heads of sections and marry a girl who wore a hat, perhaps a real middle-class woman. But he himself avoided women at all costs. What did he want with them? He would never marry, he had no other future but to be a lone-wolf and drive his engine on and on without repose. Thus all his bosses agreed that he was an outstanding driver, a non-drinker, a non-wencher too, indeed, rather the laughing-stock of his skirt-chasing mates for his exaggeratedly circumspect behaviour. But they also said that he was sometimes rather worrying, because of his moody fits, those silences when his eyes were so strangely dull, and he had earthy pallor in his cheeks. In his little lodging-room in Cardinet Street, with its view of the Batignolles yard where his locomotive was housed, what long hours Jacques Lantier did know, all his free time, indeed, when he remained shut away deliberately like a monk in his cell, absorbing the sullen trouble of that subterranean lust of his by dint of forced sleep, lying obliterated, face down.

With an effort he now tried to get to his feet. Whatever was he about, lying there on the grass, this mild, misty winter night? The countryside was still bathed in shadows, only the haze-enwrapped sky was luminous, an immense vault as of ground glass, yellowish from the moon concealed beyond. The horizon was in black slumber, still as death itself. Now come on, it must be nearly nine, far better go back to the Misards' and to bed. But, aghast, he suddenly pictured himself back there climbing the stairs to the attic, stretching out on the hay with nothing but thin matchboarding to separate him from Flora. She would be there, he would hear her very breathing. He knew too well that she never closed the door. He could easily go in to her. And again the convulsion seized him, with the thought of her stripped, her outstretched limbs warm with slumber, and he broke into sobs so violent that they brought him grovelling to the ground again. He had meant to kill her, to kill her, dear God! It was suffocating him, he went through hell at the thought that he might enter her room to kill her in her bed – immediately, if he went back. Having no weapon would be no defence, no use clutching his own head, to crush himself to death, no use, for he sensed that against his very will under the lash of that urge to take by force, under that need to avenge the wrong done his kind so long, long ago, the male in him would open that door and would strangle her. No, no, better spend the whole night tramping the downs than go back there. All at once, he leapt to his feet and took to flight.

Now, for another half an hour Jacques Lantier tore through the dark lands, as if pursued and harried by embodiments of his own horrific thoughts. He clambered up steep slopes, he tumbled down into narrow ravines. One after another, he came to two rivers and forged across them, soaked to the waist. A bramble thicket, barring his way, drove him to frenzy. His obsession was to keep dead straight on, to forge farther and farther away, to escape, to escape that double, that insane beast he felt within himself. But all the time he was carrying that lunatic with him, it raced as fast as he himself did. Having believed he had driven it out seven months since and achieved normality, he now found it still part of his being, and so he had to start all over again, again to fight the terrible battle to prevent that other man within him leaping on the first woman that chance made him touch as he passed. Nevertheless, the immense night silence and the emptiness to some extent calmed him, bringing him the dream of a life as silent and deserted as this desolate country through which it seemed that he might tread on his way for ever and never meet a soul.

63

Without realizing it, he must have made a complete circle, for at last – there he was up against the railroad from the other side. He had traversed a huge semi-circle over the blackthorn-bristling hillsides above the tunnel. He staggered back away from it, angry and troubled to have thus returned to human tracks. But then, having meant to take a short cut behind a hillock, he lost his way and merely found himself back yet again facing the hedge along the permanent-way, just where it came out of the tunnel, and at the very place where so recently he had lain sobbing! He now felt utterly defeated. He lay lifeless, indifferent, when from the depths of the hill came the thunder of a train emerging from the tunnel, for the moment but a faint murmur, but one which was rapidly growing in volume. It arrested his attention, for it was none other than the Havre express, the six-thirty out from Paris, which passed this spot at nine twenty-five, the train which he drove himself twice in every week.

First, Jacques saw the black orifice of the tunnel show lighter, like the doorway of a baker's oven opened when the brushwood is burned. Then out burst the locomotive, enveloped in its own thunder, the large circular eye of its single head-light gleaming, piercing the countryside, lighting the twin rails on which it ran. But it was gone in a flash, like lightning, to be followed at once by the coaches, one after another, with their little oblongs of lighted window, sharply bright as they revealed the succession of little compartments full of passengers, all moving at such dizzy speed that after they were gone the eye could not even be sure it had seen them. And then, suddenly, most vividly, in a clearly-limned fragment of a second, through the gleaming panes of a half-compartment, Jacques saw a man who was holding another man down on the seat and thrusting a knife into his throat, while an indefinite shape, third person or mere pile of luggage, weighed down on the struggling legs of the victim. Then the train was gone, already in far flight towards Maufras Cross, in the pitch darkness showing no more than a triangle of red points, its three rear lights.

Riveted there, he stared after the train, as its rumble grew fainter in the depths of the vast, dead peace of that barren land. Had he really seen what he thought he had seen? He was all hesitancy, fearing to be sure of that vision revealed and withdrawn in a flash. Not a single feature of the two actors in the drama remained clear in his mind. That third dark form, he told himself, must have been a

64

travelling rug, fallen over the prostrate man's legs. But yet, for a moment, did he not discern a pale face of delicate outline, under a luxurious head of hair? But it all went blurry at once and dematerialized like something seen in a dream. For a flash, when he thought hard of it again, the silhouette of a human face returned. But after that, it vanished again, for ever. It must have been his imagination. Indeed, this whole incident so made his blood run cold, was so astounding, that in the end he told himself it must be mere hallucination, sprung from the terrible fit from which he had just emerged.

For nearly an hour Jacques still went on tramping through the night, his mind heavy with a tangle of thought. He was broken now, the tension had left him, his fever was blotted out by a great wave of ice which had welled up from within him. Without consciously willing it, at last he made his way back towards Maufras Cross. Yet, when he had reached the crossing-keeper's cottage, he told himself he would not go in, he would doss down in the little lean-to woodshed built on to one end. But under the door of the cottage he saw light, and mechanically he pushed it open, to come upon a surprising scene which held him fascinated on the threshold. It was Misard, in the corner of the room. He had pulled the butter crock out and was on all fours, a lighted lantern beside him. He was tapping the wall lightly. He was sounding it. He was searching.

The sound of the door made the man rear up. But he was not in the least put out. In the most natural tones, he merely said: 'The matches, I've dropped them, somewhere here.' Then, replacing the butter crock, he added: 'I came in to take the lantern. Just now, when I came back in, I found a man stretched out beside the permanent-way . . . dead, I reckon.'

For the moment Jacques had thought that he had caught Misard hunting for Aunt Phasie's nest-egg, which would have changed his dubiety about his aunt's accusations into certainty. But now, under the sudden shock of this news that Misard had discovered a corpse, that other drama, the drama of this isolated cottage, was completely forgotten, and it was the scene in the half-compartment of the train – the brief vision of one man cutting another man's throat – which in the same flash returned to him. 'A man – beside the permanent-way?' he demanded. 'But wherever do you mean?' and the colour left his cheeks.

Misard was about to tell Jacques that he had been on his way home with a couple of eels taken on his lines, his first act as a poacher being to hurry home and hide them, but he stopped short. Why did he have to let this young fellow in on all that? So instead, with a vague gesture, Misard merely said: 'Back there, about five hundred yards, I should say . . . Have to have a light to see what it's all about.'

In the same instant Jacques heard a dull thump just overhead. He was so nervy that he started violently.

'That's nought,' said Misard, 'only Flora getting up.'

Jacques now recognized the sound of bare feet padding across the floor above. Flora must have heard them. He guessed she was listening through her open door.

'I'll go with you,' he said painfully. 'But are you sure the man's dead?'

'Looked bloody well like it,' said Misard. 'With the lantern we'll see.'

'But whatever do you think it can have been? An accident, of course.'

'Maybe. Some poor b—— taking a short cut, I reckon. If it isn't somebody fallen out of the train.'

Jacques shuddered. 'Quick then, come on, quick!' he cried.

Never before had he felt such feverish need to see. While Misard just plodded along the track, entirely unmoved, his lantern swinging in his hand, its circle of light slowly coming up along the rails, Jacques got impatient and ran on ahead. There was a sort of physical desire glowing up in him, like that inner heat which speeds the steps of lovers when the hour of meeting is nigh. He was terrified of what he might find there, so he raced to meet it, straining every sinew. And when he got there, all but stumbling over a black bundle stretched along by the down track, he stood paralysed, pinned to the ground by a shock which ran from his feet to head. Not being able to see precisely what had taken place caused him such sharp pain that he turned and swore at Misard, dawdling along, still a good thirty yards away.

'Damnation, man, hurry,' he cried. 'If there's life in him, we may still be able to help.'

Still dragging his steps, Misard came up at last, utterly unconcerned.

Slowly sweeping the lantern light the length of the body, he merely grunted: 'Hm! He's damn well had it, hasn't he?'

No doubt falling from the train, the man had landed face in the dust on his belly, at most a couple of feet from the outer rail. All that was to be seen of the head was a coronet of white hair. The legs sprawled out. The left arm thrust at an angle as if torn from the socket, while the right was folded under the man's chest. He was very well dressed, in a loose travelling cloak of navy-blue, smart buttoned boots, and had fine linen underclothing. There was no trace of the body's having been run over, only of quantities of blood having poured from the throat, staining the shirt collar.

'It's a nob,' Misard observed calmly, 'a nob who somebody's finished off.' Then, turning to Jacques, standing gaping there like a dummy, he said sharply: 'Mustn't touch him, it's agin the law ...' Then he added: 'You stay here, old chap, and stand guard, while I run along to Barentin and tell the station-master there.'

Misard took his lantern and examined a mileage post. 'Good,' he said, 'right on No. 153.' He planted the lantern down on the ground near the body and made off into the darkness at his usual slow pace.

Left alone, Jacques did not stir, but gazed at the motionless lump of blood-drained flesh. In the dim light of the lantern placed at ground-level the outlines were not clear, but the excitement which had first driven him there, and the frightful attraction which held him at the site, came to a head in a notion which suddenly thrust knife-sharp through every pore – the notion that that other man – the man he had seen for an instant, knife in hand – that other man had dared, that other man had not been faint-hearted, that other man had gone the whole hog as his lust commanded – in short, that other man had achieved satisfaction, *that other man had killed!* Oh! fantastic thought, not being faint of heart, fantastic thought, satisfying desire, plunging home the knife! And his own longing to do such a thing had been sheer pain ten long years now!

In his fevered mind Jacques now despised himself and admired the other man. And thereby became obsessive need to see it all, unquenched possessive thirst to satiate his eyes with this remains of a man, this broken doll, this flaccid rag, to which the knife before his eyes had transformed a human being. This other man had materialized his constant dream, so let him see this, the result. Had it been he who

67

killed, this is what would lie prostrate. His heart thudding seemed to burst him asunder, and at the sight of this deathly violence his own murder itch flared like the lust for copulation. He took a step forward, closer, like a hesitant child growing accustomed to the bogey. Yes, he would dare, in his turn he would dare!

But a sudden thunder at his back made him leap to one side. It was a train which he had not noticed approaching, he was so deeply engrossed. He was nearly knocked down. Only the hot breath and frightful breath of the engine warmed him. It swept by, a tempest of noise, smoke and flame. Still more multitudes, the ceaseless flow of passengers towards Havre for tomorrow's great day. A child was pressing its nose against the pane, peering out into the dark country-side; the silhouettes of men came and went; a young woman lowered a window and tossed out a scrap of buttery, sugary paper.

All cheerfulness, the train was already far away, utterly indifferent to this corpse so close to which its wheels had brushed, this thing still sprawled face down, in the dim light of the lantern, with the mournful night-time peace all round.

He was suddenly possessed with a longing to see the wound, while still alone. Misgivings held him back, thought that perhaps if he touched the head, the fact would be known. But he had reckoned it out that Misard could hardly get back with the station-master for three-quarters of an hour. He let minutes slip by, his mind on Misard. Misard was such a timid, slow-moving, unruffled little man, but he too had the guts to do it, killing slowly without a trace of fuss, by doses of poison. Was it then so easy to kill? Did everybody kill?

He crept closer. The notion of taking a look at the wound pricked him with such sharp needles that his skin burned. He had to see how it was done, see what had run out of it, see the actual red gash. If he put the head back carefully, nobody would ever know. But behind his reluctance there was another fear which he did not admit, the fear of blood itself. Always and everywhere that horror had awakened together with desire in him. But yet there was still a quarter of an hour before anyone could come, and despite all his misgivings he was about to make up his mind to do it, when a slight noise at his side made him shudder.

It was Flora, beside him, gazing down just as he was. She had always been curious about accidents. The moment she heard of an animal run into or a man cut in two by a train, she could be counted on to go racing to the scene. And now, after a first glance, she had no qualms about her curiosity. She bent down. With one hand she took the lantern and with the other the head, turning it over.

'Don't you dare,' muttered Jacques, 'it's against the law.'

She shrugged her shoulders. There was the face in the yellow light, the face of an old man with a big nose and the blue eyes of one who had once been fair. The eyes were wide open. Under the chin gaped a wound, a shocking wound, a deep gash which had all but severed the neck, a ploughed-in wound, as if the knife had dug deep and turned this way and that. Blood had flooded over all the right side of the chest. On the left-hand side the little red ribbon of a Commander of the Legion of Honour in the button-hole of the overcoat looked like a lost clot of the man's life-fluid.

Faintly, in surprise, Flora cried out: 'Good Heavens! It's him – that old bastard!'

Stooping now like her, Jacques drew closer to get a better view, his hair mingling with hers, and he caught his breath and almost choked at the lavish sight. Automatically, he repeated after her:

'That old bastard . . . that old bastard . . .'

'Yes,' she said, 'old Grandmorin . . . old Judge Grandmorin.'

For an instant more she quizzed the bloodless features, the contorted lips, the horrified, starting eyes. Then she let the head go. *Rigor mortis* had already begun to stiffen the sinews, but it fell back to the ground, closing the wound again.

'He won't lark with any more girls,' she whispered. 'I guess this was done over one. Too true . . . Poor little Louisette. The dirty old swine, he's paid for it all right!'

There was a long silence. She had put the lantern down again and now waited, glancing slyly at Jacques from time to time. With the body now between them, he was motionless. He seemed lost, as if his very being had been absorbed into what he had just seen. It must be nearly eleven. After the scene which had taken place between them, he was shy to speak first. Then came the sound of voices. It was Misard, bringing the Barentin station-master. Anxious not to be seen, Flora decided to speak first. 'Aren't you coming back to bed?' she whispered.

He shivered and for a moment he was torn two ways. Then, shrinking back in terror, with great effort: 'No, no!' he cried.

She made no sign of response, but the limp line of her shoulders and the dangling arms revealed all her powerful body's disappointment. As if to seek forgiveness for having resisted him just now, she descended to humility.

'Then, if you're not coming back – does that mean I shan't be seeing you any more?' she murmured.

'No, no,' he could only repeat.

The voices drew closer. Without even trying to take his hand in farewell – for he seemed deliberately to have put that corpse between them – and without even the 'All right, so long then' of their childhood partings, she vanished into the darkness, and her breathing came harsh, as if she were suddenly stifling sobs.

All at once, there was the station-master, with Misard and two porters. The station-master too at once recognized who it was: no doubt whatsoever, Judge Grandmorin, that's who, he knew the judge, he had often seen him get out at his station, every time, in fact, he came down to see his sister, Madame Bonnehon, out at Doinville. The body, he ordered, was to stay where it was. All he did was cover it with a coat which one of the men had brought. He had sent a clerk by the eleven o'clock train to report the affair to the State Prosecutor at Rouen. But him there was no point in expecting out before five or six the next morning. Anyway, he would have to fetch the examining magistrate, the clerk of the court and a doctor. So the station-master arranged for a rota to take turns, keeping guard all night, with a lantern.

Before making up his mind at last to go along to Barentin and find a shake-down there in one of the sheds (for it would not be till seven thirty that he would have to catch the Havre train), Jacques stood at the scene, transfixed, a considerable time. Then the thought of the examining magistrate coming out suddenly alarmed him, as if he felt he was an accomplice of the murderer.

Was he to tell what he had seen when the express passed? His first decision was to do so. After all, he had nothing to fear. Besides, his duty was clear. Then he asked himself what good it would do. He could not provide a single definite detail. There was nothing precise that he could say about the man who did it. That being so, it would be stupid to stick his nose into it, losing time and being very worried, without doing anybody any good.

No, no, he was not going to speak. So at last, off he went, turning back twice, to see the black hump of the body lying there in the circle of yellow light of the lantern. From the hazy sky which overhung the desolation of that waste land with its arid slopes, it struck a little colder now. Meanwhile, other trains had passed. Now another was coming along, bound for Paris, a very long train. Inexorable in the power of their machinery, incessantly they passed either way, bound for destinations still far-off in time, each totally indifferent to the fact that it swept so close by the all but severed head of the man whose throat another man had cut.

3

The next day, a Sunday, precisely when all the bells of Havre were busily striking 5 A.M., Roubaud strode down the main platform to take over his duties. It was still pitch dark, but the wind blowing in from the sea had grown stronger and was driving away the last vestiges of fog clinging to the slopes, the upper ridge of which stretches from Saint-Adresse to Tourneville Fort. Over to the west, above the sea, a clear patch of sky was already showing, with the last stars gleaming brightly. Under the station roof, dull in the damp chill of this early hour, the gas burners were still smoking. And there was the first Montivilliers train being assembled by the shunters, under the instructions of the night A.S.M. The waiting-room doors were still closed, the platforms deserted, in this sluggish awakening of the station.

When he left his flat up above the waiting-rooms, Roubaud had come on Madame Lebleu, wife of the booking-office clerk, standing in the middle of the famous 'corridor' which served all the residential quarters of senior station staff. For weeks now that good lady had been getting up at all hours to spy on Mademoiselle Guichon. Mademoiselle Guichon worked in the office, and Madame Lebleu suspected her of carrying on with the station-master, M. Dabadie. Not that she had ever obtained the slightest clue, no, not a suspicion of one, not a whisper. And on this occasion too she was quick to slip back into her own flat, her only harvest a certain astonishment at having observed, in the space of the three seconds which the husband needed to get out of his door and close it again, that there, at this early hour, inside the Roubauds' flat, Madame Roubaud herself, the allegedly beautiful Severine, was actually out of bed! Yes, she was actually up, already dressed, her hair done too, and her outdoor shoes on. Yes, Madame Roubaud, of all women, usually lie-abed till nine! In fact, Madame Lebleu went so far as to waken her husband, to acquaint him of this extraordinary news item. The night before, the Lebleus had stayed up till the Paris express came in, at eleven five, for they were burning with curiosity to learn how Roubaud had got on at Paris about the assistant prefect. But they had been unable to guess a thing from the bearing of the couple, who had come back just the same as any other day. And though the Lebleus had strained their ears till midnight, not a sound had come from their neighbours. The Roubauds must have gone to bed at once and slept most soundly. But since Madame Roubaud had got up at such an unearthly hour, it was now clear that their trip had not ended well. And when the booking-clerk asked his wife how Madame R. had seemed, his wife made a tremendous effort to describe her: very rigid, she said, very pale too, with those big blue eyes of hers standing out under that black mop of hair. Yes, the A.S.M.'s wife had been as still as a statue. She might have been walking in her sleep, said Madame Lebleu. Well, at least they had a clue what to keep a look out for during the day.

Down in the station, Roubaud sought out his opposite number, Moulin, who had done the night shift, and took over, while Moulin accompanied him for a moment on his round to put him *au fait* about little items, such as the capture of some pilferers, caught red-handed, trying to get into the left-luggage office, three shunters who had had to be reprimanded for insubordination, and a coupling broken while making up the Montivilliers train. Roubaud took it all in without a word, his countenance tranquil. He merely looked a little washed out. Perhaps he was rather tired. The heavy shadows under his eyes suggested he was. But when the night A.S.M. had finished his report, Roubaud seemed to be asking for further information. One might have thought that he had expected more than that to happen during that night. 'That's all,' said Moulin. Roubaud made no reply, merely stared at the platform under his feet for some moments.

Walking thus together the length of the platform, the two men reached the end of the covered-in part, at the point where, on the right, there was a bay for rolling stock come in during the previous day and intended for use on the morrow. Here Roubaud raised his head at last, and his eyes had fixed on a first-class coach with a half-compartment – No. 293 – which happened to be directly under the flickering light of a gas-jet, when Moulin suddenly cried:

'Oh, I was forgetting . . .'

Roubaud's bloodless cheeks flushed and he was unable to prevent himself starting with surprise.

'I was forgetting,' Moulin said again. 'This coach is not to leave the station. Don't let them use it in this morning's six-forty express.'

There was a brief silence before, in quite ordinary tones, Roubaud replied.

'Hm! And why is that?' he asked.

'Because there's a half-compartment reserved for this evening's express. We can't be sure of getting a coach with one in during the day. All the more reason for holding this one back.'

His eyes still fixed on this coach No. 293, Roubaud replied.

'Right you are.'

Then quite other thoughts seemed to absorb him. All at once he expostulated: 'It really is the limit! Just look at what those bastards call cleaning! That coach looks as if it had not been done for a week.'

'Pooh!' said Moulin. 'When trains come in after eleven, it's not likely the chaps are going to do much cleaning, is it? . . . We've got to be thankful if they condescend to give them the once over. Why the other evening, they actually missed a passenger sound asleep in one of the compartments, and the man never woke up till morning!'

He suppressed a yawn. 'Well, I'll be turning in,' he said. But just as he was leaving, curiosity all at once brought him back.

'By the way, that business of yours about the under-prefect. You've settled that all right, I take it?'

'Absolutely. I had a nice little jaunt, as a matter of fact, I'm in the clear.'

'Glad to hear it . . . And don't forget to hold that No. 293 back, will you?'

When Roubaud found himself alone on the platform, he made his way slowly back to the Montivilliers train, which was ready at the platform. The waiting-room doors were open now, travellers were appearing, a number of sportsmen with their dogs and two or three families of small shopkeepers taking advantage of Sunday. In a word, not many travelling. But once this train – the first of the day – had pulled out, Roubaud had to buckle to, at once. There was preparation of the slow five forty-five up to Paris via Rouen to see to. At this early hour there were few men on duty and the A.S.M.'s job involved a host of additional cares. As soon as he had supervised the shunting, each coach being brought into position separately under the station roof on the traverser, he had to scurry off to the departure to give an eye to the issue of tickets and registering of luggage. There was a dispute between a porter and some soldiers which called for his intervention. For half an hour, with icy draughts lashing him, amid a travelling public shivering with cold, bleary from early rising, cross-tempered from jostling each other in semi-darkness, he had to be everywhere at once and had not a thought for himself. The moment the departure of the slow train had cleared the station, he hurried off to the signal box, to make certain everything was as it should be there, for another train was due in, but was late – the non-stop from Paris. He returned to the platform, to be present as it came in, waited till all the passengers had given up their tickets and were on the station buses, which by then had lined up along the barrier which separated the road from the tracks. It was only then that he could breathe for a moment in a station once again deserted and silent.

It struck six. At leisurely pace, Roubaud left the covered part of the station. Once outside, with space in front of him, he raised his head and took deep breaths. At last day was breaking. The wind coming in off the open sea had finished sweeping away the mist, and it was the clear morning of a fine day. He gave a glance northwards, Ingouville way, up to the cemetery trees. The ridge of high ground stood out, a violet line against the sky, which was lighter now. Then, swinging round to south and west, he glanced at the last wisps of frail cloud, floating softly away in formation over the sea, while the whole western sky, that vast gulf of the Seine estuary, was just beginning to catch fire from the sun, about to top the horizon. With a mechanical gesture, he removed his gold-braided cap, as if to freshen his forehead in that keen, clean air. The familiar scene, the immense level lay-out of the station installations, arrival platforms to the left, locomotive depot next, goods on the right, a town in itself, seemed to soothe him, bringing him back to the tranquillity of everyday tasks which never changed. Away above the wall of Charles Lafitte Street the factory stacks were smoking. He could just see the immense piles of coal in the yards along Vauban dock. The murmur of the remainder of the harbour was also now to be heard. The whistles of good trains, all this awakening and the very smell of the water which the wind carried, reminded him of today's festivities, the ship to be launched, which was going to bring a great crush of people.

As he returned to the station proper, he came upon the shunters

75

just beginning to make up the six-forty express. And then, getting the impression that the men were about to put that coach No. 293 on the traverser, all the calm which the clean morning air had granted him vanished in a sudden explosion of rage. 'God Almighty! Not that one,' he yelled. 'Leave it be, can't you? That's not going out till this evening.'

The foreman explained that they were merely pushing the coach a few feet out of the way, to get at another, behind it. But he paid no attention, so deafened was he by that quite disproportionate flush of fury. 'You mutton-headed bastards,' he bullyragged. 'Haven't you been told not to touch that one?'

Even when at last he was brought to understand what they intended, he was still savage, lashing out about the inconveniences of a station in which there was not even room to turn a waggon round. Indeed, Havre station, being one of the first to be built on this line, with its roofing part timbered, part galvanized, with only narrow glazings, and its dismal, bleak buildings, already all cracks, and the rolling-stock shed a mere shanty of timber, was much too small and altogether unworthy of such a port.

'It's a crying shame,' he said. 'I don't know why the Company has not pulled the whole damned thing down long ago.'

The shunters stood gaping. They were astonished to hear a disciplinarian and stickler for forms like old Roubaud let his tongue go like that. All tensed up, he now saw the shunting work to its end in silence. A discontented fold cut his low forehead in two, and his rotund, beefy cheeks, with their bristling red beard, seemed to swell with mulish indignation.

But after this outburst, Roubaud recovered his customary calm. He busied himself most energetically with the express, checking every detail. Some couplings seeming to him badly made, he insisted on having them re-done under his eyes. A mother and her two daughters, whom his wife used to visit, wanted him to find them a *Ladies Only*. Before whistling to give the signal for departure, he once again made sure the train was exactly as it should be, and after it had pulled out, he followed it a long time, with that alert glance of a man conscious that a moment of forgetfulness on his part might cost human lives.

At once after this he had to go right across the tracks, to receive in a Rouen train just entering the station. There he found a post office fellow with whom he exchanged the latest every morning. In so tight-packed a morning's work, this was always a welcome little respite, nearly quarter of an hour in which he could take breath without any duty calling him away. And this morning too he rolled his usual cigarette, and chatted with great vivacity. The sun was already well up, the gas-jets had been extinguished. The station roofing was so poorly glazed that the whole place was still in greyish shadow. But beyond it the vast expanse of sky on to which it opened was already ablaze with radiant light, the whole expanse of the horizon flushed rose-pink, every object standing out clearly in the clear atmosphere of a fine winter morning.

At eight, M. Dabadie, the station-master, generally came down, and the A.S.M. then reported to him. M. Dabadie was a handsome man, very dark, very spruce, with the general style of a very wide-oh big business man. But, a practical man, he readily devolved the passenger traffic on his A.S.M. and devoted himself principally to the port traffic. There was a tremendous flow of goods, and he was in constant negotiations with leading business firms of Havre and indeed the whole world. This particular morning he was a little late. Roubaud had already looked into his office without finding him. The mail on his table was still unopened, but the A.S.M. had caught sight of a telegram among the letters. As if some fascination held him there, he hung about at the door, repeatedly returning, in spite of himself, to glance at that mail-littered desk.

At last, at ten minutes past eight, M. Dabadie appeared. Roubaud sat down and kept silent, to allow M. Dabadie to open his mail. But M. Dabadie was in no hurry, and wanted to be pleasant to his A.S.M. He held a high opinion of Roubaud.

'Of course, everything went off all right at Paris?' he enquired.

'Yes, sir, thank you.'

He had now opened the telegram. But still he did not read it. Instead, he smiled at Roubaud, whose voice had lost all its timbre, through the tremendous effort its owner had to make to keep control of a nervous tic plucking at his chin.

'We are very lucky to be able to keep you here,' said M. Dabadie.

'Well, sir, I am very pleased to be able to stay.'

Then, when M. Dabadie did at last make up his mind to glance at the telegram, Roubaud, his face quite damp with faint perspiration, watched him. But the emotion he expected simply did not appear. The S.M. merely read the telegram quietly to the end, then tossed it down on his desk. It was apparently a mere routine service communication, and M. Dabadie immediately proceeded to open the rest of his mail, while, according to their daily custom, the A.S.M. made his verbal report on the events of the night and early morning. But this morning Roubaud was rather inclined to stammer. Indeed, he had to think quite hard before recalling what his opposite number had said about the men who tried to break into the left-luggage office. There was a further brief exchange between the two men, then with a gesture as the two other A.S.M.s – those of the port and the slow goods – appeared on the scene to make their reports, Roubaud was released. The newcomers, however, brought a new telegram, which had just been handed to them as they crossed the platform.

'You may go,' said M. Dabadie, seeing his assistant hesitate at the door.

But still Roubaud waited, staring wide-eyed. Indeed, he only left when the little slip of paper had fallen to the desk, brushed aside with the same indifference as the first telegram. For a moment he now wandered about the station. He seemed puzzled, indeed, quite nonplussed. The clock said eight thirty-five, and there was no departure before the slow nine-fifty. He generally used this comparatively quiet hour to do a round of the station, and today he had gone some distance before realizing where his legs were leading him. Then, raising his head, he found himself just opposite coach No. 293. At once, he turned sharply right about and made for the loco shop, though he had nothing to inspect there. The sun had now risen well above the horizon and the thin air was full of a golden dust. But he was no longer enjoying this fine morning. Instead, he became all bustle, to all appearances very busy, in his effort to stifle his singleminded expectation.

Suddenly, a voice halted him.

'Good morning, M. Roubaud . . . Did you see my missus?'

It was Pecqueux, a tall, rakish fellow of forty-three, big-boned, thin, his face bronzed by the locomotive fires and the smoke. The grey eyes under the low forehead and the large mouth in the salient jaw had the permanent leer of a great skirt-lover.

'Oh, it's you, Pecqueux is it?' cried Roubaud, halting, and apparently

78

astonished. 'But of course, I was forgetting, your engine's broken its coupling-rod, hasn't it? You are not going till this evening. Twenty-four hours off, jolly good, eh?'

'Jolly good,' repeated Pecqueux, who still had not worked last night's binge out of his system.

By origin from a village near Rouen, he had joined the Company very young, as workman fitter. Then, at the age of thirty, getting bored by the workshops, he wanted to be fireman, with the idea of rising to engine-driver. It was at this time that he had married Victoire, a girl from his own village. But though the years were rolling by, he was still just fireman, and now would never be promoted to driver. His conduct was too poor, he was careless of his appearance, and was a persistent boozer and wencher. A score of times he would have been dismissed had he not had M. Grandmorin to take his part, and had the administration not been inured to his weaknesses, which he admittedly redeemed by his cheerful humour and his many years' experience as fitter. He was only really worrying when drunk, for then he became a real brute, capable of anything.

'And the missus, see her?' he asked again, his mouth a great gash of cheerful laughter.

'But of course, of course we saw her,' replied the A.S.M. 'We even had lunch at your place ... Ah, Pecqueux, you've a fine wife in Victoire, and you've made a great mistake not being a better husband to her.'

Pecqueux laughed more rakishly than ever. 'You don't really mean it!' he cried. 'But it's my missus' own wish for me to have a good time.'

This was true. Victoire, his senior by two years, having become enormous, obese, a regular mountain of immobility, actually used to slip a bit of silver into his pocket for him to take his pleasures elsewhere. She had never much taken to heart the continual wenching which in him seemed a physical need. Now things had rather settled down, and Pecqueux had two wives, one at each end of the route, the real one at Paris for nights at home, and another at Havre to fill in the time spent there between one train and another. By nature very sparing, a regular old cheese-parer, in fact, 'Ma' Victoire, who knew all about his goings-on and mothered him, was never tired of saying that the last thing she wanted her man to do was put out her 'opposite number' at Havre. Indeed, every time Pecqueux set out, Victoire made sure he had a change of linen. Victoire would have felt it badly if 'the other' had been able to say she neglected her husband.

'All the same,' Roubaud insisted, 'you do go a bit too far, you know. My wife is very fond of her old nursie, and she's going to give you a good talking to.'

But he suddenly became silent. A tall, lean woman had emerged from the shed they were approaching. It was Philomène Sauvagnat, sister of Sauvagnat, yard inspector. This in fact was the auxiliary wife whom Pecqueux had been enjoying at Havre for the past year. The two of them must have been having a confab there in the shed, when Pecqueux came out to hail his A.S.M. Still youthful, despite her thirty-two years, Philomène was a tall, angular creature, flat-bosomed, but her flesh devoured by insatiable sexual desire. She had the long head, the fiery eyes and the body of a rather scraggy mare constantly on heat. It was also whispered that she was addicted to the bottle. All the men on the station were said to have taken their turn in her bed, in that little house near the locomotive sheds which was allocated to her brother and kept by her in very slovenly fashion. The brother, a typical Auvergnian, was pig-headed, and a stickler for discipline, and though he stood well with his superiors, he had had a lot of bother about all this, to the point of being threatened with curtailment of tenancy. For the present he was allowed to stay on out of personal consideration for himself, while for his part he was anxious to keep it on out of a sort of need for family domesticity, which, whenever he found his sister with a man, did not prevent him knocking her about so roughly that many a time she finished up senseless on the floor. The case of Pecqueux, however, was one of a real love match. In that ourageous rake's arms Philomène found real satisfaction, while for Pecqueux this under-fleshed woman had at the outset of the affair proved a really welcome change from his frankly over-fleshed legitimate spouse. Now he just went on with it, because it relieved him of the need to look for a bit of skirt elsewhere. Severine Roubaud, from a feeling that she owed it to Victoire, was the only woman to take the matter up, and she had quarrelled with Philomène, whom out of a sort of pride she now did all she could to avoid and cut dead whenever she saw her.

'All right then old duck,' cried Philomène, brazenly to Pecqueux,

'I'll be seeing you. I'll get out of the way now, so M. Roubaud can talk pi to you on behalf of his missus.'

Incorrigible, Pecqueux just grinned.

'Come on now,' he cried, 'you needn't go, he doesn't mean no harm!'

'Oh, I must go,' she said. 'I've got to take Madame Lebleu some eggs, my hens have begun laying.'

She had thus brought in Madame Lebleu's name on purpose, because she knew all about the undercurrent of hostility between that lady and the A.S.M.'s wife, so just to make the latter mad she pretended to be on better terms with the former. But she was not going to leave the two men at once, she gave rein to her curiosity, hearing the fireman enquire what the latest was about that under-prefect business.

'You've fixed that, you're all right, I hope, M. Roubaud?'

'Perfectly all right.'

Pecqueux gave a roguish wink. 'Bah!' he cried. 'You never had any cause to worry, because with a good card like you've got, up your sleeve . . . eh? You know what I mean. My missus too has a lot to thank that old boy for.'

But Roubaud cut this allusion to Grandmorin very short, by suddenly going back to Pecqueux's service arrangements.

'So you're not going back to Paris this evening?'

'That's right. Lison'll be ready then. They're just fitting her tie-rod now . . . I'm expecting my driver back any moment. He's gone off for a breath of air in the country. You know who I mean, don't you? Jacques Lantier! Hails from your part of the country, Jacques does.'

For a moment Roubaud made no reply. He was absent, lost in thought. Then, suddenly waking up, 'What's that you say?' he cried. 'Ah, engine-driver Jacques Lantier . . . Why, of course I know him. Just enough to bid each other time of day, anyway. As a matter of fact, though, it's here we met each other. He being my junior, I never saw him at Plassans. Last autumn he did my wife a kindness, ran a little errand for her at Dieppe. She's some cousins there . . . I gather Lantier's a capable fellow.'

He was babbling on, he was talking too much. Suddenly he moved off.

81

'Au revoir, Pecqueux ... I must see what's doing over there, on the other side.'

It was only now that Philomène left the scene, loping along in her horse-like way, while Pecqueux, hands in pockets, stood grinning cheerfully. It really was a delightfully free morning, this. Besides, he was curious to observe the A.S.M. already coming back. Why, Roubaud had only had time to poke his nose into the shed. Didn't take him long to inspect, did it? And he wondered what the A.S.M. had really been after.

It was just on the stroke of nine when Roubaud re-entered the station proper. He followed the whole way through, to near the parcel office, but, looking hard, did not seem to find what he was searching for. He came back again, still striding impatiently. One after the other, he put his head in at all the various offices. At this hour Havre railway station was empty and peaceful. Indeed, he was the only person at all busy, as if the calm irritated him more and more, for he was in that over-stressed state of a man who, menaced by a catastrophe, ends up in a desperate longing for it to explode on him. His self-control was exhausted, he simply could not keep still. His eyes now did not leave the clock. Nine ... five past nine. As a rule, he did not go in for breakfast till ten, when the nine-fifty had pulled out. But all at once, thought of Severine, who must be equally on tenterhooks up there, brought him back to the flat. He reached the corridor at the precise instant when Madame Lebleu was opening the door to Philomène, who had popped in hatless to take her a couple of eggs. The two women hesitated, so that Roubaud was obliged to run the gauntlet of their four eyes aimed at him. He had his key ready and was as quick as he could possibly be, but all the same in the flash of the door's opening and closing they had time to catch sight of Severine. She was sitting on a chair in the dining room, her hands folded in her lap, her features very pale and still. At this sight, Madame Lebleu drew Philomène inside and closed her own door, then told what she had herself seen earlier that morning: it was as plain as a pikestaff, that *sous-préfet* business had turned out badly for the Roubauds! Oh no, Philomène explained, not at all, that was precisely why she had hurried round, she had news to tell Madame Lebleu – and she repeated what she had just heard none other than Roubaud say. After that the two women lost themselves in the wildest conjectures. But whenever they met it was always the same, gossip without end.

'I'll swear they've had a dressing down . . . They're shaking in their shoes, I can tell you.'

'Dear Madame Lebleu, wouldn't it be wonderful if we were to see the last of them?'

This ever more venomous antagonism between the Lebleus and the Roubauds really arose from a housing question. The whole of the first floor of the station building, above the waiting rooms, was given over to living quarters for the senior staff. There was a long central corridor just like that in an hotel, with overhead lighting, and this corridor, with its buff-coloured walls, ran through the whole breadth of the building, with brown doors at intervals on either side, all the way down it. But the flats on the right had windows which gave on to the station courtyard with its old plane trees, beyond which stretched the lovely view of Ingouville ridge, whereas those on the left had dwarfed arched windows which opened directly on to the station roofing, and this, with its galvanized ridge and sooty glazing, blocked the view. Nothing could be more delightful than the outlook on the one side, with the incessant traffic of the station approach, not to mention the greenery and the expanse of countryside, while the other flats were enough to give anyone the pip, just like a prison with the sky walled in, and hardly any proper daylight. The front flats were occupied by the station-master, the assistant station-master Moulin and the Lebleus, the back ones by the Roubauds, and Mademoiselle Guichon the clerk, while there were three more rooms on that side, reserved for travelling inspectors. Now, everybody knew that formerly the two A.S.M.s had always lodged side by side. The fact that the Lebleus had one of the front flats was due to the favouritism of a former A.S.M., the man whose place Roubaud had taken. He had had his reasons to make up to Madame Lebleu, so, being a widower without children, he had let her have his flat. Now, that being so, was it really right to put the Roubauds at the back when they had a right to be in front? But so long as the Lebleus and the Roubauds had got on well together, Severine had in fact always given way to her neighbour, who was twenty years her senior, and not a healthy woman either, so corpulent that she always had trouble with her breathing. And war was not really declared till Philomène had set the two women, Madame Lebleu and Severine Roubaud, at loggerheads by her disgusting tittle-tattle.

'I tell you,' said Philomène, returning to her pet subject, 'they're not above taking advantage of being in Paris to put in a word at head office for turning you out . . . I've been told on good authority, they have written a long letter to the General Manager claiming their right.'

Madame Lebleu choked with indignation. 'They're a lowdown couple!' she wheezed. 'And I have good reason for thinking that they are doing all they can to get that good-for-nothing office girl on their side. For the last fortnight she's hardly had the decency to say good-morning properly, the hussy! . . . A nice piece of work she is, too . . . But I've got my eye on her . . .'

She lowered her voice, to affirm that Mademoiselle Guichon had a *rendezvous* every night with the S.M. It had been he – a widower, father of a big daughter still at boarding school – who had installed that thirty-year-old faded blondie there, with her tight most untalkative lips, the sly viper. She was even supposed to have been a teacher once. But there was no taking her ever by surprise, she slipped about so soundlessly, through the least opening. In herself she did not count for much, but if she was sleeping with the station-master, that made her of decisive importance. What a triumph it would be to find out her secret and get her under their thumb!

'Ah, but I shall find out, I shall, all in good time,' Madame Lebleu assured Philomène. 'I'm not one to take things lying down. . . . We are here, and here we are going to stay. Decent folk are on our side, aren't they, my dear?'

It was true enough that the whole station was violently *pro* or *con* in this business of the flats. The corridor was particularly worked up about it. It was perhaps only the other A.S.M. – Moulin, that is – who took no interest in it. He of course was all right, in front, with a fragile, shy little wife, scarcely ever to be seen, producing another child every twentieth month.

'I don't know,' concluded Philomène. 'Even if they are shaking in their boots, as you say, they're going to weather this storm all right . . . You mark my words, if they don't. They know people with influence, they do.'

All this time she had still been clinging to her two eggs, but with

84

these words she handed them to Madame Lebleu. Really newly-laid, they were, she'd taken them warm from under her hen's bottom. The elder lady gushed her gratitude.

'Oh, how kind you are to me . . . You spoil me, my dear . . . And I see so little of you nowadays! You must come in for a chat more often. You know my hubby is always at work and I find it so dull, my dear, tied here as I am, with my legs, you see. Oh, whatever should I do if those awful Roubauds took away my view?' And then, accompanying Philomène to the door, Madame Lebleu opened it and put her finger to her lips.

'Sh! Listen!'

They stood together stock still in the corridor fully five minutes, not stirring a finger, scarcely breathing, heads bent, their ears alerted towards the Roubauds' door, but not a sound emerged therefrom, a deathly silence reigned. At last, afraid of being surprised, they separated, with a final silent nod of the head, the one to tiptoe away, the other to close the door so softly that one could not even have heard the bolt enter the socket.

At nine twenty, Roubaud was down in the station again, looking after the making up of the nine-fifty slow, and, despite the efforts he made not to do so, gesticulating too much. He was now like a cat on hot bricks, every moment turning to look the length of the platform. But he saw nothing coming. His hands were shaking.

Then, just as he was casting a glance the length of the station behind him, he all at once, close at hand, heard a young fellow from the telegraph office breathlessly crying: 'M. Roubaud, M. Roubaud! I wonder if you know where M. Dabadie and the Police Super are? . . . I have telegrams for them, I've been looking for them for the last ten minutes . . .'

Roubaud had swung round, so tense from top to toe that not a muscle of his face moved. His eyes fastened on the telegrams which the clerk was holding. This time, by the man's pent-up excitement, he was sure these were the telegrams he expected, at last the dénouement was there. Very calm, he spoke.

'I saw M. Dabadie go by only a moment ago.'

Never before had he felt so cool, his mind so clear, every faculty united on the defensive. Yes, he was sure of himself now.

'Why,' he cried, 'but there is M. Dabadie, coming this way.'

And there, indeed, the station-master was, coming from the direction of the slow goods office. M. Dabadie gave but one glance at the wire, then cried: 'Good Heavens! Roubaud! There's been a murder down the line . . . This is from the inspector at Rouen.'

'What's that you say?' cried Roubaud. 'One of our men murdered?'

'No, no,' cried M. Dabadie, quickly. 'It's a passenger . . . apparently one who booked a half-compartment at Paris . . . The body was thrown out near the end of Malaunay tunnel, just by mile-post 153 . . . What's more, the victim is one of our own Directors! It is M. Grandmorin.'

'Not Judge Grandmorin? Judge Grandmorin? Oh! how terribly upset my poor wife will be!'

The cry was so à propos, and so heartfelt, that for a moment it struck M. Dabadie forcibly.

'How right you are,' he said, thoughtfully, 'of course, you knew him well. A very decent man, was he not?'

Then, holding up the other telegram, addressed to the Police Superintendent, he ran on: 'This will be from the examining magistrate. All about the formalities, I don't doubt . . . And it's only nine twenty-five, of course M. Cauche isn't in his office yet . . . Somebody'd better go round at once to the *Café du Commerce* on Napoleon Promenade, he's sure to be there.'

Five minutes later, M. Cauche arrived, at the heels of a railwayman. An ex-Army officer, who considered his post a sort of hobby, he never turned up at the station before ten, when, after idling about for a few moments, he would go back again to his café. This dramatic intervention, falling in between two hands of piquet, had taken him quite by surprise for a moment, the business which usually came his way being far less serious than this.

The telegram was indeed from the Rouen examining magistrate, and the fact that it only arrived now, fully twelve hours after the discovery of the body, was due to the magistrate having first telegraphed to Paris to find out the circumstances of Judge Grandmorin's departure, after which, tracing out the time of the train and number of the compartment allotted him, he had merely instructed the Havre Superintendent to inspect the half-compartment of coach No. 293, 'if still at Havre'.

Immediately he had read this detailed instruction, the moroseness which M. Cauche had been exhibiting at the interruption – as he thought, probably for no serious reason – vanished, to give place to an attitude of enormous self-importance, fitting the extreme seriousness which he now saw in the case. Suddenly all anxiety and apprehension lest conduct of the enquiry slipped from his hands, he cried out that that coach was bound not to be at Havre any longer.

'It's bound to have left this morning!' he complained.

It was left to Roubaud, quite unruffled, to put his mind at rest.

'Oh no, sir, if you'll excuse me . . . It so happens that we had orders to reserve a half-compartment on this evening's up train, so that very coach is over there, in the siding.'

He led the way, the superintendent and the station-master following him. The news must have spread around already, for the shunters all slyly left their posts and tailed after them, while clerks and others first appeared at their various office doors, then filtered into the crowd, one by one, till very soon there was quite a gathering of station folk.

As they reached the coach, M. Dabadie began to think out loud.

'All the same,' he said, 'this coach will have been inspected last night, and if there really were anything to report, we should already have known.'

'That's just what we are going to check up on,' said M. Cauche, sharply.

He opened the door and entered the half-compartment. In the very same instant he cried out loudly, without giving thought to what expressions he was using:

'My God, anyone'd think they'd stuck a pig!'

A gasp of horror ran through the gathering of onlookers, and necks were stretched, to see for themselves. M. Dabadie was one of the first who had to have a look. He pulled himself up on to the running board, with Roubaud craning forward with all the others, not to be different.

There was not a trace of disorder in the half-compartment. The windows were closed and at first glance everything seemed in place. There was a frightful smell coming from the open door and then they saw that in the very centre of one of the seat cushions a pool of blood had congealed. The pool had been so copious, so broad, that a little stream had trickled from it as if there had been a spring of blood there, and the flow had dripped on to the floor-mat below. Flecks of

87

blood also adhered to the upholstery. But there was nothing else. Only this nauseating blood.

M. Dabadie was beside himself.

'Where are the men who did the inspection last night? Find them and bring them to me!'

But they were already there. They came forward, stammering excuses. Could a man see properly at night? All the same, they said they had run their hands over all the seats. They swore they noticed nothing last night.

Meanwhile, M. Cauche stood inside the compartment, pencil out, jotting down points for his report. He called Roubaud to him – he often spent a few minutes with Roubaud, strolling down the platform in off moments, smoking a cigarette.

'M. Roubaud, do you mind stepping up, you may be able to help me.'

And when the A.S.M. had placed himself astride the patch on the floor, not to tread in it, M. Cauche said:

'Just peep under that other squab, will you, and see if anything has slipped behind it.'

Roubaud lifted the seat and made a painstaking little search, his eyes expressive merely of curiosity.

'Nothing here,' he said.

Then there was, however, a spot on the back squab which attracted his attention. He pointed it out to the superintendent. Was that not a bloodstained finger-print? But no, in the end they agreed that it was only mud. Meanwhile, scenting crime, a host of people had come up to watch the search and were pressing behind the station-master, whom the queasiness of a man of refinement had persuaded to stay on the running-board. But all at once an idea came to him.

'Why, M. Roubaud,' he cried, 'but weren't you on this very train? Surely you came back by last night's express? Then you're the very man to give us some information!'

'By Jove, how right you are,' cried the Superintendent. 'And did you notice anything, M. Roubaud?'

For three or four seconds, Roubaud said nothing. Just at that moment he happened to have bent down, to examine the floormat again. But he straightened up almost at once, and his reply was made in perfectly normal tones, though possibly he was a little loud.

'But of course, of course,' he said. 'I will tell you . . . My wife was with me. If what I am going to say is to go in the report, perhaps she had better come down to check my impressions with her own.'

This to M. Cauche seemed most reasonable, and Pecqueux, who had just turned up on the scene, offered to run and fetch Madame Roubaud. Off he went, loping along with huge strides, and they all waited a moment. Philomène, who had run up to the scene with Pecqueux, now followed him again as he went for Severine. She was annoyed with him for offering to do this. But then she spotted Madame Lebleu, speeding to the scene as fast as her poor swollen legs would carry her. So she rushed to aid Madame Lebleu, and the two women raised their hands to high heaven, all gasps and excitement at the discovery of a crime so abominable. Though nobody knew a thing yet, there were stories already in circulation all round them, to be seen by frantic gestures and wild expressions on men's faces. No matter that it was all pure, spontaneous invention, Philomène herself on her word of honour, in a voice which soared above the general hubbub, asserted that Madame Roubaud had actually seen the murderer, and when Pecqueux reappeared with the lady in question there was dead silence.

'Just you look at her!' whispered Madame Lebleu. 'With those airs of a princess, whoever would think she was only the wife of an assistant station-master? I tell you, she was dolled up like that before daybreak this morning, all corseted and her hair done at that hour, just as if she was going calling.'

Severine made her way towards them with short, even steps. It was a longish stretch of platform to cover, with every eye fastened on her, but she did not falter. She merely held a handkerchief to her eyes, in the great grief she had felt the instant she learned who the victim was. Very smartly dressed in a black woollen frock, she might have been in mourning for her protector. Her heavy head of dark hair gleamed in the sunlight, for despite the cold she had not even had time to put on a hat. Her blue eyes, so gentle, so full of sorrow, as they were, swimming with tears indeed, made her a very touching figure.

'She certainly has reason to cry,' observed Philomène, under her breath. 'They are done now their fairy godfather has been killed.'

When Severine was at last there, in the centre of the crowd, against the open door of the compartment, M. Cauche and Roubaud got down on to the platform, and the latter at once began to tell what he knew.

'Darling,' he said, 'yesterday morning, as soon as we reached Paris, we went to see M. Grandmorin, didn't we? It must have been about quarter past eleven, wasn't that the time?'

He held her with his gaze, while meekly she repeated:

'Yes, quarter past eleven.'

But her glance halted on the seat black-stained with blood, she choked suddenly and deep sobs broke from her bosom. The station-master, very moved, all fuss, intervened.

'Madame,' he said, 'if this sight is too much for you . . . We are very mindful of your grief.'

'No, I only want a word from Madame Roubaud,' the superintendent interrupted. 'We shall take Madame back home at once.'

Hastily, Roubaud continued.

'Wasn't it then, after we had chatted about one thing and another, that M. Grandmorin said he was leaving Paris this morning, to go down to Doinville, to see his sister? I can see him at his desk as I speak. I sat here, my wife there . . . Am I not right, darling, he said he was leaving this morning?'

'Yes, this morning.'

M. Cauche, who was still making rapid notes, looked up.

'What's that, this morning? But he left last night!'

'Just a moment please,' resumed Roubaud. 'When he learned that we were taking the evening train, as a matter of fact he did for a moment consider travelling with us, provided my wife had cared to go on with him as far as Doinville and spend a few days there with his sister, Madame Bonnehon, as she had done once or twice before. But having a lot to do at home, my wife declined . . . Didn't you, darling?'

'Yes, yes, I declined.'

'You see, he was very kind . . . He dealt with my business, then saw us to the door of his room . . . Didn't he, darling?'

'That's right, right to the door.'

'We left yesterday evening . . . Before getting into our compartment, I had a chat with M. Vaudorpe, the St Lazare station-master. And I certainly noticed nothing wrong. I was in fact very annoyed, because I thought we would be alone in our compartment, but in the corner there was a lady whom I had not noticed, besides two others, a couple

90

who got in at the last moment . . . Nor did I notice anything special all the way to Rouen. Then, at Rouen, where we got out to stretch our legs, imagine our astonishment when three or four coaches away we saw M. Grandmorin standing at the door of a compartment. "Why, Monsieur le Président," I said to him, "you are travelling after all? And we never even knew you were on the same train!" And he explained that he had had a telegram . . . Then the whistle blew, we got back quickly into our compartment, where, incidentally, we were now alone, all three people who had been in our compartment having got out at Rouen, which of course suited us all right . . . Well, and that's all, isn't it, darling?'

'Yes, that is all.'

This story, so eminently simple, made a great impression on all who heard it. Nobody could make head or tail of the whole thing. The superintendent stopped writing and expressed the general bewilderment by putting a question.

'Are you really sure there was nobody in the compartment with M. Grandmorin?'

'No, that's a thing I am absolutely clear about.'

There was a wave of excitement. There was already an eeriness about this mystery which confronted them, and there was nobody present but felt a little creepy. If this passenger had been alone, by whom could he have been murdered and thrown out of the compartment, ten miles away, before the next train stop?

The general silence was broken by Philomène's voice.

'It really is very fishy, you know,' she was saying.

Then, aware of her eyes on him, Roubaud gave a toss of the chin, as if to say that he too thought it was really very queer indeed. Near Philomène he observed Pecqueux and Madame Lebleu, and they too nodded, all in the same way. All eyes were now turned towards him. They expected something new, they were quizzing him to discern some forgotten detail in him which might throw light on the murder. But there was not a trace of accusation in those eminently inquisitive glances. All the same, Roubaud seemed to detect the emergence of a vague suspicion, that sort of misgiving which it only needs the most trifling fact, for it to be turned into certainty.

'Astounding,' murmured M. Cauche.

'Quite astounding,' M. Dabadie repeated.

Then Roubaud gained courage.

'Another thing I am quite certain about is that the express, on that straight run from Rouen to Barentin, ran at normal speed and I noticed nothing out of the ordinary ... I mention that precisely because, since we were alone, I lowered the window, to smoke a cigarette, and while I was smoking, I kept glancing out, so I was well aware of all the sounds of the train's running ... Why, when I saw my successor at Barentin, I mean M. Bessière, on the platform, I called to him and we exchanged a word or two, and I remember that he stood on the running board a moment and shook my hand ... Didn't he, darling? You could ask him, he would confirm it.'

Motionless and pale throughout, her fine features sunk, drowned in sorrow, Severine once again confirmed her husband's statement.

'Yes,' she said, 'he would confirm it.'

From that point, any charge was out of the question, since the Roubauds, having got back into their compartment at Rouen, at Barentin had been greeted by a friend. That shadow of suspicion which Roubaud thought he had detected in their eyes had vanished, and everybody's astonishment grew greater. The whole affair was becoming more and more mysterious.

'Just a moment,' said the superintendent, 'are you quite sure that at Rouen nobody was able to get into the compartment after you left M. Grandmorin?'

This was clearly a question which Roubaud had not anticipated. For the first time, he was confused, doubtless having no ready-made answer. Hesitating, he glanced at his wife.

'No,' he said, at last, 'I don't think so ... The doors were being closed, the whistle was blowing, we only just had time to get back to our own coach ... Besides, it was a reserved compartment, wasn't it. As far as I can see, nobody could get in ...'

But his wife's blue eyes grew so large that he was afraid to be too positive.

'After all, I really don't know ... Yes, perhaps somebody was able to get in ... There was rather a crowd on the platform ...'

As he spoke, his voice regained its firmness and the new part of the story grew firm as it developed.

'You see, through the festival here, there was a considerable crowd ... We had to keep third-class passengers out of our own

92

compartment ... Besides, the station is very badly lit, you could not see anything, people were shouting and pushing as they hurried away ... Upon my word, I do think it feasible that somebody may have scrambled in at the last moment – having nowhere to go, perhaps taking advantage of the crush.' He broke off. 'What do you say, darling, that's what must have happened, don't you think?'

Severine seemed broken with grief. With her handkerchief pressed to her red eyes, she repeated:

'That must be what happened.'

From that point, however, the enquiry had its scent, and without saying a word, the superintendent and the station-master exchanged understanding glances. Gradually, the crowd came to life. Feeling the interrogation over, they all began to unburden themselves of comments, and hypotheses were immediately in circulation, each man of course having his own idea. For a moment, all station services seemed suspended, everybody was there, everybody preoccupied with the murder, and when the nine thirty-eight suddenly came in under the station roof, they were all taken by surprise. There was at once a violent scurrying about, as doors opened, and the passengers flooded out. But nearly all the more inquisitive people had stayed beside the superintendent who, being a conscientious man of method, was having a last look at the compartment.

At this instant, Pecqueux, gesticulating between Madame Lebleu and Philomène, suddenly sighted his own driver, Jacques Lantier. Jacques had just got off the train from Barentin and stood transfixed, watching the little crowd from a distance. With a pressing wave of the hand, Pecqueux beckoned him over, but at first Jacques did not stir. However, a moment later he gave way and slowly came across.

'What is it?' he asked his fireman.

He knew very well what it was, and scarcely paid any heed to the story of the murder or the hypotheses which were being made. What surprised him and moved him strangely was to have come right into the throes of this enquiry and thus meet again that compartment which he had glimpsed in the darkness as it rushed through the night. He craned his neck and peered at the pool of blood coagulating on the cushion. Once more he saw that murder scene, and also, still more clearly, the corpse, stretched out sprawling beside the permanent-way, near Maufras Cross, with gaping throat. Then, looking the other way, while Pecqueux went on with the story, Jacques noticed the Roubauds and was struck by the curious way in which they too had got mixed up in it, leaving Paris in the very same train as the victim and being, so it seemed, the very last people to speak to Grandmorin, at Rouen. Roubaud, as a matter of fact, he knew personally, they were on handshake terms and occasionally ran into each other when he was driving the express. The wife he had glimpsed only at a distance, avoiding her as he avoided other women, because of his own unhealthy impulses. But in this moment, tearful and pale as she was, with those incredibly gentle blue eyes so scared under the rich confusion of her black hair, she struck him, and he could not keep his eyes off her. Indeed, he lost himself, watching her, suddenly quite dazed, wondering why the Roubauds and he were there at all, how the facts of the case could have brought them together in this chariot of crime, they freshly back overnight from Paris and he from Barentin.

'But I know all about it,' he said suddenly, very loudly, interrupting the fireman, 'I was down there at Maufras Cross myself last night, just where the tunnel ends, and I think I saw something of it just when the train passed.'

There was at once a tremendous buzz of excitement, and they all crowded round him. He was the first to be astonished, shrinking back in amazement, staggered by what he himself had just said. Why on earth did he speak? Once he had made such a formal resolve to hold his tongue, why on earth did he talk like that? There were so many good reasons for saying nothing. But the words had left his lips automatically, while he was watching that woman. All at once she took her handkerchief from her eyes, to stare hard at him through her tears. Her remarkable eyes seemed larger than ever.

The superintendent had quickly turned to him.

'What's that? What did you see?'

With Severine's gaze steady on him, Jacques told what he had seen: the half-compartment, lighted, flashing by in the night, at top speed, the fleeting sight of two men, in profile, one on his back, the other with a knife in his hand. Close against his wife, Roubaud listened, staring keenly, wide-eyed, at Jacques.

'Then,' the superintendent enquired, 'would you recognize the murderer?'

'Ah, now, that's something I doubt.'

94

'Was he wearing an overcoat or a workman's tunic?'

'I could not be sure. Don't forget, the train must have been doing forty-five miles an hour.'

Against her will, Severine exchanged a glance with her husband, and he found the strength to observe that one would certainly 'have to have good eyes'.

'No matter,' concluded M. Cauche, 'this is a very important piece of evidence. The examining magistrate will help you to get it a bit straight ... M. Lantier and M. Roubaud, will you please give me your exact names, for the record.'

It was over. Gradually, the crowd of gapers dispersed, and the station services resumed their normal course. Roubaud in particular had to hurry, to look after the nine-fifty slow train, which was already loading up. He had shaken Jacques' hand a little more forcibly than he usually did, while Jacques, left there with Severine, behind Madame Lebleu, Pecqueux and Philomène, who were making their way from the scene in a huddle of whispers, felt himself obliged to accompany the young woman as far as the stairs up to the staff apartments. All the way he could find nothing to say to her, but yet he could not leave her side, as if some bond held her to him.

By now the day was all cheerfulness. Clear sunlight was mastering the morning mists, the sky was a depthless azure, and the sea breeze, growing as the tide came in, was filling the air with briny freshness. When at last he left the A.S.M.'s wife, once again Jacques found himself face to face with those wide-set eyes, the terrified pleading gentleness of which had stirred him so profoundly.

There came a sharp blast on a whistle. It was Roubaud signalling the nine-fifty out. The locomotive gave a long answering whistle, and the train was set in motion, gathering speed, to vanish in the distance in the golden dust of the sunlight.

4

On this particular day, in the second week of March, M. Denizet, examining magistrate, had summoned to his office at the Rouen Law Courts certain key witnesses in the Grandmorin case.

The case had been a great sensation for the past three weeks. It had shaken Rouen and was proving quite exciting in Paris, and in the violent campaign this was waging against the Empire the Republican press were making great capital out of it. Struggle was being made the fiercer by the proximity of a general election, a preoccupation which overshadowed all political activity. There had been stormy debates in the Chamber, one in which the powers of two deputies connected with the Emperor had been the subject of an acrimonious exchange and another in which the financial conduct of the Prefect of the Seine Department was challenged, and the elction of a municipal council demanded. The Grandmorin case came in just right to keep this restive state of affairs going, and the most extraordinary stories were going the rounds, every day the newspapers being full of fresh hypotheses, all equally damaging to the Government. One story suggested that the victim, who, besides being a former judge, a Commander of the Legion of Honour, and a millionaire was *persona grata* at the Imperial Palace, was given to the worst debauches. Another line, since there was no sign of the judicial investigation getting to the bottom of the crime, was to charge both the police and the magistrature with connivance. The unknown murderer was not merely becoming legendary, he was also a byword. And the fact that there was a grain of truth in all these attacks did not make them any the easier to bear.

M. Denizet was consequently very well aware of the heavy burden of responsibility which rested on his shoulders. He also had his own reasons to take it all very much to heart, for he was an ambitious man and most anxious for a case of this calibre to bring the limelight to bear on all the high-level qualities of perspicacity and assiduity with which he believed himself endowed. Son of a big Norman grazier, he had studied law at Caen and did not join the magistracy till rather late, but once in it, his peasant origin had hampered his promotion, and his father's bankruptcy aggravated the position. Deputy public prosecutor successively at Bernay, Dieppe and Havre, he took ten years to become a full public prosecutor at Pont-Audemer. Then, sent to Rouen first as deputy public prosecutor for that city, he had become examining magistrate only in his fifties, after another eighteen months. With no money at the back of him, harassed by needs which his meagre appointments were insufficient to cover, he was totally dependent on his magistrature, and that was a position badly paid, normally accepted by none but second-rate men, and within the body of magistrates rivalries tended to be fought out with cut-throat venality. Yet in fact M. Denizet was of lively, subtle intellect, and an honest man to boot. He was genuinely fond of his profession, though perhaps a little too intoxicated by the power it gave him, for of course, when sitting in chambers as examining magistrate he was absolute master of anybody he chose to subpoena. The only check, indeed, on this enthusiasm of his for his work was his own self-interest, for he had a burning desire to be decorated and transferred to Paris. It was for this reason that, after having allowed himself to be carried away at the outset of the case by his passion for the truth, he was now proceeding most circumspectly, inclined everywhere to see pitfalls likely to ruin his prospects.

It must be admitted that M. Denizet was prejudiced, for, quite early in this enquiry, a friend had given him the good tip to go to Paris, to the Ministry of Justice, where he had had a long talk with M. Camy-Lamotte, the Secretary-General, a very big figure, for not only was he in general control of all personnel matters, he was also responsible for nominations, so in constant contact with the Imperial Palace. M. Camy-Lamotte was a striking personality, having started life himself as a deputy public prosecutor, but having early got himself a grand officership of the Legion of Honour by reason jointly of his own contacts and his wife's pull. The Grandmorin case had of course been referred to him, the state prosecutor of Rouen being naturally enough a bit concerned about a squalid murder like this, with a prominent former judge as victim, for which reason he had taken the precaution of sending the file to the Minister, who in turn passed it on to his Secretary-General. In all this there was also something of a coincidence, for M. Camy-Lamotte, the junior by some years, had been at college together with Judge Grandmorin, and Grandmorin had remained so close a friend throughout his life that he had known him inside-out – including his vices. Hence he spoke of the tragic death of his friend with real grief, and the only reason he agreed to see M. Denizet at all was his anxiety to see the guilty person laid by the heels. But he did not conceal the fact that court circles were displeased by the disproportionate fuss being made about it, and he went so far as to suggest that considerable restraint was called for. In short, M. Denizet gathered that it would be wise of him to take things steadily and not venture on any further step without previous approval. He even returned to Rouen with the conviction that in his personal anxiety to get to the bottom of it, the Secretary-General had sent his own enquiry men out. There was in fact a desire to know the truth in order perhaps to be the better able if necessary to conceal it.

But time slipped by, and however patient he strove to be, M. Denizet began to be irritated by the press jibes. There were also the police, who kept returning to it, nose snuffling at the wind, like good dogs. So he came to be obsessed by the need to strike the right scent. He must have the kudos of being the first to pick it up, even if he were to be merely only to relinquish it again, should such be his instructions. So, while he awaited a letter of directive, a suggestion or a mere hint from the Ministry – and this was an unconscionably long time coming – he had applied himself vigorously to making his enquiries. But though he had made two or three arrests, it had not been possible to maintain one of them.

Then, suddenly, the opening of Judge Grandmorin's will reawakened in M. Denizet a suspicion with which he had played for a while at the very outset: the possibility of the Roubauds being the guilty ones. For the will, *choc-a-bloc* with curious legacies, included one by which Severine was to inherit a small house situated at a place called Maufras Cross. Hitherto there had appeared to be no motive for the murder. Now there was a clear one. Aware of this clause in the will, the Roubauds had possibly murdered their benefactor to be able to enjoy the property without delay. This idea haunted him the more since M. Camy-Lamotte had made special mention of Roubaud's wife, and said he had seen her years ago at the judge's house, when she was a schoolgirl, and lived there. But what unlikely elements there proved to be in this! What impossibilities, physical and moral. From the moment he began to direct his enquiry in that direction, at every step he came up against details which completely upset classically conducted judicial enquiry as he understood the process. It threw light on nothing, there was no great central source of illumination, revealing the whole thing.

There was however another likely line of enquiry which M. Denizet had not lost sight of, and that was one furnished by none other than Roubaud – the notion of a man's having been able to take advantage of the crush on the platform at Rouen to get into Judge Grandmorin's half-compartment, and this man was the notorious, legendary murderer, the man who could not be traced, the king-pin of all the press jibes. The judicial enquiry was therefore now turned on to the appearance of this individual, trying to trace this all the way from Rouen, where he first appeared, to Barentin, where he must have left the train. But out of all that work came nothing precise, some witnesses even denying the possibility of the death compartment having been entered like that – all this was, of course, prior to the introduction of the corridor train – while others offered M. Denizet the most contradictory details. Indeed, the trail was threatening to peter out altogether when, interrogating the crossing-keeper, Misard, the magistrate unintentionally stumbled on the dramatic story of Cabuche and Louisette, that is, of a young girl, raped by the judge, going to her good friend Cabuche to die. This meant a great flash of inspiration to M. Denizet, and there was a murder charge of classical perfection all ready formed in his head! He had it all, the threat of murdering the victim made by the quarry-worker, that man's shocking antecedents, and the clumsy, unprovable *alibi* he offered. And, in a moment of inspired initiative, M. Denizet the evening before this particular day had arranged for Cabuche to be arrested secretly at the cottage where he lived deep in the wood, a lost lair at the back of beyond if there ever was one, and what was more, there they found a bloodstained pair of trousers. And now, though still loth to accept the persuasion which was gradually taking possession of him, and assuring himself he ought not altogether to relinquish the hypothesis that the Roubauds did it, he felt real exultation at the thought that he alone had had keen enough a nose to ferret out the real murderer. Hence it was with the idea of achieving certainty that he had now summoned again to his chambers a number of the witnesses whom he had already once heard the very next day after the crime.

The examining magistrate's chambers were situated down Joan of Arc Street, in the dilapidated old building built on to the end of the former palace of the Dukes of Normandy, now transformed into the Law Courts – which, for that matter, it disgraced. M. Denizet occupied a vast, mournful, dreary room on the ground floor, so badly lit by daylight that a lamp always had to be lit at three o'clock during the winter. Decorated long since with a green paper which had faded, it had as furnishing two armchairs, four ordinary chairs, the magistrate's desk and a little table for the clerk, while the mantel-shelf over the unlit fireplace bore a black marble clock flanked by bronze tankards. A door behind the desk led to a second room, in which the magistrate sometimes kept those witnesses whom he wanted to keep on hand, while the main door of entry gave on to a large corridor equipped with benches for the witnesses to wait on.

Though the summons was only for two o'clock, the Roubauds were there by half past one. They had come in from Havre and had scarcely allowed themselves time for lunch, which they took in a little restaurant in the main street. They were both in black, Roubaud wearing a frock coat, his wife a silk frock, just like a lady, and they maintained the rather tired, gloomy solemnity of a couple who have lost a relative. She took her place on one of the benches and sat there quite still. He, without a word, his hands behind his back, strode slowly up and down before her. But every time he turned, their eyes met and then, like a mute shadow, their hidden anxiety crossed their faces. Though it would have delighted them to get it, the Maufras Cross legacy had begun to revive their fears, for Grandmorin's family, in particular his daughter, egged on by her husband, being outraged by all the strange legacies he had made, so many that altogether they amounted to half the total estate, was talking of challenging the will, and Madame de Lachesnaye was revealing herself particularly hard against her old friend Severine, about whom she was making the gravest suggestions. At the same time the memory of a possible clue to which at first he had not given a thought, now haunted Roubaud continuously. This was the letter which he had made his wife write to persuade Grandmorin to take the evening train, for if Grandmorin

100

had not destroyed it, this was a piece of paper they were going to come upon, and they might well identify the handwriting.

Fortunately, days had gone by and nothing had been said about it, so surely, he was beginning to conclude, the letter had after all been destroyed. Yet none the less every fresh summons to the examining magistrate's chambers gave rise in the Roubauds to cold sweats concealed by their formal bearing of decorum, as both legators and witnesses. The clock struck two, and at that moment, Jacques Lantier too entered the hall. He had come straight from Paris. Roubaud at once went up to him, hand extended, most forthcoming.

'Why, you too,' he said. 'You too have been disturbed ... Phew! I'm sick of it, aren't you. There's no end to this sorry business!'

When Jacques caught sight of Severine – she was still seated, motionless – he stopped short. For the past three weeks, every other day, every time he came to Havre, the A.S.M. had showered cordialities on him. Once he had even been obliged to consent to lunch with the Roubauds, though when he was close to the young wife he felt his old uneasy shiver. Indeed, it tended to grow worse. Did this mean that he was doomed to lust after her body too? His heart thudded, his hands went hot as fire, merely at sight of her white bosom in the opening of her corsage. Merely for this reason, he was firmly resolved in future to be resolute and avoid her.

'And what do they say about it all at Paris, eh?' continued Roubaud. 'Nothing fresh, I suppose? Because, you know, they don't know a thing about it and they never will ... But you must come and pay your respects to my wife.'

Roubaud took charge of him, and Jacques was obliged to draw near and greet Severine, who was very shy, with her timid, young, girlish smile. He made an effort to chat about trifles, while the eyes of husband and wife alike held him tenaciously, quite as if they were trying to probe beyond his thought, to read those deep-down reveries into which he himself never dared dig. They for their part wondered why he was so cold. Why did he seem to be avoiding them? Did his memory stir? Had they been summoned together with him for a confrontation? They would have given anything to make him theirs, this one witness whom they mistrusted, to bind him to them by such tight bonds of friendship that he would never dare utter a word against them.

It was Roubaud who in his dire anxiety brought the talk back to the murder.

'Any idea,' he asked, 'what on earth it can be they've summoned us for now? Is there really something new, I wonder?'

Jacques made a gesture of indifference.

'At the station, just now, when I arrived, there was talk of an arrest,' he said.

The Roubauds were dumbfounded, not only very puzzled, but also very disturbed, too. What did he say, an arrest? But nobody had breathed a word to them. Had the arrest been made, they asked? Or was it that the authorities were thinking of making one? They showered questions on him, but he had already told them all he knew.

At that point the sound of steps in the corridor caught Severine's attention. 'Berthe,' she whispered, 'and her husband.'

It was indeed the Lachesnayes. Very stiffly they brushed the Roubauds by and young Madame de Lachesnaye had not even a glance for her former playmate. What was worse, the usher immediately let them into the magistrate's room.

'Oh, well,' said Roubaud, 'we must be patient, I suppose. We are here, I know, for a good two hours . . . Better sit down.'

He placed himself on Severine's left, with a gesture inviting Jacques to sit next to her on the other side. For a moment longer, Jacques remained standing then, as she looked up at him with those gentle, timid eyes, he acquiesced. Madame Roubaud was a frail enough little figure between the two of them, and Jacques was very conscious of her submissive gentleness. Indeed, during that long wait the faint warmth which emanated from her gradually pervaded his whole body, completely stupefying him.

In M. Denizet's room, the interrogations were about to begin. The enquiry had already produced a very fat file indeed, with numerous bundles of documents in their blue folders. An attempt had been made to follow M. Grandmorin's movements from the moment of his departure from Paris. M. Vandorpe, the St Lazare station-master, had given evidence about the departure of the six-thirty express, about coach 293 being added at the last moment, about his brief talk with Roubaud, about how Roubaud had entered his compartment a little while before Judge Grandmorin arrived on the platform, and finally about M. Grandmorin's entering his special coupé, in which he was unquestionably alone. Next, Henri Dauvergne, the guard of the train, interrogated concerning what had taken place at Rouen during the ten minutes halt there, had been unable to add anything new. He had seen the Roubauds chatting opposite their compartment, and it was certainly his impression that they had returned there and that an inspector had shut the door, but it was all rather vague, seen amid the surging crowd in the semi-darkness of the station. As for asserting whether or not a man, the famous undiscoverable murderer, had been able to jump into the compartment just as the train was moving out, that he considered most unlikely, though he did admit it was a possibility, for such a thing had to his knowledge happened twice before. Other Rouen station hands, questioned on the same points, instead of bringing new light, had rather tended to muddle things by their answers, for these were mutually contradictory. Nevertheless, one fact finally emerged as proved, and that was Roubaud, inside his compartment, shaking hands with the Barentin stationmaster while that person stood on the foot-board. For that person, M. Bessière, had testified formally that this account was true, adding moreover that his colleague, Roubaud, had been alone with his wife, who was reclining and seemed to be peacefully asleep. There had also been some search for the passengers who left Paris in the same compartment as the Roubauds, and they had tracked down the stout lady and gentleman who arrived late, at the last moment. These were good middle-class folk from Petit Couronne, who deposed that as they fell asleep at once, they could say nothing. The woman in black, however, silent in her corner, had vanished like a shade, and all efforts to discover her had proved in vain. Finally, there were a number of other witnesses, the small-fry of the case, those who provided evidence of the identity of the passengers who got off that evening at Barentin. The murderer must surely have got off there, yet the tickets had been counted and they had succeeded in recognizing all the passengers except one. This was said to have been a tall fellow with his head wrapped in a blue handkerchief, but some witnesses said he was wearing an ordinary overcoat, though another avowed he was dressed in a workman's tunic. Merely concerning this person, who had completely disappeared, vanishing as utterly as a dream, there was a file of three hundred and six items. Altogether, it was a frightful muddle, every single statement being flatly contradicted by some other.

The file was further confused by the judicial items: the record of the protocol regarding the corpse made by the clerk of the court whom the state prosecutor and the examining magistrate had taken to the scene of the crime. This included a voluminous description of the section of the railway where the body had lain, the position of the body, its attire, and the contents of the pockets, which made identification possible. Next came the record of the deposition of the doctor who had likewise been taken there, an item which in medical jargon included a lengthy description of the wound in the throat, the only wound as it happened, a terrible gash, made with 'a cutting instrument, no doubt a knife'. There were also other depositions, including documents about the transport of the body to Rouen hospital, the time it had remained there, before remarkably rapid decomposition compelled the authorities to deliver it to the family for interment. However, only two or three points of any importance emerged from that further accumulation of paper.

First, there had been found in the pockets neither the dead man's watch nor his small wallet, which should have contained ten thousand-franc notes, due to be handed to M. Grandmorin's sister, Madame Bonnehon, by the victim, and expected by her. It would therefore have seemed as if the motive for the crime had been robbery, if on the other hand a big diamond ring had not been left on Grandmorin's finger. This contradiction alone gave rise to a whole series of hypotheses. Unfortunately, they had not got the numbers of the bank-notes. But the watch was known – a bulky, stem-wind watch with the judge's initials intertwined on the case and, on the works inside, the serial number, 2516.

Finally, the weapon, the knife used by the murderer, had given rise to considerable searching, in the brushwood along the track, anywhere indeed where it might have been thrown. But all searches had remained fruitless. The murderer must have hidden the knife in the same hole as the money and the watch. All they had picked up was the victim's travelling rug, some distance before Barentin station, where no doubt it had been abandoned as compromising. It was now one of the exhibits.

When the Lachesnayes entered the room, M. Denizet, standing at

104

his desk, was just glancing again through one of the first interrogation records, which his clerk had fished out of the pile for him. He was a small man, rather stout, clean-shaven, grizzled. The fleshy cheeks, the square chin, the ample nose exhibited a pallid immobility which was enhanced by heavy eyelids which sagged and concealed half the man's large, pale eyes. All the wisdom here, all the adroitness which he thought he possessed, had taken refuge in M. Denizet's mouth, one of those actor's mouths, revelatory of emotion, mobile in the extreme, and contracting to a fine line whenever he thought he was being most perspicacious. This over-cleverness as a matter of fact was frequently M. Denizet's undoing. He was inclined to be too spry, over prone to creeping round the plain, simple truth, all of course from professional fervour, seeing in his job the role of a sort of anatomist of ethics endowed with second sight and really very clever, though, for that matter, M. Denizet was far from being a fool.

He was at once all amiability to Madame de Lachesnaye, for even in his judicial capacity he was after all still a worldly magistrate, one who moved a great deal in Rouen society and that of the department too. 'Madame,' he cried, 'pray be seated,' and himself slid forward a chair for young Madame de Lachesnaye, a retiring and, indeed, rather disobliging blonde who was even ugly in her mourning. M. Denizet was however, merely courteous, with rather a sarcastic air, towards M. de Lachesnaye, who was as fair as his wife and also unhealthy looking. The reason for this was that in M. Denizet's eyes this puny fellow, court counsellor since the early age of thirty-six, with a decoration to his name too, thanks to the influence of his father-in-law and the services which his father, a magistrate before him, had given in mixed commissions, was an example of that magistracy of favour, that rich magistracy, that band of mediocrities who by reason of their relations and their money got themselves jobs and were sure of rapid advancement, whereas he himself, being penniless and without any such personal backing, was compelled constantly to lick up to others on the slippery uphill road of promotion. For this reason, M. Denizet was scarcely going to miss the chance of making de Lachesnaye feel his power as examining magistrate, his absolute power, indeed, over the liberty of any of them, power to the point of being able by one word, should it be his whim, to stigmatize a witness as hostile and have him placed under arrest on the spot.

'Madame,' he proceeded, 'you must forgive me for being obliged once again to bother you about this unhappy matter. But I know you are as keen as we all are on having daylight thrown on it and ensuring that the guilty person pays for his crime.'

He nodded to the clerk, a tall, sallow fellow, with salient cheek-bones, and the interrogation began. However, after the first few questions put to his wife, M. de Lachesnaye – who, seeing he was not going to be asked to do so, had sat down on his own accord – tried to take her place. He went so far as to unburden himself of all his bitterness about his father-in-law's will. Did it make sense, so many legacies and such considerable ones that they amounted to nearly half the estate, an estate, moreover, of three million seven hundred thousand francs? And to people whom for the most part they did not even know, women of all classes! There was even one for a little girl who sold violets and had her stand in a doorway in Rocher Street. All that really was a bit too much, and he was only waiting for the criminal enquiry to be completed, to see if there were not some means of quashing so unseemly a testament.

While he uttered this complaint, grinding his teeth, revealing what a fool he was, a typical provincial type, pig-headed over his whims and greedy for money to a high degree, M. Denizet examined him with his large, clear eyes, half hidden by their lids, and his sensitive lips expressed a jealous scorn for a man such a nincompoop as to be dissatisfied with two million francs, but whom some day no doubt, owing to all that money, he would have to see in the purple, at the very top of the ladder.

'In my opinion, Monsieur,' he said at last, 'you would be making a mistake. The will could only be attacked if the total legacies exceeded one half the estate, and that is not the case.'

Then, turning to his clerk, he remarked: 'Of course, Laurent, you're not putting all this down, are you?'

With a faint grin, as a man who knew what *verbum sap* meant, the clerk reassured him that he was not putting it down.

'Oh, but after all,' cried M. de Lachesnaye, still more indignantly, 'I do hope you don't imagine I am going to let those Roubauds have the Maufras Cross property. A present like that to the daughter of one of his servants? And why, on whatever grounds? Besides, if it is proved that they have sunk to crime . . .'

106

'Really, you think that?'

'Good heavens, if they were aware of what was in the will, their interest in our poor father's death is proved, isn't it? Besides, don't forget that they were the last persons to speak to him . . . After all, it does look a bit queer, doesn't it?'

'And you, Madame, do you think your former friend capable of such a crime?'

Before replying, Berthe de Lachesnaye gave her husband a glance. In a few few months of marriage, their displeasing manners, their mutual dryness had reacted together and become intensified. They made each other worse. It was he who had set her against Severine, to such a point that in order to get that Maufras Cross house back, Berthe would now have had Severine arrested at once.

'Besides, I really must say,' she said at last, 'that the woman you speak of had bad instincts while she was still small.'

'What exactly do you mean, Madame? Are you accusing Madame Roubaud of having misconducted herself at Doinville?'

'Indeed no,' cried Madame de Lachesnaye, 'or my dear father would never have allowed her to remain there.'

The outburst expressed all the indignant prudery of a middle-class woman unassailably *sans reproche*, a female who prided herself on being one of the most incontestably virtuous women in all Rouen, *persona grata* at the same time in all the best houses.

'All the same,' she insisted, 'when there are habits of giddiness and even dissipation . . . Well, the fact is, Monsieur, there are many things which I should once have thought impossible, but which I no longer find so.'

Once again, M. Denizet fidgeted impatiently. The fact was, he was no longer on that scent, and anybody else who was had therefore become his opponent, indeed to such a point that they seemed to be impugning the very reliability of his intellect.

'Now, allow me,' he cried, 'we must be reasonable. People like the Roubauds do not kill a man like your father to get a legacy a bit earlier, or there would be at least some signs of their haste, and I should find other hints of a lust for possession and enjoyment in them. No, the motive is insufficient, we must find another. And there is none. You yourselves do not offer any . . . Besides, go back to the facts, can't you see for yourselves the physical points which make it impossible? Nobody saw the Roubauds enter the compartment. One railway employee even thinks he can be sure that they returned to their own. And since they were certainly in their own compartment at Barentin, if they were the criminals one would have to admit they had moved to and fro between their own coach and that of M. Grandmorin, which was three coaches away, and that during the few minutes the train took at top speed over that distance. Now, is that likely? I have questioned engine-drivers and guards. They have all assured me that only great practice could give a man sufficient coolness and strength . . . But in any case, that knocks the woman out, and the husband would have had to risk it all without her. And to do what? To kill a protector who had just got them out of serious trouble? No, no, no, that's out of the question! The hypothesis won't hold water. We must find another. Impossible? Indeed no! What about a man who boards the train at Rouen and gets off at the next station – and one too who quite recently was uttering threats to murder your father?'

He was so carried away that he had actually begun to talk about his new re-construction. Indeed, he was about to say too much, when the door opened just sufficiently to admit the usher's head. But before the man could utter a word, a gloved hand had pushed the door wide open, and in came a golden-haired woman, in very smart mourning, beautiful still at over fifty, with the opulent, powerful loveliness of an aged goddess.

'My dear Judge Denizet,' she cried. 'It's only me. I am late. You will forgive me, won't you? The roads are shocking. The three leagues from Doinville were like six today.'

M. Denizet had risen to his feet, and addressed her with a courtly air.

'I trust, Madame, that you have fully recovered from last Sunday?'

'I am fine . . . But what about you, my dear M. Denizet? Have you really got over the shock my coachman must have given you? He tells me that about half a mile from the house he all but tipped you out of the brougham when he brought you.'

'It was nothing, Madame, nothing, a mere jolting. I had even forgotten about it . . . But pray be seated, Madame, and, as I was just saying to Madame de Lachesnaye, forgive me if I am obliged to re-awaken your grief by this terrible case.'

'Good gracious me, not at all, what has to be, has to be . . . Good afternoon, Berthe, my dear. Good afternoon, Lachesnaye.'

And it was Madame Bonnehon, the murdered man's sister, who took the initiative, embraced her niece and shook the husband's hand. The wife of a manufacturer who accumulated a fortune, leaving her a widow at thirty, with considerable money in her own name, too (for when she shared out with her brother she acquired the Doinville estate), she had led a delightful life, one unending succession, so people said, of love affairs, though outwardly so proper and seeming the height of unconcerned virtue that she had remained the queen of the drawing-rooms of Rouen. Fortune and taste had so disposed that she had had many lovers of the bench. For a quarter of a century, indeed, she had entertained the law world, every man jack of the law courts, in fact, bringing them out to the manor and taking them home again in her carriages. Her life had been one endless party. She had still not quite settled down. There was talk of a motherly interest in the young deputy prosecutor, a M. Chaumette, son of a counsellor of the court. While working to get the son promoted, she was showering invitations and little kindnesses on the father. She had also kept one very good friend of the old days, another counsellor of the court, a bachelor, a M. Desbazeilles, literary lion of the Rouen courts, whose polished sonnets were much quoted. For years M. Desbazeilles had had his own room at Doinville. Even now, for all that he was over sixty, he frequently dined there, though arthritis at last restricted this old flame to memories.

Thus by her kindly manner Madame Bonnehon maintained her rule despite advancing years, and nobody ever thought of challenging it. It was not till the last winter that she had felt any competition, but now she had this in the form of Madame Leboucq, wife of yet another counsellor, a tall dark woman of thirty-four, certainly most attractive, whom the gentry of the bench had latterly shown a tendency to frequent, a circumstance which had introduced a thread of melancholy into Madame Bonnehon's customary gaiety.

'Well, Madame,' said M. Denizet, 'if I may, I will ask you one or two questions.'

Though the interrogation of the Lachesnayes was over, he did not dismiss them, so his cold dismal room was now transformed into a worldly *salon*. The imperturbable clerk prepared to write again.

109

'A witness has testified as to your brother's having received a telegram, summoning him immediately to Doinville. We have found no trace of any such telegram. Did you send him one, Madame?'

Smiling, completely at her ease, Madame Bonnehon answered rather in tones of friendly chatting.

'No, I didn't write to my brother, I was expecting him, I knew he was coming, but without fixing any definite date. He usually turned up like that, and almost always by the night train. As he slept in a summer-house in the park which opened on to a lonely lane, we never even heard him come. He used to take a cab from Barentin and you wouldn't see him till the next day, sometimes quite late. He would drop in casually, like any neighbour, any old time after he actually arrived ... But if this time I was actually expecting him, that was because he was to bring me those ten thousand francs, to settle a little account between us. He was sure to have had those notes on him. That's why from the very beginning I have been convinced it was a simple murder for robbery.'

M. Denizet remained silent for a time, then, looking Madame Bonnehon straight in the face, asked what she thought of Madame Roubaud and her husband. Her immediate response was a lively gesture of protest.

'Oh no, my dear M. Denizet, don't make the mistake again of thinking those good people have anything to do with it ... Severine was such a good little girl, so gentle, indeed, she was almost too quiet, and such a lovely little thing, too, but there's no harm in that, though if you really want me to tell you again what I think, I will repeat that she and her husband are incapable of doing anything bad.'

With a nod, he agreed, and with a glint of triumph in his eyes looked across at Madame de Lachesnaye, who was stung into protest.

'My dear aunt,' she said, 'I do think you are rather easily taken in.'

Whereupon, being accustomed to say whatever came to her mind, Madame Bonnehon unburdened herself.

'That's enough, Berthe,' she said, 'on that subject you and I will never agree. Severine was a happy child, she always loved laughter, and quite right too ... Oh, I know very well what you and your husband think. What is wrong with you is that money seems to have gone to your heads, if you are going to tell us you are so surprised by your father's leaving Maufras Cross to darling Severine ... Your

110

father brought her up, he provided her with a marriage settlement, what more natural than that he should find a place for her in his will? Come now, did he not treat her more as another daughter ... My dear girl, let me assure you, money doesn't spell happiness!'

As a matter of fact, having herself always been very well off, Madame Bonnehon herself was completely uninterested in money. With the perverseness of a beautiful woman who had known much love, she pretended that beauty and love were the sole *raison d'être* of existence.

'It is Roubaud who started the story about a telegram,' observed M. de Lachesnaye, drily. 'If there never was any telegram, M. Grandmorin could never have said that he had one. Why did Roubaud invent the yarn?'

'But surely,' cried M. Denizet, getting rather worked up, 'M. Grandmorin himself may well have invented a telegram, merely to explain to the Roubauds his sudden departure. As they have stated, he was to have left on the morrow, so when they found him in the same train as they were, supposing of course that he did not wish to tell them the real reason, which, as far as that goes, we do not know, he felt he needed an explanation. But anyway, it's of no great importance, it doesn't get us anywhere.'

There was a new silence. When the examining magistrate resumed, he was very calm and trod warily.

'Madame,' he said, turning to Madame Bonnehon, 'now I want to touch on a very delicate matter, and beg you to forgive the sort of questions I have to put to you. Nobody respects the memory of your brother more than I do ... But there is a certain amount of gossip going round, is there not? ... It is said that he still had mistresses.'

With her unlimited tolerance, Madame Bonnehon could not help smiling.

'My dear sir,' she said, 'I ask you, at his age? In any case, my brother was widowed very early. I never thought I had any right to condemn what he found suited his book, and he went his own way. I never interfered in his affairs at all. All I know is that he always maintained his position and to the end moved in the best society.'

Outraged at this discussion of her father's mistresses in her presence, Berthe had lowered her eyes, while, quite as embarrassed as she was, her husband strode across to the window and stared out, with his back to the proceedings.

'You will forgive my persistence,' said M. Denizet. 'Was there not once a scandal about one of your own chamber maids?'

'Oh, of course, yes, I know, you mean Louisette . . . But, my dear M. Denizet, Louisette was a little trollop who at fourteen years of age had relations with an habitual criminal. There was, I know, an attempt to exploit that girl's death to my brother's disadvantage. And shameless it was to do so, too. I will tell you all about it.'

No doubt she believed what she said. Although she had a pretty fair idea about Judge Grandmorin's morals, and his sudden death did not astonish her, she felt it was up to her to defend the high standing of the family. However, in the wretched story of Louisette, even though she thought it quite likely that her brother had had his eye on the girl, she was equally convinced that Louisette was precociously depraved.

'Picture,' she said, 'picture a regular little hussy, a dainty, pink-and-white slip of a girl, angelically sweet and innocent, butter wouldn't melt in her mouth, any priest would have granted her the sacrament without any confession . . . Ah, but now listen! She was only just turned fourteen when she became the intimate of a regular thug, a quarry-worker named Cabuche, who had just done five years prison for killing a man in a night-bar. This man lived a wild life on the edge of Bécourt Forest, where the old man, who died of a broken heart, left the son a hut built of tree-trunks and clay. This younger Cabuche continued to work a corner of the abandoned quarries there which, once upon a time, I imagine, furnished half the stones of Rouen. It was in that out-of-the-way burrow that despite the fact that the whole countryside was terrified of him, this mere kid used to go to see her wild man, and he lived quite by himself, like a leper. This man and the girl were often seen together, wandering through the woods, hand in hand, a dainty-looking little thing like her and a coarse brute. In short, depravity of the lowest. Of course, I did not find all this out till later. I had taken Louisette into the house more from charity than anything else, to do a good deed. The parents – Misard by name – had of course taken good care not to tell me that they had beaten the hussy many a time without being able to prevent her running to this man the moment the door was left open . . . And then this accident happened. At Doinville my brother had no servants of his own. Louisette and another girl looked after him in that little summerhouse he used to use. One morning Louisette went there alone – and then disappeared. In my opinion, she had been planning for a long time to run away. It is quite possible that her lover was expecting her and took her away. But the frightful thing was that five days later the news got round that she was dead, and there was a lot of talk about my brother having tried to rape her, and in such a revolting way that she was beside herself and took refuge in Cabuche's hut, where she was supposed to have died of brain fever. What really did happen? There were so many suggestions that it is hard to tell. My own belief is that Louisette, who certainly did die of some sort of brain fever – there was the medical certificate, of course – really died as the result of sheer folly, nights spent out in the open, wandering about in the swamps – Speak for yourself, M. Denizet, can you imagine my brother misusing a kid like that? The mere suggestion is outrageous, hateful.'

Throughout this story, M. Denizet had listened carefully but non-committally, so Madame Bonnehon did not quite know how to conclude. Then with resolution, she cried:

'Heavens alive! I won't say my brother did not try a little fun with her, he loved young folk, despite his stern exterior he was of a jolly nature, well, let's go so far as to say he kissed her . . .'

But at this suggestion the Lachesnayes were all indignation and shame.

'My dear aunt!' cried Berthe.

Madame Bonnehon shrugged her shoulders. What was the point of pitching yarns to the examining magistrate?

'Yes, kissed her,' she said, 'perhaps cuddled her a bit . . . And I will tell you what makes me admit this, it is the fact that it was not the quarry-man started the story, it was Louisette herself, the little liar, it was that shameless little hussy who exaggerated things, perhaps to make her lover stick to her, till Cabuche, who, as I tell you, is a regular brute, really did come to believe that my brother had killed his sweetheart . . . And then the man was beside himself with fury and all round the country repeated in bars that if he ever got hold of my brother, he would stick him like a pig.'

113

Here, the examining magistrate, who so far had said nothing at all, swiftly interrupted.

'Oh, he said that, did he? Are there any witnesses?'

'But, my dear M. Denizet, you could find as many witnesses as ever you want . . . In short, it was all a very unhappy business, and it caused us a great deal of worry. It was fortunate that my brother's position raised him above suspicion.'

Madame Bonnehon had just realized what new trail M. Denizet was following, and she was rather worried by it. Indeed, she suddenly decided not to get any deeper, by pursuing the matter. M. Denizet, however, had risen to his feet. He did not, he said, wish to presume further on the good offices of M. Grandmorin's sorrowing next-of-kin, and, at his request, the clerk read out their depositions before asking them to sign. The record proved perfectly correct, so well winnowed of unnecessary or compromising words that when Madame Bonnehon took the pen to sign, she shot a glance of mingled surprise and condescension at the emaciated, pallid clerk, whom till now she had not even noticed. Then, when the magistrate saw her to the door, together with her nephew and niece, she took both his hands in hers and shook them.

'I do hope I shall see you soon, M. Denizet, you know you are always welcome at Doinville . . . I *am* grateful to you, you are one of my last true loves.'

Her winsome smile was wreathed in ruefulness, but her niece, formal to the end, and the first to leave, merely inclined her head.

Alone, M. Denizet first took breath. He stood where he had left them for a minute, deep in thought. Now he did seem to have it all quite clear. There had quite clearly been violence on Grandmorin's side. The man, in fact, was notorious, and that made the enquiry a ticklish one. He made a further resolution to be specially wary until the guidance he expected from the Ministry came through. At the same time, he was cock-a-hoop, for at last he had the real culprit.

'Bring in M. Jacques Lantier.'

On the corridor bench the Roubauds were still waiting, their faces expressionless, as if their very patience made them drowsy, except every now and then for a nervous twitch. But the usher's voice, calling Jacques, seemed to waken them for a moment, and a faint shiver passed over them. They followed Jacques with a stare till he had vanished through the door, then they sank back into their waiting, a trifle paler than before, and completely silent.

The whole Grandmorin case had been haunting Jacques these three weeks like an ailment, as if in the end it was liable to turn against him. That of course was unreasonable, for he had nothing to reproach himself with, not even with having held his tongue. All the same, he was unable to enter the magistrate's room without the faint tremor of a guilty man, afraid of having his crime discovered, and he took up a defensive attitude to questions, becoming all caution, from fear of saying too much. The fact was, he himself might so easily have been the killer. Was that not to be read in his eyes? Nothing therefore could be more unpleasant to him than these summonses to the enquiry, they frayed his nerves, he was on tenterhooks in his anxiety to be harassed as little as possible by all this business which was none of his.

However, on this particular occasion M. Denizet proved to be concerned exclusively with the appearance of the murderer. As the sole witness who had seen anything of this person, Jacques was obviously the only person in a position to give precise indications. But he refused to budge from his first deposition, repeated that the murder scene had been no more than a fleeting vision, the image of a single second, so swift that in his memory it remained utterly formless, abstract, merely one man cutting the throat of another man. For half an hour, with slow persistence, the examining magistrate racked him, putting the same question in every conceivable way: was the murderer big, was he small? had he a beard? had he long or short hair? what sort of clothes was he wearing? what class did he seem to belong to? And a worried Jacques continued to give vague answers.

'In short,' M. Denizet demanded sharply, all of a sudden, 'if he was pointed out to you, would you recognize him?'

Jacques' eyes flickered slightly, and while those searching eyes bored into his very skull, his inward struggle came to the surface and was uttered out loud.

'Would I recognize him . . . yes . . . perhaps I would . . .'

And then his inexplicable fear of being trapped into unwitting complicity thrust him back again into persistent evasiveness.

'But no, all the same, I don't think I should recognize him, I could never be sure. Don't forget, sir, a speed of forty-eight miles an hour.'

With a gesture of despair, the magistrate was about to send Jacques into the other room, to be ready at hand for further questioning, when he thought better of that.

'Stay here,' he said, 'you can sit down.'

And, ringing again for the usher, he said:

'Bring in M. and Madame Roubaud.'

At once, as they crossed the threshold, they saw Jacques, and their eyes at once went dull, furtive with alarm. Had he spoken? Was he being kept there to confront them with? Feeling his presence all their self-assurance vanished, and their first replies were made in a very lifeless voice. But the magistrate was merely running through their first interrogation again, all they had to do was to repeat the same phrases as before, almost word for word, while he listened without even looking at them. Then, all at once, he turned to Severine.

'Madame, you told the Havre station superintendent – I have his statement here – that you thought that at Rouen a man entered the compartment just as the train was moving out.'

She was quite taken aback. Whyever was he bringing that up? Was it a trap? Was he going to set one statement against another and make her contradict herself? With a swift glance she consulted her husband, and Roubaud warily intervened, saying quickly that he did not think his wife had been 'quite so positive as all that'.

'Excuse me,' said M. Denizet, 'but when you yourself mentioned the possibility of this, your wife did say: "That must be what happened" . . . All I wish to know, Madame, is whether you had any particular reason for saying that?'

Her anxiety ended. She saw that if she were not cautious, he was step by step going to get her to make a definite assertion. But at the same time, she obviously had to say something, so she said: 'Oh, no, Monsieur, I had no positive . . . I must have meant merely that it was reasonable enough to suppose he had, simply because it really is not at all easy to explain the murder in any other way.'

'So you did not actually see the man, you cannot tell us anything more about him?'

'Oh no, Monsieur, nothing at all.'

M. Denizet seemed to drop this point of enquiry. But only, the next moment, to take it up again with Roubaud.

'If he really did get into the compartment, however is it that you did not see this man, for your deposition goes to show that you were still talking to M. Grandmorin when the guard whistled for the train to leave.'

This insistence finally scared the assistant station-master, and he was utterly at a loss to know what attitude he ought to take. If they had some clue against him, it was frivolous for him to make the suggestion of an unknown murderer, and if he insisted on doing so, he might make his own position worse. Hoping that before long he would see what he ought to do, he temporized at some length, with a very confused explanation.

'It really is most annoying,' said M. Denizet, 'that your recollections are so hazy, for you of all people could have helped us to clear up suspicions which have fallen on a number of people.'

This seemed so close to the bone that Roubaud suddenly felt an irresistible need to prove his innocence. Thinking himself uncovered, his mind was at once made up. 'As a matter of fact,' he said quickly, 'I am more than a little worried about what is the right thing to do. You surely understand how naturally one hesitates, especially when I tell you that as a matter of fact I really do think I may have seen the man . . .'

There was a triumphant gesture from the examining magistrate, for M. Denizet ascribed this show of frankness to his own skill. He always did claim that experience had taught him how extraordinarily difficult some witnesses found it to admit all they knew. It was his pride despite their instinctive caution, to be the midwife of the knowledge such witnesses possessed.

'Now tell me all about him . . . What was he like? Short? Tall? About your height?'

'Nothing like it,' cried Roubaud, quickly, 'much taller . . . At least, that's the impression I have. For it is only an impression, you see. I just have a feeling that as I ran to get back to my own coach I brushed by somebody.'

'Just a moment,' said M. Denizet.

He turned to Jacques, and put a question to him.

'Now, was the man you caught sight of with a knife in his hand taller than M. Roubaud?'

But Jacques was getting impatient. He had begun to feel that he was going to miss the five o'clock train. He raised his eyes and

117

examined Roubaud keenly. He had the impression that he had never looked at him before, and was astounded to find him short, powerfully built, and with a striking profile, which he had seen somewhere before – or had he dreamed it?

'No,' he murmured, 'he was not, he was more or less the same height as he is.'

But Roubaud protested vigorously.

'Ah, no, much taller, a head taller at least.'

Jacques continued to stare at Roubaud, and under that quizzing glance, in which he read a growing astonishment, the A.S.M. fidgeted, as if to take flight from his own appearance, while, frozen with fear, his wife just as keenly followed the obscure writhings of memory stamped on the young man's features. It was plain that at first Jacques was himself taken by surprise at certain parallels to be made between Roubaud and the murderer. Indeed, he suddenly became quite sure that Roubaud was the man, just as the gossiping had suggested. Then he seemed to be entirely at the mercy of all the emotions which that discovery had stirred up and merely gaped, powerless to know what he was going to do, powerless, indeed, to know anything. If he spoke, this couple were doomed. Roubaud's eyes met his and the two men looked deep into each other's souls. There was a tense silence.

'So you two do not agree,' resumed M. Denizet. 'But if he seemed smaller to you, Lantier, was that not very likely because he was bending down, struggling with the victim?'

He too quizzed the two men. He had never intended to resort to this confrontation, but by professional instinct he did feel, in this instant, that he was not far off the truth. Even his persuasion about the Cabuche line was shaken. Was it possible the Lachesnayes were right? Could the guilty persons against all appearances really be this decent station-master and his so gentle young wife?

'Had the man a full beard, like yourself?' he asked Roubaud.

Roubaud managed to master his voice completely, before he answered: 'A full beard? Oh no, definitely not! I think he was clean shaven.'

Jacques could see that the same question would be put to him. What was he going to say? For he could have sworn that the murderer was not shaven at all. After all, why should he not speak the truth? These two people were nothing to him! But when he looked away

118

from the husband, it was to meet the eyes of the wife, and in them he read such a burning prayer, such an abandonment of her whole person to him, that he was staggered, and his old tremor took possession of him. Surely he did not then love her? Was this the woman whom he could love, in a normal way, to unite with her and never be plagued with that horrible longing to destroy her? In the same instant that he asked himself this, by a striking repercussion of his agitation he felt his memory go dim and he was no longer at all able to see the murderer in Roubaud. The vision became so vague that he was seized with doubts so strong that he could have bitten off his tongue for ever having spoken.

M. Denizet was now putting the fateful question: 'Had the man you saw a full beard, like M. Roubaud?'

Quite truthfully now, he answered: 'Really, sir, I cannot tell. I must repeat, it was all so swift. No, I know nothing, I can make no assertion.'

But M. Denizet became stubborn, for he wanted to rid himself of this suspicion he now had of the assistant station-master. So he urged first one, then the other, and from Roubaud in the end obtained a complete description of the murderer, as a tall, powerfully-built, clean-shaven fellow, wearing a workman's tunic, the very opposite in fact, of what he looked like himself, while all he could get from Lantier was evasive monosyllables, which all tended to bear out Roubaud's assertions. So the examining magistrate now came back to his first persuasion – that he was on the right track, and the portrait which witness Roubaud gave of the murderer was so precise that every additional feature made it the more reliable. Thus this couple, whom he had just now wrongly suspected, proved to be the very ones whose crushing deposition was going to cost the murderer his head.

'Would you wait in here,' he asked both parties, when they had signed their depositions, and he indicated the other room. 'Wait till I call you.'

At once he gave orders to bring in 'the prisoner', and was so pleased with himself that he went so far as to cry to his clerk:

'Laurent, we've got him.'

The door now opened, to admit two gendarmes, who brought in a tall young fellow of between twenty-five and thirty. On a sign from M. Denizet, the gendarmes withdrew, and Cabuche was alone in the magistrate's room. He was in a bewildered state, like a hunted beast, bristling all over. He was a powerful man, with muscular neck and enormous fists. His skin and hair were those of a very fair man, his beard sparse, no more than a silky down on lips and cheeks. The massive features and low forehead suggested the violence of a man of limited intelligence, somebody who was all immediate sensation, yet in the broad lips and squat nose there was a certain good-doggie craving for affectionate submissiveness. Snatched roughly from the heart of his lair in the early morning, torn from his forest, irritated by charges he could not understand, with his perplexity and some tears in his tunic, he had already acquired that dubious remand prison appearance which that institution can give the most respectable of men. Night was drawing near, the room had grown dark, and he shrank into the gloom. Then the usher brought in a lamp with a plain glass globe, and the light of this showed up his features clearly. Thus uncovered, he stood motionless.

All at once, M. Denizet fixed his heavy-lidded large pale eyes on him. But he did not speak. It was the tackle by silence, the first trial of strength, before the full savagery of war – a war of trickery, subterfuge, moral torture. This man was the culprit, everything now pointed to him. Cabuche therefore now had no other right but to confess his crime.

The interrogation began, very slowly.

'Do you know what crime you are accused of?'

His voice thick with impotent rage, Cabuche growled: 'Nobody has told me, but I can guess all right. There's been enough talk about it.'

'You knew M. Grandmorin?'

'I did, only too well, too.'

'A girl who was intimate with you went into service as maid of Madame Bonnehon.'

An upsurge of rage carried the quarry-man away. In his fury, he saw red.

'Any b—— who says that's a b—— liar! Louisette I never touched.'

M. Denizet observed this access of anger with some interest, and, pretending to come back from another angle, he said: 'You are very wild, Cabuche. You have already done five years for killing a man in a quarrel.'

120

Cabuche lowered his head. That sentence was his eternal shame. He muttered:

'He hit first . . . i only did four years, I had one year's remission.'

'So,' M. Denizet resumed, 'you make out there was nothing between you and this girl Louisette?'

Again, Cabuche clenched his fists. Then, in a low voice, gasping, he said:

'I'm telling you, she was only a kid, she wasn't yet fourteen. When I came back, you know where from . . . and everybody turned their backs on me, people threw stones at me, but in the forest, where I always met her, she always used to talk to me, she was kind all right, she was decent to me . . . So that's how we two became friends. We used to hold hands and walk about. It was so good, so good, in those days . . . True, she was growing up, so I did have thoughts about her. I'm not going to deny that, I might have been out of my head, I was so fond of her. And she was very fond of me too. It would have come to that, what you say, but they took her from me and put her into service at Doinville, with that lady . . . Then, one evening, when I got in from the quarry, I found her at my door, half out of her mind and so upset she was hot with fever. She had not dared go back to her parents, she came to me to die . . . Good God, that swine, I ought to have gone straight there and stuck him.'

The examining magistrate pursed his thin lips, for the sincere note in this man's words had struck him forcibly. It was plain that he would have to tread warily here, he had a tougher customer to deal with than he had bargained for.

'Yes,' he said, 'I know the outrageous story you and that hussy cooked up. But you might at least take note that the whole of M. Grandmorin's life puts him above your accusations.'

Astounded at this, eyes bulging, hands shaking, the quarry-man stammered: 'What's that you say? We cooked it up? It isn't we who lied, yet are we going to be accused of lying?'

'Why of course, and don't put it on like that, Cabuche . . . I have already interrogated Misard, who married the mother of that wretched girl of yours. If necessary, I will confront you with him. You will see what he thinks of your fine yarn . . . Now take more care what you reply to me. We have witnesses, we know everything, you would do better to tell the truth.'

121

These were his usual intimidation tactics, which he used even when he knew nothing and had no witnesses.

'Would you deny then that all over the place you said you would stick M. Grandmorin like a pig?'

'Aye, I should think I did say that, and meant it too, I'm telling you, my hand itched terrible.'

This certainly surprised M. Denizet, who had expected a tissue of absolute denial. What was this, a defendant admitting his threats? What did this cunning mean? Wary of getting to the point too quickly, he reflected for a moment, then, looking Cabuche straight in the face, suddenly put the question to him:

'What were you doing on the night of February 14th?'

'I went to bed, about six . . . I was a bit off colour, what's more my cousin Louis did me a good turn, he took a load of broken stone down to Doinville.'

'Yes, your cousin was seen with the waggon when he crossed the railway at the level-crossing. But when your cousin was interrogated, all he could say was that you left him at midday and he had not seen you since that . . . Prove that you were in bed at six.'

'Look here, that's silly, I can't prove that, I live all alone right away on the far edge of the forest . . . I was in bed, I'm telling you, and that's all there is to it.'

M. Denizet decided to have recourse to the frontal method of telling the accused all that was attributed to him. His face grew rigid with the effort of will while his lips ran through the scene.

'Now,' he said, 'I will tell you what you did on the evening of February 14th . . . At three o'clock you took the train from Barentin to Rouen, for a purpose which the enquiry has not yet elucidated. You were to return by the Paris train which stops at Rouen at three minutes past nine, and you were on the platform, among the crowd, when you caught sight of M. Grandmorin, in his compartment. Take note that I quite recognize that there was no earlier intent, that the idea of your crime only came to you at that instant . . . Thanks to all the crowds, you were able to get aboard the train and you waited till you would be in the Malaunay tunnel when actually you killed M. Grandmorin . . . Then you threw the body out, then got off the train yourself at Barentin, after first getting rid of the travelling rug . . . That is what you did.'

He closely followed every trace of emotion on Cabuche's ruddy countenance, and was most annoyed when, after seeming very attentive at the start, the man ended by breaking into roars of laughter.

'What's this yarn you tell me? . . .' he cried. 'Why, if I'd done the job, I would say so all right!' Then, quite calmly, he added: 'I did not do it, but I ought to have done. God damn me, yes, and I'm sorry I didn't.'

Nor could M. Denizet get another thing out of him. In vain, he returned to questioning, running over the same points a dozen times, with a different tactic each time. No, was the response every time, no, it was not Cabuche. Cabuche just shrugged his shoulders and said it was all tommyrot. When he had been arrested, his hut was searched, without finding weapon or money or watch, only a pair of trousers with a few spots of blood on them – devastating proof. Here again, Cabuche roared with laughter, that was a good one, that blood was – that came from a rabbit taken in a snare which he had bled dangling against his leg. And it was the magistrate who lost ground, all because of that fixed idea he had of the crime, that excess of professional cleverness, over-complicating things, going beyond the simple truth. Gradually this stupid fellow, quite incapable of playing a clever game, but invincibly strong when he said *no, no,* and *no,* seriously disconcerted him, for now M. Denizet could not but see Cabuche as guilty, so that every fresh denial merely made him more persistent, seeing the man just pigheaded in his brutality and falsehood. But he would force the rascal to change his tune.

'Then you deny it?' he demanded.

'Of course I do, when it wasn't me . . . If it was, by God, I'd be so proud of it, I'd tell you at once.'

Suddenly, M. Denizet rose and himself opened the door of the little adjoining room, and summoned Jacques in.

'Do you recognize this man?' he demanded.

'Of course I do,' replied the engine-driver, in astonishment, 'I've seen M. Cabuche at the Misards'.'

'I don't mean that . . . Do you recognize in him the man in the train – the murderer?'

Immediately, Jacques was all caution. In the very first place, he did not recognize Cabuche as the murderer. That man had seemed both shorter and darker, and he was on the point of saying so, when it occurred to him that that was being too forthcoming. So he remained evasive.

'I don't know,' he said, 'I just can't say . . . I assure you, sir, I just can't say.'

Without another word, M. Denizet now called in the Roubauds, and to them too he put the question.

'Do you recognize this man?'

Cabuche continued to grin. He was not surprised at this. He gave Severine a little nod, having known her as a girl when she came to stay at Maufras Cross. On the other hand, both Severine and her husband had caught their breath when they saw Cabuche there, for they realized that this was the man who had been arrested, of whom Jacques had spoken, this was the new defendant who had given rise to this new interrogation! And Roubaud was stupefied, even frightened by the astonishing resemblance between this fellow and the imaginary murderer whose description he had invented, merely to be different from his own. It was all no doubt pure chance, but it worried him so much that he was loth to reply at all.

'Come on,' demanded M. Denizet, 'do you recognize him?'

'Good gracious, sir,' he said, 'I must repeat, it was no more than an impression, somebody brushing by me . . . I'm not saying this man is not about the same height as the one I saw, fair too, and clean shaven . . .'

'Well, then, speak out, do you recognize him?'

At great strain, Roubaud simply shook from the frightful inward struggle. Then the instinct of self-preservation carried him away.

'I cannot say for certain,' he said, 'but there is some resemblance, there's a lot of resemblance, in fact . . .'

This time, Cabuche began to swear. They were all beginning to get his goat with their cock-and-bull stories. And as he was not the man at all, he wanted to be going. With the blood pouring at high pressure into his brain, he banged his fists together and became altogether so menacing that the gendarmes were called and took him away. When he saw this violence, this instinct, as he thought, of the cornered beast to attack, M. Denizet was triumphant. Now his mind really was made up, and he showed it.

'Did you notice his eyes?' he cried, excitedly. 'I tell you, I can always recognize them by the eyes . . . Oh yes, we've got our man in the bag, we've got him.'

The Roubauds stood like dummies, gaping one at the other. So was this all, were they saved, if the law now had the culprit? They were rather dazed and their consciences were uneasy because of the part which the facts had forced them to play. But they were also overcome with delight, and this outweighed their scruples, and they grinned at Jacques. With a sense of alleviation, but a terrible need for fresh air, they were at last waiting for the examining magistrate to let all three of them go, when the usher brought him a letter.

Swiftly, M. Denizet sat down at his desk, forgetful of the three witnesses, to read the communication carefully. For this was the letter from the Ministry, the guidance he should have had the patience to await before driving on with the investigation. And as he read on, his features gradually froze, reassuming their usual gloomy immobility. At one point he raised his head and glanced at the Roubauds, as if something he had come to in the letter had reminded him of them. Their brief happiness vanished, they fell back into their former mental discomfort, they felt they were enmeshed again. Why exactly had he looked at them? Had those three lines of Severine's handwriting, that clumsy note, fear of which haunted them, at last been discovered at Paris? Severine knew M. Camy-Lamotte well, for she had often seen him at Grandmorin's, and she knew he had been made executor. Regret burnt into Roubaud's soul that he had not had the sense to send his wife to Paris, to make a number of useful visits, in order at least to make sure of the Secretary-General's protection, if the Company, getting tired of the nasty rumours, took it into its head to turn them out. And neither of them could now take their eyes off the magistrate, feeling their anxiety grow in proportion to his gloom, for he was clearly put out by this letter which he had received.

It had, indeed, made a hash of the whole day's work. At last, he put the letter down. For a few moments, his wide-open eyes on Jacques and the Roubauds, he remained lost in thought. Then, resignedly, talking aloud to himself, he said: 'Well, we shall see what we shall see, it will all come up again.' . . . Then, after another silence, he added: 'You may go.'

But notwithstanding that he had now been advised to do no more till a certain agreement was reached about the case, then, just as they were leaving the room, he could not resist the need to know one detail and clear up a crucial point which upset his new scheme.

'Ah, no, just a moment,' he cried to Jacques, 'please, I have one more question to put to you.'

Out in the corridor, the Roubauds stopped short. The doors were open, but they were unable to leave. There was something which kept them back, the strain of what had just taken place in the magistrate's room, and they found it physically impossible to go till they had learned from Jacques what that additional question was that the magistrate had to put to him. They turned, and hovered in the vestibule, on jellied knees. Then they sat down again, side by side, on the bench, where they had already spent hours waiting, and slumped there, unable to utter a word.

When the engine-driver reappeared, Roubaud got painfully to his feet. 'We have been waiting for you, we can go down to the station together . . . Well?'

But Jacques was embarrassed, turning his head away, as if anxious to avoid Severine's eyes, fixed on him.

'He's no longer sure, he's floundering,' he said, at last. 'Here's what he's just asked me – he wonders whether there were not two people in it. And as at Havre I had spoken of something black weighing down on the old man's legs, he questioned me about that. . . . He seems to think it was not the rug. Then he sent for the rug, and I had to decide the point . . . Oh, damnation, yes, I said, it was the rug, it must have been.'

The Roubauds shivered. The sleuths were on their tracks, and now a mere word from this young fellow could be their ruin. He must know, and in the end he would talk. They left the Law Courts together, in dead silence, Severine between the two men. Out in the street Roubaud spoke again.

'By the way, colleague,' he said, 'my wife's going to have to spend a day in Paris, on business. You'll be a good friend if she needs anyone and see her about for me, won't you?'

5

At 11.15, dead on time, Europe Bridge with the regulation two hoots of its horn signalled the Havre express, coming out of the Batignolles tunnel, and in no time the turntables were a-clatter as, with a sharp blast of its whistle, the train entered the station, brakes grinding, all smoke and streaming water from the thick rain which had been driving incessantly all the way from Rouen. Before the porters had had time to put their hands to the doors, one of these opened and before the train had stopped Severine had leapt nimbly out. Her coach was at the rear and to reach the engine she had to hurry, pressing through the swift turmoil of passengers emerging from their compartments, cluttered with children and parcels. And there was Jacques Lantier, standing on the footplate of his locomotive, waiting to take it to the sheds, while his mate, Pecqueux, cloth in hand, wiped the brass.

'Cardinet Street, then,' she cried, reaching up on tip-toe, 'we meet there, at three, don't we, and you'll introduce me to your chief, so I can thank him.'

It was Roubaud had thought up this excuse of thanking the head of the Batignolles locomotive sheds for a trifling service he had done him some time previously. By this means Severine would be automatically confided to Lantier's friendly care, by which she would be able to draw him closer to her and influence him.

But Jacques, black with coal-dust, soaking wet, worn out by the struggle against wind and rain, merely looked down coldly at her, and did not reply. He had not been able to say *no* to the husband, just before leaving Havre. But the notion of being alone in this woman's company set him in turmoil, for he was now fully aware that he desired her.

'All right, then?' she tried again, with a smile and that soft, caressing glance of hers, though rather taken aback, even slightly repelled, finding him so dirty, scarcely recognizable. 'Can I count on you?'

As she had now raised herself still higher, leaning her gloved hand on a hand-hold, Pecqueux thought it only right to warn her.

'Look out,' he said, 'get yourself in a mess on that.'

Then Jacques had no option but to reply. 'All right,' he said, sullenly, 'Cardinet Street ... Provided this damned rain does not finish me off altogether. What foul weather it is!'

He looked so sorry for himself that she was touched, and as if it had all been on her account alone, she cried: 'Yes, aren't you in a state, you poor boy, and me so snug inside ... But I did think of you! How awful, I thought, in the open engine-cab in such a downpour ... But I was so happy, you know, thinking you were driving the train up this morning and back again this evening.'

But this kindly intimate talk merely seemed to worry him still more, and his face lit up with relief when there was a sudden whistle and cry from one of the station men and he had to pull the engine whistle lanyard, before backing, and Pecqueux put out his hand to wave the young woman away from the locomotive.

'At three, then!'

'Yes, at three!'

And so, as the engine drew out again, Severine left the platform, the last to go. Outside, in Amsterdam Street, just as she was about to open her umbrella, she found to her delight that it had stopped raining. She went as far as Havre Square, pondered a moment, then decided it would be best to lunch at once. It was eleven twenty-five, so she dropped into a Duvan Café-restaurant at the corner of St Lazare Street, and ordered fried eggs and a chop. Eating at leisure, she sank into the tangle of thought which had haunted her now for weeks, and that seductively sweet smile of hers vanished from her countenance which became bloodless and worried.

It was yesterday, two days after their interrogation at Rouen, that, considering it dangerous to wait, Roubaud decided to send her to see M. Camy-Lamotte, not at the Ministry, but privately, at his town residence next to Grandmorin's house in Rocher Street. She knew he would be there at one, so she could take her time, preparing her words, and trying to guess what he would reply, so that she should have nothing to worry about. For yesterday a new cause for anxiety had appeared to precipitate this visit: through the station grapevine they had learned that Madame Lebleu and Philomène were broadcasting the news that it was reliable information that the Company were going to dismiss Roubaud because he would give it a bad name, and the worst of it was that when Roubaud had tackled M. Dabadie about this, he had not been able to deny it, which certainly lent the rumour weight. It at once made it an urgent matter for her to run up to Paris to plead their cause and above all seek the support of influential M. Camy-Lamotte, just as previously they had enjoyed Grandmorin's. But behind that solicitation, which would be a wonderful pretext for calling on M. Camy-Lamotte, there was a much more imperious motive, an insatiable, burning need to know something definite, that need which eventually drives a criminal to risk revealing himself rather than remain in the dark. Ever since Jacques had told them of the authorities' suspicion that there were two murderers involved, and they felt they were definitely suspected, the uncertainty was killing them. They wore themselves out with conjecture, imagined that incriminating letter had been discovered and all the facts laid bare. Hourly, they expected cross-examination, even arrest, and the anxiety had grown so great and the slightest details concerning them had assumed such threatening shape that in the end they were brought to preferring disaster to that interminable alert. They had to end their suffering by knowing.

Severine finished her chop, so absorbed in thought that she started with sheer surprise when she suddenly realized she was in public, in Paris. Everything then turned bitter, food stuck in her throat, and she had not even the heart to order coffee. But although she had deliberately lunched slowly, it was scarcely quarter past twelve when she left the restaurant, and she had still three quarters of an hour to kill. And though she loved Paris and on the rare occasions she was there revelled in aimless window-shopping, she now felt timid and lost, impatient to get it all over and hide herself.

The pavements were already drying and a warm wind was driving away the last vestiges of cloud. She went down Tronchet Street, to find herself at the Madeleine flower market, bright with primroses and azaleas, a real March show of blossoms, showy against the dun end-of-winter skies. For half an hour she strolled up and down through this first flourish of spring, again at the mercy of confused reflections, with Jacques Lantier appearing to her now as an enemy whom she had to disarm. She felt as if her visit to Rocher Street was over and everything was in order on that front, all she now needed to do was to ensure the young engine-driver's silence, a complicated task to tackle, and though her head burst with romantic suggestions, she was baffled as to what to do. Nevertheless, these thoughts did not tire her or frighten her, but rather lulled her senses sweetly. Then, all at once, she noticed the time by a kiosk clock: ten minutes past one! She had not yet been on the errand for which she had come, and so, jolted back with a rude awakening into reality, she hurried towards Rocher Street.

M. Camy-Lamotte's town house was at the corner of Rocher Street and Naples Street, and her way took Severine past the Grandmorin house, now empty and silent, the Venetian blinds down. She looked up and hastened past. Memory of her last visit here had come back to her, and the house towered over her menacingly. A little way from it, as if hearing the noise of a great concourse of people at her back, she suddenly instinctively looked behind her, to see, on the opposite pavement, none other than M. Denizet, the Rouen examining magistrate, going the same way. She was staggered by this coincidence. Had he seen how she had eyed Grandmorin's house? But he plodded methodically on, so she let him draw ahead on the far side, and followed, though very worried. Then again fear clutched at her heart, for when he reached the corner of Naples Street, she saw him ring M. Camy-Lamotte's bell.

Terror seized her. Now she would never dare make that call. She hurried the other way, turned into Edinburgh Street and followed this through to Europe Bridge. Not till there did she feel safe. And now, not knowing where to go or what she should do, she leant on the railing in a dazed state and gazed down at the vast station yards beneath her, with their incessant movement of trains. With terrified eyes, she followed their movements, convinced now that the magistrate had called on M. Camy-Lamotte about their case, and that the two men were now discussing her, deciding her fate at that very instant. A prey now to despair, she suddenly felt she would rather fling herself under a train than go back to Rocher Street. There was one at that instant, coming out from the main line platforms. She watched it approach, then pass beneath her, puffing up to her very cheeks warm tufts of white vapour. Then the stupid pointlessness of her expedition, the terrible anxiety which she would be taking back with her, if she failed to find the strength to go on and obtain that definite answer, became so painfully vivid to her that she gave herself five minutes only to pull herself together again. Locomotives whistled, and she followed one of them with her eye, a small one, shunting a suburban train out of the way, after which her glance rose towards the left, where, up above the parcels yard, at the very top of the building in the Amsterdam *cul-de-sac*, she recognized 'Ma' Victoire's window, and pictured herself as she had been that day when she propped her elbows on the sill side by side with her husband, looking out, just before that frightful scene which was the starting-point of all their misfortune. And that evoked their dangerous position with such a violent stab of pain that she immediately felt prepared to brave anything, could she but end the strain. Blasts on a signal horn and a prolonged rumble deafened her, while dense smoke blotted out the horizon and billowed into the limpid Paris sky. She then made her way back up Rocher Street, forcing her pace suicidally, in sudden fear that M. Camy-Lamotte would already have gone out again.

When Severine had given a tug at the bell-pull she was again frozen by fear, but a butler quickly opened, took her name, and seated her in an ante-room. Through doors gently left ajar she clearly caught the lively interchange of two men in discussion, then sudden silence, silence profound and absolute, which enveloped her whole being. The only thing she was aware of was the blood throbbing through her temples. She told herself that the Rouen examining magistrate was still there closeted with the Secretary-General, they would be sure to keep her waiting a long time, and the waiting would be unbearable. Then came a sudden surprise: the butler was calling her by name and showing her into another room. Yet she was sure that M. Denizet was still there, and imagined him lurking behind a door.

It was a large study, with sombre furniture, thick carpet, heavy curtains, so solemn, so shut away, that not a sound penetrated from without. Yet there were flowers, pale pink roses, in a bronze basket. And with undemonstrative charm that detail indicated that behind all this severity there was a taste for pleasant living. And there stood the master of the house, impeccably dressed in a close-fitting frock coat. With his fine-lined features, relieved somewhat by the generosity of his grizzled side-whiskers, he too was severe in appearance, yet with

131

the grace of the one-time dandy, despite his years still slender, and beneath the deliberate rigour of his formal dress one sensed an unexpected geniality. In the dim lighting he looked very tall.

As she entered, Severine was conscious only of the oppression of the stuffy warmth, and of M. Camy-Lamotte examining her carefully as she made her way towards him. He made no motion to her to be seated. It was his affectation never to be the first to speak. Instead, he waited for her to declare the purpose of her call. This prolonged the silence till, reacting swiftly to this manner of reception, she all at once in her peril felt complete mistress of herself, very self-possessed and very wary.

'Monsieur,' she said, 'you must forgive me for my boldness in coming to request your favour. You know the irreparable loss I have just suffered, and in my present desolation I have dared think you might take our part and to some extent prolong the moral support which your friend, my own much-grieved protector, used to show me.'

After that, M. Camy-Lamotte could not but offer her a chair, which he did with a gesture. For she had made her little speech in so perfect a manner, without either exaggerated humility or exaggerated grief, in short, with all the innate art of feminine hypocrisy. But he still said nothing himself, merely sat down and waited for her to proceed, which she did, perceiving that she must at once come to the point.

'May I refresh your memory,' she said, 'and recall that I have had the honour of seeing you down at Doinville. Oh, what happy days those were for me . . . But now bad times have come and I have only you, Monsieur, to call on, so in the name of him whom we have just lost, I turn to you. You were his friend. Will you please add to his benevolence and be to me what he was.'

He listened and watched her, shaken, she seemed so unaffected, and so charming, in both her grief and her request for help, that all his suspicions were shaken. Yet, that note which he had come upon among Grandmorin's papers, those few unsigned words he had thought could be from nobody else but her, for he knew of the favours which she in turn had used to grant to Grandmorin. Indeed, the moment that just now she had been announced, the mere fact that she thus called had finally convinced him, and he had broken off his discussion with M. Denizet merely to get his proof positive. But now he had seen her, so gentle and so sweet, however could he think her capable of murder?

However, he still wanted to get things straight, so, without relinquishing his air of severity, he said: 'Tell me exactly what it is you require, Madame . . . Of course I recollect you, and, provided there is no obstacle to such help, ask nothing better than to be of service to you.'

Very succinctly, Severine now told him of her husband's danger of dismissal: there were many who were jealous of him because of his merits and also because of the elevated support which he had hitherto enjoyed. And now that they thought him defenceless, they had hopes of beating him and were making great efforts. She was, however, not going to mention names, and despite their great immediate danger, spoke with great moderation. She said frankly that before bringing herself to come to Paris like this she had had to be firmly persuaded of the need to act quickly. Tomorrow, it might be too late. It was immediately that she craved his aid, his support. All this she put before him with such a logical tissue of details and such good reasons that it really did seem out of the question that she should have made this effort for any other purpose.

M. Camy-Lamotte followed even the almost imperceptible little quiver of her lips. Then he struck his first blow.

'But I still don't quite see,' he said, 'why the Company should dismiss your husband. It has nothing serious against him.'

She followed his features with equal keenness, alive to the slightest wrinkle of his countenance, wondering all the time if he had found that letter. And now, despite the innocence of the question which he had put, she was at once convinced that that letter was present, was even in some article of furniture in that very room! He knew, and he was trying to trap her. He wanted to see whether she would dare speak of the real reasons for the threatened dismissal. He had indeed asked her a trifle too emphatically, and she felt that tired man's eyes probing her very soul. With great courage, she plunged to meet her danger.

'Before Heaven, Monsieur,' she cried, passionately, 'it is a frightful thing, but we had recently actually fallen under suspicion of having murdered our benefactor, and all on account of that miserable legacy.

133

It was not difficult for us to prove our innocence, but the terrible charges have inevitably left an after-taste, and I can only suppose the Company wants to avoid tongues wagging.'

Again he was astonished, disconcerted, indeed, by her frankness, particularly by the sincerity of her tone. What is more, though at first glance he had thought her rather uninteresting, he now began to find her most attractive, with that ingratiating meekness of the blue eyes under that turbulent mass of jet-black hair. With envious admiration, his mind flashed to his old friend Grandmorin. How on earth did that damned old rascal, ten years his own senior, manage to have such delicious morsels right up to his death, while to conserve his own dwindling energies he himself had already had to renounce all such delights? This really was a wench of very great charm, great subtlety too, and the chill, high-official haughtiness which (with such a troublesome case on his plate) he certainly felt, M. Camy-Lamotte allowed to be subtly suffused by the smile of one who, though maybe now merely an onlooker, certainly had also once been a great lover of womanflesh.

Here, however, Severine was carried away by the bravado of sensing her feminine powers, and she made the mistake of adding:

'Folk like us don't murder for money. There would have had to be some other motive, and there wasn't any.'

He shot a glance at her, and detected a quiver at the corner of her lips. Ahah! She was the culprit! From that instant, his conviction was absolute. And she too at once understood that she had given herself away. It was plain from the way the Secretary-General's smile suddenly shut off and the chin pursed.

This *contretemps* produced a gulf of weakness in her, as if her very substance had left her. Nevertheless, she still bore herself upright, and heard her own voice continuing to speak in the same even tones, now confining herself solely to what was necessary. The conversation continued, but from now on neither party had anything to learn, and, regardless of the words they spoke, their talk was an exchange of unspoken things. He had the letter, and she was the woman who wrote it. That emerged precisely from the things which were not said.

'Madame,' said M. Camy-Lamotte, at last, 'I am not going to refuse to say a word to the Company, if you really deserve my support. It so happens that this afternoon I am expecting the Business Manager to come to see me about another matter . . . But I shall have to have some details. Perhaps you would not mind jotting down for me your husband's name, age, and service details and anything else I ought to know about your position.'

And ceasing to watch her closely, so as not to frighten her, he pushed a small table over to her. She started. So he wanted a specimen of her handwriting, did he – to compare with the letter. For a moment she desperately sought an excuse, telling herself that she would not write. Then came the thought – what good would that do, since he already knew? Besides, they could always get a specimen of her hand. So, without revealing the slightest concern, in the most direct manner possible, she wrote down what he wanted, while he, standing behind her, was able to see that even though it was now more distinguished and less shaky, it was exactly the same hand as that of the note.

M. Camy-Lamotte was now beginning to find this little slip of a girl very courageous. He smiled again, now that she could no longer see him, and it was the smile of a man whom, for all his experienced blaséness, sheer female seductiveness could still disturb. But there was nothing like the appearance of weighing it all up carefully. He was most careful about the window-dressing of the régime he served.

'Very well then, Madame,' he said, 'if you will let me have that, I will make enquiries and do whatever I can.'

'I am very much in your gratitude, Monsieur,' she said. 'So you will see my husband is kept on, I can consider the matter settled?'

'Oh, good gracious me, no, I make no promises . . . I must enquire into it and think it over.'

He really was still uncertain, not quite sure what attitude he was going to take regarding this couple, while Severine, feeling herself at his mercy, had only one cause of anxiety: this hesitancy of his, the toss of whether she was going to be saved or ruined by M. Camy-Lamotte, without any possibility of guessing his motives.

'But Monsieur,' she cried, 'just think what agony we are in. You are surely not going to let me go back to Havre without giving me a definite answer?'

'But good Heavens, yes, Madame, I certainly am. I am not my own master in this. You will really have to wait.'

He was already guiding her to the door, and she was leaving in a state of terrible agitation, on the point indeed of confessing everything in a loud voice, in her pressing need to compel him to state plainly what he intended to do with them. And then, in her hopes of discovering a way round, to gain another minute, she cried:

'But I am forgetting, I also wanted to ask your advice about that wretched legacy. Do you think we should perhaps refuse it?'

'The law is on your side,' he replied, cautiously. 'It is all a matter of how you feel about it and of your circumstances.'

On the threshold, she had a final effort. 'Monsieur,' she pleaded, 'I beg you, don't let me go like this, tell me if I may hope?'

On a desperate impulse, she had taken him by the hand. He withdrew it. It was those lovely eyes, so ardently supplicatory, that suddenly moved him.

'Very well,' he said, 'come back at five o'clock. I may have something to tell you.'

She took her leave, emerging from that house more agitated than she had entered it. The situation had taken definite shape, and now her fate was clearly in suspense, under the threat of arrest at any moment. However was she going to live till five? Suddenly she remembered Jacques Lantier, whom she had quite forgotten. Yes, there was another person who could be her ruin, were she arrested. Though it was scarcely half past two, she hastened away up Rocher Street towards Cardinet Street.

After she left, M. Camy-Lamotte stood facing his desk. An intimate at court, to which he was summoned nearly every day, as Secretary-General of the Ministry of Justice, as important a person as the Minister of Justice himself – indeed, often involved on more intimate tasks than the Minister – he was well aware to what extent the highest levels were annoyed and worried by this case of Grandmorin's murder. The opposition press was maintaining its noisy campaign, some of the papers actually accusing the police of being so busy with political spying that they had not sufficient time to deal with murderers, others ferreting out the secret life of the dead judge, constantly underlining that he had been one of the Palace favourites and that this was a hotbed of squalid debauch. As the general election drew near, this campaign was getting really serious. This was why it had been intimated to the Secretary-General that it would be desirable to bring it to an end as soon as possible, no matter how. As the Minister had passed the responsibility for this ticklish operation to him, he was sole arbiter, which was just what necessitated due consideration, for he did not want to foot the general bill by being clumsy.

Still deep in thought, M. Camy-Lamotte crossed the room and opened the door leading to the neighbouring room, where M. Denizet was waiting. And as he entered the room that worthy, who had of course eavesdropped, cried:

'Didn't I tell you, we have been wrong to suspect those folk. . . . It's plain that the woman is only concerned with keeping her husband's job for him. She did not utter one suspicious word.'

The Secretary-General did not answer at once. Deep in reflection, his eyes on the examining magistrate, whose combination of heavy features and thin lips suddenly struck him, he was at this instant weighing up M. Denizet's work, which as behind-the-scenes head of personnel was his concern, and he found himself astonished that despite his poverty Denizet should have remained so upright and despite his occupational stupidity so intelligent. There was also no doubt about it, however subtle M. Denizet thought he was, with those eyelids covering half his eyes, when he thought he had the truth, he was passionate in his pigheadedness.

'So you persist, do you, in thinking this man Cabuche was the murderer?'

M. Denizet started violently, he was so astonished. 'But of course I do,' he said . . . 'Everything points to him. But I have given you all the proofs. I would go so far as to say they were classical proofs. Not one link is missing . . . I have made considerable effort to find any accomplice, such as a woman in the compartment, as you so strongly suggested. That did seem to fit in with evidence of the engine-driver, who actually saw the murder, but when I gave the man a searching cross-examination, he did not stick to his original statement, and even recognized in the travelling rug the dark shape he had spoken of . . . Oh, indeed, I have no doubt whatsoever, Cabuche is the man, the more so since, if it is not Cabuche, we have nobody else.'

The Secretary-General had waited till now to inform M. Denizet of the piece of evidence in writing which he held, but now that his own mind was made up, he was less and less in a hurry to establish the truth. For what was the point of disposing of the false trail of M. Denizet's judicial enquiry, if the real trail was going to lead to the exposure of far more embarrassing details? All that needed careful thought before deciding on it.

'Heavens!' he cried, with his tired-man smile, 'I really am inclined to admit that you are on the right track ... I asked you to come merely to run through certain serious points together with you. This case rather stands out, you see, and now it has taken on quite a political tinge. I am sure you've noticed that, haven't you? But that means that we may well find ourselves forced to act as government men ... Now look here, all cards on the table, your enquiries went to show that the girl – Cabuche's little tart, I mean – was raped, eh?'

The examining magistrate turned down the corner of his mouth squeamishly, and his eyes all but vanished behind his lids.

'I certainly think it damned likely,' he murmured, 'that Judge Grandmorin did make a bit of a mess of her, and that of course is going to come out at the trial ... What is more, if the defence is in the hands of an opposition man, we can certainly expect to have a lot more very dirty linen washed in public. Heaven alone knows, our poor country has enough of it.'

The moment he ceased to be subservient to professional routine, insisting on the dignity of his absolute power and absolute perspicacity, M. Denizet was no fool. He had very well understood why he had been summoned, not to the Ministry of Justice, but to the Secretary-General's private residence.

'In short,' he concluded, seeing that the Secretary-General was not going to stick his neck out, 'we're in for a pretty dirty case.'

M. Camy-Lamotte merely nodded. He was trying to estimate the results of the alternative trial, that of the Roubauds. There was no doubt about it, if the husband was indicted, he would spill the whole story, about his wife too having been seduced, and while still a minor, and about her subsequent liaison with the judge, and the fit of jealous indignation which drove him to commit the deed – not to speak of the fact that it would no longer be the case of a scivvy and an habitual criminal, and that this railwayman and his pretty wife were going to rally a good section of the bourgeoisie of the railway world. Besides, how was one to know what else would not come out, with a man like Grandmorin? There was a fair chance of stirring up shocking things which nobody envisaged. No, there was no question, thought M. Camy-Lamotte, trying the real culprits, the Roubauds, would be

138

far dirtier a business. And for him, that was the end of the argument. He ruled that out, absolutely. To be sure of a trial, if he was going to have one at all, he would rather stick to that of innocent Cabuche.

'I incline to your scheme,' he said, at last, to M. Denizet. 'Assuming that he had something to avenge, there are indeed good *a priori* reasons for suspecting the quarry-man . . . But what a dismal business it all is, good Heavens, and what a lot of mud is going to be stirred up! . . . I know of course that justice must remain indifferent to the consequences, and that, rising above the interests . . .'

But he did not complete the sentence. He ended it off with a mere gesture, while the examining magistrate, silent in turn, waited gloomily for the instructions which he thought were now coming. Once this fiction of his own mind, which was now his notion of the truth, was accepted by M. Camy-Lamotte, he did not really mind about anything else, and was quite ready to sacrifice the notion of justice to the convenience of the Government. But despite his usual skill in transactions of this sort, the Secretary-General was rather in a hurry, spoke too quickly, as if obedience went without question.

'In short,' he said quite brusquely, 'what we want of you is to find there is no true bill in either case . . . So will you arrange to have the case pigeon-holed?'

'I am very sorry,' said M. Denizet, most emphatically, 'but I am really not the master in the matter, I must be guided by my conscience.'

A smile immediately leapt to M. Camy-Lamotte's countenance, and he was again the formal high official of state, with that polite but rather disillusioned air which exuded scorn of the world at large.

'But of course,' he cried. 'It is precisely to your conscience that I am addressing myself. It is up to you to take whatever decision your conscience may dictate, and I am sure that you will weigh the *pros* and *cons* most fairly, with a view to the triumph of sound ways of thought and of public ethics . . . You know even better than I do that it is sometimes the brave man's course rather to resign himself to a wrong than to cause a greater one . . . But of course we appeal solely to your high sense of public duty and your personal integrity. There is not the slightest thought of limiting your freedom of action. That indeed is why I repeat that you are the complete master of the case. As, for that matter, the law requires.'

139

Jealous of that infinite power, particularly when he was on the point of using it badly, the Rouen examining magistrate accepted each of M. Camy-Lamotte's pronouncements with a self-satisfied nod of the head.

'For that matter,' the latter continued, with such an increase of kindliness that the exaggeration of it was really almost ironical, 'we know whom we are talking to. We have been watching your efforts for some time now, and I may mention that were a vacancy to occur, you would at once be asked to come to Paris.'

M. Denizet started. What was this? If he rendered the service asked of him, they were going to satisfy his great ambition, his dream of a post in Paris? But M. Camy-Lamotte had noticed his reaction, and was already adding:

'There is definitely a place for you, it is only a question of time. But since I have already been rather indiscreet, I think I should add that I am glad to be able to tell you that your name is already down for the *Cross of the Legion of Honour* – next August 15th.'

Swiftly, M. Denizet turned all this over in his mind. He would have preferred the promotion, for he reckoned that in the last resort this would increase his salary by about 166 francs a month, and in the respectable penury in which he lived, that was more than affluence. It meant new clothes, better food for his good Melanie and a less cantankerous Melanie too. There was no doubt, it was a good cross to bear. And this was a promise. In his heart of hearts, he who would never have sold himself, being nourished in the tradition of a magistrature which if materially poor, was honest, without more ado now yielded to a mere hope, to this rather nebulous undertaking on the part of the administration to favour him. The judicial functions, after all, had become a trade like any other, and he had certainly had his nose on the grindstone a long time, always ready to bend to orders from above and always solicitous of promotion.

'Will you kindly tell the Minister,' he murmured, 'that I really am very grateful.'

He rose, feeling that now any further exchange between them would be embarrassing to them both. And his eyes were dull, his features expressionless, when he wound up by saying:

'And so I will get on with my enquiry, of course, keeping your particular misgivings in mind. It goes without saying that if we cannot establish a cast-iron case against Cabuche, it would be better not to risk the pointless notoriety of a trial . . . In such case, the man would have to be released and an eye kept on him.'

On the threshold the Secretary-General proved himself amiability itself to the very last word. 'Monsieur Denizet,' he said, 'we rely completely on your great sense of what is fitting and on your impeccable honesty.'

As soon as he was alone, M. Camy-Lamotte was curious enough, however pointless it now was, to compare Severine's hand with the unsigned note which he had found among Judge Grandmorin's papers. Yes, the resemblance was complete! He folded up her letter again and pressed it carefully, for though he had not breathed a word about it to the examining magistrate, he still thought a weapon like that worth keeping. And when his memory pictured the features of that little lady, so frail yet so strong in her battle of nerves, he again shrugged his shoulders with that cynical, indulgent shrug of his. Oh, the little darlings, when they wanted something!

At twenty minutes to three, before the time, Severine was at the Cardinet Street meeting-place where she had agreed to meet Jacques. Though she did not know it, he lived there, at the very top of a large block, occupying a cramped little room, which scarcely ever saw him except at night when he went home to bed, apart from which of course he slept away two nights a week, at Havre, in between the evening express to that port and the morning one back to Paris. But on this occasion, being soaked to the skin and worn out, he had gone to his room to lie down for a while, and Severine might easily have waited for him in vain, had a couple next door not had a quarrel, the husband beating the wife and the wife yelling out. Then, looking out of his attic window and seeing Severine on the pavement below, Jacques had a speedy wash and dressed in very bad humour.

'Ah, there you are, at last!' she cried, when with some surprise she saw him emerge from the courtyard. 'I had begun to think there was a misunderstanding. But you did say at the corner of Saussure Street . . .'

She threw a glance at the block and without giving him time to answer her, said:

'Is this where you live, then?'

Without telling her, he had in fact fixed the *rendezvous* at his own door, because the depôt they were to visit was more or less opposite. But her question irked him, he was afraid she was going to push her palliness to the point of asking if she could see his room, and this was so sparsely furnished and so untidy that he was ashamed of it.

'Oh, I don't live there, I just stable,' he said. 'But let's hurry, I am afraid the chief may have gone out.'

He was right, for when they called at the little house just behind the depôt in the station yard where the yard chief lived, he was not there, and they then wandered fruitlessly from shed to shed, everywhere to be told to come back at half past four, if they wanted to be sure of finding him in the repair shops.

'That's all right,' said Severine, 'we will come back.'

Then, outside again, alone, in Jacques' company, she said: 'If you've nothing to do, you don't mind if I spend the time with you, do you?'

He could not refuse. Besides, in spite of the dull unrest she caused in him, she also charmed him more and more, so strongly, indeed, that the deliberate moroseness with which he had proposed to protect himself melted under her gentle glances. As he told himself, with those sweet, elongated features and that timid manner, when she did love she must be like a faithful dog which one cannot ever bring oneself to strike.

'Of course I won't leave you,' he replied, a little less harshly than heretofore. 'But we have more than an hour and a half before us . . . Shall we go to a café?'

She smiled back at him, pleased to feel him friendly at last. But she quickly rejected his suggestion.

'Oh, but no, I don't want to shut myself up . . . I would much prefer to take your arm and walk about, wherever you like.'

Without a word from him she slipped her arm softly into his. Now that he was no longer black with smoke, she found him distinguished looking, with his get-up of a clerk on holiday. Indeed, he had quite a middle-class manner, emphasized by a sort of free pride, being used to the open air and everyday dangers. Never before had she really noticed that he was quite a handsome man, with regular features set in an oval face and very dark moustaches against a pale skin. It was only those fugitive eyes of his, those gold-speckled eyes which kept avoiding her, that continued to make her mistrustful. Did he avoid

142

looking her in the face because he did not want to get entangled, wanted to remain free to act as he thought fit, even against her? From that instant, because of the general uncertainty in which she still found herself, at the mercy of a palsy each time her mind went back to that study in Rocher Street where her fate was being decided, she had one aim only, to feel that this man whose arm she now held was all hers and that whenever she raised her head she could make him abandon his eyes to hers, and hold nothing back. Then he would really belong to her. She did not in the least love him. She did not even think of loving. She was merely making an effort to make him her tool, so she might have nothing more to fear.

For some minutes they walked on without a word, through the continual flow of foot-passengers which generally crowds that common residential district. Sometimes they were obliged to leave the pavement, and crossed the street weaving through between vehicles. Then they found themselves facing the Batignolles Gardens, almost deserted at this time of the year. But the sky, washed by the morning's downpour, was of a very gentle blue, and the lilacs were breaking into bloom under the warm March sun.

'Shall we go in?' asked Severine. 'All these crowds begin to make me dizzy.'

But Jacques had in any case meant to go into the gardens, with no thought of doing so just to please her, he merely wanted to get away from the crowds too.

'Here or anywhere,' he said, 'come on.'

Slowly, they sauntered between the lawns, with their leafless trees. There were some women taking their babies for an airing, others using the gardens as a short-cut, striding hard. They crossed the river and climbed the path between the rock gardens. Then, idling, they came down again, to follow the path through the firtree plantation, whose needles gleamed a sombre green in the sunshine. Then, coming upon a bench in an isolated corner, hidden from watching eyes, they sat down, this time without even discussing it, but as if brought there by common understanding.

'It's turned out lovely after all, today, hasn't it?' she said, after a silence.

'Yes,' he replied, 'there's the sun again.'

But that is not all what they were thinking of. He, who shunned

143

women, had just been running over the events which had brought them together. There she was, touching him, threatening to invade his life, and it was all a continual source of surprise. Since that last interrogation at Rouen, he was quite sure this woman was implicated in the Maufras Cross murder. But how? Through what circumstances? By what passion or interest had she been goaded to it? All these questions he asked without being able to give himself any clear answer. Yet he did finally concoct some sort of story: the husband's greed, a dominant character, in a hurry to get hold of the legacy, perhaps afraid of the will's being changed, to their disadvantage – perhaps it was even a scheme to bind her more closely to him by a bond of bloodshed. To this version he stuck, and the dark corners of it attracted him, intrigued him, without prompting him to try to clear them up. He had also been plagued by the notion that it was his duty to tell all this to the authorities. This indeed was the thought which now preoccupied him, when he found himself seated so close to her on a public bench that he felt the warmth of her thigh against his.

'In March,' he said again. 'Astonishing, isn't it, to be able to sit out of doors, like this.'

'Ah! As soon as the sun is out, it always feels good,' she murmured.

She, for her part, was reflecting that this boy would really have to be very stupid, not to guess that they had done it. They had thrown themselves at his head too blatantly. Why, she was pressing her leg against his at this very instant. Thus in the long silence, broken only by empty words, she followed his line of thought. When their eyes met, she came to read that he was just beginning to wonder whether she were not the thing he saw pressing as a dark mass with all its weight on the victim's legs. What, oh! what was she to do, to bind him to her by bonds indestructible?

'It was very cold this morning at Havre,' she said.

'Not to speak of all the water that's come down,' he replied.

It was at that moment that Severine suddenly had her inspiration. She did not argue, did not debate it. It came to her by sheer instinct, from the depths of her mind and her heart, for, had she argued about it, she would have said nothing. But she felt that this was as it should be, and by just talking of it, she would win him over. Softly, she took hold of his hand, and looked at him. The tufty conifers concealed them from people passing along the other alleys. They could hear

144

only a dull distant rumble of wheels, muted in the sunny isolation of the gardens. Just where the alley turned there was one child, all alone, playing silently with a little spade, filling a bucket with sand. And with all her being in it, half whispering, she plunged.

'You think me guilty, do you?'

He shuddered slightly. Her eyes held his.

'Yes,' he said, in the same agitated half voice.

At this she squeezed the hand she held more firmly. She said nothing for some moments, feeling their fevers mingle.

'You are mistaken,' she said, at last. 'I am not.'

She said this in point of fact less to convince him, than merely to indicate to him that in the eyes of everybody else she must be innocent. It was the declaration of a woman who says *no* because she just wants it to be *no*, despite everything, always.

'I am not guilty . . . You must stop hurting me so by thinking I am.'

She was now very happy, seeing that he let her hold his eyes in hers and drink them down into her. There was no question about it, what she had just done was to render her body up to him, and if later he claimed it, she would not be able to refuse him. But the principal thing was that the bond between them was tied and indissoluble. Now she could dare him to tell, for he was hers and she was his. Their silent avowal had made them one.

'You will not hurt me any more, you will believe me?'

'Yes, I believe you,' he said, with a smile.

Why indeed should he be so cruel as to press her to talk of that terrible thing? Later, she could tell him everything, if she needed. This way in which she found peace by confessing to him, without saying a word, touched him profoundly. It was the indication of affection without limits. She was so confiding, so tender, with those periwinkle-blue eyes, and revealed herself moreover to him so womanly, so utterly a man's woman, ever ready to submit, and be happy in submission. And what delighted him above all else, while their fingers were still interlocked and their eyes could not quit each other's, was the fact that she alone did not seem to prompt that *malaise* of his, that frightful spasm which usually took possession of him in the close presence of a woman and the idea of possessing her. He had not been able to touch the flesh of any other without experiencing that terrible urge to bite deep into it, in a loathsome

145

thirst for laceration and blood. Did this really mean that here was a woman he could love without it ever coming to murder?

'You surely know I am your friend and you have nothing to fear from me,' he murmured at her ear. 'I do not want to know your business. That is up to you . . . Do you understand me? Use me as you want.'

He had drawn so close to her face that he could feel her warm breath stirring his moustaches. As recently as the morning he would have shaken with fear lest in such circumstances a terrible attack take possession of him. What was this that had happened to him, for hardly a quiver to trouble him? He was engulfed now in the glorious weakness of convalescence! The notion that she had killed, becoming certainty, made her seem totally different to him. She was greater, a woman apart. It might well be that she had been not merely the accessory, but had actually struck the blow. Though he had no proof, he was sure this was possible. And therefrom she was sanctified to him, a being beyond reason, superior to the terrified desires she awakened in him.

Now they could both talk cheerfully, like any couple in the early stages of a courtship.

'You ought to give me your other hand, to warm.'

'Oh no, not here, somebody might see.'

'Who? Why, we are alone . . . Besides, what's the harm? Holding hands doesn't make babies.'

'I should hope not.'

She laughed uproariously, in the delight of being saved. She did not love this young fellow. At least, she thought she was sure that she did not love him. And even if she had in a sense promised herself to him, she was already musing about how to wriggle out of paying. He seemed so nice, he would never pester her. It would all work out quite well.

'Then it's agreed, isn't it, we are friends, and nobody, not even my husband, can point the finger at us . . . Please let go my hand now, and don't keep looking at me like that, you'll wear your eyes out.'

But he kept her delicate fingers in his, and in a very low voice stammered: 'You know I love you.'

With a swift gesture she jerked her hand free. Standing now facing him as he still sat there, she cried:

'Now we are getting silly, upon my word we are! Behave yourself, somebody is coming.'

As a matter of fact, a nurse had just appeared, her baby asleep in her arms. Then a very preoccupied young girl came along. The sun was sinking, lost in an horizon of purplish mists. Its rays crept back from the lawns, dying in gold dust beyond the green tips of the firs. The incessant rumble of the traffic seemed suddenly to stop. They heard a nearby clock strike: one, two, three, four, five . . .!

'Oh, good gracious me!' cried Severine. 'It's five o'clock, and I ought already to be at Rocher Street!'

Her happiness vanished, all the anxiety of the unknown which awaited her in M. Camy-Lamotte's house flooded back and reminded her that she was still not safe. The colour left her cheeks, her lips quivered.

'But what about the yard superintendent you had to see?' asked Jacques, getting up and taking her arm again.

'Oh, bother it, that will have to do another time! . . . Listen, my dear, I do not need you any more now, you must let me hurry to my appointment. But thank you again, thank you from the bottom of my heart.'

Tearing herself away, she took both his hands and squeezed them.

'We'll meet very soon, at the train.'

'Yes, we'll meet soon.'

She was already hurrying away, as fast as she could go. She vanished between the laid-out hillocks of the gardens, while Jacques slowly made his way back to Cardinet Street.

At his residence, M. Camy-Lamotte had just had a long interview with the Business Manager of the Western Railway Company. Summoned on another matter, the Manager also began to discuss the Grandmorin murder, and remarked how much this worried his Directors. In the first place, there were the press complaints of the lack of security for travellers in first-class compartments. Besides that, the whole personnel of the railway felt involved, a number of its men were under suspicion, not counting this fellow Roubaud, the most compromised of them all, liable to be arrested at any moment. Finally, the gossip about the shocking behaviour of Judge Grandmorin, one of the Directors, seemed to reflect on them all. Thus this crime, which was presumably committed by a petty A.S.M. and was part of a sordid, dirty, indecent story, by complex stages of gearing had begun to shake the whole apparatus of one of France's principal railways, upsetting even the principal executives. The shattering effects were going even higher, reaching the Ministry, even threatening the State in its present unhealthy political condition. It was an hour of crisis and any further complication might be fatal to the fever-stricken body politic. So when M. Camy-Lamotte elucidated from the Business Manager that that very morning the Company had decided to dismiss Roubaud, he attacked the decision very fiercely indeed. Oh no, he said, nothing would be more clumsy and unfortunate. If they chose to make Roubaud out to be a political martyr, that would only intensify the press campaign. Then there would be a thundering scandal, from top to bottom, and who on earth could say what nasty discoveries either party might not make. The scandal had gone on too long already. It must be hushed up. So, convinced by M. Camy-Lamotte, the Business Manager promised to keep Roubaud on, not even to transfer him to another post. Then alone people would see that everything was really decent and above-board. In any case, M. Camy-Lamotte said, it was all over, the case was going to be pigeon-holed.

When Severine, quite out of breath, once more found herself in M. Camy-Lamotte's forbidding study, it was to be subjected again for a few moments to his silent quizzing look, for the astounding effort she made to appear calm fascinated him. There was no gainsaying it, she was a very charming little thing, was this dainty little criminal with the periwinkle-blue eyes.

'Well, Madame . . .'

He paused for a few more seconds, to take his pleasure in her anxiety. But her eyes were so penetrating, he felt her whole being cling to him in such dire need to know, that he took pity.

'Well, Madame, I have seen the Business Manager, and have secured his assurance that your husband will not be dismissed . . . The matter has been arranged.'

At this, weakness overcame her, for the flood of sheer happiness which flooded through her quite took her breath away. Her eyes filled with tears. She could not speak, but only smiled.

Insisting on the phrase, to bring out its precise meaning, he repeated:

'The matter has been arranged . . . You can return to Havre at peace.'

She understood all he meant: he was saying that they would not be arrested, they were being pardoned. Not merely was her husband's station-mastership safe, this terrible drama too was over, consigned to oblivion, buried. With an instinctive caressing movement, like a lovely domestic animal which fawns gratefully, she bent over his hands, held them pressed to her cheeks, and kissed them. And this time he did not withdraw them, but was himself very moved by the delicate tenderness of this expression of thanks.

'One thing only,' he added, striving to be stern again. 'You must not forget yourselves, you must behave yourselves.'

'Oh, Monsieur!'

But he still wanted to keep them dependent on his mercy, both the woman and the man, so he made a reference to the letter.

'Do not forget that the file remains here, and at the slightest lapse, it might be opened again . . . Above all, do advise your husband to drop politics. On that score, we shall be most exacting. I know how involved he is already, I have heard all about a wretched and most unfortunate quarrel with a deputy-prefect. Indeed, he is considered to be a declared republican, and that is detestable . . . Don't you think so? Let him be a good boy, or we shall make no bones about sitting on him.'

She stood there, all eagerness now to get outside, to give freer air to the delight which was choking her.

'Monsieur,' she said, 'we shall follow your advice, we shall do what you want of us . . . No matter when or where, you have only to say the word: I am at your service.'

The smile had crept back to his face, that sluggish smile, with in it a hint of the man who had so long imbibed the vanity of all things.

'Of course, Madame,' he said, grandiloquently, 'I shall never make ill or cheap use of your complaisance.'

With his own hand he showed her out. Radiant, she turned back twice on the landing, to thank him.

Once out in the street, her legs carried her like a mad thing. She suddenly noticed that for no reason whatsoever she was going up Rocher Street, and she turned back down the hill, crossing over to the other side, also for no apparent reason, at risk of being run over.

She felt a compulsion to keep moving, she wanted to wave her arms, shout out. She had already seen through to the reason why they were being pardoned, and caught herself saying: 'Why, damn them, they are afraid, there's no fear now that they will stir all that up, what a ninny I have been to worry so! How obvious! But what luck! Now, I am safe, I am really safe ... No matter, I'm going to give my husband a good scare, to keep him in his place ... I am saved, saved, what luck!'

As she came out into St Lazare Street, she caught sight of the clock outside a watchmaker's shop, and saw it was twenty to six. 'Upon my word,' she thought, 'I'm going to treat myself to a good dinner, I have the time.'

She chose the best restaurant opposite the station and there, at a very white little table, against the huge plateglass window, where she could get full enjoyment of all the people going by, she ordered a really nice little dinner: oysters, fillet of sole and roast chicken. At least she owed it to herself to make up for her rotten lunch. She ate greedily, found the fancy white bread lovely and next treated herself to another dainty, *beignets* of puff pastry. Then, after black coffee, she made haste, for she had only a very few minutes left before the train.

After leaving her, Jacques first went back to his room, to don his working clothes, then went straight to the locomotive yard, where as a rule he did not turn up till half an hour before his engine pulled out. He had come to rely on Pecqueux for the check-over, though two out of three times his fireman was drunk. But today, in his sentimental state, without realizing it, he was overcome with conscience, and wanted to make sure for himself that everything was working perfectly, the more so since that morning on the up run from Havre he had thought he detected a tendency in Lison to overlabour to poor result.

In the huge closed, sooty-black locomotive hangar, lit by tall dusty windows, Jacques' locomotive was among all the others at the head of one of the tracks, ready to leave first. A yard fireman had just re-stoked her and red-hot ashes were falling into the pan below the riddling grate. It was one of those express engines with twin coupled axles, a giant of delicate grace, its huge but light driving wheels with their steel coupling-rods, a broad-bosomed engine, long and powerful in the loin, with all the logic and precision which constitute the sovereign beauty of these metal creatures of precision and power.

Like the other engines of the Western Railway Company, in addition to its serial number, it bore the name of a station, in this case *Lison*, a place in the Cotentin country. But in his sentimental love for his engine, Jacques had turned Lison into a girl's name. My Lison, he would say, in a fondling, lover's way.

But it was true, he did love his engine with a lover's fondness. He had been driving her for four years now. He had driven others, some easy to handle, some difficult, some full of pluck, some idlers, and he was very clear that every single one had its own character, that many a one was not worth tuppence, just like, as everybody knows, with women of flesh and blood, so that, if he did love this Lison of his, that was because she really had all the qualities of a fine woman. She was gentle, she was responsive to his word, she was easy on the pull off, and, thanks to a good boiler system, she was a steady puller on the road. It was argued that if she got under way so readily, that was due to the fine quality of her wheel tyres and still more to the fine tuning of her slide-valve gear, just as the fact that she always gave a good head of steam on very little fuel was put down to the quality of the copper of her tubes and the satisfactory layout of her boiler. But Jacques knew that there was something besides that in it, for other engines, identically built, fitted with the same care, failed to exhibit a single one of Lison's qualities. There was a soul, a mystery of engine construction, in it all, a something which the hazards of the hammer add to metal, or the touch of a masterman's hands lends to a vital part: the personality of the engine, its life.

Thus he loved Lison as a grateful male loves a woman, loved her for her quick get-away and quick stopping, for her qualities of a really good mare. He loved her too because in addition to his regular salary she earned him a bonus, being so economical with fuel. She built up her head of steam so well that he was able to save a considerable amount of coal. He had only one thing to reproach her with – she was greedy on lubrication, her cylinders in particular eating up oil at a quite unreasonable rate, she was always hungry for oil, her lust never sated. He had made efforts to tune this out of her, but in vain, she got breathless at once. It had to be put down to her temperament. He was now resigned to putting up with this greediness of hers, just as one turns the blind eye to a little failing in people who otherwise are all good qualities, and he was reduced to joining with his fireman in

151

joking about it and saying that, just like any pretty woman, she needed greasing too often.

While the furnace roared and Lison's pressure mounted, he made a tour of inspection, looking at every part and trying to find out why that morning she had been greedier than ever on lubrication. But he found nothing wrong, she was clean, and gleaming with that happy cleanliness which bespeaks the loving care of the engineer. He was always to be seen wiping her and polishing. Especially when he reached his destination he would rub her down vigorously, just as horse folk do their steaming nags at the end of a long ride, and he would profit by her being warm, the better to clean up spots and dribbles. Nor did he ever force her violently, but kept up a steady pace, avoiding unnecessary slowing down, because this only made it necessary to put on harmful spurts of speed later. In this way the couple had lived throughout in the greatest harmony. Not once in four years had he complained of her in the depôt register, where engine-drivers note down any repairs they need and you find that the bad drivers, those who are idlers or drunkards, are always at loggerheads with their engines.

But all the same, on this particular occasion he could not get out of his mind that looseness she had with her oil, and there was another feeling too, something vague deep down in him that he had not experienced before, an uneasiness, even a lack of confidence regarding her, as if he was not quite sure of her and was doing his best to reassure himself that she would behave properly on the way back.

Another thing was that Pecqueux had not turned up, and when at last he did appear, white-tongued from the lunch he had indulged in with a friend, Jacques flew off the handle at him. The two men as a rule got on well together, having for years now worked together up and down the line, rattling side by side on their silent job, united by the common tasks and common dangers. Though the junior by ten years, Jacques always adopted a paternal attitude towards his fireman, hushing up his delinquencies, leaving him an hour to sleep it off when he was too drunk, and Pecqueux returned the kindness with canine devotion. And apart from his drunkenness it must be said that Pecqueux was a first-class man, who knew his job inside-out. It must also be said that he too was fond of Lison, which all helped for the two men's mutual understanding, so that they and the engine constituted a real triangular set-up, though one with never a quarrel. It was for this reason that when Jacques suddenly fired off at him like that, Pecqueux was amazed, and he stared at him in real astonishment when he heard him grinding out his suspicions of Lison.

'What on earth do you mean?' he demanded. 'She goes like an angel!'

'On the contrary,' said Jacques, 'I am far from satisfied.'

And notwithstanding the good condition of every part, he kept on tossing back his head, trying the levers, making sure the valves were functioning properly. He climbed round her and with his own hand topped up the cylinder lubrication, while the fireman wiped the dome, where there were slight traces of rust. The sander linkage worked all right, and everything should have set his mind at ease.

The truth was, Lison no longer had the monopoly of his heart. Another attachment was already growing there. That dainty, frail little creature, whom he could still see as if close by his side, on the bench in the Batignolles Gardens, so weak and appealing, so in need of affection and protection, had entered his heart. Never before when for any reason he was delayed and had to drive his train at top speed, had he given the slightest thought to the dangers which the passengers were running. But now the mere thought of taking back to Havre that little woman whom only that very morning he had almost hated, and had been annoyed to feel on the train, filled him with tremendous anxiety, tremendous fear of an accident, in which he imagined her injured by his fault and dying in his arms. From now on he was burdened with love. Lison, fallen under suspicion, would do well to behave herself properly, or she risked losing her reputation of a good puller.

It struck six. Jacques and Pecqueux climbed on to the little sheet-iron bridge which connected tender and locomotive, and when at a nod from his chief Pecqueux opened the cleaning cocks, a cloud of white vapour filled the black shed. Then, obedient to the slowly opened regulating wheel, Lison moved out from the depôt and whistled for a track. Almost immediately, she was able to plunge into the Batignolles tunnel. But at Europe Bridge they had to wait, and it was not till the scheduled hour that the signal sent them on to the 6.30 express, to which two shunters coupled Lison securely.

The train was on the point of leaving. There were only five minutes·

to go. Jacques leant out, surprised not to see Severine among the crowd of passengers. He was absolutely convinced that she would not get into the train without coming to see him first.

At last, late, there she was, half walking, half running. And indeed, she did pass the whole length of the train, not halting once till she reached the engine, high colour in her cheeks, exultant with delight. her little feet stretched up on tiptoe, her countenance reached up at him, wreathed in a broad smile.

'Don't worry,' she cried, 'here I am.'

He too began to laugh, happy now she was there.

'Fine,' he called back. 'Fine, all's in order.'

But still she reached up towards him, and, less loudly, cried:

'My dear friend, I am so happy . . . Such luck I've had . . . Exactly what I wanted.'

He understood it all, he too was very pleased. Then she started to run for a seat, but turned back yet again, to cry jokingly:

'Now then, you just look out, don't you tip me out.'

On top of the world, he shouted back:

'The idea, you don't fear!'

Doors were already being banged, Severine only just had time to climb in. Then, as the guard signalled, Jacques whistled and opened the regulator. They were off. It was the same departure as that of the tragedy train in February, at the same time, amid the same station throngs, the same noises, the same clouds of smoke. The only difference was that now it was still daylight, a clear dusk, a light of infinite gentleness. At the window, Severine looked out. Jacques, on the right of Lison's footplate, warmly dressed in over-trousers and a woollen over-tunic, with goggles furnished with cloth ear-pieces tied behind his head, under his peaked cap, now had eyes only for the track, every instant leaning out for a moment behind the wind-screen, to get a better view. Constantly shaken by the violent vibration, though oblivious of this, he kept his right hand on the speed regulator, like a pilot's on the helm, incessantly adjusting it imperceptibly this way and that, while with his left hand he tugged again and again on the whistle cord, for the exit from Paris is a difficult one, full of hidden dangers. He whistled at level crossings, through stations, entering tunnels, on sharp curves. When a red signal showed far ahead in the failing daylight, he shrilled with long blasts for an open

154

track, and thundered by. And at intervals his eye flashed to the pressure gauge and his fingers turned the little injector control the instant the needle marked over 160 pounds. It was to the track ahead that his gaze ever returned, incessantly on the alert for the slightest thing, his attention so keen that he saw nothing else and did not even notice the hurricane-like wind rushing past him. Then the pressure-gauge dropped, and with his foot he flung open the furnace door and raised the grate, whereupon Pecqueux, who knew the gesture so well, took his hammer, broke coal and pitched it evenly in over the whole fire-box area. The blazing heat scorched their legs and then, when the door banged to, the icy draught resumed its sway.

Night was falling, and Jacques increased his caution. Rarely had he felt Lison so obedient. He possessed her, he rode her in his own way with absolute will, as her master, yet never once relaxing his severity, treating her like a wild animal he had tamed, but whom he could never quite trust.

At his back, in the train rushing through the night at high speed, he could see a dainty feminine body, which yielded itself to him, and, smilingly, trusted him. It gave him a subtle thrill, he gripped the speed regulator more harshly, and his keen eyes peered into the thickening darkness in search of red lights. After the junctions of Asnières and Colombes, he breathed a little more freely. As far as Mantes all went well, the track was level as a billiard table, and Lison ran smoothly. But beyond Mantes he had to push her, to master rather a stiff gradient of more than a mile. Then, without slackening speed, he put her down the gentle slope of Rolleboise tunnel, and she cleared the two and a half kilometres of it in under three minutes.

There was now only one more tunnel, that of Roule, near Gallon, before Sotteville station, which was a recognized teaser, with its confusion of tracks, permanent shunting going on, always cluttered up, making it really dangerous. All his strength was now concentrated in his watchful eyes and governing hand and so, whistling and hissing wildly, he put Lison all out through Sotteville, and did not halt again till Rouen, out of which at last she pulled rather more steadily up the long gradient which runs as far as Malaunay.

The moon had risen, very clear, with its white light, by which as they flashed by Jacques could distinguish every bush, even the stones of the roads. When they were leaving Malaunay, alarmed by the

155

shadow of a tall tree which barred the track he shot a glance to the right, and recognized the out-of-the-way country, even the brushwood on the heath from which he had seen the murder. Wild, waste land, this countryside flashed by with its incessant hills, its dark deep wooded ravines, its wild desolation. Then, at Maufras Cross, under the motionless moon, that house set cock-eyed suddenly flashed into view, deserted and sorry, its shutters for ever closed, gruesomely dismal. And, without knowing why, this time too, though more now than ever before, something clutched at Jacques' heart, as if he was seeing his own misfortune.

Nevertheless, an instant later, his eyes recorded another sight. Near the Misards' house, against the level-crossing gate, Flora was standing. She did not move, she only turned her head, to follow him on with her eyes, in the lightning-flash which bore him on, away from her. Against the white light her tall outline stood clearly out, and in the pallid gold of the moonlight her golden hair caught fire.

Now, having pressed Lison hard to get her over Motteville ridge, he let her breathe across Bolbec plain, then at last speeded her up, from Saint-Romain to Harfleur, on the steepest down gradient of the line, seven good miles which engines all devoured ravenously, cantering like mad mares which scent the stable. At Havre, he was broken with weariness when, under the station roof, with all its re-echoing din and eddying smoke, before hurrying indoors, Severine ran up to him, so cheerfully and so sweetly to cry:

'Thank you; see you tomorrow.'

6

One month passed, and everything was again very, very quiet in the apartment which the Roubauds occupied on the first floor up of the station building, immediately above the waiting-rooms. Their life, like that of their fellow-denizens of 'the corridor', all that little community of officials of the railway, under their regular régime determined by clock and time-table – their life had resumed its old, monotonous tenor, and one would have said that nothing violent or out of the ordinary had ever happened.

The notorious, scandalous Grandmorin murder case was quietly fading from memory, on the way to being pigeon-holed for ever because of the apparent inability of the authorities to discover the murderer. And at last, after remanding Cabuche for another fortnight, M. Denizet issued a finding of 'no-bill' against him on the grounds of insufficient evidence, and the legend was already taking shape of a mysterious killer on whom the police could never lay their hands, a virtuoso of crime who was everywhere at once, charged with all manner of murders, but who vanished in smoke at the mere approach of a detective. Nevertheless, jibes about this mythical figure were already losing their bite. Solely in the opposition press, burning hot with pre-election fever, rather distant, rare, sly allusions to this mythical figure still appeared from time to time. The oppressiveness of the régime, indeed, and the arbitrary acts of prefects, every day now provided new stories round which to weave indignant articles. Thus the case was dropped from the headlines and gradually ceased to excite the feverish curiosity of the masses. It had practically ceased to be a subject of conversation at all.

What however had completed the restoration of tranquillity in the Roubaud *ménage* was the happy way in which another difficulty, the threatened trouble over Judge Grandmorin's testament, was smoothed out. On the considered advice of Madame Bonnehon the Lachesnayes had at last agreed not to challenge the will. Their motives were a fear of reawakening scandalous talk, but also some dubiety as the possible outcome of a lawsuit. Thus, with the acquisition of their legacy, the Roubauds had now been the owners of Maufras Cross for a week, house and garden together valued at forty thousand francs. They had at once resolved to sell a place so befouled by bloodshed and debauchery. It haunted them like a nightmare. They would never dare to spend a night there, so frightful were the ghosts of that past. What was more, they proposed to sell, together with all the furniture, just as it stood, without even so much as passing a duster over it. But as sale by public auction would have fetched far too low a price, purchasers prepared to withdraw to so lonely a spot being rare, they had decided to bide their time till somebody who really fancied it should come along, and all they did was to put up a board with the words TO BE SOLD big enough to be read easily from all the many passing trains. However, that board and the desolate nature of the site, all served to aggravate the dismal look of those closed shutters and bramble-grown garden. As Roubaud flatly refused even to look at the place, and make one or two essential arrangements, Severine went down one afternoon, then left the keys with the Misards, charging them with the business of showing the property if anybody wanted to see it. Any purchaser could have moved in within a couple of hours, for there was everything they might need, even linen in the cupboards.

And now that there was nothing left to worry the Roubauds, they let each day follow sluggishly on till it merged into drowsy expectation of the next. In the end, they told themselves, the house would be sold. Then they would invest the money, and all would be well. Indeed, in time they even came to forget all about Maufras Cross, living as if they were never to leave that three-roomed flat which they occupied – a dining-room opening straight on to the corridor, a rather large bedroom on the right, and the kitchen, very small and unventilated, on the left. Even the station roofing rearing its galvanized sheeting slopes immediately under their windows, and barring the outlook like a prison wall, instead of exasperating them as it had once done, seemed to bring them calm. Being thus shut away tended to build up a sensation of infinite tranquillity, of a comforting peace in which they could lose themselves in sleep. At least they had no neighbours to overlook them, they were not always at the mercy of quizzing eyes, and they no longer complained of anything except the stuffy heat and blinding glare from the galvanized roof when it warmed during the first days of sunshine. For now spring really had arrived.

After the terrible shock, which for nearly two months had kept them continually tense with fear, they revelled blissfully in the torpidity which now engulfed them. All they asked was to be left alone, happy merely to exist, once they were free of the agonies of apprehension. Roubaud had never been so reliable, so conscientious, in his work. When on day duty he was down on the platforms by half past five, never went up for his breakfast before ten, was back on duty again at eleven, and worked on till five, thus giving eleven full hours' service. He never even gave himself the brief respite of a meal at home, but took a snack in his office, and this exacting service he bore with a sort of satisfaction, seeming even to enjoy it, supervising the least detail, insisting on seeing everything, doing it all himself, as if in thus wearing himself out he found oblivion, a resumption of balanced, normal life.

Severine, for her part, almost always alone, a grass widow every other week and even when not, seeing her husband only at lunch and dinner, seemed to have been infected with the fever of housekeeping. It had formerly been her way to sit over a piece of needlework, with a detestation of ordinary house work, which an elderly char, Mother Simon, used to come in every morning at nine to do. But since the resumption of peaceful life, with the certainty of preserving it, she had been seized by notions of thoroughly cleaning and re-arranging the house, and never sat down till she had thoroughly done the whole flat.

Apart from this, husband and wife slept like logs. In the rare moments they had for talking, at meals, or those nights when they slept together, they never spoke of the past. They had every reason to believe it was a closed book, all over.

Particularly for Severine, life now became quite pleasant. Like any young lady brought up only to sew a fine seam, she gradually relapsed back into idleness, once again relinquishing house work to Mother Simon. She had as a matter of fact started a very big piece of needlework, an embroidered quilt, which threatened to be a life's work. She rose rather late, enjoying lying in, lulled by the arrival and departure of trains, which came to mark the passage of the hours for

159

her as exactly as any clock would. In the early days of her marriage all those harsh station noises, whistles shrilling, turntables clattering, wheels grinding and thundering, the very walls shuddering from time to time as if there were an earth tremor, had exasperated her madly. Then, little by little, she had grown accustomed to them all and the station, all sound and vibration, became an integral part of her life, till now it actually gave her pleasure and her peace of mind really depended on all that agitation, that din and clatter. Till lunch, she wandered from room to room, gossiping with her char, her own hands idle. Then came the long afternoons, seated by the dining-room window, happy to do nothing, her needlework more often than not fallen to her knees. During those weeks in which her husband came back at daybreak, she listened to his snores till evening. Indeed, those had become her good weeks, weeks like those of former days, before her marriage. She could sprawl out over the full width of the bed, and amuse herself as she pleased, free the whole day long. She scarcely ever went out. All she saw of Havre was the smoke of nearby factory chimneys, the black billowings from which blotched the sky above that galvanized roof-ridge slicing off the horizon a few yards from her eyes. Havre itself was over there, beyond that eternal barrier. At first she was hyperconscious of its invisible presence, but in the end her annoyance at never being able to see it had subsided, and the half-dozen pots of wallflowers and verbenas which she kept in the gutter just under her window provided her with a miniature garden, blooming there, cut off from the world. Sometimes she would speak of it as of mysterious flowers blossoming deep in a forest land. When he was off duty her husband would sometimes slip out of the window on to the roof and walk the length of the guttering, then climb the galvanized slope and perch right on the ridge, at the front end above the station approach, to smoke a pipe up in the fresh air, the whole city spread out at his feet, the docks thick planted with their lofty copse of masts, and beyond, the vast pale green ocean stretching away to infinity.

It seemed that the same lethargy had overtaken the Roubauds' neighbours, the other officials' households, and this corridor too, down which used to blow the terrible draught of all their gossip, was at rest. When Philomène came to see Madame Lebleu, one could scarce hear the murmur of their voices. Astonished, both of them, to see how things had turned out, they never mentioned the A.S.M. now but in tones of scornful pity. It was obvious that to keep him in his job his wife had had to go up to Paris and go to fine lengths, for whatever was said or done, Roubaud was now a marked man, he would never completely wash that shadow of suspicion away. And now that the booking-clerk's wife felt sure that from now on the Roubauds were powerless to get her out of the better flat, she merely despised them, very loftily too. Head high in the air, she would sweep right past them without even a nod of acknowledgment. Indeed, the Lebleus carried their high airs so far that she even choked Philomène off. Gradually Philomène ceased altogether to visit her, finding her far too haughty and quite uninteresting. Madame Lebleu, however, continued spying on the station-master, M. Dabadie, and Mademoiselle Guichon. It had become her great pastime, though she never once succeeded in catching them out. Thus all that one ever heard in the corridor now was the shuffle of Madame Lebleu's felt slippers. Everything had bit by bit settled down, and a whole month thus went by, a month of sovereign peace, like any great sleep following a great catastrophe.

There was, however, in the Roubauds' household a corner of the parquet in the dining-room which remained painful and disturbing, a point which their glance could never even accidentally touch on without once again great uneasiness possessing them. This was where, on the left of the window, they had detached the oak skirting and under the parquet boards tucked away that watch, and the ten thousand francs which had been taken off Grandmorin's person, together with about three hundred francs in gold which were in the leather purse. These objects, the watch and ten thousand francs in notes, Roubaud had removed from Grandmorin's pockets merely to suggest theft. He was not a thief. Indeed, he said he would rather die of hunger than sell the watch or take advantage of a farthing of that money he now held. That old scoundrel's money? The money of the man who had sullied his wife, and to whom he had merely dealt justice? That money, stained with filth and blood? No, no! That money was not clean enough for an honest man to handle! Even though he had accepted the gift he did not even place any pretensions on the Maufras Cross house. What was more, the actual fact of having rummaged in the murdered man's pockets, the mere circumstance of those notes carried off in those abominable moments of the crime, disgusted Roubaud, prompting his conscience to repugnance and fear. At the same time, he had never felt any impulse first to burn the notes, then go out under cover of darkness and throw watch and purse into the sea. Whatever the most obvious prudence may have counselled, a dull instinct deep within him revolted against such destruction. The fact was, he had an involuntary respect for so big a sum of money as such, and would never have consented to destroy it. His first impulse, the first night, was to thrust it away under his pillow, for he felt no other cranny to be safe. For some days following, he exterted all his ingenuity to discover a hiding-place, and tried a new one every morning. The slightest sound then worried him, for he was obsessed with fear of the authorities searching his home. Never before had he so exerted his imagination. It was thus, exhausting all devices and weary of constant apprehension that at last the day came when he could not make the effort to remove watch and banknotes from their last hiding place behind the skirting, and now he would not have put his hand into that hole for anything in the world, it was like a sort of cold storage place which was at the same time a pit of horror and death, where ghosts awaited him. He even avoided walking on that particular board of the parquet every time that he crossed the room, the very feeling of putting his foot there was unpleasant, he seemed to feel an electric shock through his feet when he trod on it. When she sat by the window in the afternoon, Severine always pushed her chair well back, not to be exactly over that corpse which they thus preserved under their floor-boards. They never mentioned it to each other, forcing themselves to think that they were bound to get used to it, but in the end they found themselves at constant strain from realizing that it was still there, feeling it incessantly, more and more obsessing, under their footsoles. And this mental discomfort was the more remarkable in that the knife which Roubaud had used never upset them at all, that lovely new knife which his wifie had bought him and he had forthwith plunged into her ex-paramour's throat. All they had done was to wash it, and there it lay, in the kitchen drawer. Mother Simon sometimes used it as a breadknife.

However, though they had thus achieved a peaceful life, by forcing Jacques Lantier to be a frequent visitor, Roubaud felt compelled to introduce a new source of unrest which gradually grew. The round of the engine-driver's duties brought him to Havre three times weekly,

Mondays, from ten thirty-five P.M. to six forty A.M. on Tuesdays, and Fridays and Saturdays from eleven five P.M. to six forty A.M. on Saturday. The very first Monday after Severine's trip to Paris to see M. Camy-Lamotte, Roubaud was most insistent.

'No, no, my dear fellow, you really can't refuse to have a bite with us . . . Damn it all, you were so kind to my wife, I owe you some sign of gratitude.'

Thus Jacques came to accept lunch with them twice in a month. It would seem that Roubaud was now so badly irked by the long silences which developed when he was eating a meal alone with his wife that it was an alleviation to be able to set a guest between them. He was immediately prolific of anecdotes, all chatter and humour.

'But you must come often, my dear boy, you can see it's never the slightest trouble to us to have you.'

One evening, a Friday, just as Jacques had had a wash and was about to turn in, he ran into Roubaud, who was mooching round the engine-yard, and despite the lateness of the hour, Roubaud, disliking to go home alone, had made Jacques go with him, first as far as the station, then right up to the flat. Still not in bed, Severine was reading. A bottle of liqueur was dug out, and the three of them played cards till past midnight.

After that, lunches on Mondays and little parties on Fridays and Saturdays became quite habitual. If on any occasion the partner was missing, it would be Roubaud who ferreted him out and brought him round, full of protests about his negligence. To be frank, as time went on Roubaud was getting more and more morose, and only cheered up a little when he had his new friend there. This younger man, who at first had worried him so terribly, and now ought to have been hateful to him as a real witness of what had been done, thus a living evocation of those terrible things Roubaud would have liked to forget, had on the contrary become necessary to him, perhaps for the very reason that Jacques Lantier knew but had never spoken. This lay between them as that powerful bond – complicity. Many a time Roubaud would shoot the other a knowing glance, or shake his hand with a sudden vigour which went far beyond expression of any friendship between them.

The principal thing, however, was that in the domestic circle Jacques took the Roubauds' minds off each other. For Severine too used to give Lantier a glad welcome. When he appeared she would utter the cheerful cry of a woman stirred by sudden delight. She would drop anything she was doing, needlework or reading, and in laughter and smail talk escape for a while from the state of sullen soporification in which she passed her days.

'Oh, how nice of you to come round!' she would cry. 'I heard the express come in and wondered if we should be seeing you.'

When he lunched with them, it was always a party. She now knew his tastes, she would go out herself to get fresh eggs for him, and all so sweetly, so much the good housewife welcoming the friend of the family, never the suggestion of anything more in it all than a mixture of a desire to be hospitable and the need to take her mind off things.

'Now, you must come round again next Monday, we shall have cream!' she would cry, as he left.

The only unfortunate thing was that when, after a month, he had become a regular fixture, the gulf between the Roubauds became deeper. More and more, the wife found pleasure in having the bed to herself and contrived to share it as little as possible with her husband, nor did he, who had been so hot, indeed, so rough, in the early stages of their marriage, do a thing to keep her there. He had always loved her indiscriminatingly, and she had been resigned to his caresses with the submissiveness of a dutiful spouse, thinking that this was how things had to be, though certainly getting no pleasure out of it herself. But since the murder, though she could not tell why, the sexual act had become quite hateful to her. It frayed her nerves. It even frightened her. There was an evening when the candle had not been put out first, and she suddenly shrieked. In the blood-charged, convulsed features bearing down on her she seemed to see the face of a murderer, and after that she shook every time he touched her, and had a horrible sensation of murder – as if he had thrown her on to her back and was raising a knife to strike at her too. It was all very silly, but her heart simply thudded with fear.

For that matter, however, Roubaud made less and less demand on her, finding her too unco-operative for him to get pleasure from it. The weariness and indifference that time brings seemed to have been all at once produced between them by that terrible climax, by the blood that had been spilt. Now, on nights when they could not avoid the common conjugal bed, they tended to keep each to their own sides, and there was no doubt but that by the mere fact that his presence would make them forget their obsession with each other, Jacques Lantier was helping this divorcement to become complete. He was, in fact, liberating them from each other.

Yet Roubaud lived without any sense of remorse. He had merely been afraid of consequences – until the case was shelved – and his principal worry then had been that of losing his job. Now, he had no regrets whatsoever. It is however possible that if he had been able to do it all over again, he would have kept his wife out of it altogether, for women so soon get unbalanced, and he saw he was losing his own wife because he had put too heavy a burden on her. Without her in it, he would then have remained the master and would not have sunk together with her to the present uneasy pull devil, pull baker of accomplices in crime. But that was how it had turned out, and he could but make the best of it, particularly as now he had to make a real effort to get back into that state of mind in which he had been immediately after her confession, thinking that killing Grandmorin was essential to be able to live. It had then seemed that if he did not kill the other man, he would not have been able to go on existing. Now that the fire of his jealousy had burned itself out and he could never recapture that unbearable smart, but was in a stupefied state, rather as if his heart had been made much more compact by all the blood he had spilled, there were even moments when he wondered whether it had really been worth while doing. But that was nevertheless no kind of repentance, at most it was a disillusionment, just as one so often has notions one would never admit to of what would make one happy without really being a jot the happier for them. A most talkative man by nature, he now had long periods of taciturnity, plunged into an undergrowth of thought from which he emerged still more gloomy. To avoid sitting face to face with his wife after meals, he had now begun to make it his daily custom to climb up on to the station roofing and sit up on the gable, where there was always air, and he would smoke pipe after pipe, lost in vague dreams, staring out beyond the port at the packet steamers hull down on the skyline, bound for distant climes.

But one evening Roubaud had a sudden return of his former frightful jealousy. He had gone to fetch Jacques at the locomotive shed, and was taking him back with him for a drink, when he met Henri Dauvergne, leading guard, coming down the stairs, and Dauvergne looked embarrassed, then gratuitously explained that he had been to see Severine on an errand for his sisters, though the truth was that for some time he had been pursuing Severine and imagined he would get her, too.

Roubaud had no sooner stepped inside the flat than he assailed Severine violently.

'What did that fellow Dauvergne want poking round here? You know I can't stand the man!'

'But, my dear, all he wanted was an embroidery pattern.'

'Embroidery pattern, I don't think! Do you imagine that I'm such a fool I don't know what he comes hanging round here for? You'd better watch your step, let me tell you, my lady!'

He strode across to her, his fists clenched. She fell back away from him, white as a sheet, astounded by the vehemence of his anger, especially since they now lived so coldly one regarding the other. But the storm was already passing, and Roubaud turned to Jacques.

'Too true, smart fellows like that meddling in family life, as if a man's wife were going to fling herself straight at their heads and the husband be pleased to turn the blind eye! I don't mind telling you, if anything like that did happen, I'd wring my wife's neck like a shot, I would. And see that fellow doesn't come again,' he cried, 'or I'll settle his hash for him . . . It's disgusting, don't you think so, Lantier?'

Jacques was most embarrassed by this scene and did not know quite what to do. Was that exaggerated show of anger really aimed at him? Was Roubaud warning him? But his mind was at rest on that score when Roubaud ran on, quite cheerful again:

'The scoundrel, I know very well you'd be the first to show him the door, darling . . . Come on, find some glasses, we'll have a drink, we three.'

And he was clapping Jacques on the shoulder, with Severine, quite herself again, smiling at both men. And they drained a glass together and spent a very pleasant hour or two.

It was in this way that Roubaud brought together his wife and this friend the engine-driver, all in seeming camaraderie, apparently without even dreaming of the possible consequences. Yet that very display of jealousy was precisely the cause of knitting a closer friendship, indeed, of a clandestine exchange of sentiment, shot with mutual confidences, between Jacques and Severine, for when, the next day, Jacques saw Severine again, he commiserated with her for having been so buliied, and she with eyes swimming with tears by the very spontaneity of her self-pity revealed how little happiness she now found in her marriage. From that moment the two had a private topic of conversation. There was a conspiracy of friendship between them, which led to their being able to converse by mere nods. Every time he came, Jacques' eyes questioned her whether she had had new reason for unhappiness, and she would reply in the same language, by imperceptible movements of her eyes. Then their hands began to touch behind the husband's back, after which, getting bolder, they exchanged long eloquent hand clasps, when their warm fingers told each other of the growing interest they took in the most minute facts of each other's existence. It was rarely that they had the luck to meet for a few instants without Roubaud. He was always there, between them, in that gloomy dining-room, nor did they make any effort to escape him, or ever even think of suggesting to one another a *rendezvous* in some out-of-the-way corner of the station. Up to that point, it was only a genuine friendship, an impulse of lively emotion, which Roubaud scarcely hindered, since merely a glance or a hand-squeeze was needed to make manifest their mutual understanding.

The first time that Jacques whispered in Severine's ear that the following Friday at midnight he would be waiting for her behind the loco sheds, she quickly snatched her hand away from his. This was her week of freedom, when her husband was on night duty. But she was overcome with terrible anxiety at the mere thought of going outside, and so far away, through the dark station, to meet this young man. She felt an embarrassment she had never known. It was the fear of virginity innocent of sex, when the heart thuds. And despite the fierce desire which she too felt for this suggested stroll by night, she did not give way at once. It was the beginning of June.

The evenings were beginning to be sultry, but slightly cooled by the sea breeze. Though she said *no*, he had already waited for her on three previous occasions, always hopeful that she would come. This evening too she had said: *no*, but it was a moonless night, the sky cloudy, not a star shining, everything cloaked in sultry mist. And while he stood there in the shadows, he saw her come at last, tiptoeing, dressed all in black. It was so dark that she could have

167

brushed by him without seeing him, had he not halted her by seizing her in his arms and kissing her. She uttered a low cry and a shudder shook her frame. But that was all that took place. She steadfastly refused to sit down inside one of the locomotive sheds looming all round them. So they walked, talking scarcely above a whisper, pressed close one to the other. The space occupied by the locomotive depôt and offices was enormous, the whole area between Verte Street and François Mazeline Street, each of which crosses the railway tracks, by a level-crossing. This was a vast world of its own, a confusion of rails leading into loco sheds, to reservoirs and so forth, with two huge hangars for the locomotives, a little dwelling house, occupied by the Sauvagnats, with a little patch of kitchen garden all round it, some ramshackle sheds which contained workshops, and a dormitory block for engine-drivers and firemen. Nothing was easier than to hide oneself there, lost as if in the depth of a wood with a veritable maze of deserted rides criss-crossing all ways. For an hour they enjoyed delightful seclusion, assuaging each other with all the soft words of dear friendship which for so long had been accumulating – for Severine would only hear talk of a friendship between them. She had immediately told Jacques that she would never be his, that it would be too horrid to soil the purity of this understanding friendship of which she was so proud, for above all else she needed esteem. Then he saw her on the way home as far as Verte Street, their lips touched in a profound kiss, and she went back.

At this moment Roubaud was just beginning to drowse in the assistant station-master's office. He was sunk in the depths of an ancient leather armchair, from which, stiff-limbed, he would rise a score of times in a night. Up to nine, he had to accept in and despatch out the evening trains. The boat-train was his particular care, with shuntings and additional coaches and consignment notes to be minutely inspected. Then, once the Paris express had come in and been shunted to a siding, he supped by himself in the office on a fat meat sandwich sent down for him, which he ate at the corner of his desk. The last train, a slow one from Rouen, came in at half-an-hour after midnight, whereupon the platforms sank into their great silence, with only here and there a gas-jet burning, the whole station then sound asleep in the small light, stirred by little winds. The only staff left on duty were two inspectors and four or five men, under the orders of the assistant station-master. They would lie snoring, fists clenched, on the benches in the guard-room, whereas Roubaud, whose duty it was to waken them at the least alarm, could only take a cat-wink of sleep. For fear lest as daylight drew near he should oversleep, he set his alarm-clock at five, for then he had to receive the first train in from Paris. But sometimes, particularly latterly, he would have fits of insomnia, and turn and turn in his chair. Then he would go out and do a turn through the station, as far as the signal-box, where he would exchange a few words. The vast blackness of the sky and the sovereign tranquillity of night would in the end reduce his fever. Because of a fight he had once had with some pilferers, he had been equipped with a revolver, which he always carried in his pocket, loaded. And often enough he would mooch about like that till day broke, stock still the instant he thought anything stirred in the night, eventually proceeding again, rather regretful at not having had to fire his gun. But at last he would be relieved to see the sky whiten and begin to rescue the great grey phantom of the station from darkness. Now that it was daybreak at three, he would go back to his office to fling himself down in his armchair and sleep like the dead till his alarm-clock wakened him with a violent start for the Paris train.

Every fortnight, on Fridays and Saturdays, Severine now went to meet Jacques, and one night, just as she had been telling him of the revolver which her husband carried, that weapon gave them a bad scare. As a matter of fact, Roubaud had never gone as far as the yards, but that did not rob their night meetings of a haunting sense of danger which always marred the delight. They had however found a particularly lovely corner, a sort of alley between enormous heaps of coal behind the Sauvagnats' house, which transformed the scene into a deserted street between black marble palaces. There, they were absolutely hidden. At the end of the alley there was a little tool shed in which a pile of unused sacks would have made a very soft couch. But when, one Saturday, a sudden downpour forced them to take refuge inside, Severine insisted on remaining standing, yielding only her lips, in endless kisses. Here she made no pretence of shame, but out of her affection let him draw in her very breath, drinking greedily of her. And when, afired by that brazier of love, he tried to take her, with tears and ever again the same reasons, she struggled against it. Why did he insist on making her so unhappy? It seemed so lovely to

169

her just to adore each other like friends, without dirty sex coming between them. Sullied at sixteen by the debauchery of that old beast whose bleeding ghost now haunted her, and taken by force later to satisfy the brutal lusts of her husband, Severine had retained the innocence of a child, she was virgin from top to toe, with that delightful shrinking when desire is still unconscious. What she found ravishing in Jacques was his gentleness, his obedience in keeping his hands from roaming about her body, the moment she took them in the tips of her own frail fingers. For the first time in her life she now loved, and the reason why she would not yield her body was that it would quite simply have ruined her love had she let herself at once be his, as she had had to let those two other men. It was her instinctive desire to draw out for ever so exquisite a sensation as that which she now knew. She had to become quite young again, as she was before Grandmorin dirtied her. She wanted a dear kissing sweetheart such as one has at fifteen, mouth absorbed in mouth behind doors. And apart from rare instants of high fever, he too was not insistent, but readily lent himself to this incessant postponement of full delight. Just like her, he seemed to return to childhood and the first steps in love, which anyway had hitherto been such a terrible sensation to him. If he was so manageable, withdrawing his hands the instant she guided them away, this was because deep down in his emotion he was aware of a numb fear, a frightful uneasiness of terror of again confusing sexual desire with his old urge to kill. This woman who had killed was as it were the dream of his own flesh. With every day he grew more confident of being cured, for had he not held her now for hours with his arms round her neck? With her mouth on his, had he not drunk of her soul, without a hint of that mad lust to master her by cutting her throat? But he was still afraid of the final step, hence it was so good to wait, to leave it to their passion itself to unite them when the moment should come and in each other's arms they would at last know the final annihilation of will. Thus one glorious *rendezvous* followed another, and they were never tired of these brief meetings when they walked together through the darkness, with those huge heaps of coal darkening the night on either side of them.

One July night, to reach Havre on time, by eleven five, Jacques had to flog Lison, as if the stifling heat had made her lazy. From Rouen there was a following storm on his left, down the Seine valley, with

170

dazzling flashes of lightning. Every now and then Jacques peered about him in concern, for this was one of the nights that Severine was to meet him. He was afraid lest the storm should break too soon and keep her in. So, having reached Havre before the rain began, he eyed the passengers with impatience. It seemed they would never stop emerging from the carriages.

Roubaud was on the platform, pinned to the station for the night.

'You're in a damned hurry to get between the sheets, Jacques,' he laughed. 'Sweet repose!'

'Thanks,' said Jacques, and with a shrill whistle he ran the train out and took Lison to the loco sheds. The huge doors were open, and Lison plunged into the narrow hangar, which had two tracks about seventy yards long, with room for six locos. It was very dark inside, the four gas-jets scarcely dispelling the darkness, and it was only the intense flashes of lightning which every now and then turned the roof glass and the tall windows on either side to flame, lighting the place, and in those brief conflagrations one could see the cracking walls, the smoke-blackened girders black and all the poverty of this long-since insufficient building. Two engines were already there, asleep.

At once, Pecqueux set to work quenching Lison's fires. He riddled her violently and the red-hot cinders rained into the pit beneath her.

'I'm too hungry for words,' he said. 'I'm going to have a bite, coming?'

Jacques did not reply. In spite of his urgency, he did not want to leave Lison before the furnace was clear and the boiler empty. He was always conscientious about that good driver's habit of his, he never left her without seeing the job completed. Whenever he had time, he even stayed on till he had gone all over Lison and wiped her down, with the care a man gives to a favourite horse.

The water was now gushing into the pit in great gouts, and all he said was:

'Come on with it, come on.'

A terrible clap of thunder interrupted him, and this time the tall windows were so clearly limned by the inflamed heavens that one could have counted the broken panes. On the left, the length of the repair benches, a sheet of galvanized standing against the wall resonated with the persistent ring of a bell. The whole upper part of the iron framework of the hangar seemed to groan.

171

'B——!' the fireman muttered.

Jacques gave a gesture of despair. That was that, he told himself, the more so since now a regular deluge was pouring down on the shed, the downfall so heavy that it seemed the roof glass must give way. There must be panes broken up in the roof too, for dense gusts of rain were now spattering down on to Lison. A furious hurricane came in through the doors, which were still open, and one would have thought the old building was going to be carried right away.

Pecqueux had finished putting Lison away.

'That'll do,' he growled, 'perhaps I shall be able to see what I'm doing tomorrow . . . No need to fuss any more tonight . . .'

Then, coming back to his proposal.

'Must have a bite . . . Besides it's raining too hard to go round there yet.'

The canteen was indeed very handy, being next door to the loco shops, and connected with it by a small service door, whereas the building which the Company had had to hire as lodging house for firemen and drivers who had to spend the night at Havre was at some distance, in François Mazeline Street, and they could easily get soaked to the skin before they got there.

Jacques could not do better than follow Pecqueux. That worthy had already taken his driver's food basket, as if to help him by carrying it, though really because he knew that there were still a couple of good slices of roast veal, some bread and most of a bottle of wine in it. Indeed, that was really what had given him an appetite. The downpour grew heavier, and fresh peals of thunder shook the shed. When the two men left, Lison was already cooling down, to sleep all by herself in that frightful lightning-rent darkness, huge rain drops quivering on her loins. Nearby, a badly shut-off water hydrant was streaming away, forming a constant pool in the pit between the rails.

But before eating, Jacques wanted to wash. In one of the canteen rooms there was always hot water and a row of buckets. Black from the journey, he took a piece of soap from his basket and scoured face and hands, and as he always took the precaution, well advised in an engine-driver, of taking a spare suit of clothing with him, he was able to change completely, which indeed was his custom every evening that he met Severine at Havre. Pecqueux was already getting impatient, for all he chose to do was give a cat-lick to his hands and the tip of his nose.

The canteen was no more than a bare room with yellow, washed walls, one stove to warm up food on, and one table, bolted to the floor, with a galvanized top in lieu of cloth, the furniture being completed by a couple of forms. Men had to bring their own food, which they ate off the paper wrappings, using their clasp knives. The room was lit by one large window.

'What awful rain,' grumbled Jacques, standing and staring out.

But Pecqueux had sat down at the table.

'Well come along man, aren't you going to have anything?'

'No, thanks, *mon vieux*,' said Jacques. 'You take my bread and meat, if you have a mind . . . I'm not hungry.'

The other man did not need twice asking. Immediately, he attacked the veal and finished off the bottle. He often got such little extras, for his chief was not a big eater, and with his dog-like devotion he liked Jacques the more for all these pickings which came his way. His mouth full, after a silence he suddenly said:

'What the hell's the rain matter? We're inside all right! Though if it goes on, I shall have to get wet, I've a job on,' and he began to laugh. For Pecqueux had never hidden his movements and in order not to cause astonishment by the frequency with which he slept out, spending so many nights in Philomène Sauvagnat's bed, he had let Jacques in on his liaison. As Philomène had a ground floor room near the kitchen in her brother's little house, all Pecqueux had to do was tap on the shutter and she let him in through the window. It was said that this had been the route of every man jack on Havre station, but now Philomène was very constant to her fireman, who seemed to answer her needs.

'Blast it and blast it!' Jacques growled, morosely seeing the rain come on again, harder than ever, after having slackened a bit.

Once again Pecqueux, who on the tip of his knife was just conveying to his mouth the last chunk of veal, roared with his rascally laughter.

'Damn it, you too got a job on this evening, eh? It's a b——, the Company can hardly reproach us two for wearing out their mattresses, can it?'

Jacques swung round in a flash.

'What do you mean?'

'I'll be hanged, you've been as bad as me since June, not back till two in the morning or after.'

Pecqueux must know something. Was it possible that on some occasion he had been seen with Severine? In every room of the lodging-house, the beds were in pairs, fireman and driver together, for the existence of these little teams of two was tied up together as tightly as possible. So it was really not so very astonishing if Pecqueux had noticed the rather irregular life his chief was now leading.

'I get headaches,' ventured Jacques, 'it does me good to go for a breath of air.'

But his fireman was quick to withdraw.

'Oh, don't you fear, you please yourself . . . I was only pulling your leg . . . Even if any time you did have any troubles you can always tell me, you know, if ever you want anything I'm your man.'

Without explaining more clearly what he meant, he took Jacques' hand, shook it with a crushing grip, offering his entire loyalty. Then, crumpling up the paper in which the meat had been wrapped and throwing it away, he put the empty bottle back in the basket, all with the air of a painstaking valet, well used to clearing the table neatly. Then, as the rain was still pouring down, though there was no more thunder:

'Well,' he said, 'I'm off, I'll leave you to your own business.'

'Hm,' Jacques replied, 'as it doesn't look like stopping, I think I'll stretch out in the doss-room.'

Next to the loco sheds there was a large room with mattresses and tarpaulins where the men could go to rest in their clothes whenever they had only three or four hours to wait at Havre. And, as soon as he saw the fireman vanish in the downpour in the direction of the Sauvagnats', he ran the gauntlet of the rain himself to the doss-room. But he did not lie down. Instead, he stood on the threshold, for inside it was stifling hot. There was one driver, snoring on his back, his mouth wide open.

Some minutes more passed, and Jacques could not bring himself to give up hope. He was so exasperated by this stupid storm that at last the crazy idea grew in him that he should go along to their meeting-place despite it. At least, even if there were no Severine he would have the satisfaction of having gone. Every fibre of his body seemed to leap as at last he plunged into the night through the rain, and down the alley between the coal piles, to their favourite corner. And as, lashing his face, the huge drops of the rain blinded him, he continued all the way to the tool shed, where they had sheltered on that one previous occasion. He felt somehow that he would be less alone in there. He entered the complete obscurity of that retreat and in the same instant two slender arms were flung round his neck and hot lips pressed moist on his. It was Severine!

'Good Lord, you! You're here, already!'

'Yes,' she whispered, 'I saw the storm coming up, so I ran here at once, before it began . . . But how late you are!' She sighed heavily, her voice seeming to fail her.

Never had he known her to lie so yielding against him. Then she slipped from him. He felt her sink to those piles of empty sacks, that soft bed which occupied a corner of the shed. He sank down beside her. Their arms still enlaced about each other, he felt her legs lie on his. They could not see each other, they were wrapped dizzily in each other's breathing, everything about them was utterly blotted out. The burning kiss which followed unlocked words of the most intimate endearment, words such as they had never used before, words like the very blood of their hearts commingling, she waiting there, ready for him, and he so long to come. And suddenly, after a mere minute of this, almost speechless now, she suddenly drew him on to her and forced him to take her. She had certainly not intended this. Indeed when he arrived, she had already given him up. But this was the very reason why she was suddenly swept off her feet by the sheer delight of holding him, and all at once there came the irresistible need to be his, a desire beyond intention and beyond reason, something which was merely so because it had to be so, the rain lashed at the shed roof. The last train in from Paris roared by, grinding and whistling, shaking the very ground.

When at last Jacques withdrew from her, he was astonished to hear the sound of the storm come back to him. He could not make out where he was. And when on the ground he came upon the handle of a hammer which he had felt when first he lay down with her, he felt happiness flood through him. What triumph at last! He had possessed Severine and he had not taken up that hammer to smash in her brain. She had rendered herself to him without making him fight for her and without a hint in him of that instinctive lust to fling her dead over

175

his shoulder, like prey snatched from other would-be lovers. He no longer felt that thirst for revenge of ancient, long-forgotten injuries, the sullen hatred accumulating from male to male since the first deception in the darkness of the cave. Instead, the possession of this woman had been a marvel of beauty. She had cured him, because for him she was different from all others. In her frailty she had once been strong, she had on her the blood of a man and that was like an armour of horror. It was she who had mastered him. He would never have dared. And it was in a flood of yielding, highly emotional gratitude, a longing to melt away in her, that he took her in his arms again.

Severine too gave herself unrestrainedly, as dizzily happy as he was, freed at last from a struggle which had no longer meant anything to her. Whyever indeed had she held herself back from him so long? She had promised herself to him, therefore, since in love there should be but enjoyment and loving kindness, she should have yielded herself. Now she saw quite clearly that even when it had seemed so lovely to keep it at a distance, she had been longing for this. Her heart and her body alike lived now solely by their need for love absolute, love unending, and the course of her life which had cast her terrified into all those abominable things was monstrous and cruel. Up to this point, life had used her ill, muddied her and stained her with blood, so brutally that even though they had preserved their innocence, her lovely blue eyes had beneath that tragic helmet of jet-black hair thereby grown permanently large with terror. Despite everything, she had remained virginal and had in fact just yielded her flesh for the first time, to this young man whom she adored. She had given herself in yearning to lose herself in him, to be his servitor. To him she belonged, of her he could dispose according to his whim.

'Darling, dear love, take me, keep me, I want only what you want.'

'No, no, sweetest one, you are the mistress. I exist but to love you and do your bidding.'

Hours passed. The rain had long since stopped, intense silence invested the station, silence disturbed by but one confused and far-off voice, that of the murmuring sea. They were still in each other's arms, when a flash of light brought them trembling to their feet. Day was about to break, above the Seine estuary a patch of sky was spread with frail light. But what could be that sudden crack of a gun? Their

176

rashness, their madness in staying so late filled their swift imagination with Roubaud, Roubaud pursuing them with revolver shots.

'Stay here! Wait: I'll go and see.'

Whispering, Jacques crept cautiously to the door. In the darkness, still dense, he heard men running their way, caught Roubaud's voice, urging on the watchmen, shouting that there were three thieves, he had seen them clearly, three thieves stealing coal. For some weeks now there had scarcely been a night but Roubaud had thought he saw robbers. This time, gripped by sudden terror, he had fired a random shot into the darkness.

'Quick, quick, we must not stay here,' whispered Jacques. 'They will certainly come this way . . . Run for it!'

Madly they took each other in full embrace again, mouths abandoned each to each. Then, nimbly, Severine raced along beside the loco sheds, under the high wall, while Jacques crept off among the heaps of coal. Just in time, too. Roubaud was indeed making for the tool-shed, swearing that the thieves must be in there. The watchmen's lanterns danced about at ground level. Then, fed up with this stupid chase, the men began to squabble and finally the whole party made off in the direction of the station. And just as Jacques felt himself safe and thought he had better go along to the François Mazeline Street railwaymen's dormitory, he was startled almost to collide with Pecqueux, who was just finishing pulling on his clothes and swearing like a trooper.

'What on earth's up with you?' Jacques demanded.

'Pah! Bloody hell! Don't say a word, those loonies woke Sauvagnat and he heard me with his sister. He came down in his nightshirt and I had to skedaddle through the window . . . I say, just listen!'

Into the night air rose the cries and sobs of a woman being chastised, mingled with the loud voice of a man piling insults on her.

'Did I tell you? Now he's at it, giving her a hiding. She can't be less than thirty-two, but whenever he catches her he whips her like she was still in short skirts . . . Ah, b—— if I care, after all it's none of my business, he's her brother, isn't he?'

'Why,' said Jacques, 'I always thought he put up with you and only blew off the handle when he found her with someone else.'

'Pah! You never can tell. Sometimes he does seem to turn the blind eye. Then, as you see, there are times when he wallops her. All the same, he is fond of his sister, he would rather anything happen than lose her. You see he insists on keeping things within bounds. . . . Bloody hell, though, I believe she's taking a pasting today.'

The shrieks tailed off into loud whimpers, and the two men withdrew. Ten minutes later, both were sound asleep, side by side, in a dormitory room with buff distempered walls, sparsely furnished with four beds, four chairs, a table and a single zinc washing-bowl.

After that, every night that they met, Jacques and Severine enjoyed great delights. They did not always have the same protection of a storm about them. Clear skies and bright moonlight nights were a worry to them. But on such occasions they crept into dark corners, discovering shadows in which it was so good to press close together. Thus, in August and September there were wonderful nights, so entrancing that, overcome in the end with drowsiness, they would have let the sun overtake outside, had not the wakening sounds of the station, the distant breath of locomotives, parted them. Even the first chill nights of October did not upset them. She came more warmly clothed, wrapped in a heavy cloak, in which he too nearly disappeared. They had now begun to bar themselves in at the far end of the tool-shed, which they contrived to close from the inside with an iron bar. There, they had their own snug little corner, and November storms and hurricanes could strip tiles from the roofs without touching even a hair of the nape of their necks. Nevertheless, after their very first intimacy, he always had the desire to possess her in her home, in that constricted dwelling-place where she seemed different, and still more desirable to him, with all the grace and well-being of middle-class domesticity, but she had consistently refused, less from fear of the spies of 'the corridor' than from a last vestige of scruples, by which, despite everything, the conjugal bed must be kept sacrosanct. But one Monday, in broad daylight, when he was to lunch at the flat, but Roubaud was slow to appear, being retained by the station master, Jacques started playing about and suddenly carried her to the bed. It was so far all no more than a daring game which occasioned them both merriment, till all at once they both forgot all scruples.

From then on, Severine abandoned all resistance, and on Fridays and Saturdays, as soon as it had struck midnight, Jacques would go up, to lie with her. It was terribly risky. They were afraid to move about, because of the neighbours, yet it afforded them a new wave of love for each other, and new delights. Even so, sudden whims, or the need to find full liberty, would still quite often send them like wild creatures at large, into the inky solitude of icy nights. During a terrible frost one December night they actually possessed each other out under the stars.

Jacques and Severine had lived four months thus, in a love which grew stronger and stronger. They were, it is true, both of them new to it all, in the childhood stage of the heart, the astonished naïvety of first love, in which the slightest caress can turn the head. And he no longer had any doubts, he certainly had found the cure to his terrible hereditary twist, for since he had possessed her the idea of killing had never troubled him more. Was it then possible that physical possession satisfied that need of death? In the obscure depths of the beast in man, were sexual possession and killing synonymous?

But he was too untutored to analyse, he simply did not attempt to open that terrible door. There were occasions when with her in his arms he recaptured for an instant the memory of what she had done – the memory of the murder – yet he never felt the slightest desire to know more about it. But Severine, on the contrary, seemed driven more and more by a need to tell everything. When she clutched him in her arms he could clearly sense that she was breathlessly swollen with her secret. He knew that her only reason for seeking absorption in him was to ease herself of that which she kept stifled within her. From her loins would suddenly rise a profound shudder, stiffening her lustful nipples, and emerging on her lips in a confused tangle of whispers. Was that murmur, dying on her tongue at the height of her orgasm, was it now at last going to babble all? But then he would be frightened, and swiftly with his own lips always sealed hers before she could speak. Why thrust that unknown between them? Could he really be sure that it would make no difference to their happiness? He sensed danger and he trembled with inward horror at the thought that together they should rake again over that story of bloodshed. And there was no doubt but that she guessed this, for, lying pressed to him, she would once again be all sweetness, caressing him, a creature of love made but to give and to receive the joy of sex. Then a madness of mutual possession would sweep over them, till on occasion they lost consciousness in each other's arms.

Since the summer, Roubaud had grown still stouter. In proportion to his wife's return to the gaiety and freshness she had known at twenty, he had aged and appeared more gloomy. In four months, as he himself said, he had changed greatly. He always shook Jacques' hand with vigorous cordiality and said he was to be sure to come round to see them. Indeed, he seemed only happy when Jacques was at table with them. But that distraction did not suffice. With the excuse that he found it stuffy and needed to get some fresh air, he often went out after the first mouthful, sometimes leaving the engine-driver with his wife. The truth was that he had now begun to frequent a little café in Napoleon Square where he met M. Cauche, the Station Superintendent of Police. He did not drink much, merely nips of rum, but had acquired a taste for gambling, which soon became a passion. He was not cheerful or able to forget it all except cards in hand, lost in endless games of piquet. Then M. Cauche, who was an absolute addict, suggested they should add an incentive to the game, so they played at one franc, after which Roubaud, not knowing himself, simply glowed with the lust to win, the scorching fever of card winnings which can harry a man to the point of risking job and even life for a toss of the dice. Up to that point, his work had not deteriorated. Those nights when he was not on duty he just slipped off after hours, and did not return till two or three A.M. His wife never complained. All she had against it was that he was still more morose when he did come home, for he had astonishing runs of bad luck, and ended up by getting into debt.

One evening, a first squabble broke out between Severine and Roubaud. Though she did not hate him yet, she had got to the point of finding it hard to bear with him, for she felt him to be an incubus encumbering her life. She could have been so airily happy, had she not been burdened by his presence. As far as that went, she had not the slightest remorse about deceiving him, for was it not his fault? Had he not more or less driven her to lapse as she had done? In the slow break-up of their marriage, they had each found their own consolation and alleviation for the mental discomfort which troubled them. If he had his gambling, she had a perfect right to her lover. But what more than anything else aggravated her and she found it difficult to accept without revolt was the embarrassment which his continual losses were causing her. Since franc after franc of the household money had dribbled away to that Napoleon Square café she sometimes did not know how to pay the laundry-woman. She lacked many a little comfort, many a ribbon.

And on this particular occasion when they quarrelled about it, this was purely over the necessary purchase of a pair of boots. On the point of going out, unable to find the bread knife, he had taken the big knife – the weapon – which was in a dresser drawer. She stared at him as he refused her fifteen francs for the boots, the reason being that he had not got them and did not know where to find them. Obstinate, she repeated her request, gradually working him up, and forcing him to repeat his refusal. Then, suddenly, she pointed to that corner of the parquet underneath which lay those ghostly objects, and said there was money there, and she wanted some of it. Every drop of colour drained from his cheeks and he let the knife drop back into the drawer. For a moment she thought he was going to strike her, for he went close up to her, but he only stuttered that that money could rot away, he would cut off his hand before he would take it out. And, clenching his fists, he threatened to slaughter her if when he was out she raised the skirting and dared take were it only a farthing of it. Never and never! That was all dead and buried. She was certainly now as deathly pale as he was, equally aghast at the thought of breaking into that fund. Even if poverty overcame them, they would rather starve to death one beside the other. Nor did they ever mention the subject again, even when they did come to be very hard pressed. The impression of burning whenever they trod there had grown so unbearably great that in the end they used to skirt round the spot.

But instead, other quarrels appeared, about Maufras Cross. Why could they not sell the house? They charged one another with having failed to do this, that and the other to facilitate the sale. He still refused savagely to have anything at all to do with the property, and when she did write one of her rare notes to Misard, all she got was a very indefinite answer, there had been no applicants, the apples had had the canker, the vegetables had not grown for lack of watering. Gradually the great calm which had descended on this couple after their danger had passed was stirred up in this way and threatened to be ended by a new surge of fever. All the germs of trouble – that hidden money, a paramour in the house – had developed, and these now kept the Roubauds apart and exacerbated one against the other. And in this augmenting unrest life was tending to be hell.

What was more, by a fatal coincidence, everything round the Roubauds now began to go wrong. There was a fresh outburst of gossip and backchat in 'the corridor'. Philomène had suddenly quarrelled violently with Madame Lebleu, owing to that lady's suddenly levelling the charge of Philomène's having sold her a hen which had died of disease. The real reason for the break, however, was a new friendship between Severine and Philomène. When one night Pecqueux saw Severine in Jacques' arms, Severine silenced her former scruples and was very nice to the fireman's mistress, while Philomène, being much flattered by this intimacy with a lady who was incontestably the *belle* and the distinguishing feature of the station, had come to turn against the cashier's wife, who, she said, was an old bitch quite capable of setting the mountains at loggerheads. She put Madame Lebleu in the wrong all round, noising it everywhere now that the flat which fronted on the street did really belong to the Roubauds, and it was disgusting of the Company not to let them have it. Things were looking pretty black for Madame Lebleu, the more so for her malicious persistence in spying on Mademoiselle Guichon, to catch her with the station-master, who was also threatening to cause her serious trouble. For, though she got no nearer catching them at it, Madame Lebleu made the mistake of letting herself be seen with her ear to other people's doors, till M. Dabadie, in annoyance at being spied on like that, told the other A.S.M., Moulin, that if the Roubauds still wanted the front flat, he was ready prepared to sign the necessary bit of paper. And when Moulin, otherwise not a gossiper, had put that about, passions were so inflamed that there was nearly a battle from one end of 'the corridor' to the other.

Amid all those increasing disturbances, Severine had only one good day, Thursdays. Since October she had had the cool effrontery to invent a pretext, the first that came into her head, of pains in the knee, said to necessitate the attention of a specialist, and every Thursday left by the 6.40 A.M. fast train up – the one Jacques drove – and then spent the day with him at Paris, returning by the 6.30 P.M. At first she felt under an obligation to give her husband reports about her knee – now it was a bit better, now worse – then, seeing that he paid no attention, she simply ceased to bother. Indeed, there were times, watching him, when she wondered whether he knew. However had that savagely jealous man, who in lunatic rage, blinded with

182

blood, had murdered on that account, however had he come to tolerate her having a lover? But she could not credit it, and concluded that he was just losing his grip.

One freezing night in the early part of December, Severine waited up late for her husband. The next morning, a Thursday, she was to take the express before dawn, and she was accustomed on the evenings before these trips to make great preparations getting every garment ready so as to be able to dress the instant she slipped out of bed. At last she lay down, and in the end, towards one, fell asleep. Roubaud had not appeared. There had already been two occasions when he had not appeared till the small hours, being absorbed in his growing passion, unable to tear himself from the café, a small back room of which was turning into a regular gambling den, where in seclusion they played now for big stakes. Happy, after all, to be able to sleep alone, and cradled by her expectation of how lovely it would be all day tomorrow, the young woman slumbered soundly in the yielding warmth of her blankets.

But just as it was about to strike three, a strange sound wakened her. At first she could not understand it, thought she was dreaming, even fell asleep again. Then came a dull sound of levering, of timber creaking – just as if a door were being forced open. Finally, there was a sharp crack and a sharper, rending sound which made her start up. Then she was seized with alarm. There must be somebody forcing the corridor lock. For a minute she dared not stir, merely listened, with buzzing ears. Then she found the courage to get up, to find out. Soundlessly, barefoot, she opened the bedroom door, so pinched with fear that she was like a frail little ghost in her shift, when what she saw in the dining-room froze her with astonishment, and horror! It was Roubaud, on the floor, crouching, propped on his elbows. He had just broken the skirting away with a chisel. He was lighted by a candle beside him, which threw his shadow large on the ceiling. And in this very instant, his face bent over a dark gulf slit in the flooring, he was staring, big eyed, while the blood purpled his cheeks till he looked a real murderer. Then with a brutal gesture he plunged in his arm, but his movements were so nervous that at first he found nothing. He had to hold the candle to the hole, when, tucked well back, he revealed the purse, the bank-notes, the watch.

Involuntarily, Severine cried out. Roubaud swung round in terror.

For an instant he did not recognize her, thought that in the white figure staring at him aghast with terrified eyes he was seeing a ghost.

'What do you think you are doing?' she demanded.

Then, as comprehension came to him, he could only groan, and stared at her, embarrassed by her presence, wishing she were back in bed. But not one word of argument came to his lips, all he could think of was boxing her ears, as she stood there shivering, half naked.

'Very fine,' she said, 'you refuse me fifteen francs for boots I need, but you can take it for yourself all right when you lose.'

In a flash, that infuriated him. Was she going still further to ruin his life, hindering his pleasure, this woman he no longer desired, to sleep with who was merely a violent rupture of his peace of mind? Now that he found his pleasure elsewhere, he had no more need of her. He dived his hand in again, but took only the purse, with its three hundred francs in gold. And when he had ground the skirting back into place with his heel, he went up to her and through clenched teeth ground out: 'You make me sick, I shall do what I like! Do I ask you what you're going to do tomorrow in Paris?'

After that, with a furious shrug of his shoulders, he went back to the café, leaving the candle where it was, on the floor. Severine took it up. Frozen to the heart, she went back to bed, keeping the candle alight, unable to sleep again, eyes wide open. Now it was definite. The break-up of their marriage had taken place by steady stages, as if the crime which was destroying the man in him had filtered into any bonds between them and rotted them away. About Jacques, Roubaud knew!

7

This Thursday morning, folk who were proposing to take the 6.40 fast train up to Paris had a shock when they woke up: since midnight it had been snowing, and so heavily that there was already a foot of it in the streets. Under the station roofing, Lison was ready, breathing smoke and vapour, with seven coaches in her train, two third class and four first. When, at half past five, Jacques and Pecqueux had reached the locomotive sheds, to check her over, they had grunted with some concern at those persistent white flakes still falling from the night sky. Now, on the footplate, they stood in expectation of the warning whistle, their eyes far ahead, beyond the gaping triangle of galvanized iron and glass, following the thick flakes still falling silently and without cease.

'I'll be damned if I can see a single signal,' muttered Jacques.

'We'll be lucky if we get through,' said his fireman.

Roubaud had turned up just in time to take over, and was there on the platform, with his lantern. Every now and then his worn-out eyelids closed from weariness, but he still did not relax his supervision. When Jacques asked him if he had had no reports in on the state of the track, the A.S.M. went up to him, took his hand and said there was still nothing in, and when, at that moment, Severine came along the platform, he himself led her to a first-class compartment and saw her in. He could not have failed to detect the glance of anxious emotion exchanged by the two lovers, but he did not even make the effort to tell his wife that it was rash of her to travel on such a morning, and she would be wiser to put it off.

Passengers appeared, heavily wrapped, carrying hand-luggage, quite a crush, indeed, despite the bitter wind. The snow on their boots showed no signs of melting. Doors were hastily closed, everybody sealing himself in. The platform was left empty, under the poor flicker of rare gas jets, the locomotive headlamp, just at the foot of the chimney, the only bright spot, like a giant eye thrusting its sheet of light into the enwrapping darkness.

Then Roubaud raised his lantern, giving the signal, the leading guard whistled and as soon as he could open the regulator and thrust forward the little gear lever, Jacques responded. They were off. For another minute the A.S.M. followed with his eyes as the train withdrew into the blizzard.

'And look out,' cried Jacques to Pecqueux. 'No joke, today.'

He had not failed to notice that his companion too, just like Roubaud seemed about to drop with weariness. Pecqueux had obviously spent the night on the randan.

'*Phew!*' cried Pecqueux, 'there's nought to worry about!'

The instant they emerged from the station, the two men were deep in snow. There was an east wind blowing, in other words, a head wind, lashing them in savage gusts, but behind their screen they did not feel it too badly at first. Besides, they were warmly dressed, in thick cloth coats, their eyes protected by goggles. But in the darkness the dazzling light of their head-lamp seemed lost at once in the fluffy mass which was falling. Instead of being lighted two or three hundred yards ahead, the track seemed to be lost in milky fog, out of which objects appeared only at very close range, as if from the depths of dream. And, as he had feared, what raised Jacques' anxiety to a peak was to realize, at the first section, that he definitely could not distinguish the red signals at the regulation distance from them. After that he drove with the utmost caution, though he dared not slacken speed, for the wind was offering tremendous resistance and any relaxation would have been as great a danger.

As far as Harfleur Lison made good time. The depth of snow which had fallen was still not enough to worry Jacques, for there was at most a couple of feet, and the snow-fender in front of the engine could handle a good three feet. His chief concern was to maintain his speed, knowing that apart from temperance and loving his engine, the real merit of an engine-driver was in keeping up a steady speed, without any spurts, all at maximum pressure. Indeed, his only fault was in this insistence on keeping going, in his stubborn insistence on not halting, in disregarding signals, sure he would always have time to bring Lison to a stop. He even went so far sometimes as to drive on after running over fog-signals – 'corns', in railway jargon – which might have meant a week's suspension every time. But now, in the great danger of which he was aware, the thought that Severine was on

186

board, that he was responsible for that precious life, rallied all his will-power and held it all the way through to Paris, the whole length of that double line of tracks, through all the obstacles he had to negotiate.

Thus, balancing despite the continual jolting, on the footplate which linked engine to tender, and leaning out to the right, Jacques contrived to see despite the snow. Through the water-washed glass windscreen he could see nothing, so he kept his head outside, his cheeks lashed by thousands of needles and nipped by such cold that it felt like razors cutting. From time to time he drew back, to take breath, taking off his goggles, to wipe them, then returned resolutely to it, braving the full blast of the storm, his eyes steely hard in their anxiety to make out the signals, and he was so absorbed in his own efforts that twice he imagined mistakenly that he saw red flashes in the greyish curtain trembling before his vision.

Then, all at once, in the darkness, he felt his fireman no longer by his side. So as not to dazzle the driver, the water-level indicator was lit by only one small glimmer, and then, on the pressure gauge, Jacques suddenly noticed that the little quivering blue needle was swinging rapidly back. The fires were dying down. Overcome by fatigue, Pecqueux was stretched out, sound asleep on the tool chest.

'You bloody whoreson!' cried Jacques, in an absolute fury, shaking him.

Unintelligibly muttering excuses, Pecqueux staggered to his feet. He could hardly stand, but force of habit sent him, hammer in hand, straight back to his stoking, cracking the coal and shovelling it on to the bars in an even layer, then giving a quick sweep with the broom. And while the furnace door was open, the glow of the fire lit the train following behind, and it became like the flaring tail of a comet, kindling the cross-falling snow and turning the flakes to large drops of gold.

After Harfleur came the long three leagues up-gradient as far as Saint Romain, the steepest climb on the whole line. Now all attention, the driver applied himself to his task, ready, over this rise which was bad enough in fine weather, for a sudden overload. His hand on the gear lever, he kept his eye on the flashing past of the telegraph poles, and endeavoured by these to estimate her speed. It was dropping

187

sharply and Lison was breathing hard. He could also feel the pressure on the snow-plough. The resistance there was growing.

With one foot he flung the furnace door open, and despite his drowsiness Pecqueux again tumbled to it, coaxing the fire, to bring the steam pressure up still further. The furnace door glowed red now, lighting the two men's legs with lurid violet light, but in the draught of icy air which enveloped them they were not conscious of the fierce heat. On a gesture from his chief, Pecqueux next raised the flue-rod, to make the fire draw still more fiercely. Rapidly the needle rose to 160 pounds, and Lison began to give of her utmost. There was even a moment when, seeing the water-level drop, Jacques had to open the injector, even though this might reduce pressure. But it rose rapidly again and Lison roared and belched into the night like an overladen beast, lurching and straining her loins till one could have thought one heard her limbs crack. And, no longer having the love for her which he once had had, Jacques abused her, like any woman growing older and feebler.

'The lazy bitch,' he ground out, between his teeth, who ordinarily never spoke a word on a journey, 'she'll never do it.'

However, somnolent as he was, Pecqueux gaped in consternation. What on earth had Jacques Lantier got now against Lison? Was she not the same good, obedient engine, who pulled the dead weight of a train out so easily that it was a pleasure to travel behind her, and with such good vaporization that on the run between Paris and Havre she saved ten per cent of her fuel? When an engine had valves like hers, so beautifully adjusted, sealing off her steam so miraculously well, one could allow her many an imperfection, just as one could shut one's eyes to a woman being a bit crotchety about a trifle if on the whole she behaved and kept house well. True, Lison was heavy on oil. But so what? Oil her, then! That was all!

Just at that very moment, however, Jacques lost his temper with her about that.

'She'll never get up if she isn't oiled extra,' he said.

And he did what he had scarcely ever done before, took his oilcan to lubricate her on the road. Clambering over the rail, he followed along her boiler side, a most perilous manoeuvre. His feet slithered on the narrow steel plates, wet with snow. He was blinded, too, while the frightful wind threatened to sweep him away like a piece of straw.

With her diminutive man thus clinging to her loins, Lison roared on her breathless course into the night, through the vast white field of snow, in which she cut so deep a furrow. She shook him as she swept him on. Reaching the front cross-member, he crouched down at the right-hand cylinder lubricating cup, and with the utmost difficulty, clinging with one hand to the rail, topped it up. Then he had to clamber round on her like an insect, to do the same to the left-hand cylinder. When at last he got back, exhausted, to the cab, he was terribly white, having felt the breath of death.

'Foul bitch!' he muttered.

Astounded by this unusual harshness regarding their Lison, Pecqueux could not but try one of his customary wisecracks.

'Ought to have let me do that, mate, right up my street, oiling bitches!'

Back at his controls, peering out on the left-hand side of the cab, his eyes on the track, he felt somewhat enlivened by this effort. As a rule, he had good sight, better than Pecqueux's, but in this blizzard every landmark became invisible and, familiar as they both were with every mile of the road, it was with the utmost difficulty that they could recognize even what country they were passing through. The track seemed to be under snow, the hedges, even the houses beside the railroad, were swallowed up in it, it had become all one endless level expanse, a confusion of uncertain varying degrees of whiteness, through which he had the impression that Lison was galloping madly, out of all control.

Never before had this team, driver and fireman, felt so powerfully the bond of fraternity which united them as they did now on this locomotive roaring through all the dangers. On their footplate, they were more alone, more cut off from the world, than in any closed room, and on their shoulders they had the crushing extra burden of responsibility for all the human lives behind them.

Thus, though Pecqueux's wisecrack about oiling his bitches would ordinarily have been the last pinprick to infuriate him, Jacques now could not resist a smile. He restrained the anger which was mounting in him. This was certainly no moment for quarrelling. The snow was deeper than ever, the white curtain on the edge of their field of vision denser. They were still climbing, when far ahead Pecqueux in his turn thought he sighted a red danger signal and warned Jacques. An

189

instant later, they could no longer see it. As Pecqueux said, their eyes were dreaming dreams. Nevertheless, though he himself had seen nothing, Jacques felt his heart still thudding. He was becoming jittery by the hallucination of the other man, he was losing confidence in himself. All they seemed able to make out beyond the pale turbulence of the snowflakes were looming dark shapes, immense masses, like giant fragments of the night, which seemed to break away and swoop down against them. Were those shapes the debris of landslides, or hills that barred their way, into which the train would crash? A prey to wildest apprehension, Jacques tugged at the cord and Lison uttered a long-drawn-out, desperate whistle. It floated wailingly away into the tempest. An instant later, he was suddenly astonished to see that he had whistled just at the right time, for they were rushing at top speed through Saint Romain station, which he had thought still nearly a mile away.

However, once she had mastered that terrible gradient, Lison now began to run more easily, and Jacques could relax for a moment. From Saint Romain to Bolbec the line climbed scarcely perceptibly, everything would be all right till the far edge of the plain. Nonetheless, when he reached Beuzeville, during the three minutes time-table halt, seeing the station-master on the platform, he called him up, feeling he had to tell him his concern at the ever deeper snow. He would never get through to Rouen, he said, and, seeing he was at a locomotive depôt where there were always engines available, it would be better to add another engine at once, but the S.M. said he had no orders to that effect, and thought he ought not to take it on himself. All he offered was – half-a-dozen wooden shovels to clear the tracks if needs be. These Pecqueux accepted and stacked in one corner of the tender.

On the level stretch which now followed, Lison certainly continued to make good speed without too much effort, though it certainly did take it out of her. Every few minutes now, Jacques had to make that gesture of his, kicking open the furnace door, for the fireman to stoke up, and every time this was done, the glowing comet's tail cut into the night over the train's dismal black body as it tore through this countryside shrouded in white.

It was nearly seven forty-five, day was breaking, but one could only just distinguish the sky as a somewhat whiter area, so full was the air of the close-packed flurry of snow filling the world with its own whiteness from skyline to skyline. That abnormal daylight, in which one could still distinguish nothing, worried the two men even more than the darkness as, eyes streaming with tears despite their goggles, they strained to see well ahead. Without releasing hold on the valve controls, the driver's fingers also kept hold of the whistle cord and from caution almost continuously kept going a lament of distress from out of that desert of snow.

Without trouble they passed Bolbec, then Yvetot. But at Motteville Jacques enquired of the assistant station-master there but, in vain, for information regarding the state of the track ahead. No train had come through so far. There was only a telegram stating baldly that the Paris slow down was safe, but held up at Rouen. So off went Lison again, down the gentle slope to Barentin at a weary, labouring gait. Day was now definitely breaking, a very pallid day, one might have thought that the light was supplied by the snow. This was falling more thickly, like an icy hoar-frost, as if drowning the earth with fragmentary dust of the high heavens.

As the sun rose, the wind grew fiercer, the flakes driven like bullets. Pecqueux had constantly to shovel the snow off the coal in the tender. The countryside was now visible on either side, though so unrecognizable that they both felt they were rushing along in a dream. The huge level fields, the lush pastures with their hedges, the walled-in orchards, were now only an uninterrupted sea of white, merely swollen here and there by sharp undulations. It was all one vast uncertain whiteness, in which every object was dissolved away. And now Lison's driver, his countenance lacerated by the blast, his hand constantly on the driving wheel, began to suffer terribly from the cold.

At last came the halt at Barentin. M. Bessière, the station-master, himself went up to the locomotive, to warn Jacques that there were reports of heavy drifts towards Maufras Cross.

'I think you can still get through, but it will be tough going.'

Then the young driver lost patience.

'God Almighty!' he cried. 'Just what I said, back at Beuzeville! What harm would it have done them to give me an extra engine? A fine fix we're going to be in!'

The leading guard had come along from his van, and he too was getting annoyed. He was icy cold in his box and avowed that he could not distinguish a signal from a telegraph pole. They were merely feeling their way in all that whiteness.

'Well, anyway, I've warned you,' said M. Bessière.

But the passengers were now getting uneasy at the long halt in that snowed-up station, with not a porter's voice to be heard, not a door banging. Windows were being lowered, heads appeared. There was a stout lady with two charming fair-haired young girls, doubtless her daughters, all three certainly English, and, further along, there was a very pretty dark young woman, whom an elderly man was pressing to shut the window again, and there were also two men, one young, the other old, leaning out of their windows, talking about it. But when Jacques glanced back, all he saw was Severine, who was also leaning out, anxiously looking his way. The darling thing, how worried she must be, and how his heart ached, knowing her there, so near and yet so far, in this dangerous position. He would have given his life already to have reached Paris and brought her in safe and sound.

'Well, better be going,' said the station-master. 'No use frightening people.'

He gave the signal. The guard went back to his van and whistled, and, after a long wail, once again Lison set off.

At once, Jacques could feel that the condition of the track was different. It was no longer level country. There was an end to endless trundling on through a thick snow carpet, like a tramp steamer steadily furrowing a heavy sea. They were entering more broken-up country, with continual hills and vales all the way to Malaunay, and here the snow had drifted for stretches clean off the track, but elsewhere had piled deep. Sweeping the embankments clear, the wind accumulated the snow in the cuttings. This meant a continual succession of new obstacles to fight through. They ran through stretches of clear track always barred at last by real ramparts. It was now broad daylight, and under that covering of snow the waste countryside of narrow gorges and steep slopes, frozen in twisted immobility, was as desolate as any arctic scene.

Jacques had never before felt cold penetrate so badly to his bones. Under the thousand needles of the snow his cheeks felt as if they were bleeding, and he was losing all consciousness of his tingling hands, which had suddenly become so indifferent to feeling that with a shudder he realized that without looking he could not even tell whether he had hold of the gear control or not. When he raised his hand to pull the whistle control, from the shoulder down his arm was as heavy as a dead thing. He could not have said whether his legs were supporting him or not, and was conscious only of the continual jolting which seemed to be eviscerating him. The cold, this iciness which had now crept up nearly into his brain, brought with it immense fatigue, to the point of no longer being aware that he was the driver of the train. He had ceased even automatically to adjust the steam feed. In a state of bewilderment he found himself watching the pressure-gauge needle slip back. Through his brain whirled all the stories he had heard of hallucination – was that thing there ahead not a fallen tree across the rails? Just above that thicket – was that not a red flag? Were those not fog-signals snapping again and again under his wheels?

He could not have made any clear answer. All he knew was that he ought to stop the train. But even for that he could not summon the will-power. This crisis tortured him for some minutes. Then, all at once, the sight of Pecqueux, who had again collapsed on to the tool chest, knocked out by the same accumulation of cold from which he himself was suffering, made him so furious that he felt quite warm again. The drunken sot! All his usual consideration for his tippling fireman went to the wind, and he awakened Pecqueux with his boot, kicking incessantly till the lanky form staggered to an upright position. Still dazed, Pecqueux merely grumbled, then took up his shovel again.

'All right, keep your wool on, we're off again.'

The furnace full, up went the steam pressure again, and time too, for Lison was just entering a cutting, where she had to force her way through a drift which was more than a yard deep. She pressed forward only with extreme effort, which revealed itself in shuddering which shook her through and through. There was a moment when, exhausted, she almost grounded, like a ship on a sandbank. What overcame her was the quantity of snow, which had gradually piled on top of the coaches till it lay there in a dense layer.

They crept on for some time, like this, a black line in a furrow of white, itself immersed in whiteness. Lison herself was trimmed with ermine. The snow lapped round her dusky flanks, where it steadily melted, to stream away like rain. Once again, despite the weight on the train, she got free and carried on. Then, rounding a long curve on an embankment, they could see the whole train again behind them, as it rolled on easily, a ribbon of darkness lost in a legendary country of dazzling white. But farther on there were more cuttings and Jacques and Pecqueux, who this time had both felt Lison nearly run aground, braced themselves against the cold, fast at their stations, which, whatever it cost them, they could not abandon. Once again the engine began to lose speed. Lison had plunged into a sharply banked ravine, and this time she slowed down steadily, without any shock, as if she was gently but surely bogging in, caught by all her wheels, more and more tightly gripped, till she had no breath left. And she was stationary. This was it! The snow gripped her. She was powerless.

'Now we're caught,' Jacques growled. 'Bloody hell!'

He stayed at his controls some seconds longer, his hand on the wheel, opening her up completely, to see if the obstruction might not give way. Then, hearing Lison cough and gasp in vain, he shut off steam and in a rage uttered still worse oaths. The leading guard was leaning out of his van door. Now Pecqueux too stuck his head out and he too shouted.

'We're caught, we're stuck!'

The guard leapt down quickly, and the snow reached his knees. He came up slowly. The three men discussed the position.

'We can't do anything else but try to clear it,' Jacques said, at last. 'Fortunately, we have got shovels. Call up your rear guard, and we four'll soon get the track clear.'

They signalled to the rear guard, who had also climbed down. He got to them with some difficulty, lost in snow at times. By now this halt in open country, in the midst of that white desolation, together with the clear sound of the train officials' voices, debating what was to be done, and the sight of the guard scrambling with difficulty along past the train, deep in snow, had alarmed the passengers. Down came the windows. They were all shouting and asking questions. A general confusion was growing.

'Where are we? Why have we halted? What's wrong, then? Good gracious me, is something wrong?'

The guard felt he had to quieten them. As he came up, the Englishwoman, on either side of whose plump red cheeks appeared the delightful countenances of her daughters, asked with a strong foreign accent if there was any danger.

'No, no, Madame,' he replied, 'only a little snow. We shall soon be off again.'

The window closed again, shutting off the lively chatter of the girls, with all the music of their English tongue, so lively on their rosy lips. They found the situation most entertaining, and were laughing heartily.

Farther on, the elderly gentleman summoned the guard, while from behind him his young wife also thrust her dark and pretty head out of the window.

'However comes it that you did not take precautions? This is intolerable . . . I am on my way back from London. I have to be in Paris on business this morning! I tell you I shall make the Company responsible for any delay!'

'We shall be off again in three minutes, sir,' was all the guard could say.

It was frightfully cold. The carriages chilled rapidly. All the heads vanished again. Windows were closed. But now inside the coaches there was a persistent excitement and alarm, finding expression in a dull murmur of voices. Only two windows remained down, while, three compartments one from another, an American in his forties and a young man who lived at Havre had a great conversation and were most interested in the work of clearing the track.

'In America, sir, everybody would get out and take a hand.'

'Oh, but this is nothing at all, I was held up twice, last year, my job takes me to Paris every week.'

'I have to be there roughly every three weeks, sir.'

'Not all the way from New York?'

'Yes, indeed, sir, all the way from New York.'

Jacques took command. He had caught sight of Severine leaning out of one of the doors of the first coach, where she always travelled, to be near him, but with his eyes he had begged her to draw back, and she had understood at once and withdrawn, not to stay in the icy wind which scorched her cheeks. From that moment, his mind on her, he worked most heartily. But he now observed that the cause of the hold-up was not the snow under the wheels, for these sliced cleanly through the thickest of it, but the low-slung cinder-box under her belly, which piled up the snow and compressed it into huge blocks.

'We shall have to strip off that cinder-box,' he said, suddenly.

At first, the leading guard opposed him. Drivers were under guards' orders, and he refused to authorize any interference with a locomotive. But at last, Jacques convinced him.

'All right then, if you will take the responsibility.'

It was however a tough job. On their backs under Lison, the snow melting beneath them, Jacques and Pecqueux had to labour for nearly half an hour. It was a good thing they had the right spanners in their tool-chest. At last, nearly burned and nearly crushed a score of times, they succeeded in getting the cinder-box off. It was a heavy casting, and was now badly caught between wheels and cylinders, but with all four men heaving on it, they at last got it out and on to the side of the cutting.

'Now let's finish clearing that snow,' said the guard.

The train had by this time been held up nearly an hour, and the passengers were getting really alarmed. Windows were now constantly being lowered again and people insisting on knowing why the train did not move. Passengers began to be panicky, angry, tearful even, quite losing their heads.

'No, that'll do, we've cleared enough,' cried Jacques to the guard. 'Up you get, I'll manage the rest.'

He and Pecqueux resumed their stations, and when the two guards had reached their vans, he opened the steam cocks, and a jet of super-heated steam gushed almost soundlessly into the snow, and finished clearing what still stuck to the rails. Then, hand on control, he reversed her. Slowly, they ran back about three hundred yards, to get a good run. Then, with the fire well stoked and pressure up above the limit, he drove Lison hard at the wall of snow which barred them, and crashed her into it, head-on, with all the weight of the train behind her. There was a tremendous grunt, like that one hears when a timber-feller brings down his heavy axe into the heartwood, and Lison's powerful frame groaned. But still she could not get through, still she was halted, belching smoke, quivering from the strain. Twice more he tried the trick, drew back, rushed at the snow, to carry through it. Each time, loins straining, Lison forced her broad bosom against the mass, her breath angrily hissing, then seemed to get

196

second wind, gathered her steel muscles in a supreme effort and got through. Slowly, the train lumbered behind her between the two walls of snow into which she had carved her way. And she was free.

'She's grand, all the same,' muttered Pecqueux.

Blinded, Jacques took off his goggles and wiped them. His heart was thumping hard, and he no longer felt the cold. But he had suddenly recalled the very deep cutting about three hundred yards from Maufras Cross. It lay open to the wind, and there must be a lot of snow drifted in there. In that same instant he felt sure that this was to be the reef on which he was to be shipwrecked. He leant out. Beyond a curve, he sighted the cutting, dead ahead, still some distance from him, a long trench, filled with snow. It was broad daylight, the whiteness unlimited and dazzling, though snow was still falling.

Nevertheless, Lison continued, at moderate speed, without so far encountering any other obstacle. As a precaution, they had lit their front and rear lamps, and the white headlight at the base of the smoke-stack gleamed in the daylight like a cyclopean eye. On she rolled, nearer and nearer the cutting, with that one eye wide open. Then she seemed to give a little snort, like a frightened mare. She was shaken by a profound shuddering, she bent her back, and still made some progress solely because her driver so willed it. He had kicked open the furnace door, for his fireman to quicken the fire, and now it was not a comet's tail setting fire to the night, but a vast belching of dense black smoke which fouled the pale shimmering of this limitless sky.

Lison approached. At last, she had to plunge into the cutting. On either side the slopes were covered, and ahead the track was completely invisible. It was like the bed of a mountain torrent, now slumbering deep under the snow settled there. She entered, she rolled on about fifty yards more, more and more slowly, breathing desperately. She thrust snow aside and it piled high before her, a frothing, overtowering mountain which struggled against her and threatened to bury her. For an instant she indeed did seem to be covered, beaten, yet with a last lurch of her loins freed herself once more and carried on another thirty yards. But that was the end. There came an agonized jolt. Impacted blocks of snow fell away from her and encumbered the track again. Every moving part was full of snow, binding her mechanism together with ropes of fresh ice. And there she halted finally, puffing fruitlessly into the icy air, till even her breath died out and she was motionless – and dead.

'Now we're stuck all right,' said Jacques. 'Just what I expected.'

But at once he tried to pull back, to attempt his former manoeuvre again. This time, however, Lison would not stir from where she was. She refused to go either backward or forward. She was blocked everywhere, glued to the ground, inert and unresponsive. Behind her was the train, equally dead, buried up to the windows in the deep drift. Nor had the downfall ceased, and now in long bouts the flakes were falling bigger. They were thoroughly bogged in. Soon engine and coaches would vanish beneath this. They were already half covered by the quivering silence of that black solitude. Now nothing stirred, only the snow, weaving the shroud.

'What do you know?' cried the leading guard, leaning from his van. 'Do we dig out again?'

'We're b——,' Pecqueux shouted, graphically.

This time the situation was indeed serious. The rear guard ran to lay a series of fog signals to protect the train behind, while the driver sent out a long desperate chain of swift whistles, which ricocheted lugubriously over the snowy waste. They were only four, they could never dig out such a mass of snow. It would need a whole team. They had no other course but to run for help.

The worse thing was that the passengers were panicking again. A window opened and the pretty dark woman jumped down, all worked up, thinking there had been an accident, while her husband, the elderly business-man, followed her, shouting:

'I shall write to the Minister, this is outrageous!'

Women were weeping, men's voices rose angrily as they emerged from their compartments, other windows came banging down. Only the two young English girls seemed still to get fun out of it. They were all smiles, not in the least worried, and when the leading guard began to try to calm them all, the younger one asked in French with a slight British lisp:

'So is it *all change* now?'

Several men had now got down, despite the thick snow, which was waist high. The American came up with the young man from Havre, and the two went on as far as the engine, to see.

'That's a good four or five hours' work,' they agreed, 'before we're out.'

'A good five hours, provided we have at least twenty men.'

Jacques had now persuaded the leading guard to send the junior back to Barentin for assistance. Neither he nor Pecqueux could leave the engine. The man set off and was soon lost to sight along the cutting. He had over two miles to go, and with the best of luck could not be back before two hours. So Jacques, really worried now, left his post for a moment and ran to the first coach, where he saw that Severine had lowered her window.

'Don't worry,' he said, quickly. 'There's nothing to fear.'

She spoke quickly too, and formally, in case they were heard.

'I'm not afraid. But I have been so worried on your account.'

This exchange was made so tenderly that they were both much relieved, and exchanged smiles. Then, as he made his way back to the engine, Jacques was startled to see Flora, then Misard and two other men whom he did not at once recognize, coming along the embankment towards them. They had heard the distress signals, so Misard, who was not on duty, had hurried along with two friends whom he happened to be treating to a bottle of white wine. These were the quarryman, Cabuche, who could not work on account of the snow, and pointsman Ozil, who had come through the tunnel from Malaunay, to court Flora, whom despite the way she rejected him he never ceased trying to win. And Flora, wild girl as she was, strong and tough as any boy, had come with them just to see, out of curiosity. Indeed, for her and for her father too, this was an outstanding event, an astonishing adventure, a train being stopped like that right at their door. In the five years they had lived there, what trains had they not seen or heard go by, at all hours of the day or night, in fine weather or foul, but all of them swift as the wind. Every one of them seemed to be borne on the tempest which brought it, not one had ever even slowed down, they saw them fleeting by and vanishing in the distance without ever being able to find out anything about them. The whole world whirled by, a mass of humanity swept by at top speed, and all they could ever know of them was of faces glimpsed for a brief instant, faces they would never see again and faces which became familiar, from always seeing them on definite days, but still, for all that, anonymous faces. And here was a train in the snow with everybody getting out at their very door. The natural order of things was reversed, they stared from top to toe at this stranger world expelled by chance on to the track, they gaped round-eyed, much as savages come running down to the rocks where European folk suffer ship-wreck. These opened train doors revealing fur-wrapped women-folk and men emerging in massive overcoats, and all this luxurious comfort stranded there amid that icy scene froze them with astonishment.

Flora, however, recognized Severine. Regularly on the look-out for the trains which Jacques drove, for some weeks she had noticed this woman in the Thursday morning express, the more so since every time she passed, Severine looked out at this spot, to catch a glimpse of her Maufras Cross property. And Flora's glance grew sombre when she saw Severine's surreptitious exchange with Jacques.

'Why, but that's Madame Roubaud!' cried Misard, who too had just seen who it was, and immediately assumed an obsequious air. 'What good fortune! . . . You must not stay out here, you must come along to our cottage.'

Jacques shook hands with the crossing-keeper and supported the suggestion.

'He is right . . . We may be here for hours, you might die of cold.'

Severine would not go, said she was well wrapped-up. Besides, the idea of three hundred yards to go through the deep snow rather alarmed her. Then Flora went up to her. Staring at her with those steady, wide-open eyes of hers, she addressed her.

'Do come, Madame, I will carry you.'

And before Severine had accepted, Flora had taken her in her powerful man's arms and raised her high as if she were a little child, to put her down on the other side of the track, where the snow was trodden, and she would not sink in. Some passengers standing nearby marvelled and laughed. What a lass! With a dozen like her, it wouldn't take a couple of hours to clear that snow away!

Meanwhile Misard's suggestion, and the thought of the crossing-keeper's cottage where they could get warm by the fire and perhaps find bread and wine, ran from coach to coach. The panic died down as soon as it was realized that there was no immediate danger, though they were in a dismal situation all the same. The footwarmers were

200

cooling off. It was nine o'clock. They were going to be hungry and thirsty long before help could come. It might take a long time too, to get them free. Who could say they would not have to spend the night there? They split into two camps, those who got scared and refused to leave the coaches, withdrawing into them as if intent on dying there, wrapped in whatever they had and stretched out ill-humoured on the seats, and the others who would rather risk the passage through the snow, hoping to be better off when they got there, and above all anxious to get away from this nightmare of a train broken down, dead, and cold. A fairly large party got together, the elderly business man and his young wife, the Englishwoman with her two daughters, the young man from Havre, the American, a dozen others, ready to set off.

Jacques in an undertone succeeded in convincing Severine, swearing at the same time that if he could get away for a moment he would come along and tell her what was happening. And as Flora was still gazing at him with those sombre eyes, he addressed her kindly, as an old friend:

'Well, so that's all right, you'll take these ladies and gentlemen along, won't you, Flora lass . . . I'll keep Misard and the others here, we'll all lend a hand and do what we can while we wait for more help.'

And indeed, Cabuche, Ozil, Misard at once took shovels, to join Pecqueux and the leading guard, who were already shovelling at the snow. The little team made every effort to get the engine free, scraping it away from under the wheels and pitching it up on the slope. Not a man spoke, the only sound that of their furious efforts lost in the dismal white waste, which absorbed every movement. When the little party of passengers had drawn some distance away, they had a last sight of the train as a little black line, all alone, on which the deepening snow weighed heavily. All doors were closed, all windows firmly to. It was still snowing and with mute persistence was slowly but surely burying them.

Flora would have carried Severine, but she refused, and insisted on walking with the rest of them. It was hard work covering those three hundred yards. Particularly in the cutting, they sank in over their knees and twice the fat Englishwoman had to be rescued, half buried in the snow. But her two girls were still all laughter, and delighted

with it. Having fallen once, the young wife of the elderly business-
man had found herself obliged to accept a hand from the younger
man from Havre, while her husband expatiated to the American on
the shortcomings of France. It was however easier once they got out
of the cutting, but they now had to walk strictly in Indian file, in order
to keep to the embankment, the edge of which was not very easy to
distinguish. But at last they were there, and Flora led them straight
into the kitchen, where there was of course not a chair for everybody,
for there were now twenty of them. Fortunately, it was a large enough
room to hold them all. All Flora could do was to bring a couple of
planks and with these between the chairs she contrived a couple of
benches. She threw a bundle of wood on to the fire in the hearth, and
then with a gesture indicated that she could do no more for them.

All this she had done without a word, and she now stood staring
with her large greenish eyes at the strangers, all with the insolent but
rather wild look of a stalwart blonde savage. There were only two
faces which she knew, from having seen them at the windows of
trains for months – that of the American and that of the young man
from Havre, and these she examined rather as one examines buzzing
insects which one never has a proper chance of seeing when in flight,
but now at last has motionless. Though she had known nothing of
them, beyond their features, she had never thought that they were
quite like this, and they looked peculiar to her. As for the others, they
all looked like a different species, the inhabitants of an unknown
world, fallen suddenly from the skies, bringing to her kitchen clothes,
habits and ideas she never thought to see. The Englishwoman
confided to the businessman's young wife that she was on her way to
India to join her eldest son, who was a high official there, while the
Frenchwoman was joking about her own bad luck, now that for once
she had had the whim of going to London with her husband, who
visited that city twice every year. Everybody was complaining about
being held up in so dismal a place. They were going to be hungry,
going to need sleep. Good gracious, what on earth were they going to
do? After she had listened for some time to this without a sign of life,
Flora suddenly looked across at Severine, who had a chair near the
fire, and, catching her eye, nodded to her to accompany her into the
adjoining room.

202

'Mother,' she said, as they went in, 'this is Madame Roubaud. Wouldn't you like to talk to her?'

Phasie was in bed, her face sallow, her legs swollen, so ill that she had not got up at all for the past fortnight. In this miserable room, in which a tiled stove maintained a stifling heat, she spent hours and hours turning her single thought over and over, her only other distraction being the vibration caused by the trains rushing by.

'Oh, Madame Roubaud,' she whispered, 'all right.'

Flora explained what had happened and told her mother about all the people she had brought to the house. But Phasie was not interested. She merely raised her head an instant and said:

'If Madame Roubaud wishes to have a look at her house, you know where the keys are, hanging near the cupboard.'

But Severine declined. The mere thought of Maufras Cross in this snow, under such a sky, made her shudder. No, she did not want to see it, she would rather wait there, in the warm.

'You must sit down, Madame,' Flora interjected. 'You will be more comfortable here than in there. Besides, we can never even try to feed so many, but if you are hungry, we can easily find something for you.'

And she brought up a chair, persistently trying to be obliging, in an obvious effort to overcome her usual roughness. But she could not keep her eyes off this young lady, as if trying to read through her and get the true answer to the question which had worried her latterly, and this obligingness was only an excuse to draw close to Severine, to peer into her face, to touch her, all in order to find out.

Severine thanked her and sat down next the stove, for it was true, she would rather be shut away here with this ill woman, hoping that Jacques would eventually find ways and means of joining her. Two hours crept by and at last, after talk of country things, she gave way to the extreme warmth and had just dozed off, when Flora, who was constantly called back to the kitchen, opened the door and in her hard voice said:

'Come in then, as she's in here.'

It was Jacques, who had slipped away to bring good news. The guard sent to Barentin had just brought a large team along, about thirty soldiers, sent to danger points by the authorities, in case of trouble and they were now all at work with picks and shovels. Only it would take some time, and they might not get away before night.

'But you're really all right, aren't you? Just be patient! You won't let Madame Roubaud die of hunger, will you, Aunt Phasie?'

At the sight of her big boy, as she called him, Phasie had painfully raised herself to a sitting position and was drinking in the sight of him. The mere sound of his voice revived her and made her happy.

'Of course not, of course not,' she cried, when he went near her bed. 'Oh, my darling big boy, how lovely to see you! To think it was you got stuck in the snow. And that idiot girl had not the sense to tell me.'

And, turning to her daughter, she scolded her:

'You might at least have the manners to go and look after the company, we don't want them telling the management we're savages.'

Flora had indeed planted herself firmly there, as if permanently fixed between Severine and Jacques. Even now she seemed to hesitate, uncertain whether or not to insist on staying where she was, despite her mother. But she would see nothing, her mother being there would keep them from giving themselves away, so sweeping them with a lingering glance from head to foot, without another word she went out.

'But whatever's this, my dear Aunt?' Jacques demanded, with a worried air. 'Not really on your back? Don't tell me it's bad?'

She made him come closer and sit on the edge of the bed, and without any more concern for Severine, who had discreetly drawn back, she unburdened herself in a low voice.

'It's very bad indeed, my dear boy, it's a wonder you find me still in the land of the living . . . I was not going to write and tell you because it was not anything I could write about . . . I very nearly passed away, but I am a little better now and I think I may slip out of his grasp once again.'

Jacques' eyes flitted over her countenance. He was frightened by the progress of her disorder. There was now not a trace of the lovely, healthy body he once had known.

'So you still keep having your cramps and dizzy fits? Poor Auntie!' he murmured.

She gripped his hand so fiercely that the bones cracked. In a still lower voice, she ran on:

'Would you believe it, the other day I caught him out . . . You know I had begun to think I never should find out what he was

204

drugging me in. I never drank anything he had touched, nor ate, but all the same every night my stomach was always on fire. . . . What do you think, he was putting it in the table salt. One evening I actually saw him doing it . . . To think I used to use such a lot of it too, to cleanse myself.'

Since the possession of Severine had seemed to cure him, Jacques had sometimes reflected on his aunt's story of slow, persistent poisoning, in rather the sceptical mood that one recalls a nightmare. Now it was he who held the sick woman's hands firmly in his, in a desire to soothe her.

'No, no,' he said, 'look here, I don't really think . . . Before you say things like that you have to be very sure . . . Besides, it is far too slow. I really do think it must be one of those funny complaints doctors don't know much about.'

'It's an illness and no mistake,' she cried, scornfully, 'an illness he has planted in me right enough . . . But you're right about the doctors, I've had two and they couldn't make anything of it, and they could not agree. I don't want any of that tribe poking their noses in here . . . I'm telling you, he's been putting it in the salt. But I assure you I saw him. Just to get that thousand francs of mine which poor father left me. He kids himself that when he has done away with me he'll be sure to find them. But I'll defy him to. They are in a place where nobody will ever find them, never, never! . . . I can die all right, my mind's at rest, nobody's ever going to get my little bit.'

'Why, my dear Aunt,' he said, 'if I were only as sure as that, I'd tell the police at once.'

She made a gesture of real horror.

'Oh no, that's the last thing . . . This is our private business, betwixt him and me. I know he wants to get rid of me, and of course I don't want to let him. So it's up to me to fight back, isn't it, and not be such a silly woman as I was about the table salt he doctored . . . Besides, who would ever believe it, a little abortion like him, a little squirt you could put in your pocket, mastering a big woman like me, with his rat's teeth too.'

She was overcome by a brief fit of shuddering, and before she finished speaking, her breath came hard.

'No matter, he hasn't succeeded this time. I'm better now, I shall be on my tootsies before the fortnight's out . . . And then he'll have

205

to be mighty clever to catch Phasie again. I'd like to see him! If he does manage to give me that drug of his again, that'll mean he really is the better man, and if that's the case, I'm through, I'll just fade away . . . But I don't want any meddling, mind you!'

Jacques felt sure her disease was going to her brain, to cause these frightful delusions. To take her mind off, he tried to joke, when suddenly she began to shake visibly under her blankets.

'Here he comes,' she whispered, 'I can always feel when that man is coming.'

She was right. A few moments later, in came Misard. All the colour had left her cheeks. She was at the mercy now of that unreasoning terror which large animals can feel of some small insect which bites and poisons them. The fact was that in her obsession about defending herself alone, she was increasingly terrified of Misard, though she would never admit it. True, though the moment he entered the door Misard's eye flashed over his wife and Jacques with their heads together, he subsequently appeared not to notice them at all, but was all attention for Severine, fawning before her with those dull eyes and that timid little mouth. He had thought perhaps Ma'am would care to take advantage of the occasion to glance at her property . . . If she would care for him to go along with her, he was at her service. And when Severine again declined, he continued in his rather whining manner: 'I thought, Ma'am, perhaps, about the apples and the rest, you see, I mean, what with the worm, it really wasn't worth the packing . . . Then there was that gale which did so much damage . . . It's such a pity there's nobody wants to make an offer for the property. There was one gentleman, but he wanted a lot of repair work . . . But I am at your service, Ma'am, you can count on me to act for you as if you were here yourself.'

After this he insisted on bringing some bread and some pears, the pears were out of his own orchard, and nice sound fruit they were too. She accepted them.

In the kitchen, Misard told the passengers that they were making great strides with clearing the track, but there was another four or five hours' work. It was past mid-day now, and this announcement brought forth a further burst of lamentation, for everybody was now getting really hungry. Flora had just said flatly that they had not enough bread in the house to go round. There was some wine, though, and she had brought up a couple of gallons from the cellar, and put it out on the table. The only thing was, they were short of glasses, they would have to share, the Englishwoman and her two girls had one, there was another for the elderly gentleman and his young wife, though the latter was finding a most zealous and resourceful cavalier in the young man from Havre, for he went out and actually found her some apples and a loaf of bread, tucked away in the wood-shed, which made Flora angry, for that was a loaf put away for her sick mother, but the young man without more ado sliced it up and passed it round to the ladies, the young wife first, of course, all smiles and gratification. Her husband, by now in a state of permanent indignation, was preoccupied duetting with the American on the commercial ethics of New York. The young English misses had never crunched an apple with better heart. Their mother was now very sleepy and inclined to doze. Two other ladies had been reduced to squatting on the floor by the hearth. Some of the men had gone outside for a smoke, and then came back all shivers, chilled to the bone. Gradually the general discomfort increased, their hunger merely titillated and their fatigue increased by impatience and embarrassment. The Misards' kitchen had turned into an encampment of shipwrecked folk, a handful of civilized beings demoralized by being cast on a desert isle.

Now Misard's coming and going, leaving the communicating door open, enabled Aunt Phasie to view the scene from her sick-bed. So these were the folk whom she had seen thunder by her, were they, in the past twelve months which she had dragged out between mattress and chair? It was only rarely now that she could go outside, and she spent all the twenty-four hours nailed there, eyes on the window, her only company those trains flashing by. She had always complained about this wild country, where there was never a visitor, but now a whole party of people had suddenly emerged from the great unknown. To think that of all those folk so impatient to rush away on their own business there was not one to suspect anything or guess at the foulness which had been put into her table salt!

The fact was, Aunt Phasie was bursting with this new notion of hers, and would have liked to know whether it was right in the sight of the Almighty to be so craftily dirty and nobody notice it. True, an enormous number of people did come their way, thousands and thousands, but all at such speed, not one suspecting that in that little cottage down there a man was murdering his wife at his ease, and not a soul the wiser. So she watched those strangers fallen from the moon and told herself that if folk were so preoccupied as they seemed to be, it was after all not so remarkable as all that to move among unclean things and be innocent of what was happening.

'Are you going back to the train now?' Misard asked Jacques.

'Certainly,' said Jacques. 'I'll come along in a minute.'

Misard went out, closing the door behind him. Phasie held the young man's hand firmly in hers and whispered again:

'If it's going to be my last, you just watch his face when he finds he can't discover my little bit . . . It doesn't half make me laugh, I can tell you, when I think of it. After all, I shall die happy.'

'But my dear Aunt,' expostulated Jacques, 'that's going to do nobody any good. Won't you really leave it to your daughter?'

'Flora? For him to get out of her? Not likely! . . . I wouldn't even let you have it, my dear boy, you're too soft like her, he'd get hold of part of it all right, if you had it. No, nobody shall have it, only the dear earth where I shall lie with it.'

She had worn herself out, and Jacques tucked her in again, soothed her and gave her a kiss, with the promise of coming again soon to see her. Then, seeing her apparently doze off, he slipped across to put Severine, still by the stove, between him and Phasie, and with a smile raised his finger to enjoin caution. But in a lovely gesture, she merely flung back her head and without a word offered him her lips, and he bent down to glue his to hers in a cautious but drawn-out kiss. Their eyes closed, they drank each other's breath. But when they looked up again they saw Flora standing at the door, watching them!

'Didn't you want any bread, Ma'am?' she demanded, hoarsely.

Most embarrassed and annoyed, Severine stammered vaguely:

'No, no, thank you.'

For a moment, Jacques' eyes blazed furiously at Flora, and his lips quivered, as if he was going to say something, then, waving his fist threateningly at her, he thought it better to go, and the door banged behind him.

Flora stood there, tall, a virgin amazon, her massed fair hair like a tall helmet on her head. So the ache at her heart which she had known ever since she noticed that smart townswoman travelling every Thursday in the train Jacques drove had not been for nothing. Now

208

indeed, by keeping the two of them there together, she had the certainty she had wanted. The man she loved would never love her. It was that miserable little piece of fluff he had chosen. And her regret for having warded him off, that night when he had suddenly tried to force her, gnawed at her again so agonizingly that she could have sobbed, for by her simple logic, had she given herself to him before this other, it would be her whom he would now have been kissing. Where could she get him alone now, to fling her arms around his neck and cry: 'Take me, I was so silly, because I did not know.'

But, being so frustrated, rage against that fragile creature, embarrassed and stammering before her, boiled up within Flora. She needed but crush that other woman in her wrestler's arms and at one go she could stifle the life out of her, as easy as wringing a tiny bird's neck. Whyever was it she did not bring herself to it? Instead, she inwardly swore vengeance, for she knew things about her rival which could bring her to prison, allowed to go free as she had been, like all the other trollops sold to rich, powerful old men. In an agony of jealousy, with rough gestures of her powerful hands, this child of nature swept the remains of the bread and the pears into her apron.

'If Madame doesn't want the food, there's others do,' she said.

It struck three, then four. For that company broken by fatigue and increasing annoyance, time dragged on endlessly. They could already see night returning, with dull, glowering light over the vast white expanse. Every ten minutes or so some of the men would go out, to con the scene from afar, but always returning to say the engine was still snowed up. Even the two young English girls at last began to find it not too funny.

In a corner, the pretty dark lady had gone to sleep against the shoulder of the young man from Havre, but for that matter, so much had they all lost their standards that the elderly husband did not even seem to notice it. The kitchen was getting colder, and they shivered without even the gumption to put on more wood, till suddenly the American left, saying he reckoned he would be better off stretched out on a seat in the train. This idea infected them all, and there was a general moan that they would all have done better to stay where they were, at least they wouldn't be on tenterhooks like they were now, not knowing what was happening. Then with some difficulty they had to persuade the Englishwoman not to leave the cottage and go back to

209

the train. Next, a lighted candle was planted at the corner of the table, to give them a little light in this gloomy kitchen, and that put the cap on their depression. They all sank into gloomy despair.

Meanwhile, the track was in fact pretty well cleared, and while after freeing the engine the soldiers were busy on the track ahead, the engine-driver and his fireman resumed their stations. Jacques was more confident now that the snowfall was at last ceasing. Pointsman Ozil had confirmed that on the far side of the tunnel, towards Malaunay, there had been an altogether lighter fall. Once again Jacques questioned him.

'You say you walked through the tunnel, and it was easy to get in at both ends?'

'But I keep telling you, you'll get through, I guarantee.'

Cabuche, who had worked with the zeal of a kindly giant, withdrew into the background, since his last brush with justice more timid and furtive than ever. Jacques had to shout to make him hear.

'I say, mate, pass 'em up, those shovels of ours, there on the bank! Who knows, they might come in useful yet.'

And when the quarryman had rendered him this last service, he shook his hand warmly, to show, having seen how he worked, how much he appreciated him.

'You're a damn good chap, you are, Cabuche,' he said.

This little mark of friendliness moved Cabuche unexpectedly. Tears started to his eyes.

'Thanks for that,' he said.

Misard, who had drawn back by his side – Misard who had given evidence against him to the examining magistrate – nodded approvingly, his thin lips twisted into a wry smile. For some time, Misard had not helped a bit, but had merely eyed the train from end to end with a jaundiced look, peering under the wheels as if to see what he might pick up.

At last, the leading guard agreed with Jacques that they might make an attempt to proceed, but at that moment Pecqueux, who had got down on to the track, called Jacques over.

'Look at that cylinder,' he said, 'she's had a crack.'

Jacques too bent down. When he had gone over Lison a while before, he had noticed the injury. When they cleared the track they found that some oak sleepers left on the side of the cutting by the linesmen had been brought down across the rails by the snow and the wind, and it was quite feasible that it was in fact this that had stopped the train, for the engine had certainly halted dead up against the sleepers, and not only was the cylinder casing clearly scored, the piston rod seemed slightly out of truth. That however was the only damage visible, so that at first glance Jacques had not been too worried. Nevertheless, there might be serious trouble inside, for nothing was more delicate than the complicated valve mechanism, the very heart and soul of a locomotive. He went back to the cab, whistled, and opened her up, to try Lison's working. There was a prolonged shudder, like that of somebody shaken by a fall and slow to feel their feet again, but at last, breathing painfully, Lison moved a few turns of her driving wheels, though she was still sluggish and confused. But it was all right, she could run, she would make it, though Jacques certainly shook his head ruefully, knowing her so thoroughly as he did, for she suddenly responded strangely, seemed a different woman, had all at once grown old, mortally injured somewhere. It had happened in this snow, a heart blow, the chill of death, just as many a strong young woman suddenly goes chesty after one drenching with cold rain after a dance.

After Pecqueux had cleared the jets, Jacques whistled again. The two guards climbed aboard. Misard, Ozil and Cabuche jumped up and hung on to the front van, and the train slowly emerged from the cutting, between the double row of soldiers standing on both banks armed with their shovels. It ground along for three hundred yards, then pulled up at the crossing-watchman's cottage, to pick up the passengers who were there.

Flora had not moved away. Ozil and Cabuche stood beside her, close, while Misard was all fuss, busily touching his cap to the ladies and gentlemen who emerged from his home, and collecting gleaming coins. So at last they were saved! It had, however, taken far too long, and they were all shivering with cold, hungry and exhausted. The English lady practically carried her two girls, who were half asleep. Offering his services to the husband, the young man from Havre got into the same compartment as the dark, pretty young woman, who was very tired indeed. And as these people paddled about here and there in the snow, climbing in, one might have thought it was a demoralized army unit, so thoughtlessly they jostled each other, so indifferent were they to appearances. They were not even clean!

For a moment, at the closed window of the cottage, Aunt Phasie's face appeared, curiosity having drawn her from her bed, to drag herself across the room and peer out. Her enormous, diseased eyes drank in the scene of these wraiths now being removed from her which the storm had brought in from that moving outer world she would never see again.

Severine was the very last to come out. She turned to give Jacques a smile, and he leant out of the locomotive cab, to follow her with his gaze all the way to her compartment, while Flora, watching and waiting for this, went white as a sheet at this unruffled exchange of tenderness between them. On sudden impulse, she drew close to Ozil, whom till this instant she had always rejected, as if in the hatred which now burned her she felt need of a man.

The leading guard gave the signal, Lison responded with a mournful whistle, and this time Jacques started her up, not to halt till they reached Rouen. And suddenly, in that leering light, there was the Maufras Cross house, cock-eyed to the line, looking even more sombre and dilapidated amid all that snow, with its FOR SALE board nailed to the shuttered frontage. It was six o'clock. Night had now fallen, to wrap the white countryside in darkness, though a pale reflection which was of infinite sadness clung low to the earth, lighting all the loneliness of a ravaged land.

8

The train did not reach Paris till ten forty that evening. It stopped at
Rouen for twenty minutes, to give the passengers time for supper,
and there Severine at once wired to her husband to tell him that she
would not be back till the express of the following evening. A whole
night to spend with Jacques, the first they would pass together, locked
away between four walls, completely untrammelled, with no fear of
being disturbed!

Leaving Mantes, Pecqueux had an idea. His wife, Victoire, had
been in hospital for the past week because of a bad ankle sprain she
had sustained in falling, and as he had – as he put it with his raucous
guffaw – another bed open to him in town, he could offer his
apartment to Madame Roubaud. She would be far better there than
in one of the nearby hotels, and she could make herself at home there
right through till the following evening. Jacques immediately perceived
how convenient this would be, particularly as he had no idea where
he could have taken her. So when at Paris Severine made her way
through the crush of passengers to the engine, he advised her to
accept Pecqueux's offer, and proffered her the key which the fireman
handed him. She was inclined to hesitate and say no, because
Pecqueux's roguish grin upset her, she felt sure he knew.

'No,' she said, 'I have a cousin who'll put me up.'

'Come on now, that'll be all right,' Pecqueux at last spoke up, with
his boyish rascality glinting in his eyes. 'The bed's soft enough, I can
assure you, and it's big enough for four.'

Jacques' eyes were so persuasive that she took the key, and now,
leaning down, he whispered:

'Expect me.'

Severine needed only to go to the end of Amsterdam Street and
turn into the *cul-de-sac*, but the snow was so slippery that she had to
walk very carefully. She had the good luck to find the hall door still
unlocked, and got upstairs without even being seen by the *concierge*,
who was busy playing dominoes with another woman, and at the

fourth floor, she opened the door and closed it again so softly that she was sure none of the neighbours had any idea anyone was there. As she crossed the third-floor landing, she had clearly heard the laughter and singing at the Dauvergnes', no doubt one of the two sisters' little parties, when they had friends in, to play and sing together. And now that she had closed the door, the sombre stillness of the room was broken by the lively merriment of those young folk, still audible through the floorboards.

For a few instants, the darkness seemed absolute. She was quite startled when out of it the cuckoo-clock suddenly struck eleven with a lugubrious sonority she knew only too well. Then, her eyes growing accustomed to the dark, the two windows stood out as pale oblongs, throwing on the ceiling the white reflection of the snow. She could already see her way about and in the corner of the dresser found a box of matches where she remembered having seen some. But it was harder to find a candle. At last she came upon a stump at the bottom of a drawer. And when she had lit this, she threw a swift, uneasy glance round the room, as if to make sure she was really alone. Every object was familiar: the round table, at which she had lunch with her husband, the bed with its red cotton counterpane, on to which he had felled her with a blow of his fist. Nothing had moved, nothing changed in this room in the ten months which had passed since she was there.

Slowly, she took off her hat. But when about to take off her cloak, she shivered, and realized that it was freezing cold in the room. Beside the stove there were coals, and kindling in a box, so her first thought, before she took her coat off, was to light a fire in the stove. It distracted her, moreover, it took her mind off the uneasiness she had at first felt. This little domestic preparation for a night of love, the thought that they would soon both of them be warm, concentrated her thought on the delightful emotions of this little adventure, after so long, and when they least hoped for it, to be able to contemplate such a dream of a night.

When the stove was at last purring away, she put her mind to other little preparations. She re-arranged the chairs, she found white sheets and completely re-made the bed, a considerable task, as it really was a very large bed. Her only concern was to find nothing in the dresser sideboard to eat or drink: clearly, in the three days during which

Pecqueux had kept house he had cleaned up the last crumb. Just like the light, for there was only this little stump of candle. But going to bed does not demand much light, and now that she was nicely warm she felt very cheerful indeed, as she stood in the centre of the room, looking round to see if there was anything else she should do.

Just as she began to feel surprised that Jacques had still not turned up, a whistle took her to one of the windows. It was the 11.20 through train to Havre, about to leave. Below her, the vast area, the cutting which runs from St Lazare station to the Batignolles tunnel, was one single carpet of snow, on which one could only distinguish the rails, branching out fanwise. Engines, coaches and sheds alike were nothing but white ermine mounds, apparently asleep, while, between the clear glass of the station roofing and the girders of Europe Bridge, all fringed with snow, in the darkness the houses of Rome Street opposite stood out dirty and yellow-stained against the surrounding whiteness. The Havre train now appeared beneath her, the engine a dark towering mass, with its single headlamp, piercing the darkness with its sharp rays, and she saw it disappear under the bridge, its three red rear lamps staining the snow with blood. When she turned back into the room, for a moment she was seized with shivers: was she really alone? She thought she felt a hot breath on her neck and a rough hand sweep over her flesh – she felt it under her clothes. Her wide-open eyes again searched the room. No, there was nobody there.

Whatever was Jacques thinking of, being so late? Ten more minutes passed. Then a faint scratching, the sound of nails on wood, alarmed her, for some instants before, suddenly, she understood, and ran to open the door. It was indeed Jacques, with a bottle of malaga and a pasty!

Shaken by laughter, in a wild caress, she hung round his neck.

'Darling, aren't you a pet, to think of it!'

'Sh! sh!' Swiftly, he silenced her. Then, thinking the porter had followed him up, she lowered her voice. But as a matter of fact, Jacques had been very lucky. Just as he was about to ring, the door opened and a young girl and her mother, no doubt visitors of the Dauvergnes', came out, so he was able to slip up without anybody knowing, except that next door the newspaper-woman's door had been open and he saw her soaping some linen in a basin.

215

'Darling, we'd better not make any noise,' Jacques cautioned again, 'let's whisper.'

By way of reply, she crushed him passionately in her arms and covered his cheeks with silent kisses. She found it most thrilling to be so mysterious and began to whisper in the teeniest voice she could ever make.

'But of course, sweetie, like this, we shall make no more noise than two little mousies.'

With every possible precaution she laid the table, two plates, two glasses, two knives and when she did put a knife down noisily and it clattered against a plate she had difficulty in not bursting into loud laughter. He too, watching her, began to find it all very funny.

'I guessed you'd be hungry,' he murmured.

'I should just think I am! I'm starving. It was such a rotten meal at Rouen.'

'What if I go and see if I can raise some roast fowl somewhere about?'

'Oh, no, you might not be able to get back in again . . . No, let's make do with this!'

They at once sat down, side by side, to all intents on the same chair, and the pasty was shared between them, eaten to the last crumb, with all the little tricks of lovers. Then Severine discovered a thirst, and drained two glasses of the malaga, one straight after the other, and that really did bring the colour to her cheeks. The stove at their backs was beginning to glow red and they could feel its intense radiation, but when Jacques suddenly began to plant fat, noisy kisses in the nape of her neck, she waggled an admonishing finger.

'Sh! sh!'

They both listened. Somebody else was breaking the night silence, somebody else no doubt coming up to the Dauvergnes'. A few moments later, and a subdued throbbing sound rose, against the rhythmic background of music. Heavens! those girls had organized a regular hop. Next door the newspaper-woman came out, to pour away her water in the landing sink. Then her door banged to again. For an instant the dancing ceased and all they could hear was a train pulling out, a dull, snow-muffled rumbling, coming in through the window, together with the faint wailing sound of the locomotive whistle.

'An Auteuil train,' he murmured. 'The 11.50.' Then, in cosseting tone, soft as a breath of air: 'Well my pet, hush-a-bye? Shall us?'

She did not reply. Amid this fever of happiness she had suddenly been plunged into memories of the hours she had spent there with her husband. She found herself wondering if this pasty they had just eaten at the same table, amid the very same noises, were not really a continuation of that lunch. The objects in that room were beginning more and more to agitate her, memories overcame her. Never before had she felt such a burning desire as she did now to abandon herself completely to Jacques, and tell him everything. It was like physical desire, no longer to be differentiated from the sheer demand of sex. It even seemed to her that this would make her be still more his, that if she could but confess it all into his ear while he lay in her, she would attain the grand climax of the delight of being his. Details came to life, her husband was present with them, and she looked behind her, with the hallucination of seeing Roubaud's hirsute hand pass beyond her shoulder, to take up the knife.

'Shall us, pet, hush-a-bye?' murmured Jacques again.

She shuddered as she felt the young man's mouth crush into hers, as if, once again, he intended to seal in her confession. Silently, she rose to her feet, swiftly undressed, slipped into bed without even picking up the petticoats lying on the floor, the table too uncleared, while, flickering wildly, the candle stump guttered to its end. And when he in turn had undressed and entered the bed, there came a swift tangle of limbs, a possession so frenzied that it robbed them both of their very breath. Against the unbroken background of the music below them, without a cry, without a sound, the dead air of 'Ma' Victoire's room was galvanized by the immense, united, desperate shudder of the flesh, a spasm which reached the dizzy summit of obliteration.

By now Jacques no longer recognized in her the Severine of their first meetings, that once gentle, passive young woman with limpid blue eyes. With every day the body crowned by that sombre mass of black hair had grown more impassioned and Jacques' very arms had felt that persistent icy virginity out of which neither Grandmorin's senile perversities or Roubaud's unsubtle conjugal demands had known how to draw her, gradually thaw to life. She who had once been merely complaisant was now a creature of love who rendered

217

her flesh with no vestige of reservation and whenever her pleasure was accomplished manifested feverish gratitude. She had attained to wild enjoyment of sex, and with it a worship of this man who had at last taught her what her flesh could feel. It was the height of delight at last to clench him to her without any restraint, to hold his body hard against her breasts, to be bound herself by his two arms in a grip which at this instant even sealed her lips, so that she could not emit as much as a sigh.

When at last they opened their eyes again he was the first, astonished, to cry:

'Heavens, the candle has gone out!'

She made a little movement as if to indicate how little she cared. Then, bursting again with repressed laughter, she whispered:

'I have been a good little girl, haven't I?'

'You have indeed,' he whispered back. 'Nobody heard a thing. . . . Two real little mousies.'

They lay down again and at once she re-clasped him in her arms and snuggled close into him, pressing her nose into the hollow of his neck. Sighing luxuriously, she whispered:

'Heavens, isn't it wonderful?'

They spoke no more. The room was in darkness. They could hardly distinguish the pale rectangles of window. On the ceiling there was only the round pool of light of the stove. It glowed blood-red. Eyes wide open, both staring at it. The music now had ceased. Doors closed noisily. Gradually, the whole building sank into the ponderous peace of slumber. Below them, the Caen train coming into the station shook the turn-tables, but all sounds were dulled, and the noise reached them only faintly.

But, holding Jacques like that, Severine was soon again afire with desire, and with her lust the need to confess was also born again. For such long weeks this had been torturing her. The pool of blood-red on the ceiling grew larger. It seemed to spread, like real blood. As she watched it, she began to see things, and the objects in the room regained the gift of speech and shouted it all out loud. She felt the words come to her own lips. Borne by the wave of nervous tension which was stirring her flesh, how wonderful it would be to hide nothing more, to melt entirely into him!

'Darling, I have never told you . . .'

218

Jacques, whose eyes were equally fascinated by that pool of blood, knew very well what she was about to say. In that delicate body pressed to his and intertwined with his own, he had followed the mounting flood of that gruesome matter which lay dark between them, and of which without ever speaking of it they both constantly thought. Hitherto, out of fear of that inward tension which always used to precede his own former malaise, he had always silenced her out of apprehension too lest speaking of the blood that lay between them changed their lives. But so deep into his body had the exquisite relaxation penetrated as he lay in this warm bed, in the soft arms of this woman, that this time he was powerless even to bend his head and seal her lips with a kiss. He knew now that the die was cast, that she would insist on telling everything. Yet, when she seemed hesitant and worried, he was, in his tense expectancy, momentarily relieved.

An instant later, she drew slightly away from him and spoke.

'Darling, I have never told you,' she began again. 'Roubaud has an idea I sleep with you.'

At the very last, against her own will, in place of the confession, it was merely the memory of the night before at Havre which came to her lips.

'Hm! Think so?' he murmured, disbelievingly. 'But he seems all right. Why, he shook hands with me this morning.'

'I assure you, he knows everything. At this very instant, I am sure he is saying to himself that we are like this, loving one inside the other. I have my proofs.'

She was silent and hugged him more tightly, the happiness of love given new edge by the rancour excited by Roubaud. Then, after agitating reflection, she cried out.

'Oh, I hate him, I hate him!'

Jacques was startled. He felt no particular animosity for Roubaud. Indeed, he found the man most accommodating.

'But whyever?' he demanded. 'He's not much in our way.'

She did not answer. She merely repeated her hatred.

'I hate him . . . It's come to torture merely to feel him beside me. Oh, if only I could, how gladly I would escape, and be with you for ever.'

He was moved by this burst of passionate sentiment, and now drew her closer to him, from foot to shoulder her flesh against his, all his.

219

But once again, thus fused in him, almost without withdrawing her lips from his neck, she murmured:

'Dearest, that's because you don't know . . .'

This then was to be the confession, the inevitable confession, it was coming out. This time he saw quite clearly, nothing in the world would hold it back, for he sensed that in her this avowal grew out of her desperate desire again to be taken, again possessed. Not a breath more was to be heard in the whole house, even the newspaper-woman was sound asleep. Outside, Paris buried under snow was enveloped in silence, not a cab wheel to be heard. The last Havre train, which left at 0.20 A.M. seemed to have carried with it the last trace of life in the station. In the stove flames no longer leapt noisily, the fire was all of hot cinders, slowly collapsing, casting that rounded red stain on to the ceiling. It was like a horrified eye. The room was so hot now that a heavy, stifling fog seemed to weigh down that bed in which these two, their passion satiated, still interlaced their limbs.

'Darling, the truth is, you don't know . . .'

To which, automatically, he responded.

'But yes, yes, I do.'

'No, you may suspect, but you cannot know.'

'I know he did it to get that legacy of yours.'

She started. She could not help it, a hysterical little laugh broke from her.

'Oh yes, yes, his legacy!'

And then, in a low voice, so low that an insect buzzing on the window-pane would have made more noise, she told him of her childhood in Judge Grandmorin's household. At first she thought she would prevaricate and not admit all the things she did with that old man, then succumbed to the demands of frankness, finding assuagement, almost delight, in telling him it all. After that, her soft murmur flowed on and on, inexhaustible.

'Just think, it was here, in this very room, last February, remember, just when he had that bit of trouble about the deputy-prefect . . . We had just had a very nice little lunch, like our supper just now, at that table. Of course, then he still knew nothing, I did not want to tell him about it . . . But all over a ring, an old present, which Grandmorin made me for no particular purpose, I don't really know how, suddenly

220

he saw through it all . . . Oh, darling, never, never could you imagine how vilely he treated me then.'

She shivered and he felt her slender fingers stiffen on his naked flesh.

'With one blow of his fist, he knocked me down . . . And then he dragged me about by my hair . . . And then, he held his heel over my face, as if he was going to crush it in. Dearest, as long as I live, I shall never forget it . . . And he kept on hitting me, oh dear God, and if I told you all the things he insisted on knowing. You see, I am frank, telling you it all, I'm not telling you because I have to, am I, but because I want to, yet darling, I tell you, I could never bring myself even to hint all the filthy questions he made me answer, if I didn't he would have slaughtered me, that's dead sure. I suppose he must have loved me and it hurt him terribly when he found all that out, and I admit it would have been more decent of me if I had told him before we were married, but you must see my point of view, it was all so far back, all forgotten, only a real savage could have been so mad with jealousy . . . Tell me, dearest one, are you going to stop loving me because you now know it all?'

Jacques had throughout been still as stone, lifeless, considering it all, in the arms of this woman who pressed close into his bosom and his loins, so that they were like snakes knotted together. He was in fact very astonished, he had never suspected anything at all like this. How this did complicate it all, whereas that legacy would have been sufficient by itself to explain the murder away. Nevertheless, he did prefer it so, the thought that Severine and her husband had not killed for money did relieve his mind of the tinge of scorn which under Severine's kisses had at times clouded his heart.

'Me, stop loving you,' he murmured, 'why ever should I? I don't care a fig about your past. That's not my business . . . You are Roubaud's wife, but you might equally well have been anybody else's.'

There was a silence. They clung to each other to the point of suffocation. He could feel her nipples rise, hard points on her round breasts, pressing into his side.

'So that's it,' he murmured. 'You were that old judge's mistress, were you. Well it certainly is a queer business!'

Here she drew herself slowly up him till her lips met his mouth, to kiss and as she did so murmur:

'I don't love anyone else but you, dearest one, I never loved anyone before you ... Ugh! Those others! If only you knew! With them, darling, I merely giimpsed what love might be. But you, my love, have taught me real happiness.'

With deliberate caresses, she begin to excite him, offering herself, desiring him, her fingers seeking wildly for him and taking him into her again, but though he too was afire with desire just as she was, he was forced to hold himself back, and to do so he gripped her as in a vice.

'No,' he cried. 'Not yet, wait, wait ... Tell me ... So that was why you ... why old Grandmorin was ...'

Scarce audible, drawn from the shuddering depths of her, she confessed:

'Yes. Then we killed him.'

The surge of desire merged into a new surge, the surge of death, reborn in her, the throes which came at the height of every orgasm, again possessed her. For some moments she was stifled by a drawn-out dizziness, before, once more plunging her muzzle into the hollow of her lover's neck, she continued her whisper:

'He made me write to the judge to take the same express that we were taking, but not to let us see he was there till Rouen ... I huddled into my corner. I was shivering from head to foot. I was horrified by the misfortune into which we were rushing. Opposite him he had a woman in black who never spoke and frightened me terribly. I could not even see her features, but I felt that she could read our brains and was well aware what we were going to do ... The whole two hours from Paris to Rouen passed like that. I did not say a word, I did not stir, I shut my eyes to pretend to myself that I was asleep. I felt him at my side. He too never once stirred, which was oh! so horrible to bear, when I knew the awful thoughts revolving in his head, but could not even guess exactly what he had made up his mind to do ... Oh, that journey, with that swarm of thoughts whirling, amid all the whistling and the jolting and the grinding of the wheels!'

Jacques, his mouth buried in the thick, scented fleece of her hair, at regular intervals automatically implanted long kisses on her crown. Then he murmured:

'But as you were not in the same compartment, however did you manage to do it?

For of course, there was no connection between compartment and compartment.

'Wait, I'll tell you it all . . . My husband had his plan, though, as a matter of fact, it was sheer luck that it came off. You see, there was a ten minutes' stop at Rouen. We got out and just as if we wanted to stretch our legs, he made me walk as far as the judge's compartment, which was a coupé. There, he pretended to be astonished, seeing the judge in the doorway, just as if he had not known that he was on the train. There was a big crowd on the platform, and a big rush of people for the third-class coaches, because of the festivities there were to be at Havre the following day. When they began shutting the doors, it was the judge who suggested we should get in with him. I stammered something about our travelling-case, but he insisted, said it was safe enough, nobody would steal it, and we could go back when we got to Barentin, because he was getting out there anyway. For a moment I thought my husband was really worried and was going to run back for the case, but just then the guard whistled. That made his mind up, he pushed me in, got in himself, and closed the window. There were people running everywhere, the station officials all excitement. So there just wasn't a single person who really noticed what happened. And then the train pulled out.'

She was silent for a while, seeing it all again in her mind's eye. Quite automatically, a tendon began to pluck in her right thigh and her loosely outstretched limbs rhythmically rubbed the young man's knee.

'Oh, that first moment in that little half compartment, when I felt the ground rushing away beneath us. I was utterly unable to think. My mind could not get away from our case. How were we to get it back? Would it not give us away, now we had left it in the other carriage? It all seemed so foolish, impossible, a nightmare murder, all childish imagination, a murder which anybody would be mad to commit. But I made an effort to calm myself. I persuaded myself my husband would shrink from it. It would never be, could not be. But no, merely seeing him talking to the judge made it clear to me that his mind was unshaken in its ferocity. Yet outwardly he remained quite calm, even chatted cheerfully, in his usual lively way. It could only

223

have been in the steely glance he turned on me from time to time that I read his stubbornness and determination. He would kill Grandmorin in another mile or so, at some point he had decided on, but which I did not know. It was unquestionable. It even blazed out of his eyes when he looked at the judge, the man who so soon would cease to exist. I did not speak, my whole inside shivered and I was trying to hide it, pretending to smile whenever they looked my way. You may well ask why it never occurred to me to prevent it all. But it was only later, when I tried to fathom it all out, that I was astounded I never shouted out of the window or pulled the alarm cord. But at the actual time I seemed to be paralysed, I felt myself absolutely powerless to move. No doubt I thought my husband was in the right, and as I am telling you everything, I ought to confess this too: despite myself, I was through and through with Roubaud against that other man because, you see, I had been loved by them both, and one was young, whereas the other, *ugh*! Jacques, oh! that old man's awful way of making love . . . Besides, do we ever know our own minds? We often do things we would have said we never could do, don't we? When I think that I could never bleed a chicken! Oh that frightful feeling, like a stormy night, that terrible night which cried out of my very inside!'

And in that moment Jacques sensed that this fragile young woman, so slender in his arms, had become dense, impenetrable, like the black depths of which she spoke. In vain he could enlace her more tightly, she was impenetrable now to him. But this story of murder, whispered broken in their embracement, made him all fever, and he insisted.

'Tell me then, did you help kill the old bastard yourself?'

'I was in a corner seat,' she continued, without taking any notice of him. 'There was my husband between me and him. He was in the far corner seat. They were talking about the elections which were due . . . Every now and then, I saw my husband lean forward and peer out, to make sure where we were. He seemed impatient . . . Every time, I followed his glance and at the same time noticed how far we had gone. It was not a very dark night, the trees flashed by clearly, and all the time there were the wheels grinding. They had never sounded like that before, it was a frightful din, all angry, menacing voices and eerie cries of animals bellowing at death. The train was running at top speed. Suddenly lights flashed and the rattle echoed

224

against the buildings of a station. It was Maromme. We were already over five miles from Rouen. Next came Malaunay, then Barentin. So when was it going to be done? Did he have to wait to the very last minute? I lost all sense of time and distance, I just let myself be swept on senselessly, I felt like a stone falling noisily through the night when, as we swept through Malaunay, I suddenly understood: it was to be in the tunnel, one kilometre from there . . . I looked at Roubaud . . . Our eyes met! Yes, in the tunnel! Two minutes to go! . . . The train rushed on, we passed the Dieppe fork, I caught sight of the signalman at his post. There are slopes there, where I definitely thought I saw men waving their arms, shouting at us. Then came a long whistle from the engine. It was the tunnel entrance. And when the train plunged in, what a roar there was against that low-pitched vaulting. You know what I mean, that metallic clanging, like hammers on an anvil, and in that mad moment I turned it all into peals of thunder rolling.'

She shivered like a leaf, then broke off to resume, in quite a different voice, almost laughing:

'Isn't it ridiculous, sweetie, I can still feel the chill of it right inside my bones. Yet I am quite warm, and so gloriously happy, here with you . . . Besides, as you know, there's nothing more to fear, they've given up the case, not to mention that the big-wigs of the Government are even less anxious than we are to bring it into the open . . . That's the truth of it. I'm not worried.' Then, laughing outright, she added; 'I can tell you, my poppet, you gave us a jolly good scare . . . And now we come to it, tell me, I've always wondered, how much of it did you really see?'

'Why, what I told old Denizet, of course, that's all: one man cutting another man's throat . . . You two were so queer about it that in the end I doubted my own eyes. There was a moment when I did think I recognized Roubaud . . . As a matter of fact, though, I was not really sure till much later . . .'

She interrupted him excitely.

'I know, in the Batignolles Gardens, that day I said *no*, remember? The first time we were ever here in Paris alone together. Isn't it funny! I remember I said it was not us and I knew quite well you understood the opposite. Anyone would have thought I'd already told you, really, wouldn't they, darling? Sweetie, I have often thought

225

about it, I really believe, you know, that that is when I fell in love with you.'

There was an upsurge of emotion between them, they crushed close, seeming to fuse, and she resumed:

'The train was running in the tunnel. It is a very long tunnel. It takes three minutes. I could have sworn we had been in it an hour. . . . The judge had stopped talking, because of the frightful clatter of all that iron. And at that last moment my husband must have weakened for a moment, because he made no sign to move, except in the flickering light of the lamp I suddenly saw his ears go purple . . . Was he going to wait for open country again? From then on, it was so much destiny, destiny, so inevitable, that my only longing was to be relieved of the agony of expectation, to be free. Why then did he not do it, now he was to do it? I was so torn by fear and strain that I could have taken the knife myself, to be done with it . . . Roubaud shot me a glance. My thoughts must have been written on my face. And suddenly he flung himself on Grandmorin, who had turned to the window, and grabbed him by the shoulder. Grandmorin of course tried to shake him off. He was frightened and reached up for the alarm signal. His fingers had just reached it, when Roubaud got at him and brought him down on the seat with such a crash that he was doubled in two. He was flabbergasted. He was terrified and opened his mouth, but he only uttered indistinct cries, and the noise of the train in the tunnel swallowed them up. But I distinctly heard Roubaud repeating: "You swine, you swine, you swine," in a wheezy voice, but so fiercely, terribly fiercely. Then the noise suddenly lifted, the train came out of the tunnel, the countryside appeared again, all dusk and trees flashing by . . . I stayed in my corner, stiff, pressing against the antimaccassar as long as I could. How long did the struggle last? Only very few seconds. But to me it seemed it would never end, that all the passengers on that train must be hearing Grandmorin's cries, that the trees could see us. All this time, though Roubaud had the open knife ready, he could not strike, because Grandmorin was kicking so. Then my husband staggered, nearly fell to his knees, the train rocked so, rushing us on at top speed and the engine whistling as we drew near to Maufras Cross . . . It was then that I flung myself on the struggling man's legs, and I never have remembered how I came to do it. But it's a fact. I just let myself fall on him like a bundle. I crushed his legs

226

down with all my weight, I prevented him kicking. But I did not see a thing. I only felt it: I mean the thud as the knife went through into his throat and the drawn-out shudder of the body. Death came in three big hiccoughs, like a broken watch running down . . . Ugh! I can still feel those death throes in my bones!'

Jacques was all eagerness to ask questions, and would have interrupted, but she insisted on rushing on.

'No, wait a moment . . . Just as I was getting up, we passed Maufras Cross at top speed. I distinctly saw the shuttered front of the house, then the crossing-keeper's hut. There were two and a half or three miles more to go before we reached Barentin . . . The body lay crumpled up on the seat, the blood gushing out in a regular flood, and my husband stood there, speechless, staring at it, while the train shook him and he wiped the knife on his handkerchief. That lasted a minute without either of us doing a thing to save ourselves. And if we kept the body there with us or stayed in that compartment, there was a chance of everything being discovered when we stopped at Barentin . . .

'But then I saw that Roubaud had put the knife back into his pocket, and seemed to come back to reality. I saw him run his fingers over Grandmorin's pockets, take his watch, his money, all he could find. Then he opened the door and tried to push the body out, without getting hold of him at all, because of the blood.

'"Come on, there, help me," he cried, "Let's push together." I made not the slightest attempt, I had no control left of my limbs. "God in Heaven!" he cried, "will you push, or won't you?" The head went out first and dangled down on the running-board, but the body doubled up and got stuck. And all the time, the train was rushing on. Suddenly, with a stronger heave, the corpse tipped up, then vanished in the grinding of the wheels.

'"Ah! The swine! That's done!" he cried. Then he gathered up the judge's travelling rug and threw that too out of the door. There remained only us, standing there, and the pool of blood on the seat, where we dared not sit down again, and the door still swinging open. I did not understand at once, I was so exhausted and confused, when I saw him getting out. He vanished for a time. Then he came back. "Come on, quick, follow me, unless you want us both to lose our heads." I did not stir. He lost patience.

227

'"Good God!" he cried, "are you coming? Our compartment is empty, we shall go back to it." Our compartment empty. Did this mean that he had really been there? That woman in black, who did not speak, whose face you couldn't see, was he sure she had not stayed in the corner? "Will you come along," he shouted at me. "If not, I'll tip you out like I did him!" He had got back inside. He was livid with rage and very rough with me. So I found myself out on the running-board, clinging to the brass hand-rail. He got out after me, and shut the door ever so carefully. "Get along, get along," he shouted. But I was afraid to move, I was overcome with the dizziness, rushing along as we were, with the wind lashing at me, a gale was getting up, my hair began to come undone, I thought my numb fingers would never hold that rail. "Get along, God damn you!" he cried, and kept pushing me. So I had to go on, hand over hand, clinging to the carriage side, my skirts flapping all round me, entangling in my legs. Away far ahead, beyond a curve, you could see the lights of Barentin station, and the engine began to whistle. "Get along, God damn you!" he nagged.

'Oh, what hellish din and terror I was in as I crept along. I felt as if the gale had taken hold of me and was whirling me about like a piece of straw, to smash me far away there against a wall. Behind me the countryside rushed at mad gallop, the trees spun, twisted one after the other. They seemed to gasp with horror. At the end of the carriage, when I had to stride out to reach the running-board of the next one and get hold of the next hand rail, I stopped and lost courage. I should never be able to do it. "Get along, God damn you!" he shouted and leapt at me and pushed me. I closed my eyes. I do not know how I got across, it was only instinct, I was like an animal which gets its claws in, and refuses to fall. Another thing I cannot tell is how we were not seen. We had to go along three coaches, and one of them was a third-class and crammed full. I recall the ranks of the heads clearly lit by the lamp. I believe I should recognize them if I ever met them, particularly one of a stout man with red side-whiskers, and those of two young girls, leaning forward laughing. And I kept hearing "Get along, God damn you! Get along, God damn you!" I gave up. Barentin lights drew close. The engine whistled. My last impression is of being dragged, tugged, lifted up, by the hair. He had to grab hold of me, open the door over my shoulders, and heave me into the compartment. There I was, out of breath, only half conscious, in a corner, when suddenly, the train stopped, and without moving a muscle, I heard him exchange a few words with the Barentin station-master. Only when the train had started again did he sink to the seat. He was exhausted too. We did not speak a word all the rest of the way to Havre. Darling, how I hate him, how I hate him, for all the horrible things he made me go through. But you, my sweetest one, I love you, you have brought me so much happiness.'

After the violent climax of this long story, this cry of Severine's expressed all her cravings to be possessed by him amid such foul memories. But though Jacques was burning like her, she had shaken him to the core, and he hesitated.

'No, just a moment. So you lay on Grandmorin's legs and felt him die?'

That unknown something was stirring to new life in him, a force surging in frenzied waves from his very bowels, veiling everything with scarlet. He was obsessed with sheer inquisitiveness about the details of the act.

'The knife, tell me, did you actually feel it go in?'

'Yes, a sort of thud.'

'I see . . . A sort of thud . . . No feeling of cutting? Sure?'

'Oh no! Only a sort of thud.'

'Then he heaved back, you said, didn't you?'

'Yes, three times. *Ugh!* From one end of his body to the other, such drawn-out heaves I could follow them through, down to his feet.'

'And those heaves stiffened him, did they?'

'Yes, the first very strong, the others feebler.'

'And then he was dead. Now what exactly did you get out of that, I mean, feeling him dead like that, by a knife blow?'

'Me? I . . . I don't really know.'

'You don't really know? Why lie about it? Do tell me what you got out of it, everything, come on . . . Did it hurt?'

'Oh no, it didn't hurt.'

'Pleasure?'

'Pleasure? Why, darling no, of course not, not pleasure.'

'Then what, my love? Do tell me! Everything! I beg you! If you only knew . . . Tell me what anybody feels when they do it!'

'Good Heavens, can such things be told? It is terrible. You feel, oh, you feel so far away! I went through more in that minute than in all my life before.'

Only now, teeth tight closed, able only to stammer incoherently, Jacques took her and she him too, and again they possessed one another, finding love in the depths of death, in a spasm of accomplishment as fraught with agony as that of those creatures to whom copulation spells evisceration. The only sound was their hoarse breathing. The blood-like glow on the ceiling had now vanished. The stove was going out. The room grew chill in harmony with the bitter frost outside. From snow-muffled Paris not a voice was to be heard. For a few moments there were snores from the newspaper-woman's room, next door, then everything was blotted out in a dark gulf as that tenement house slept.

Suddenly Jacques, who had kept Severine in his arms, felt too her succumbing as if thunder-struck to impenetrable sleep. The journey, the long wait in the Misards' cottage and now this fevered night, had slain her. Whispering a baby good-night, she was already breathing evenly, gone from this world. The cuckoo-clock had just struck three.

For more than another hour, Jacques kept her on his left arm, which gradually became numbed. He was unable to close his eyes. Every time he tried to shut them in sleep an invisible hand seemed stubbornly to force them open in the darkness. He could no longer make out any object in that room engulfed in night. All was uniformly black, stove, furniture, walls. Only when he turned did he see the two pallid rectangles of window immobile and immaterial as in dream.

Physically exhausted though he was, he was kept awake by incredible cerebral activity, for ever unravelling the same tangle of ideas. Every time that by effort he thought he had sunk to sleep, the same haunting thoughts reappeared, the same pictures flashed before him, awakening the same reactions. And while his staring eyes filled with the shadows, this scene which with machine-like regularity whirled through him, was the murder, in all its detail. It kept coming back, again and again, unchanging, all-pervading, maddening. The knife entered with a dull thud, the body gave three long heaves, life gushed out in a flood of warm blood, a red flood which he could imagine streaming over his own hands. Twenty times, thirty times, the knife entered and the body jerked. It all loomed over him, stifled him,

230

expanding till the night itself exploded. How wonderful it would be to deal such a knife blow as that, thus satisfy that deep-down longing, know what one really experiences in the act of killing, taste those instants in which one lives more than in all one's life before!

As this sense of suffocation increased, it occurred to Jacques that it was merely the weight of Severine on his arm that was preventing him from sleeping. Gently, he freed it, laid her beside him, without wakening her. Eased for a moment, he breathed more freely, thinking that sleep would come at last. But despite his efforts those invisible fingers again raised his eyelids, and there in the blackness was the murder, the knife entering, the body heaving. Red rain shot through the darkness, the wound in the throat, gaping wide, was like the wedge-shaped cut of a hatchet.

He gave up struggling, lay on his back, prey to this persistent vision. He seemed to hear the brain-engine racing in his skull. It all sprang from his early youth. But he had thought himself cured, for with the possession of this woman months back that urge had ceased, yet he had never before felt it so powerfully as when now stirred up by this murder, which, while pressed to him, flesh to flesh, legs intertwined, she had whispered in his ear. He had drawn away from her, avoided her touch, because the least contact of her skin scorched him. An unbearable burning crept up his spine, as if the mattress under his loins had turned into a grill. At the nape of his neck there were prickings like points of fire. For a moment he tried putting his arms out of bed, but they were chilled immediately and made him shiver. He was seized with fear of his hands, he drew them back in, first folding them on his stomach, then, to crush them, sliding them under his buttocks, imprisoning them there, as if in terror lest they do some foul thing, an act which he repugned but was forced to commit.

Every time the cuckoo-clock struck, Jacques counted the hour. He longed for daylight, in the hope that it would drive the nightmare away, and because of this he turned over to face and watch the windows. But there was still only the faint light of the snow to be seen. At a quarter to five, only forty minutes late, he heard the through train from Havre come in, which proved that traffic had been resumed. But it was not till after seven that he saw the windows whiten, with slow, milky light. At last the room was lit by that faint luminosity in which furniture seems to float. The stove reappeared, followed by the cupboard and the sideboard. He was still unable to close his eyes. On the contrary. The light exacerbated them, but he felt he had to see. Suddenly, before it was quite light, he more guessed than saw, on the table, the knife he had used the evening before to cut the pasty. Then he could see nothing else but the knife, a small knife, a pointed one. The growing daylight, all the whitish light of the two windows now poured in solely to find reflection in that slender blade. And his fear of his own hands made him thrust them still deeper under him, for he felt them too exacerbated, too rebellious, more powerful than his will. Would they now cease to be his, to turn into hands coming to him from another man, hands which were the legacy of an ancestor of the age when men roamed the woods wild and strangled animals?

So as not to see the knife, Jacques turned towards Severine. She was sleeping very peacefully, with the breathing of a child, utterly worn out. Her heavy black hair, falling loose, made a dark pillow for her head and tumbled over her shoulders, while under her chin, among those locks, was revealed her bosom of milky, rose-tinted fineness. He gazed at her as if she were a complete stranger. Yet he adored her, bore her image within him wherever he went, desiring her, sometimes to the point of pain, even when he was driving his Lison. Indeed, one day he had come to himself as out of a dream, rushing at full speed through a station, against the signals.

Now the vision of this bosom absorbed him with sudden fascination from which there was no escaping and within him, with horror of which he was still conscious, he felt grow the imperious need to get up and take that knife from the table and return, to thrust it into that female flesh to the hilt. He heard the dull thud of the knife as it entered, he saw the body heave three times, then stiffen in death, with a red flood gushing from it . . . Struggling, striving to escape from this haunting vision, with every second he lost more of his will, so overcome by the one single idea that he reached the very extreme at which, defeated, one gives way to the drive of sheer instinct.

Everything grew confused. His hands, in revolt, triumphing over his attempt to conceal them, broke loose and escaped from him. And he realized so clearly that from now on he was no longer their master, that if he continued to look at the woman his hands would drive on to their brutal self-satisfaction, that with his last remaining strength he

232

flung himself from the bed and rolled on the floor like a drunken man. Then he picked himself up, nearly to fall again, tripping in the pile of petticoats on the floor. Staggering, he felt wildly about for his clothes, his one thought to dress quickly, take that knife and go out to kill some other woman, in the street.

This time his desire was too painful, he must do this thing at last. He could not find his trousers. Three times he took them up before he realized that he had done so. Putting on his shoes caused him infinite trouble. He was shivering with fever. But at last he was dressed, had taken the knife and slipped it into his sleeve, convinced he would kill some female, the first he should meet in the street, when a rustle of linen and a long sigh coming from the bed, halted him. He stood by the table still frozen, bloodless. Severine was wakening. She murmured.

'Whatever is it, darling, you going out already?'

He made no answer, did not look at her, hoping she would go to sleep again.

'But wherever are you going, darling?'

'It's nothing,' he stammered. 'I must go on duty . . . You sleep on, I'll be back.'

Then sleep overcame her again, she murmured something incomprehensible, her eyes had closed again.

'Oh, how sleepy I am, how sleepy . . . Come, kiss me, darling.'

But he did not stir, for he knew that if he went back with that knife in his hand, if he saw her again but for an instant, so delicate, so lovely, in her unkempt nakedness, it would be the end of the will which held him still, so close to her. Despite his will, the hand would then be raised, to plant the knife in her throat.

'Darling, come, kiss me . . .'

Her voice faded out, she was asleep again, so gently murmuring a caress. Aghast, he opened the door and fled.

It was eight o'clock when Jacques found himself on the pavement of Amsterdam Street. The snow was still unswept, and the steps of the very few people to be abroad were muffled. But immediately, there was an elderly woman. She, however, turned down into London Street and he did not follow her. A number of men brushed past him. He made his way down the street to Havre Square, the knife in his hand, but with the point thrust out of sight up his sleeve. When a

233

young girl of about fourteen emerged from a house opposite, he crossed the road, only to see her slip into the baker's next door. He was so worked up that he did not wait, he rushed on, searching for another. From the moment he went out with that knife he had ceased to direct his actions, it was the other man in command, the man he had so many times felt stirring uneasily within him, the stranger from far away, burning with the hereditary thirst to kill. That other had killed before and he wanted to kill again. And all about Jacques thus passed in a dream, because everything now reached his senses solely through his obsession. His normal life seemed blotted out, he walked as a sleep-walker walks, his past life unknown to him, his future obscured, only the compulsive present known, and in that moving body the personality was totally absent. Two women who overtook him and brushed close by him made him quicken his pace. He had just caught up with these, however, when a man stopped them, and all three chatted and laughed. Put off by this stranger, he began to trail another woman, a shy, poor-looking little figure wrapped in a black shawl, who was passing. She took tiny steps, no doubt towards a task she detested, hard work, meanly paid, for there was no hurry in her and she looked desperately unhappy. Nor was he in any hurry, now he had his victim, but waited for the right spot, to strike at his ease. She must have noticed that she was being followed by the young man, and turned to look at him with inexpressible outrage that anybody could be after her. She had already led him as far as halfway along Havre Street, and twice had turned round at him, just in time to prevent him slitting her throat with the knife, which he had now slipped out of his sleeve. Her eyes were those of sheer poverty, such pleading eyes. He would strike at the bottom of the street, just as she stepped off the pavement. Then all at once, he swung round and began to pursue another woman, walking the other way, for no particular reason, unintending, turning on to her just because she came along and he had to follow her instead of the other.

Following this victim, Jacques drew near the station again. This one was an agile little person with smart little steps, adorably pretty too, no more than twenty, already plump, a fair girl with lovely dancing eyes which laughed on life. She had not even noticed that she was being followed by a man. She must have been in a hurry, for she tripped nimbly up the steps on the Havre side. She scurried

234

through the big departure hall, almost at a run, rushed up to the suburban ticket office and asked for a first to Auteuil. Jacques bought one too, then followed her through the waiting room on to the platform and into the train, where he sat down beside her. The train pulled out immediately. 'I've got time,' he said to himself, 'I will kill her in the tunnel.'

But an old lady opposite them, the only other person to get in, had just recognized the young woman.

'You, of all people,' she cried. 'And wherever are you off to, so early?'

The other laughed cheerfully and with a wry gesture, said:

'Well, well, I might have known I should have to meet somebody who knew me. I hope you won't give me away ... Tomorrow's my husband's birthday, so the moment he left for his office, off I went, I'm going to a gardener out at Auteuil, where he saw an orchid which he simply craves to have ... I want to make him a surprise, of course.'

The elderly lady nodded with good-natured approval.

'Is baby all right?'

'Oh, my little daughter's a real pet ... I weaned her, you know, just a week ago. You should just see her wolfing her soup. ... We're all three frightfully well, shockingly so.'

She laughed still more heartily, revealing teeth dazzling white between full-blooded lips. Jacques, who was on her right, holding the knife behind his thigh, told himself now that this was the right moment to strike. He had only to half turn round and raise the knife and there she was, just in the right position. Then, in the Batignolles tunnel, he remembered her bonnet ribbons. 'The knot,' he thought, 'the knot will get in the way, I'm sure it will.'

The two women went on chatting merrily.

'Anyone can see you are very happy.'

'Happy? Oh, if only I could tell you. It's like a dream. Two years ago, I was nothing. Remember how dull life was at my aunt's, and not a penny of dowry ... When he came, I used to shake all over, I so wanted to love him, but he was so handsome and so rich. ... And now he is mine, my hubby, and we have a baby! I tell you, it is too good!'

When he examined that bonnet-ribbon bow, Jacques now realized

235

that under it there was a big gold locket on a black velvet ribbon. He weighed everything up. 'If I take hold of her neck with my left hand, all I have to do is brush that locket aside and there's her throat all bare.'

But every minute or so the train stopped at a station. One short tunnel came after another, Coucelles, Neuilly. In a moment! It only needs a second!

'Did you go to the seaside last summer?' the elderly lady asked.

'Yes. Brittany, for six whole weeks, oh, such an out of the way little place, so unspoilt. Then we spent September in Poitou, at my father-in-law's, he has a lot of woodland down there.'

'But weren't you going to the Riviera for the winter?'

'Yes, we're going to Cannes, about the fifteenth . . . We have taken a house. It has a lovely little garden, facing the sea. We've sent somebody down to get everything ready for us . . . Not that we're exactly chilly mortals, either of us, but it's so good to have the sun. We shall be back in March, of course. Next year, we shall stay in Paris, then, in two years' time, when baby is a big girl, we shall travel. I don't know whether I'm on my head or my heels. It's all holiday.'

She was so bubbling over with happiness that in her expansiveness she even turned to Jacques, a complete stranger, to give him a smile. The movement of her head pulled the bonnet-ribbon aside, this disturbed the locket, and he saw the velvety skin of her neck, the hollows gilded by shadow, and his fingers stiffened on the knife handle, while he made an irrevocable resolution. 'There, that's the spot where I shall strike. Yes, in a moment, in the tunnel, before we reach Passy.'

But at the Trocadéro station a railwayman got in who knew him and at once began talking shop, all about the recent conviction of a driver and his mate for stealing coal, and after that, everything was confusion, and afterwards he never did get clear what happened. There was more laughter, more radiant happiness, so intense that it filled his very soul and made him drowsy. He may have gone all the way to Auteuil with those two women, he certainly could not recall their getting out. All he knew was finding himself on the bank of the Seine without knowing how he got there. His only clear memory was of standing on the bank high up, and throwing the knife into the river. After that, oblivion, his body mindless. Even that other mind had gone, together with the knife. He must have tramped for hours through streets and squares, blindly. There were people, there were endless houses, veṛy faint. He must have gone in somewhere, taking a meal in a large room full of people – he had a clear memory of white plates. He also had the persistent impression of a red placard on a shop which was closed, after which everything dissolved into blackness, a gulf of nothingness, devoid of time and space, where he lay inert, maybe for centuries.

When he came to, he was in his little Cardinet Street room, collapsed crosswise across his bed, fully dressed. Instinct had brought him there, like a fagged-out dog to its kennel. He did not even recall climbing the stairs, let alone going to bed. He awakened from dead sleep, startled by the sudden return of consciousness, he might have been unconscious. He could not tell whether he had slept three hours or three days, till suddenly it all came back to him: the night spent with Severine, her murder confession, his rushing out like a carnivorous animal in search of blood.

He had been out of himself, but now he returned, staggered by all that had taken place apart from his will. Then, suddenly realizing that Severine must even now be waiting for him brought him leaping to his feet. He glanced at his watch, saw it was already four. His head empty, calm as if he had been well bled, he hastened back to the *cul-de-sac* of Amsterdam Street.

Severine had slept through to midday without stirring. Then, waking up, and startled to find him no longer there, she had re-lit the stove. Dressed, but dying of hunger, she at last brought herself to go down to a nearby restaurant. She had now only just come in again after some shopping errands, when Jacques appeared.

'Oh, darling, how you have worried me!' she cried, and clung to his neck, gazing close into his eyes. 'Whatever happened?'

Exhausted, cold too, he soothed her without a hint of worry.

'Trifles,' he said. 'Just a dull job down at the locomotive shops. Once they get hold of you, there's no getting away.'

Then, ever so abjectly, wheedling him, in almost a whisper:

'Just think, and me imagining . . . Oh, such horrid thoughts, I was so worried . . . I don't know, I thought, after all I confessed to you, perhaps you would want no more of me . . . So I began to think you had left me and would never, never come back.'

237

Tears overcame her, she burst into a fit of sobbing, and clung desperately to him.

'Dearest one, oh, if only you knew how I need your kindness . . . Love me, oh do love me, dearest, I tell you only your love can make me forget . . . Now I have told you all my troubles, you can't leave me, can you, darling, please!'

This display of feeling entirely overcame Jacques. Gradually, all his defences collapsed and he was as wax. He stammered:

'Sweetest, of course not, I love you, you must not worry.'

Shattered himself by the destiny of the hateful urge which had again taken possession of him, and from which he would never recover, he broke down and wept with her. It was such degradation, such limitless bleakness of outlook.

'You love me too!' he cried. 'Love me as I love you! Love me with all your strength, because I have just as much need of you!'

A shudder shook her. She wanted to know all about it.

'You have troubles too? You must tell me.'

'Not troubles, no, not that. Intangible things, fits of melancholy which make me frightfully miserable, yet I can never describe to you.'

They clutched each other in fast embrace, commingling the terrible sadness of their sad state. Life was all pain, unforgettable pain, merciless, and they wept, feeling at the mercy of blind life forces, constant struggle and death.

'Come,' said Jacques, freeing himself at last, 'it is time we thought of going . . . This evening you will be back there.'

After a silence, during which she stared dismally into space, Severine murmured:

'Were I but free, were Roubaud no longer alive . . . Oh, how quickly we might forget it all!'

Violently thrusting the thought from him, Jacques said, slowly and clearly:

'Yet we cannot possibly kill him.'

She stared at him, statuesque, and he shivered through and through, astonished himself at what he had said, for he had never of his own volition argued out such a thought. For, if he had an urge to kill, why indeed not that man, the creature who stood in their path? As at last he was leaving to run down to the locomotive sheds, she took him in her arms again, covering him with kisses.

'Dearest sweet, do love me! I shall love you now more than ever. . . . Run along, we are going to be so happy!'

9

During the days immediately following, Severine and Jacques were extremely cautious. Indeed, they were anxious. For now Roubaud knew all, was he not going to spy on them, to catch them at it and suddenly have his revenge, coarse working-class type that he was? Their minds went back to the jealous fury he had already shown, to his brutality. At bottom he was always the coarse porter he had once been, the physical labourer always ready to resort to bare knuckles. There was indeed no mistaking his appearance, as they saw him. He was dour and dumb, a preoccupied worried look in the eyes, from which they concluded that he must be cogitating some savagely dirty trick, some trap, indeed, by which to get them into his power. So for the first month they only met subject to a thousand precautions, and were ever on the alert.

Roubaud was certainly increasingly out of the house, though, of course, one could never be sure, those absences might be merely the prelude to a sudden return, to catch them in each other's arms. However, their fears were never justified. On the contrary, Roubaud's absence began to be so persistent that he was in fact never there at all. He made off the moment duty ended and he did not return till on the stroke of taking over again. Weeks when he was on day duty, he came in at ten, to wolf a scrap of lunch in five minutes, and after that never showed his face till he turned up for a midday meal, while in the evening, when five o'clock came round and his counterpart took over, he simply cleared out, often for the whole night. He scarcely took any sleep, and the same thing became the rule even when he was on night duty, for then he was free from five A.M., and must have taken his meals out. At least, he never returned before it was time to go on duty, at five in the evening. For a considerable time, despite this irregular living, he continued to be a most punctual officer of the company, always present on the dot, sometimes, it is true, so fagged out that he could scarcely stand, yet there nonetheless, and conscientious about his duties too. But in course of time shortcomings did

240

appear. The other A.S.M., Moulin, had on two occasions now had to wait a whole hour for him to turn up. There was even one occasion – it was after lunch one day – when, hearing that his relief had not put in an appearance, being a decent fellow Moulin ran round to remonstrate with Roubaud and get him out of his gambling den, were it only to avoid a black mark on his record. From then on all Roubaud's work was affected by the slow disintegration of his ego. On day duty he ceased to be the assiduous nigger-driver he had been, the man who would neither send a train out or accept one in without seeing to every detail himself, a stickler for work who reported to the station-master the least failing of any man, hard on everybody, but hard on himself as well.

On the night watch he would now vanish, to sleep like a log in the office armchair, and when awakened he would seem still half asleep as he strode up and down the platform, hands behind back, issuing orders in a dead voice and never following up as he used, to see them carried out. Yet, thanks to routine, everything nevertheless still ran smoothly enough, except once when owing to his negligence a train full of passengers was switched into a siding before it had time to empty, but his colleagues did what they could to minimize that blunder. The story put out was that he was just having rather a gay time.

The truth was that now Roubaud really lived in the little private room on the first floor of the Café du Commerce, which had turned into a gambling-den. It was said that every night there were also women there, but in point of fact one would have found only one, a sexless creature of at least forty, the mistress of a retired sea captain, herself a gambling addict. At the Café du Commerce Roubaud satisfied no more than the mere passion of gambling, awakened in him, soon after his killing of Grandmorin, by a chance rubber of piquet, which had thereafter grown into something totally different from a game. It had been transformed into a habit which dominated Roubaud's life because of the complete distraction it afforded him. It wiped out all else. It had so taken possession of this man, by nature of coarse masculine sexuality, that it had superseded every thought of sex and held him in complete thrall. It was now the only pleasure, either physical or mental, which satisfied him. But this was by no means because remorse was troubling him so much that he had to seek oblivion. It was a consolation that he found in gambling, a consolation because he was so shaken by the break-up of his marriage.

Roubaud felt his whole life was ruined. In gambling he found a real solace. It afforded him a selfish pleasure which numbed all sensation by selfish happiness, for it was a pleasure which he could enjoy all by himself. Because of this, everything was now subordinated to the obsession and it was this which was threatening completely to break him up. Alcohol could never have afforded him gayer, easier, freer moments. His gambling liberated him even from everyday cares. He had the impression of living a life apart, at great pressure, a life disinterested, absolutely untouched by petty worries which formerly would have made him furious. He also maintained very good health, despite the exhausting nights he led. He even grew stouter, he put on solid fat. Indeed, he turned quite sallow, his heavy eyelids shutting away the worried eyes. When he did come home, his movements were sluggish, as if he were half asleep, and he maintained a sovereign indifference to everything in the house.

That night when Roubaud had come home to take those three hundred francs cash, hidden under the floorboards, it was to pay M. Cauche, the Superintendent, after a long run of losses. Cauche was an old hand at gambling, always cool, and that made him a tough adversary. For that matter, he always declared that he only gambled for the fun of the thing. Indeed, he even suggested that he gambled to keep up the standing of his present job, that it was to preserve the outward appearance of a retired officer and confirmed bachelor, and that was why he spent his days at the café. But this high reasoning about it did not prevent him many a time playing all night, raking in other men's money. Tongues indeed had wagged. He had been charged with being so unreliable in his job that those in authority were considering forcing his resignation. But the matter dragged on, there was so little for him to do, so why demand greater zeal? And he felt he was doing all he need merely by putting in an appearance on the station platforms, taking salutes all round.

Three weeks after the above incident, Roubaud again owed M. Cauche nearly four hundred francs. He had made out that his wife's legacy had left them comfortably off, but would add with a laugh that it was the missus kept the key of the kitty, and this explained his tardiness in paying up when he lost. Then the morning came when, being alone and worried, he once again raised the parquet, this time removing a thousand franc note from the hiding-place. He certainly trembled all over. He had not felt as upset as that night when he took the purse of hard cash. There is little doubt that in his eyes the gold coins were only a casual matter. But with this note for 1,000 *frs.* he really had begun thieving. He felt sick to the point of gooseflesh when he thought of this cursed money, which he had sworn he would never touch.

At one time he had indeed declared that he would rather die of hunger than touch it, and he could not possibly have explained how his scruples had so decayed. No doubt they had rotted away imperceptibly every day in the slow corrosion of the murder he had committed. He had the curious impression that in that cavity in the floor his nose sensed damp, a sort of mustiness, and it was this that nauseated him and revolted him. Swiftly, he put the skirting back, and again swore to himself that he would rather cut off his own fist than open the place again. All this, his wife had not seen, and when it was over, he breathed a sigh of relief, then swallowed a large glass of brandy to pull himself together. Then his heart leapt cheerfully, thinking that now he could both pay the debt and have a nice little sum left over to gamble again with.

But when it came to changing that note for 1,000 *frs.*, Roubaud's anxiety began all over again. There was a time when he would have been plucky and he would now have set about it right away, had he not been such an idiot as to mix his wife up in it, but as it was, the mere thought of the police sent him into a sweat. His knowledge that the authorities had not got the numbers of the missing notes served no purpose, nor did his information that in any case the matter was filed for good and all. He was just overcome with sheer terror whenever he contemplated asking for change anywhere.

For five days he carried the note about with him and all the time he had to keep on fingering it and moving it, not to speak of keeping it close to him all night. He elaborated the most complicated plans, because he was continually discovering unforeseen risks. First, he thought of the station cashiers: why should not one of the booking clerks who were colleagues and handled cash take it? Then that seemed frightfully dangerous. So he thought of going to the far end of the town, without his uniform peak-cap on, and buying some trifle.

243

But then, would any shop not be surprised to see him bring out so big a note to pay for a mere trifle? Thus it was that he came down to the idea of changing it at the tobacco kiosk in the station courtyard, where he went every day. Was that not the simplest way? They were well aware he had had a legacy, so the assistant was surely not going to be surprised, if he seemed in the money, but, having got as far as the door, he lost heart and had to walk down as far as the Vauban dock to get his courage back. After walking about for half an hour he came back, his mind still not made up.

Then, that evening, at the café of all places, M. Cauche being there, sudden bravado made him bring the note out there and ask the proprietress to change it for him. She, however, simply had not enough cash, so she had to send a waiter, of all places, to the tobacco kiosk. There even followed leg-pulls about the note, which looked very new, though it was ten years old. The Superintendent himself had taken it and turned it all ways, then remarked that he was sure it had been tucked away in a hole somewhere for a goodish time, which set the retired captain's mistress off on an endless yarn about somebody having hidden the family nest-egg before they died, then how they discovered it at last under the marble seat of a night-commode.

Weeks went by, and having this money in hand finally infected Roubaud completely with the gambling passion. Not that he played for high stakes. But he had a long run of bad luck, so persistent and uninterrupted that trifling daily losses in the end mounted up to a big sum. Towards the end of the month he again found himself penniless, owing a few score francs and so sick about it that he was afraid to touch a card. However, he did fight against the passion, though this very nearly made him ill. The thought of those nine other notes lying there idle under the dining-room parquet became an obsession from which he could never escape. He could see them through the boards. They burned his feet. To think that if he wished he could take more! But he really had sworn that he would not do it again and he would rather have stuck his hand in the lighted stove than take any more of that money.

Then, one evening, when Severine had gone to bed early, so utterly miserable that his eyes swam with tears, he went quite mad and took up the board again. Yet, he asked himself, what good did that highmindedness of his do him? It only meant pointless suffering. For now he realized that he was going to take those notes, all of them, one by one.

The following morning, by sheer chance, Severine noticed a fresh scratch on the chamfer of the skirting. She bent down and saw the unmistakable trace of its having been forced. Clearly, her husband had gone on taking that money. She was so angry that she was surprised at herself, for as a rule she was not greedy about money, not to mention the fact that she too believed she would rather die of hunger than touch those bloodstained notes. Yet were they not as much hers as his? Why should he dispose of them, hiding it from her too, not even asking her her opinion? Until dinner-time she was tormented by a need to be sure, and she would have pulled the board up herself, to see, had she not felt a cold breath blow through her hair at the mere thought of probing under there all by herself. Might not the dead man come out of the hole? This infantile notion made the dining-room so repugnant to her that she took her work into the other room and shut the door.

But that same evening, when in silence they were finishing off a stew, she was irritated afresh by noticing his involuntary glances at the corner of the room.

'You've taken some more, haven't you?' she suddenly demanded.

He raised his head, amazed.

'More what?'

'Come on, don't be so innocent, you know very well what I mean. Now, you listen here, I don't want you to do it again, because it's no more yours than mine, and it makes me ill to think of you touching it.'

As a rule, he avoided quarrelling with her. Their joint *ménage* was no more now than the forced contact of two persons tied together, who passed whole days without exchanging a word, coming and going at will, for ever strangers now, indifferent one to another, individuals who merely lived in proximity. So all he did was shrug his shoulders, refusing any explanation.

But she was very worked up, having suffered because of it ever since the crime, meant to have this question of that money out, once for all time.

'I insist on an answer,' she said. 'Dare you tell me you have not touched it?'

'What the dickens is it to do with you?'

'Because it makes me want to puke, that's why! Only today I was afraid again, I could not sit in this room. Every time you touch that, I have three nights of hellish dreams ... We never talk about that, so put your mind at ease. Only don't make me come back to it.'

Staring at her with his large, stony eyes, he repeated ponderously:

'What the dickens is it to you if I touch it, if I don't make you touch it? It's on my account, it concerns me.'

She would have started up violently, but restrained herself. Then, terribly upset, her countenance expressive of pain and disgust, she spoke out.

'Upon my word, you puzzle me ... You used to be honest, all the same. Yes, you never took a penny from anyone ... And what you did can be forgiven you, because you were out of your mind, just as you put me out of my mind ... But that money, oh come, that wretched money, which should have ceased to exist in your eyes, that you really ought not to touch, yet you steal it, bit by bit, for your pleasure ... Whatever is happening to you, Roubaud, how have you really fallen so low?'

He heard her out and in a minute of lucidity was surprised himself that he had fallen to such a level as to steal. The stages of his slow demoralization had indeed vanished. He was unable to piece together all that the murder had destroyed around him. He could not make out how it was that a different life, almost a new being, had begun, his household ruined, his wife separated from him and hostile. But almost at once the irreparable won the day and all he did was hopelessly wave aside these reflections which merely worried.

'When a man is fed up in the home,' he growled, 'he finds a bit of pleasure elsewhere. Seeing you do not love me ...'

'You're certainly right there, I do not.'

He gaped. Then his cheeks flushed red and he banged the table with his fist.

'Then bloody well leave me alone!' he shouted. 'Do I stand in the way of your bit of fun? Do I make myself your tutor? There are a lot of things a decent man might do in my place which I don't do. The first is that I might send you packing, with my foot up your backside. Then perhaps I might stop pilfering.'

She had turned very pale, for she too had often thought that when

246

a man who was jealous by nature was eaten by an inward ache so bad that he put up with his wife having a lover, it was a sure sign of a moral gangrene slowly eating him up, killing all other scruples, eating away his whole conscience. But she fought back and refused responsibility. Stammering, she cried:

'I forbid you to touch that money.'

He had finished his dinner, and now calmly folded his napkin. Then, standing up and leering at her, he said:

'If that's what you're after, we can split it.'

He was already bending down, as if to open up the floor. She was forced to rush forward and plant her foot there.

'Oh no,' she cried. 'You know I would rather die . . . Don't you dare pull that up. Oh no, not while I am here.'

She was due to meet Jacques that evening, behind the goods yard. When she returned, after midnight, the scene she had had that evening with Roubaud came back to her, and she locked herself in her room, double-turning the key. Roubaud was on night service, she had no fears about his coming back to sleep, for that had rarely happened. Nevertheless, the bedclothes drawn up to her chin, and the lamp left a-glimmer, she could not get to sleep.

Why had she refused to share? For now, suddenly, she no longer felt her honesty revolt against the notion of making use of Grandmorin's money. Had she not accepted the Maufras Cross legacy? Then she might as well take this money too. But that made her flesh creep again. No, never that! Money in a legacy she might take, but what she dared not touch, for fear of burning her fingers, was this money stolen from the corpse, this revolting murder money.

Then she was calm once more, reasoning that she would not take it to spend, no, she would take it to hide it away somewhere else, where only she knew and it would rest for eternity, and even now that would be to save half the sum from her husband. He would then not triumph by keeping it all, he would not go gambling what belonged to her.

When the clock struck three, she was terribly sorry she had refused to share out. The thought followed, hazy and distant at first, of getting up, and taking all the money out, so he would have no more. The only thing was that at the thought she felt such ice chill her bones that she would not contemplate it. Yet what a tempting thought,

247

to take it all, keep it all, and he not even dare complain! And gradually this idea forced itself on her, while another will, more powerful than her resistance, welled up out of the very depths of her being. She did not want to do this, yet she suddenly leapt out of bed, being unable not to do so. She turned up the wick and went into the dining-room.

From that moment, she had no more tremors. Her fears had vanished, she acted coolly, with the slow, precise movements of a sleep-walker. She had to look for the poker which was used to lever the skirting away. When the hole lay open she brought the lamp forward, as she could not see properly. Then, as she bent there, stupefaction held her rigid. The hole was quite empty! Apparently, while she had been to her meeting with Jacques, Roubaud too had had his afterthoughts, and had come back and done the job before her – with the same idea – of leaving nothing! She knelt down, and could see only the watch and chain, well back, the gold gleaming in the dust between the joists. Icy anger held her rigid there for some moments, half naked as she was, while, out loud, she repeated over and over again, a score of times: 'Thief!'

Then, with a furious gesture, she took the watch, when an enormous black spider which she disturbed raced away over the plaster. With her heel she got the skirting back and went back to bed, with the lamp on the bedside table. When she was warm again, she examined the watch, which she had been clenching tight all this time. On the outer case the judge's interlaced initials drew her attention. Inside, she read the number – 2516 – a manufacturer's mark. This was certainly a dangerous treasure to keep, for the authorities had that number. But she was so angry at having been able to save only this that all her fears left her. She even had the feeling that now there was no longer a corpse under her dining-room floor, her nightmares were at an end. At last she would be able to stand anywhere she wanted in her own house. And so, tucking the watch under her pillow, she put out the lamp and went to sleep.

The next day, Jacques, who had a holiday, had to wait till Roubaud had gone to his habitual corner at the *Café du Commerce*, to go up to lunch with her. From time to time they risked such little parties, and on this occasion, while they were at table, Severine, who was still all indignation, told Jacques about the money and what she had found when she opened the hiding-place. She was still just as bitter about

248

Roubaud, and again and again the cry came to her lips, 'the thief!' Next, she brought out the watch, which, in spite of the repugnance he exhibited, she insisted on giving to Jacques.

'But sweetie,' she murmured, 'nobody will ever think of going to you in search of it. If I keep it, he may still take it from me. And let me tell you this, I would rather he tore a piece of my flesh than that . . . No, he has had too much. I never wanted a penny of that money. It horrified me and I would not have spent a penny of it, but does that mean that he of all people had a right to profit by it? How I detest him!'

It even came to tears, and she pressed him so entreatingly that in the end Jacques did put the watch into his waistcoat pocket.

An hour later, Jacques had Severine, still half undressed, on his knees. She had an arm round his neck and was leaning back over his shoulder in a languishing caress, when the key turned in the lock and in came Roubaud. Severine leapt to her feet. But there was no use denying it, they were caught. Roubaud was taken aback and stopped short, but Jacques just went on sitting there, utterly flabbergasted. Then, without a hint of feeling that she had anything embarrassing to explain away, Severine rushed up to Roubaud and assailed him with infuriated cries of: '*Thief!*'

For some instants, Roubaud did not know what to do. Then, with that shrug of the shoulders with which now he dealt with any difficulty, he went through to the bedroom to take a service daybook which he had forgotten. But she followed him.

'Coward! Are you afraid to admit that you pilfered it – and took it all, you thief, thief, thief!'

Without a word, he strode back through the dining-room. Only at the kitchen door did he turn round and eye her dully.

'You bloody well leave me alone, won't you?' he said.

And he was gone, without even banging the door. He might well have seen nothing. He had made absolutely no allusion to the fact that her lover was there. There was a deathly silence. Then she turned to Jacques.

'Would you believe it?' she cried.

Only now Jacques got up, and spoke.

'He's a gone-er,' he said.

They found that they agreed. Their astonishment that the man

249

who had murdered one paramour now tolerated another was followed by their utter scorn for the husband complaisant. Once a man sinks to that, he certainly is in the gutter all right.

From that time on, Severine and Jacques enjoyed complete liberty, and they profited well by it, without the least concern for Roubaud, though now that the husband no longer worried them, their great concern was the prying eye of Madame Lebleu, who undoubtedly had her suspicions. It was of no use Jacques trying to tread softly whenever he came, for he still saw the door opposite open a trifle and an eye watching him through the crack. This surveillance became so unbearable that he no longer dared go to the flat, for his presence was immediately known, and then there would be an ear at the key-hole and they did not dare even kiss, let alone talk freely.

It was then, exasperated by this new obstacle to her pleasure, that Severine revived the old squabble with Madame Lebleu about the flat. For everybody of course knew that Madame Lebleu's flat was really by rights the A.S.M.'s. But it was no longer the lovely view or the windows opening on to the station yard and the heights of Ingouville that tempted Severine. Her sole reason, unspoken of course, was that the front flat as well as a main entrance had a back door opening on to the back-stairs, and Jacques would be able to go up and down that way, without Madame Lebleu having the least idea that he was there. And then they really would be free!

The battle was terrible. Now revived, this question, which had already once roused the corridor, with every hour became more embittered. Madame Lebleu put up a frantic defence against the threat, said she would die if she were shut up in that dark back flat, hemmed in by galvanized roofing, as dismal as in a dungeon. How could anyone expect her to live in such a hole, after being accustomed to her lovely bright room, opening on an expanse of sky and lively with the continual coming and going of the travelling public? Besides, her legs ruled out walking for her, she would be reduced to seeing a galvanized roof, that was enough to kill her at once.

Unfortunately, these were only reasons of a sentimental order, and she was obliged to admit that Roubaud's predecessor, the former assistant station-master, a bachelor, had given up the flat to her in the first place out of sheer gallantry. There was even apparently a letter signed by her husband agreeing to give it up if a new A.S.M. ever wanted it. But as this letter had hitherto not been discovered, she denied its existence.

However, the weaker Madame Lebleu's case became, the fiercer and more aggressive she showed herself. At one point she tried to make an ally of Madame Moulin, the other assistant station-master's wife, and alleged that this new friend of hers had seen men kissing Madame Roubaud on the stairs. This thoroughly put up Moulin's hackles. His wife, a gentle, insignificant little thing, never seen anywhere, wept and swore she had neither seen any such thing or said she had.

For a week the storm gathered among the women of 'the corridor'. But Madame Lebleu's great error, which involved her in disaster, was finally to have exasperated Mademoiselle Guichon by her continual spying. Here Madame Lebleu had a bee in her bonnet, being convinced that Mademoiselle Guichon went to the stationmaster every night, and feeling she simply must catch them at it, till the intention became quite unhealthy and the fixation the worse because in two years' spying she had not been able to get the slightest scrap of evidence. And as she was convinced those two did sleep together, this made her really mad. Therefore Mademoiselle Guichon, no longer able either to go out or come in without being spied upon, brought her pressure to bear to have Madame Lebleu consigned to the back flat, when there would be another flat between her and that lady, at least Madame Lebleu would not be plumb opposite her, and she would not have to pass Madame Lebleu's door. This all made it plain that M. Dabadie, the station-master, who so far had held aloof in the matter, day by day leant more to the Roubauds' side, which was a bad omen.

Certain squabbles further complicated the situation. Philomène, who now brought her fresh eggs to Severine, became openly abusive every time she came across Madame Lebleu, and as the latter left her door open on purpose to annoy people, every time Philomène came there were high words between the two women. This intimacy between Philomène and Severine went as far as confidences, till it came to the former bringing Severine messages from Jacques, when he dared not come himself. Philomène would bring some eggs and at the same time indicate a new *rendezvous* or explain why Jacques had had to be cautious the day before and she would recount all the things Jacques had talked about when he called in to see her. There were indeed now occasions when, hindered from visiting Severine, Jacques rather enjoyed spending a little time in yard chief Sauvagnat's house, following on his mate Pecqueux, so to speak, as if he was now obliged to seek some sort of distraction or afraid to spend the whole evening alone. Indeed, whenever Pecqueux now vanished, having a good time somewhere in a tavern with some seamen, he would drop in to see Philomène, ostensibly to give her a message for Severine, then sit down and linger on, while Philomène, thus drawn into this love affair, gradually got rather sentimental, for hitherto all her lovers had been rather coarse, so that this really rather nice, melancholy young fellow Jacques Lantier's delicate hands and gentlemanly manners were new dainties to her. Moreover, her affair with Pecqueux had now settled down to a sort of domesticity, with Pecqueux having regular bouts of drunkenness and doing more bullyragging than caressing, whereas, whenever she had to convey a tender word from the engine-driver to his love, Philomène was afforded a wonderful opportunity for tasting forbidden fruit.

One day, indeed, she unbosomed herself, and complained of the fireman, a loutish fellow, she said, despite that laughing exterior, one who might turn very nasty, whenever he was drunk. Jacques noticed that she had begun to pay more attention to the care of her gawky, fevered, equine body. And after all she was really most attractive, with those lovely, sensuous eyes of hers, and particularly now that she drank less and kept the house in less slovenly a fashion. One evening, her brother caught the sound of a man's voice and burst into her room with his hand already raised, to strike her, but seeing who it was in conversation with her, confined himself to offering a bottle of cider. Thus made welcome – and free here too of that obsession of his – Jacques seemed rather to like Philomène's company. Hence she for her part showed increasing tenderness towards Severine and became the furious opponent of Madame Lebleu, that 'old bitch', as she called her everywhere.

One night, coming upon the two lovers at the bottom of her little patch of garden, she accompanied them into the shadows, as far as the tool-shed, where they usually took refuge.

'All I can say,' she said to Severine, 'is that you are too soft about your flat. Since it's really yours, if I were you I'd drag that old bitch out by the hair, I would . . . Why don't you put some pressure on?'

But Jacques was against that sort of show-down.

'Now it's in M. Dabadie's hands,' he said, 'far better wait for things to sort themselves out through the proper channels.'

'I shall be in her flat before the end of the month,' Severine told him, 'then we can meet at all times.'

Despite the darkness, at these words of hope Philomène felt him give his mistress's arm a loving squeeze. She then left them, to make her way back home, but when she was thirty paces away, hidden in the shadows, she halted and turned back. It affected her terribly, knowing those two together. Yet she was not being jealous. She merely had an innocent craving to love and be loved like that.

Jacques was now becoming increasingly gloomy. On two occasions when he might have seen Severine, he had invented excuses, and he also tended to dawdle now at the Sauvagnats', to avoid her. Yet he still loved her with an impassioned desire which seemed to grow, not diminish, in intensity. But now, in her arms that terrible malaise began to take possession of him again and he would become so dizzy that he would withdraw from her at once, paralysed by terror lest he cease to be himself, and again feel the beast in him ready to rend flesh with its teeth. He tried taking refuge in the fatigue of long runs as driver. He applied for supplementary tasks, spending up to twelve hours on his feet on Lison's footplate, his body broken by the constant vibration, his lungs strained by the wind. While his fellow drivers were full of complaints of their hard lot, and maintained that their job wore a man out in twenty years, his desire was to be worn out as soon as possible. He was never tired enough, happy solely when borne like a hurricane by Lison, for then thought in him ceased and he had attention only for the signals. And when he reached his destination, sleep would overcome him before he had even time to clean himself up.

Yet with wakening the torment of that obsession always returned. He even tried to revive his affection for Lison, again spending hours cleaning her, and insisting on Pecqueux keeping all the steel surfaces like silver. When inspectors jumped on board on a run, they were all congratulations. He would nod, as if with satisfaction, but he was just as unhappy as ever, for he knew quite well that since that hold-up in

253

the snow all had never been right with his engine, once so lusty. Most likely, in the repair of her pistons, she had lost her soul, lost that ineffable balance of life which was pure chance of assembly. And this truth hurt him, and Lison's shortcomings ended in a gloomy rancour on his part, to such point that he plagued his superiors with unreasonable complaints, applying for pointless overhauls, suggesting unrealizable improvements. These were invariably refused, making him still gloomier, convinced that Lison was very ill indeed and there was no good work to be expected from her. His love for her was thereby broken down, for what was the point in living, when he was condemned to kill whomever he loved. So it was that his mistress was now offered this frenzy of despairing love, which neither suffering nor fatigue could wear down.

Severine had not failed to notice the change in him, and she too lost heart, thinking that she had been the cause, since he knew everything. When she felt him shiver on her bosom or draw back sharply to avoid a kiss, was that not because he was recalling it all, and was horrified by her? She had never dared re-open the subject. She was all regrets for having spoken, astonished too that her urge to confess had thus carried her away in that strange bed where they were both in a state of conflagration, and, since now they were both engulfed in the secret together, she was satisfied merely to have him with her, and did not even remember how then, in those distant days, she had craved for somebody to confide in. For she not only loved him, but unquestionably loved him even more since he knew all there was to know. It was an insatiable love too, the woman in her fully awake at last. She had become a being made for nothing but caresses, the essential mistress woman devoid of maternity. She lived now solely for Jacques and it was no lie when she spoke of her effort to dissolve into him, for she had but one dream – for him to bear her away and embody her in his own flesh. Invariably excessively gentle, excessively passive, and he her sole source of pleasure, she would have liked to sleep on cat-like, indefinitely, curled up on his knees, from morning till night. Just as she seemed to have remained virginal and innocent, despite all the perverse debauch of her childhood, all that remained in her of the terrible event of the murder was astonishment at ever having been involved in it. All that was distant, she could smile about it, and she would not even have been angry with her husband, had he not been in her way. But her detestation of Roubaud increased in proportion to the growth of her passion and her need for Jacques. Now that Roubaud knew and had given her *carte blanche*, it was Jacques who was the master, Jacques whom she followed, and who could dispose of her as his chattel. She had even made him give her his picture, a postcard photograph, and she took this to bed with her, sleeping with her lips on it, and now that he was unhappy she too was very unhappy, without being able even to guess what it really was that troubled him so.

Meanwhile, they went on meeting outside, till such time as they could meet at her flat in peace, that is, when she had won the front flat. Winter was drawing to a close, and February had been a very mild month. They went for ever longer walks, for hours, in fact, wandering about the vast spread-out area of the station. For Jacques now avoided stopping and standing still, and when she hung on his shoulders and he was compelled to sit down and take her, he always insisted on its being quite dark, so terrified was he of striking her, if he saw anything of her white bosom. So long as he saw nothing, he might be able to resist. In Paris, where she still went with him, every Thursday, he carefully drew the curtains, inventing a yarn about not really liking it if he could see at all.

This weekly trip was now made by Severine without any explanation to her husband, while the old excuse about her knee was good enough for the neighbours. She would also talk about going to give her old nursie, Victoire, a hug in hospital, where she was still only convalescent. Both Jacques and she herself still found those trips most exciting. On those days he would take great interest in Lison's working well, and Severine would be delighted to see him less gloomy, and the journey itself delighted her, although she was beginning to know every little ravine and thicket on the route. From Havre to Motteville there were meadows and level fields, intersected by hedges with apple-trees. After that, as far as Rouen, it was undulating waste land. After Rouen, they followed the Seine, crossing it at Sotteville, Oissel, and Pont-de-l'Arche, while it flowed through vast level stretches of country, constantly reappearing, broad and meandering. After Gaillon, they kept to its left bank, and here it was a sluggish stream, bordered by willows. They skirted hilly country, leaving the river at Bonnières, only to come out on it suddenly again at Rosny, when they emerged from Rolleboise tunnel. It was their friendly guardian all the way. Before reaching Paris, they crossed it three more times. Then came Mantes with its church tower among the trees, Triel with the white patches of its plaster-kilns, Poissy, which they ran through the heart of, next, the two green walls of the St Germain Forest, at Colombes, cuttings with lilac-covered slopes, then at last the suburbs, all the feeling of Paris, a glimpse of Asnières Bridge, and the Arc de Triomphe in the distance, towering above leprous industrial sites bristling with their smoke-stacks. The engine then plunged into the Batignolles tunnel, coming out into the echoing reverberating station, and then, till evening, they were free and belonged but to one another.

On the return journey it was usually dark, and she closed her eyes, reliving her happiness. But every time she passed Maufras Cross, be it morning or evening, she leant forward and peered out, cautious not to be observed, and could rely on seeing Flora standing at the crossing-bar, holding up the little flag in its sheath and flashing a malevolent glance at the train.

Ever since that girl, on the day of the snowstorm, had seen them kissing, Jacques had warned Severine to beware of her. He was no longer ignorant of the untamed passion with which Flora had pursued him from childhood, and he sensed that she was now bitterly jealous. He also knew her masculine strength, her unbridled murderous bitterness. Another thing was that she must know quite a lot, for he had not forgotten her allusion to the murdered judge's relations 'with a certain young person' whom 'nobody suspected', but whom he 'had married off'. If she knew that, she must surely have guessed who committed the murder. There was no doubt, she might talk, or write about it, finding revenge by denouncing Severine.

But days and weeks passed, and nothing happened, and he merely found her always there at her post beside the track, rigid, with her flag. However far off she was when she sighted his engine, Jacques could feel her fierce eyes on him. Despite the smoke, she saw him, his whole figure, and as he flashed by, her eyes flashed in pursuit of him amid the din of the wheels. At the same time the train was probed, transfixed, investigated, from the first to the last coach. And every time Flora discerned that other woman, the rival whom she now knew to be there, every Thursday. Useless for that other merely to

256

move her head slightly in her irresistible need to see out, she was always observed, and the eyes of the two women met like naked swords. Then the train would fling past the spot, and one of the two was left behind, on the ground, unable to follow, but maddened by the happiness those wheels bore with them. Flora seemed to grow, she seemed taller every time to Jacques, and he became more and more uneasy precisely because she still did nothing. He could not help wondering what plans were ripening in the head of that dour amazon whose statuesque form he could never escape.

Another who worried both Severine and Jacques was a colleague of the Western Company, Henri Dauvergne, in fact. It was he who was the leading guard of that Thursday train, and he would insist on showering little attentions on young Madame Roubaud. In the morning, before the train pulled out of Havre station, Roubaud himself used to leer, so transparent was Dauvergne's attention, reserving Severine a compartment, seeing her in, feeling the foot-warmer to make sure it was hot. Indeed, this went so far that when one day Roubaud was talking to Jacques he gave the young driver a plain hint by casting his eyes pointedly towards Dauvergne, as much as if to ask if he was going to put up with that sort of thing. Indeed, whenever they squabbled, Roubaud now accused his wife of sleeping with both men. Severine even thought for a moment that Jacques believed this too, and that this was the cause of his melancholy fits. Sobbing bitterly, she protested that she was innocent, told him he was to kill her, if she were ever untrue to him. But, deathly pale, he laughed it off, kissing her and assuring her that he never doubted she was true and that the last thing he wanted to do was to kill anyone.

Nevertheless, the first evenings of March were terrible, they had to stop seeing each other, and the few hours of liberty offered by those tiresomely long trips to Paris no longer satisfied her. She felt an increasing need to have Jacques completely hers, for them to live together day and night and for him never to leave her side. Her detestation of her husband grew greater, the mere presence of the man set her nerves hysterically and unbearably on edge. For all the sweet, yielding femininity of her nature, she was all nerves the moment Roubaud was in question, flying into a rage if he hindered her and Jacques in the slightest way. In such moments it looked as if the shadowy mass of her hair dimmed the bright blue of her eyes.

257

She became morose, charging him with having ruined her life, till now it had become unbearable to live with him. Was he not the sole culprit in this? If their marriage had gone utterly to pieces and she had a paramour, was that not his fault? Finally, all that ponderous calm which he presented her, the impassive way he would just glance at her when she was in a fit of rage, his rounded shoulders and his nascent paunch, all that dismal corpulence of his which suggested well-being, had exhausted her patience, for she of course was the victim.

She had in fact now begun to dream of nothing less than a complete break, to get right away from him and go to live somewhere else. If only she could begin all over again, above all make the past non-existent, resume living as from before all these dreadful things, be once again what she was at fifteen, then love and be loved and live as she dreamed of living in those days! For a whole week she nursed a plan to run away: it would be with Jacques, they would find refuge in Belgium, and there set up house, a young, hard-working couple. But she did not even mention the plan to him. Obstacles arose at once – the irregularity of their position, the constant anxiety in which they would have to live, but most of all the sheer annoyance of leaving Roubaud her fortune, both the money she had and Maufras Cross. They had willed everything to each other as next of kin and she would be in his power, in that legal subordination of a woman, and that would tie her hands. She would rather have died than go away and leave a farthing behind her.

One day, when Roubaud came back to the house white as a sheet and said that crossing the tracks he had all but been knocked down by a locomotive and had actually felt the buffer brush his elbow, she reflected that she would be free, were he but dead. She stared wide-eyed at him, wondering why he did not simply die, since she no longer loved him, and he was in everybody's way.

After that, Severine's dream changed. Roubaud was killed in an accident and Jacques and she went to America. But now they were married. They had sold Maufras Cross and realized all their capital. Behind, they left no fears. If they were going to a new country, that was to be re-born in each other's arms. Out there would be none of those things she longed to forget and she would be able to believe that life was new. Having made one mistake, she would start the

258

investigation of happiness afresh. He would be certain to find a job. She would do something herself. They would be well off, they would probably have children, they would make a new life of work and happiness. The moment she found herself alone, in the morning in bed, during the day, at her needlework, she withdrew into those fantasies, correcting them, extending them, ceaselessly adding happy details, till she felt herself smothered with happiness and good things. In this period, whereas formerly she had gone out so rarely, she acquired a passion for going down to the port to watch the steam packets leave. She would go and lean on the jetty railing and follow the smoke of the steamer till it mingled in the mists of the horizon, and she would not be alone, either, for she would feel that she was on deck, with Jacques, already far from France, *en route* for the paradise of her dreams.

One evening in mid-March, when the young driver had risked going up to see her in the Roubauds' flat, he told her that in his train he had just driven to Paris an old school pal, who was going to New York to develop a new invention, a button-making machine, and as this friend needed somebody who was an engineer to be his partner, he had suggested Jacques should take it up. It was really a magnificent offer, at most he would have to bring in about 30,000 francs, and there might easily be millions to be earned. All this he told Severine as no more than idle talk, and went on to say that he had of course said *no*. But of course he did rather regret it, because when all was said and done it was hard to renounce a rich future when the offer came.

Severine stood listening, staring into space. Was this not her dream, now to be realized?

'Oh,' she murmured, at last, 'we would leave tomorrow . . .'

He stared at her in astonishment.

'How on earth could we leave?' he asked.

'Why, if he were dead, of course.'

She had not named Roubaud, merely indicated him with her chin, but of course Jacques understood, and replied by a vague gesture, meant to say, yes, it was a pity, Roubaud was not dead.

'We could leave,' she resumed, speaking slowly and gravely, 'we should be so happy out there. As for the 30,000 francs, why, I should have the money if Maufras Cross were sold, and enough left over, too, to set ourselves up well. You would soon get the capital back, and I would make such a lovely little home where there would be nothing to limit our love. Oh, how good, how good that would be!' And in a whisper, she added: 'Far from all these memories, nothing but new life before us.'

This made him feel very sentimental. They took each other's hands and instinctively squeezed them. Neither could say another word. They were immersed in that hope. Then she spoke again.

'All the same,' she said, 'before your friend goes, you ought to see him again, and ask him to give you first refusal.'

Again he was astonished.

'But whatever for?'

'Good Heavens,' she cried, 'how are we to know what may not happen? The other day he was within an inch of being run over ... well, if he had, I should have been free ... Alive in the morning, you know, dead in the evening.' Her eyes were hard on his. 'Oh, if only he were dead!' she cried.

'All the same, you don't want me to kill him, I hope?' he said, with an attempt at a smile.

She said: *no*, three times, but her eyes kept saying: *yes*, and those gentle womanly eyes were made inexorably hard by love. Since Roubaud had killed a man, why should he himself not be killed? That thought had suddenly sprung up in her mind as a logical consequence of the situation. What simpler than to kill him and go away? If he were dead, it would all be over and she could begin life altogether anew. She no longer saw any other possible end, her resolution was taken, absolute, though since she had not the courage of her violence, she continued unconvincingly to say: *no*.

Leaning against the sideboard, he continued to force a smile. He had just seen that knife lying to hand.

'If you want me to kill him,' he said, 'you had better give me the knife.' He laughed boisterously. 'I already have the watch. It'll make quite a nice little museum.'

But in grave tones she said: 'Take it.' And, when he had put the knife into his pocket, he gave her a kiss, as if to ride out the joke to the very end.

'All right, my pet, so now I'll say good night ... I'll go and see my friend at once and tell him to give me a chance ... So, if it doesn't

260

rain, we meet behind the Sauvagnats'. Agreed? But don't you fear, there's not going to be any killing, I am only joking.'

Nevertheless, late though it was, Jacques did go down to the harbour to call at the hotel and see the friend who was leaving on the morrow. To him he spoke of the possibility of a legacy and asked for a fortnight to think the offer over. Then, making his way back up the main avenues to the station in darkness, he was astonished at what he had just done. Did this mean that he had made up his mind to kill Roubaud, now that he had both the man's wife and his money? But of course not, he had made up his mind to do nothing of the kind, or he would never be thinking like this. Then Severine came to his mind, the hot pressure of her hand, those staring eyes which said: *yes* while her lips said: *no*. Clearly, she wanted him to kill Roubaud. He was suddenly terribly worried. Whatever was he to do?

In bed next to Pecqueux, who was snoring, back at the railway lodging house, Jacques was unable to sleep. Against his will his brain would work on that idea of killing Roubaud. It became like thinking out the whole action of a play, down to the most remote consequences. He sought and debated all the reasons for, and all against. The result was that when the notion was examined quite coolly without any heat, there seemed to be every reason in favour. Was not Roubaud the sole obstacle to his happiness? Were Roubaud dead, he could marry Severine, whom he loved passionately, and there would be an end to hiding. He would have her, all his, for ever. Next, there was the money, quite a fortune. He would be able to give up his arduous profession and be his own master in that America where, so friends told him, an engineer could just shovel up gold. And then as if in a dream there unrolled his American life, with a wife who loved him passionately. In no time he made millions, prospects were great, there were no limits to his advancement, it was ideal. And in order to realize that dream, he had nothing but one single gesture to make, he merely had to eliminate one man – no, an animal, a noxious weed, to be trodden under foot. The man in question was not even worth preserving in himself. He was already obese and lethargic, except when engaged in his idiotic passion of gambling, which had set the seal on his pristine vigour. Why spare him? There was not a thing, no, not one single thing, in Roubaud's favour. Everything added up to condemnation, for on every point it was in other people's interest for the man to die. It seemed both stupid and cowardly to hesitate.

Lying still, thinking, Jacques' back had got hot, so he had turned on to his stomach. Now he suddenly jerked himself again to his back, as a thought struck him which, though hazy at first, had suddenly become so acute that he felt it like something pricking inside his skull. Why, why should not he, who since childhood had craved to kill and was always painfully haunted by that obsession, why should he not kill Roubaud? Perhaps by killing this selected victim he might for all time assuage his craving to kill, which meant that he would not merely be doing a good piece of work, but also be cured of his ill. Cured? Oh dear Heaven! what would it not be to live free of that fever of the blood, to be able to possess Severine and not know the primeval male awaken in him and lust for the blood of the eviscerated female. He was drenched with perspiration, seeing himself, knife in hand, striking at Roubaud's throat, exactly as Roubaud had struck Judge Grandmorin, and filled with contentment and relief as out of the wound the blood gushed on to his hands. He would kill him, he was determined, because there at one blow lay his cure, his beloved, and riches. If he was fated to kill and must have a victim, let this be the one he would slaughter, knowing that at least he had killed with logic, by reason, to advantage.

This decision taken, he tried to sleep, for it was now three A.M. He was just going off when a profound jerk brought him again to a sitting position. He was choking. Kill Roubaud? God in Heaven! What right had he? When a fly worried him, he crushed it with a blow. Once a cat got under his feet, and he broke its back with a kick, though, true, that was done quite unintentionally. But – this man, his fellow-creature? He had to run through all the arguments again to prove to his conscience his right to murder – the right of the strong hindered by the weak, whom the strong therefore destroy. Now he was the man whom the wife of this fellow-human-being loved, and she wished to be free, to marry him and bring in her worldly goods. He was merely removing the obstacle, no more. When in the forest two wolves met in the presence of a female wolf, did not the stronger get rid of the other with its jaws? And in primeval times, when like the wolves men found shelter in caves, did the desired female not belong to that member of the herd who could win her by spilling the blood of his rivals? If so, this being the law of life, he ought to obey it, regardless of scruples invented later for living in common. Gradually his right seemed absolute to him and he felt his full resolution revive in him. Tomorrow he would at once choose the place and hour and prepare the act. The best thing would most likely be to knife Roubaud one night, in the station, on one of his rounds, so that it might be suspected that pilferers had killed him when Roubaud surprised them. There was an excellent spot away behind the coal piles, if he could only get Roubaud there. Despite his efforts to sleep, he now began to organize the scene, debating where exactly he should stand, how he should strike, to finish Roubaud off quickly. But even while he was thus going into the minutest details of how he would kill, his loathing of the very idea was surreptitiously coming back, an inexorable inward protest which gradually assumed possession of him, till he cried: no, no, he would not strike, that was a monstrous, impossible thing to do, it was out of the question! The civilized man within him, the force which education and the slow and indestructible piling up of man's heritage of thought had created, was in revolt. It was wrong to kill. That conviction he had sucked with the milk of the generations before him. Finely attuned, equipped thus with scruples, his horrified brain rejected the very notion of killing in the same instant as it began to consider it. He could admit killing in self-defence or when carried away by instincts, but kill at will, kill by calculation, kill from mere self-interest, no, that he never, never could do. And day was already breaking when at last Jacques succeeded in falling to sleep, but with so light a sleep that he was still mistily aware of the horrible debate.

The following days were the most unhappy he had ever known. He avoided Severine. He sent her a message not to come to the meeting-place on Saturday, for he was afraid of her eyes. But on the Monday he could not avoid seeing her again, and, as he had feared, her wide-open blue eyes, so gentle and so profound, filled him with agony. She said not a word about it, or made a single gesture. Not a word was spoken to thrust him on to it, only her eyes were full of it, questioning him, pleading with him. He did not know how to avoid their impatience and reproachfulness. They were incessantly seeking out his, so full of amazement that he could hesitate to make them happy.

When he left her, he kissed her and pressed her sharply to him, to give her to understand that his mind was made up. Indeed, it was, as far as the bottom of the stairs, when he was again plunged back into his battle of the conscience. When he saw her again, the following day, he had the uncertain pallor and the furtive look of a coward flinching from something he has to do. Without a word, she burst out sobbing on his breast, terribly unhappy, and he was so upset that he was brimful of scorn for himself. There must be an end to this.

'Friday, down there, yes?' she whispered.

'Yes, Friday, I shall be there.'

This particular Friday it was a very dark night the sky starless, completely clouded, with sea fog. As usual, Jacques was there first at the back of the Sauvagnats' watching for Severine. But the darkness was so complete and she came up so swiftly and so lightly that he started violently when without his even noticing her, she brushed against him. But she was already in his arms, worried to find him shaking so.

'Did I frighten you, darling?' she whispered.

'Of course not, sweetie, I was waiting for you . . . Let's walk about, nobody can see us.'

Arms enlaced about each other, they began their usual slow lovers' meandering through the network of yards. On this side of the sheds, the lights were sparse. There were large patches of complete darkness, with no lighting at all, whereas towards the station the flares were thick, like clouds of sparks. For a long time they walked thus, without speaking. She rested her head on his shoulder, raising it from time to time to kiss his chin, while he would bend down and return one on her temples, just where the hair began. The solemn single stroke of one had just sounded from the distant churches. If they did not speak, it was because while they held themselves thus they could sense each other's thoughts. And they now thought only of that, for they could not be together without being obsessed by it. The debate continued. But why utter useless words, when all that was needed was action? When she stretched up against him for a caress, she suddenly felt the knife in his trousers pocket. Had he then come at last resolved to do it?

Her thoughts could not help spilling out, her lips stirred, and almost inaudibly she whispered:

'He went upstairs just now, I could not think what for . . . Then I

264

saw him take his revolver. He had forgotten it . . . That must mean he is going on a round of inspection.'

Silence fell again, but, twenty paces farther on, he in turn spoke.

'Last night, some thieves got away with some lead out here . . . He'll be along soon, that's sure.'

She gave a little shudder, then they were both dumb again, but their steps came more slowly. She had suddenly begun to wonder if it really was the knife that she felt in his pocket. Twice she kissed him, just to get a better idea. Then, as merely rubbing against his leg did not tell her, she let one arm hang to her side and thus, kissing him again, she felt. Yes, it was the knife. But he at once guessed what she was about, and crushed her against him till she could not breathe. Then he whispered in her ear:

'He'll come all right, you'll be free.'

The liquidation was decided on. They seemed not to be walking, but drawn over the ground by an outside force. Their senses had suddenly acquired extreme sharpness, particularly a keenness of touch, their hands, one in the other, painful from the contact, the least brush of lip on lip like the scratching of a nail. They were also highly aware of sounds which a little while before they had not noticed, the distant breathing of engines, sending dull thuds, stray footsteps deep in the darkness. They also saw the night, the black mass of objects stood out, as if a mist had been swept from their eyes. A bat flashed by, and they could follow its swift cornering. They had halted by a heap of coal and there they stood, ears and eyes all awake, their whole being tense. Suddenly they began to whisper.

'Hear that, over there, someone calling for help?'

'No, that was a truck being shunted.'

'But over there, to the left, someone – walking. Surely the sand creaked.'

'I don't think so. Just rats in the pile, loose coal subsiding.'

Minutes passed. Then it was Severine who gripped him violently.

'Here he is!'

'But where? I can't see a thing.'

'He's just gone round the slow goods shed. He's coming straight towards us. Look, there's his shadow against the white wall.'

'Think so? That dark patch? Is he alone?'

'Yes, he's alone, quite alone.'

And in the crucial moment, what did she do but fling her arms passionately round his neck and press her burning lips to his. It was a long drawn out kiss, a kiss of flesh all bared, a kiss in which she strove to render her blood to his. How she loved him, how she detested that other! Oh, had she only dared, she would already have done the necessary deed twenty times over, to spare him the horror of it. But her hands failed her, she felt herself too weak, it needed a man's sinews. And this never-ending kiss was all the courage she could instil into him, her promise of complete possession of her, the sacramental gift of her body.

At some distance, an engine whistled, a drawn-out cry of distress given to the night. From the darkness, too, came a din, ill-defined in place, the blows of a giant hammer, while the sea mist sweeping in loose clouds over the sky in chaotic procession, at moments threatened to extinguish the gas jets. When at last she took her lips from his, she was a mere shell, she felt that all her being had passed into his flesh.

Swiftly he took out the knife and opened it, then muttered an oath.

'Blast! We're b——, he's going back!'

He was right. After having drawn towards them, within about fifty paces, the shadow had turned left again and was receding, at the steady pace of a night watchman who finds nothing to worry about.

She gave him a push. 'But get along, get along!' she cried.

They both followed, Jacques in front, Severine on his heels slinking in the tracks of the victim, careful to make no noise. For a moment, at the corner of the repair-shops, they lost sight of him, then, cutting across the locomotive shed tracks, they came on him again, not more than twenty paces away. They had to make use of every piece of walling to hide behind, one false step and they were discovered.

'We're going to lose him,' Jacques muttered, angrily. 'If he reaches the pointsman's box, he's slipped us.'

She kept whispering behind him.

'But get along,' she insisted, 'get along then.'

In this moment, amid this vast expanse of ground lost in shadow, with the night-time desertedness of a large railway station about him, he was indeed determined. Yet even while he crept cautiously forward into the darkness, working himself up, his mind was still fighting it out, concocting reasons for this murder being a sensible act to commit, a legitimate, an act logically thrashed out and proved justifiable. For was he not merely exercising a right, the fundamental right of life, since the blood of this other man must be shed, to make the completion of his own feasible. He had nothing to do but plunge in that knife, to conquer happiness.

'We're going to lose him, we're going to lose him,' he muttered, angrily, seeing the dim form pass the pointsman's box. 'Now we're done! Look, he's got away!'

But with tense fingers she seized his arm and held him still against her.

'See, he's coming back.'

He certainly was. He had turned to the right, but was now returning. Perhaps he had vaguely sensed the murderers trailing him. But, conscientious watchman unwilling to go in before he had had a look everywhere, he had continued to plod along as steadily as before.

Halted thus suddenly, Jacques and Severine did not stir. Chance had planted them at the actual corner of a coal stack. They pressed themselves against it, leant back into it, seeming to merge with it, lost against the inky mass, and held their breath.

Now Jacques watched Roubaud come straight towards him. There was scarcely thirty paces between them, every step brought Roubaud nearer by an amount as regular as a pendulum's swing, the swing of fate. Twenty paces more, ten paces more. He would have the man there, he would raise his arm – like this – he would slice the blade into the throat with a right to left slashing movement, and stifle a cry.

The seconds had become interminable, such a flood of thoughts sweeping through the vacuum of his brain that all sense of time was obliterated. All the reasons for doing it filed through once again and the murder, together with its causes and its consequences, was distinct before his eyes. Though stretched to breaking point, his resolution was unbreakable. He meant to kill and knew why he was killing.

But at two paces, at one pace, came the rout. Suddenly everything in him collapsed. No, never would he kill! He could not kill a defenceless fellow-man like that. Reason would never produce the murder, when the instinctive drive to do it was not there. He lacked the upsurge of venom by which one leaps at the victim, he lacked the hunger or the passion which destroys. What difference did it make that he told himself this conscience was no more than an accumulation of notions built up by a slow legacy of justice, when he did not feel

267

the right to kill and no matter how he argued, he could never force into his inner self the conviction such a right could be assumed.

Unruffled, Roubaud passed by, close to them. His elbow almost touched them as they pressed back into the coal. One breath would have revealed them, but they were as transfixed as dead bodies. The arm did not rise, the hand did not thrust in its knife. Nothing disturbed the deep shadows, not even a shudder, either of lust or of fear. And Roubaud was already distant, ten good paces away. Neither Severine nor Jacques had stirred. Backs to the black pile, they had not even breathed, in their terror of that one unarmed man who had so nearly touched them as he peaceably strode by.

Then Jacques gasped, a sob of anger and shame, and he cried:

'I cannot, I cannot!'

He would have taken Severine in his arms again, leant on her in his need for her forgiveness and consolation, but she slipped away from him without a word. He reached out towards her, but clutched only her skirt, and that slipped from his fingers. He heard her quick, fleet steps as she hurried away. Vainly for a moment he followed. This brusque disappearance about finished him. Did it not mean that she was angered by his weakness? Did she now despise him? But prudence prevented his going to her. And so, finding himself thus suddenly alone in the heart of that huge, featureless space, spotted by the little yellow tongues of the gas jets, frightful anguish overcame him and he hurried away, to bury his head in a pillow and blot out the horror of life.

It was about ten days after this, towards the end of March, that the Roubauds at last triumphed over the Lebleus. The management had recognized the justness of their request, which had M. Dabadie's support, particularly since that notorious letter from the cashier undertaking to give up the flat if a new assistant station-master should want it had just been unearthed by Mademoiselle Guichon, who found it when looking up some old account-sheets. Outraged by losing the day, Madame Lebleu declared she would move out at once. If they wanted to kill her, better get it over without waiting.

For three days that unforgettable house-moving set 'the corridor' on fire. Even self-effacing little Madame Moulin, otherwise never seen in her goings or comings, even she took sides, carrying Severine's work-table from one flat to the other. But it was especially Philomène who fanned the flames, there from the start, tying bundles, heaving furniture about, invading the front flat before the Lebleus were out. She it was too, who amid all the confusion of the two lots of furniture, hopelessly intermixed in the interchange, finally turned Madame Lebleu out. Indeed, in the end she showed such zeal for Jacques and all that he loved that Pecqueux's eyes were opened at last. Really suspicious, in his most narking, spiteful, drunken manner, he asked her if this happened to be the time of day when she slept with his chief, and he added that if ever he caught them at it he'd settle the hash of them both. Philomène's sentimental leaning for the young engine-driver had certainly grown stronger, and she behaved like the servant of both him and his mistress in the hope, between the two of them, of getting a little of him to herself. When she had carried in the last chair, she banged the door to. Then once more it flew open, for she had discovered a stool which Madame Lebleu had forgotten, and this she simply flung across the corridor at that old bitch's door.

Little by little life now resumed its monotonous course. While in the back flat, glued to her deep armchair by her rheumatism, Madame Lebleu was dying of depression, her eyes swollen with tears, for now she could only see the endless galvanized iron of the station roof, blotting out the sky, Severine at the front-flat window worked away at her interminable counterpane. Beneath her she had the cheerful excitement of the station entrance, with its continual flow of vehicles and foot-passengers. An early spring was already decking with green buds the tall trees bordering the pavements, while in the distance Ingouville made a backcloth of wooded hills pointed here and there by the white walls of the homesteads of the countryside. Severine was however rather surprised to find so little pleasure in the dream she had at last realized, in being established in the flat she had coveted, in having before her space, daylight, sunshine. Indeed, she even found it irritating, when her housekeeper, Mother Simon, grumbled because this or that was different from what she was used to. There were moments when she actually regretted 'the old hole', where, as she said, the dirt showed less. As for Roubaud, he was a passive partner in the whole business. He did not even seem aware that he had changed his stable. Indeed, he often forgot, and only noticed it when the new key refused to go into the old lock. He was, it is true, less and less at home, for the Roubauds' domestic break-up continued unabated, though there was one moment when he seemed to recover his old vigour, because of a resurgence of his political ideas. Not that these were very precise or passionately held, but he could never get out of his mind that business about the assistant-prefect which had nearly cost him his job. When the general election really shook the Empire, and the régime entered a very critical period, he was suddenly cock-a-hoop, and went about telling people that 'those gentry' would not always be the bosses. However, a friendly hint from M. Dabadie, who had learned of this talk from Mademoiselle Guichon, in front of whom Roubaud had let his tongue wag, soon put him back in his place. After all, now that 'the corridor' was at peace and everybody lived in harmony, with Madame Lebleu killed by mortification, growing weaker, why seek new troubles with Government business? So with a vulgar gesture Roubaud dismissed politics, just as he had dismissed other things, and his conscience torpid, and growing stouter daily, he went his way, slouching about heavily, with drooping shoulders.

Now that they could meet at any time, the sense of embarrassment between Jacques and Severine had increased. There was nothing any more to hinder their happiness, he went up to her by the back stairs whenever he pleased, without fear of being spied on, the flat was theirs, he could even have slept in the conjugal bed with her, had he had the daring. But that abortive business, that deed desired and approved by them both, but which he could never commit, festering in their minds from now on, created a sense of malaise between them, and that proved an impassable barrier to their free love. Within him Jacques constantly bore the shame of his own weakness and he found Severine increasingly morose, sickened by the fruitless expectation of it all. Their lips no longer sought each other's, for they had exhausted all the pleasures of such semi-possession. The only happiness which they now craved was precisely that of getting away from all this, of marrying in America, of starting a new life.

One evening, Jacques found Severine in tears, and when she saw him she did not stop, but sobbed more bitterly than ever, clinging to his neck. She had already wept before, but his arms holding her had been able to assuage her grief. But now, deep in his heart, he realized that she was lacerated by a despair which grew but greater the more firmly he held her. He was aghast. At last, he took her head between

270

his hands, and, peering at close quarters deep into her swimming eyes, he cursed inwardly, for he saw without question that her terrible unhappiness came from the fact that she was a woman and in her passivity and gentleness herself could never dare strike.

'Forgive me!' he pleaded. 'Just a little longer . . . I swear I will do it now, as soon as ever I can.'

Immediately, she glued her lips to his, as if to seal that oath, and they kissed again with one of those bottomless kisses in which they commingled in an ultimate communion of their flesh.

10

Aunt Phasie died on a Thursday evening at nine, in a final stroke. Misard, who was looking after her, vainly tried to close her eyes, but they stayed obstinately open, with her head settled down a little on one shoulder, as if she wanted to keep watch on the room, while the tendons controlling the lips persisted in drawing the corners down into a caustic grin. A single candle, placed at the corner of a table, kept vigil near her and ignorant of this still-warm corpse, every train which after nine o'clock came by made Phasie shiver for a moment under the vacillating light of the little flame.

At once, to get rid of Flora, Misard despatched her to Doinville, to report the death. She could not get back before eleven, so he had two hours before him. First, he calmly carved himself a slice of bread, for he felt empty, having had no supper because his wife's death-throes had lasted so long. He ate standing, constantly coming and going, re-arranging things in the house. Spasms of coughing interrupted him, doubled him in two. He was half a corpse himself, so thin, so wan, with those dull eyes and that colourless bleached hair, that he did not look as if he would enjoy his victory long. No matter, he had devoured her, the strapping creature, tall and handsome, that she once had been, eating into her much as an insect eats into an oak, till here she was for ever on her back, reduced to nothingness, whereas he was still going. Here, suddenly remembering, he knelt down to take from under the bed a crock of bran water, which had been prepared for his dead wife to douche with. Ever since she had suspected what he was at, he had stopped doctoring the salt and had been putting the arsenious rat poison in her douche water and she had been just too stupid to suspect anything of that sort, so, in spite of all her suspicion, she'd had her dose, and at last with good effect. When he had emptied the crock outside, he returned and sponged down the tiles, which were well splashed with water. Bah! what had been the use of her being so stubborn? She had thought herself mighty clever, so serve her right. When one party in a marriage thinks it's going to bury

272

the other without outside interference, it does open that other party's eyes. He was proud of his spryness, and a broad grin stretched his face. It made a darned good yarn, she taking the dope in so innocently by the back parts all the time she took such fine care he got nothing into her by the top end!

At that instant, a passing express swept the cottage with such a hurricane of air that, used to it as he was, he turned to the window and shook. He spat silently. They were never tired of rushing on, coming from heaven knew where, and indifferent to what they crushed on their road to hell. After the train had passed, leaving behind it a lengthy silence, he again found himself face to face with the dead woman's wide-open eyes, the rigid pupils of which seemed to follow his every movement, while the upturned corners of the mouth grinned.

Otherwise phlegmatic enough, Misard could not resist a gesture of anger. He knew well enough what she was saying: 'Now find them, if you can, find them!' But nobody was going to tell him she could take them to purgatory with her. Hence they were somewhere about, and in the end he was bound to find them. Now, would it not have been more decent of her to have handed them over decently? It would have avoided such a lot of bother.

Those eyes followed him everywhere. 'Find them, if you can!' He ran his eyes over this room of hers, which he had never dared search while she was alive. The wardrobe, first. He found the keys tucked on top of the beam, then rummaged through the shelves of linen, emptied the two drawers, even took the drawers right out, to make sure there was no hiding place inside. But there was nothing. Then he thought of the night commode. He took off the marble top of that and turned the whole thing upside down, but without result. He also probed behind the mirror over the mantelpiece, a small thing bought at a fair, held up by a couple of nails. He slipped a flat rule behind it, but all he got out was some dusty black fluff. 'Find them, if you can!' Now, to escape those large fixed eyes which he could feel on him, he went on all fours and thumped all over the floor, in case a change of resonance should suggest a hollow. A number of tiles had come away from the plaster and these he prised up, but all without any result. When he stood up again, those eyes once more took him in charge, so he swung round, to meet the dead woman face to face, and then the corners of her mouth seemed to accentuate the terrible grin.

He was sure now. She was mocking him. 'Come on, find them!' He flushed violently all of a sudden. With sudden suspicion he went up to her. The sacrilegious thought which then came to him drained the blood from his cheeks. Why had he so facilely assumed that she could not take her thousand francs into the grave with her? Perhaps that was just what she was going to do. And he found the courage to uncover her, strip her, examine her, every crack and cranny of her limbs and body, since she thus defied him to find those francs. But there was nothing under her or behind her or in her. He overturned the bedding and thrust his arm full length into the mattress, but still found nothing. 'Then find them!' And that head, fallen back crooked on to the lopsided pillow, still goggled leeringly at him.

He was just trying to put the bed straight, when Flora came in, back from Doinville.

'The day after tomorrow, Saturday,' she said. 'At eleven.'

She was thinking of the funeral. Suddenly she guessed what he had been at, to get so out of breath while she was gone. But she dismissed it with a scornful gesture of indifference.

'Drop it,' she said, 'you'll never find them.'

For a moment, he thought she too was challenging him. He went up to her and challenged her.

'She left them to you, you know where they are!'

But the notion that her mother could have given those francs to anyone, least of all to herself, her daughter, made her shrug her shoulders.

'I don't think!' she said, scornfully. 'Give them to me? She's given them to the soil all right. Look, they're somewhere out there, you can find them all right.'

With a sweeping gesture, she indicated the whole house, the garden and its well, the railway tracks, the vast countryside. Yes, there it was, in a hole in some wild spot where nobody would ever discover it. Then while without the least embarrassment he went on anxiously heaving the furniture about and sounding the walls, Flora stood by the window and continued softly musing.

'What a lovely, mild night it is, outside . . . I walked quickly. The stars were like daylight . . . And oh, what a lovely sunrise it will be!'

She stayed by the window for a while, staring out into the peaceful countryside, softened now by the first warmth of April. She had come

274

back moody, her wounded heart opened up again, more unhappy than ever. But when she heard Misard leave that room and continue his savage search in the rest of the house, she too went up to the bed, and sat there, her eyes on her mother. The candle was still burning brightly and steadily at the corner of the table. A train came by and shook the cottage.

Flora had resolved to spend the whole night beside the corpse, and she gave herself up to thought. For a while the sight of the dead woman distracted her from her obsession, from the thing which haunted her, which she had been fighting out in the peace of the dark night, under the stars, all the way to Doinville and back. And now astonishment deadened her pain: why, she wondered, was she not more sorry, now her mother was dead? And why, even now, was she still not able to cry? For all her wildness and taciturnity, always running out of the house to wander through the fields, when not on duty, she had certainly been fond of her mother. A score of times, during the former bout of attacks, which had threatened to be her mother's death, she had come and seated herself there, to beg her mother to have a doctor, for she too suspected Misard's doings and hoped that alarm might halt him. But she had never got more than an angry no from the sick woman, as if in her struggle with Misard her mother had made it a point of pride to accept help from nobody, being sure to win in the end, simply by taking her money to the grave with her. After that, Flora had ceased to try to interfere, her own misfortune absorbing her, and she would vanish and race about to find forgetfulness. That, it was no doubt which now sealed her heart. When one has one grief which is too great, there is no room for another. Her mother had gone, she saw her there, destroyed, so pale, but however she tried, she could not be more sad than she already was. Call the police and denounce Misard? What good would that do, when everything anyway was going to ruin? Thus, little by little, though she was looking at the dead woman, she ceased to see her, preoccupied by her inner sight, entirely at the mercy of an idea which had gained a foothold in her brain, and now aware only of the profound impact of the trains whose passage were her clock.

For the past few moments she had heard the distant grind of the slow down from Paris. When at last it passed the window, with its

275

headlight, there was a momentary flash in the room, as if the walls had caught fire.

'One eighteen,' she said to herself. 'Seven hours more. When morning comes, at eight sixteen, they will pass.'

Every week, for months now, this expectation had been her obsession. She knew that on Thursday morning the express which Jacques drove would also be taking Severine to Paris. Now, completely absorbed in jealous self-torture, she lived only to look out for them and see them pass and tell herself that there, in far-off Paris, with nothing to come between them, they would revel in each other's bodies. Ah, that train so fleet, bringing the hateful realization that she could never attach herself to its tail, to be carried on with it. She felt as if every wheel sliced through her heart. She had suffered so much that one evening she hid herself and meant to write to the authorities, for if she could have that woman arrested, that would be the end of it, and as she had years before by accident actually seen some of the filthy things that town girl who married Roubaud did with the old Judge Grandmorin, she was sure that if the examining magistrates were but told all that, she would have delivered Severine up to them. But, pen in hand, she found she simply did not know how to put it. Besides, would the authorities even listen to her? Without doubt all those fine folk understood one another, dog did not eat dog. Indeed, as likely as not she would find herself instead in prison, just as they had once tried charging poor Cabuche.

No, what she wanted was revenge, and she would get her revenge by herself, without need of any man's aid. Nor was it a mere notion of vengeance such as she had heard tell of, doing harm to cure one's own hurt. Oh, no, what she needed was to put an end to it all, to bring it all crashing down, as if a thunderbolt had swept them away. She had her own pride, too, she knew she was stronger and lovelier than that other woman and she was convinced of her true right to have been the loved one, and when she wandered alone through that wild country with her heavy head of golden hair open to the sun, what would she not have given to have that other woman under her hands, to have their quarrel out deep in a wood, like rival warriors. No man had ever touched her yet, she could master any male, and therein was her essential invincibility, so now too she would be victorious.

It was a week before the idea had suddenly come to her, deep set in her, as if a hammer of unknown provenance had driven it deep into her brain: to kill them, so they should never pass that way again, never again go to Paris together. There was no reasoning in this, she merely obeyed a wild instinct of destruction. If she had a thorn in her finger, she would pluck it out – or cut off her finger. Kill them she must, and do so the very next time they passed. To achieve that, she must crash the train by dragging a sleeper on to the track, or unbolting a rail, so as to be sure of smashing it all, involving it all in death. He on his engine would certainly be one victim, sprawling prostrate, nor would the woman escape, who, to be as near as possible to him, was always in the front coach. As for the others, all that incessant flood of people, she simply did not think of them. They were not even people to her. Did she know them? Thus that destruction of a whole train, that sacrifice of so many lives, became the obsession of every moment of her life, unique catastrophe, which should be of sufficient compass and profundity in blood and human suffering to wash clean again her great tear-swollen heart.

Come Thursday morning, however, she had momentarily weakened, unable yet to decide exactly where or in what way she would remove a rail. But come evening, when she was off duty, the idea came to her, and she made her way through the tunnel to the Dieppe fork. This was one of her regular walks, this underground passage a good mile and more long, a straight, vaulted avenue, where she had the constant thrill of trains coming at her with their blinding head-lamps. Every time she went through she just escaped being run over, and it must have been that danger and a need to dare fate, which attracted her. But this evening, after escaping the eye of the watchman and getting half-way through the tunnel – keeping to the left, to be sure that any train coming towards her passed on the other side – she was imprudent enough to turn back to follow with her eyes the tail lights of a train bound for Havre, and when she went on again, a false step made her swing round, and then she no longer knew which way the red lights had vanished. Despite her pluck, dazed as she was by the roar of the wheels, she halted, her hands icy, her uncovered hair standing on end in a wave of terror. Now, if another train appeared, it suddenly seemed to her that in the complete darkness she would no longer be able to tell whether it was on the up track or the down one, and she might fling herself to the wrong side and be cut into pieces.

With an effort she strove to be cool and think it out. Then, suddenly, her fear carried her rushing on madly, straight ahead. No, no, she did not want to be killed before she had killed those two. Her feet caught in the rails, she slipped and fell, then she ran faster than ever. She was seized now with tunnel madness, the walls seeming to close in on her, the vaulting all echoes of imaginary sounds, menacing voices, ominous grinding. Every instant, she looked behind her, sure she felt the hot breath of an engine. Twice she had the sudden conviction that she was mistaken and that where she was she would be killed and this made her run back again. On she raced, on and on, when suddenly, far ahead, she saw a star, a round spot of light, a flaming eye, which was growing larger. But now she withstood the terrible impulse to run back yet again. The eye became a brazier, the all-devouring mouth of a furnace. Blinded, she leapt to the left, without knowing she was doing so, and the train thundered by, blasting her with its hot breath. Five minutes later, she had emerged safe and sound, on the Malaunay side.

It was nine o'clock, and in a few minutes the Havre express would come by. She immediately went on farther, at walking pace, as far as the Dieppe fork, two hundred yards away, her eyes probing the track, to see if there might not be some circumstance which would make it easier for her. And there, on the Dieppe line, which was being repaired, what should she see but a ballast train for which her friend pointsman Ozil had just set the points, and in a sudden flash she perceived and confirmed her plan: all she had to do was to prevent re-setting the points to the Havre track, and then the express would crash at top speed into the ballast train. Ever since the day when, drunk with desire, Ozil had tried to take her, and she had almost cracked his skull with her stick, she had had a warm spot in her heart for him, feeling the sort of friendship which led her, like a young nanny goat escaping from its mountain fastness, to enjoy dashing through the tunnel to pay him unexpected visits.

An ex-soldier, very thin and rather taciturn, zealous to the extreme in his work, Ozil had never given cause for the slightest complaint of negligence. He was on the alert day and night. But this untamed hussy who had given him a hiding and was as tough as any man had got under his skin. Flora only needed to beckon with her little finger, for him to obey. Though he was fourteen years her senior, he craved

278

for her and he meant to have her too. He told himself he would bide his time and try by gentle means, since the frontal attack had got him nowhere. So when this dark night she went up to his hut and called him out, he forgot everything and went to her. She robbed him of his senses. She led him now out into the open hill side, with a tangled yarn about her mother being ill and she having no intention of staying at Maufras Cross if she died. Far-off, his ear had already caught the sound of the express as it left Malaunay and steamed full throttle his way. And now, as she too felt its approach, she turned back, to see. Unfortunately for her, however, she had forgotten all about the new brake release equipment, by which, the moment the express was on the Dieppe line, it automatically set the signals against it, so that the driver had time to stop a few paces short of the ballast train. With the cry of a man alerted only as his house collapses, Ozil raced back to his post while Flora stood transfixed, out of the darkness following the express's movement as it was shunted back, to proceed normally when the points were properly set. Two days later, dismissed, Ozil came to say good-bye. He suspected nothing and pleaded with her to come to him if anything should happen to her mother. So much for that. A misfire. She would have to find some other means.

And now, as she recalled all this, the brooding cloud which darkened Flora's countenance vanished. Once again she saw the corpse in the yellow light of the candle. Now that her poor mother was no more, should she after all leave, to marry Ozil, who wanted her and might make her happy? But her gorge rose again at the idea. That, on no account! If she were such a poor thing as to leave those two a full life and for herself accept mere existence, better by far tramp the roads, better work as another woman's scivvy, better anything than belong to a man whom she did not love.

A strange noise struck her ear, and she suddenly realized that Misard was using a pick on the beaten earth floor of the kitchen. He was getting frenzied in search of her mother's nest-egg. He would gut the whole house. And she realized that she did not want to stay with him either. Then what was she to do?

There was a sudden salvo of hissing steam, the walls shook, and over the dead woman's white countenance passed the glow of a locomotive's fires. It stained the wide-open eyes and the fixed leer of

279

the lips with blood. The last all-station train down from Paris had passed, drawn by a slow, heavy locomotive.

Flora turned and examined the glittering stars in the peace of this spring night.

'Three ten,' she said to herself, 'in five more hours, they will pass.'

She would have to try again, the agony was too much. It was more than she could bear to see those two every week travelling to their love meeting. Now that she was sure she would never have Jacques to herself, she would rather he ceased to be altogether. She would rather everything ceased to be. And that miserable room where in her grief she kept vigil wrapped round her in ever greater need of destruction, for nothing to remain. As there was now nobody to love her, and her mother too was gone, let them all be wiped out of the world. By that act there would be dead upon dead, a multitude of death, a multitude for one grand, mass funeral. Her sister dead, her mother dead, her love now dead, what did that leave for her, but to be alone, whether in this awful house or elsewhere, always alone. And should she thus exist alone, while those two made a happy pair? Of course she should not, and if so, then better that everything should be brought low. Let death, already present in this smoke-ridden hovel, breathe on that railway track that passed the window and sweep the whole world from hence!

Thus, after long self-questioning, her mind made up, she again pondered the best method of realizing her plan, and in the end came back to the idea of removing a rail. That was the most certain and the most practical method, and easy to accomplish. She had only to take a sledge-hammer, drive out the chairs, then heave the rail off its sleepers. She had the tools, and in this lonely country nobody would see her working. The best place to choose was unquestionably the curve beyond the cutting on the Barentin side, where the track crossed a little valley by a twenty-seven-foot embankment. There the derailing was a certainty and the smash would be terrible.

Nevertheless, when next she came to draw up her time-table, she was worried. On the up track, before the Havre express, which passed the spot at eight sixteen, there was only one train, a slow, at seven fifty-five. Now, that would give her twenty minutes for her task, and this was enough. Yes, but in between those two timetabled trains, especially when the big steamers came in, there were often goods

280

trains which were not scheduled. How was she to know that it would really be the express which came next, and smashed?

For a long time she turned this over in her mind. It was quite dark outside. The candle was still alight, but she had omitted to snuff the wick, and it had burned long and charred, with the wax streaming down the sides.

Just as a goods train came by from Rouen, Misard entered the room. His hands were grimy with the soil, for he had been grubbing in the wood-shed. He was out of breath, baffled by all this vain searching, and so inflamed now with impotent anger that once again he began moving all the furniture, probing the mantelpiece, prodding everywhere.

The goods train was interminable, with its monotonous clank of heavy wheels, each thud of which shook the corpse on the bed. And when he reached out to take down a small picture from the wall, once again he caught sight of those dead eyes watching him, wide-open, and the lips with their grin seemed to move. The colour left his cheeks and he shuddered and in mingled terror and rage stammered: 'Yes, yes, "now you find it" ... Don't you fear, I shall find that money, the hell I will, if I have to turn every stone of this house and every clod of earth in the country.'

The black train had at last gone by, grinding slowly on into the darkness. Still once again, the dead woman continued to eye her husband, and she was so scornful, so convinced she would defeat him, that he slipped away into the darkness again, leaving the door wide-open.

Disturbed in her meditation, Flora rose to her feet. So that he should not come again to disturb her mother she closed the door that Misard had left open. As she did so, she was astonished suddenly to catch her own voice saying out loud:

'Ten minutes beforehand will be quite enough.'

Indeed, it was true. She would have time in ten minutes. Yes, if no goods train was signalled, ten minutes before the express, she would start work. And then, the matter thus settled and certain, her anxiety vanished and she felt very calm.

It began to be light a little before five. The day dawned fresh, the sky without a cloud. Notwithstanding the sharp air, she flung her window wide open, flooding that dismal room, full of smoke and the

281

odour of death, with the lovely morning air. The sun had not yet risen above the hill-crest of the horizon, topped with trees. Then at last it appeared, gilding the world, pouring its light down the slopes, flooding into the sunken roads, with all the lively joy of mother earth whenever spring comes round anew. She had not been wrong the evening before: it would be a lovely morning, one of those rare hours of youth and radiant health in which men all love to live. Oh! How lovely it would have been to roam at will by goat tracks through that wild country of narrow ravines and ridge upon ridge of downland. When she came back into the room, she was astonished to see the candle seem dead, too feeble already to add to the broad daylight more than a ghostly tear of light. Her dead mother still seemed to be watching the railroad through the window where trains came and went their ways, regardless of the pale vigil light beside her mortal body.

Flora was not due on duty till daylight, and did not leave her room till the Paris slow train at six twelve. Misard too was to come on, taking over from his night-time colleague, at six, and it was at his blast on the horn that she went out to take her place at the barrier, flag in hand. For a moment her eyes followed the train into the distance.

'Two hours more,' she said to herself, out loud.

Her mother no longer needed any help. Besides, from now on she felt an invincible horror of going back into that room. That was all over. She had kissed her mother farewell. Now she could dispose of herself and of others as she wished. Usually, between trains, she made off into the thickets around, but on this particular morning some special interest seemed to keep her at her post at the barrier. She sat on the seat which was there for the purpose, a simple plank beside the track.

The sun rose high above the horizon, golden showers of light fell slanting through the limpid atmosphere, but she did not stir, she sat on, bathed in the peace of it, lost in the heart of this untamed country, her whole being pulsating with April's throbbing sap. For a while she took an interest in her step-father whom she could see in his matchboard cabin on the far side of the line. Misard was plainly in a state of agitation, roused from his usual sluggishness. He kept coming out, fiddling anxiously with his instruments and levers, shooting swift glances at his cottage, as if his soul was still there, searching for that money. Then she forgot all about him, even forgot that he was there at all. She was absorbed, all expectation, her face closed and dead, her eyes straining down the line towards Barentin, for that was where, under the dancing sunlight, she expected her vision, there was the persistent goal of those wild eyes of hers.

The minutes crept slowly. Flora did not stir, till at last, at seven fifty-five, with two blasts of his horn, Misard signalled the Havre slow on the up-line. Then she rose, closed the crossing barrier and stood against it, flag in hand. An instant later, the train was already vanishing, after shaking the ground where they stood. She heard it plunge into the tunnel, when every sound ceased. But she did not now go back to her seat. She remained standing, once again counting the minutes. If, in ten minutes, no goods train were signalled, she would rush away there, beyond the cutting, to loosen the rail. She was very self-possessed. The only strain she felt was a certain tightness about the chest, as if her task were a terrible weight pressing on her. But at the last moment the renewed thought that Jacques and Severine were already drawing near, that unless she halted them they would once again pass by on their road to love, was enough to prevent any debate in her, confirm her, blind and implacable in her resolution. The act was now irrevocable, like the blow of the she-wolf which breaks the back of the fleeing sheep. Self-centred in her vengeance, all she could see now was their two mutilated bodies. The crowd of other folk did not exist for her. That human flood which for years had constantly passed her by, a stranger world, meant nought to her. There would be many dead, there would be much blood spilt, perhaps the very sun in the heavens would be darkened, but no matter, that gentle lightness of the balmy spring air did but exasperate her.

Two minutes more . . . one minute more . . . and she would go! Indeed, she had already set out, when the dull, heavy sound of wheels jolting on the road from Bécourt way halted her. A cart, no doubt a waggon. They would want to get through, she would have to open the crossing to them, she would have to exchange a word, she would have to stay there. She could not act. Her blow was frustrated. With a gesture of furious indifference, she turned and ran on her chosen way, abandoning her post, abandoning the waggon and its driver. Let them manage as best they knew. Then a whip cracked sharply in the early air, and a cheerful voice hailed her: 'Flora! Flora-a-a!'

It was Cabuche. She stood glued to the ground, halted thus in her first rush, halted only a few feet from the barrier itself.

'Eh, what's the idea?' he cried. 'Are you still asleep, on a lovely morning like this? Come on, let me through before the express comes along!'

In her heart there was a landslide. Her blow was indeed frustrated. Those two would go on their way to their happiness, and she would have done nothing to destroy them there. And while she tardily unfastened the ancient, half-rotted barrier, the hinges of which groaned with rust, she was all at heart searching for some obstacle, anything she could fling across the track, even here, desperate to the point of flinging herself down, had she but thought her flesh and bones hard enough to derail that love train. Then her glance fell upon the waggon, a heavy, low drag, laden with two blocks of stone so heavy that five fine horses were making hard work pulling it. And there was her solution, in those enormous, towering granite blocks, a tremendous mass to bar the track, and in her eyes there swiftly flared the fire of illicit possession, the wild desire to take that stone in her arms and plant it across the rails. She flung the crossing barrier wide. Gleaming with sweat, the five panting horses awaited the order.

'What be it with you this morning, Flora lass?' demanded Cabuche. 'You look queer this morning.'

Then she spoke.

'My mother died last night.'

Cabuche uttered a cry of friendly compassion. He put down his whip and took her hands in his.

'Flora. Poor dear! It's been coming a long time. But all the same, it's hard. She's home, is she?' Then he added: 'I must see her. If it hadn't been for that misfortune, she and I would have come to an understanding.'

He walked slowly to the cottage with her. On the threshold he glanced back at the horses, but swiftly she reassured him.

'They'll never budge. Besides, it's some time yet before the express.'

She lied. For, above the soft tremulousness of the countryside, her alerted ear had just caught the sound of that train already pulling out of Barentin. Five minutes more, it would burst out of the cutting and be there, only a hundred yards from the crossing. While the quarry-man, greatly agitated, stood at the dead woman's door, his thoughts

284

on poor little Louisette, Flora stayed outside, listening carefully to the steady approach of the express. All at once her mind turned to Misard. Misard! He would be bound to see her, he would prevent her. She nearly choked, then, swinging round, found that she could not see him at his post, then detected him, unable to resist his mad urge to search, no doubt suddenly feeling that the money must be hidden there, on the far side of the house, grubbing in the ground under the coping of the well. This was the final goad. Circumstances all connived for her. And suddenly, one of the horses whinnied.

Beyond the cutting, the roar of the locomotive grew loud, like the breathing of a man in a terrible hurry.

'I'll run and quiet them,' Flora called to Cabuche. 'You needn't worry.'

She raced down, took the trace horse by the bridle and heaved forward with all her savage force. The horses strained their withers. For a moment, the clumsy drag with its heavy load refused to budge, then, as if she had herself turned into a draught animal and harnessed herself, the huge load moved and just as the express flung out of the cutting at them, was dragged on to the tracks. Then, fearing the horses might get right across with their load, Flora hauled back suddenly against the whole team, with such a superhuman effort that her joints cracked. With her legendary strength, of which such astonishing feats of strength were told – a runaway waggon halted on a hill, a truck pushed out of the way of a train – she now did this thing, her sinewy fists of steel against the five horses heavy and neighing in their apprehension of danger.

There came a bare ten seconds of unending horror. The two enormous blocks of stone seemed to blot out the sky. Its copper pipes and steel surfaces gleaming, the train rushed forward, a lissom, living thing, thunderous of speed, swift through the golden haze of the lovely morning. The inevitable was already there. Nothing on earth could prevent the crash. Yet for Flora, time dragged painfully long.

Back at his post now, Misard was yelling, arms waving, in a crazy effort to warn and halt the train. Brought out of the house by the clang of the iron wheels and the neighing of his horses, Cabuche had reached their heads and he too yelled and heaved, to get them forward. But Flora had now rushed to his side, and was holding him back – which saved his life. He thought she had not been strong

285

enough to master the horses, that it was the horses which had dragged her. He stood blaming himself, sobbing, choking in abysmal terror, while, eyes staring wide and burning, she towered beside him and watched. In the very instant when the front of the locomotive was about to crash into the stone, when there were yet some three feet to go, for the briefest flash of time she clearly saw Jacques, his hand on the locomotive control, but his face turned her way, and in a glance which to her was infinitely long, their eyes met.

That very morning, when she came down the platform at Havre to take the express as she did every week, Jacques had given Severine a smile. What good was it going to do them to ruin life with nightmares? Why not profit by what days of happiness they could seize? Perhaps in the end everything would come out right. Anyway, he was determined at least to taste the delights of today's trip, his mind busily making plans for it, thinking of where they would go for lunch. Besides, he particularly wished to console her with a cheerful smile, because she looked so dismayed when because she found that there was no first-class coach in front, she would be obliged to travel far away from him, at the rear. For after all they would both get there together, they could make up then for this slight separation. Indeed, he was so full of high spirits that, having leant out to look back till he saw her find a seat, right at the tail, he had to chip Dauvergne, who was the guard, and still sweet on Severine. The week before, indeed, Jacques had had the distinct impression that Dauvergne was getting bolder and that she was even encouraging him, either from need of a change, or anxious to escape the terrible life she had made for herself. Perhaps Roubaud was quite right, she would end up in that young man's bed too, not because she wanted to be there, but simply because she would be bound to try something new. So this morning Jacques had twitted Dauvergne, asking him to whomever it was hidden behind one of the elms in the courtyard that he had been blowing kisses, a remark which made old Pecqueux, busy stoking Lison prior to departure, roar with laughter.

From Havre to Barentin the express had run on time without incident, and it was Dauvergne, at his guard-van look-out, who first sighted the obstacle on the tracks as they came out of the cutting. The front van was packed with luggage, for this train was full of the passengers of a steamer which had come in the evening before.

Tight-packed among all those trunks and suit-cases, which were rocking a great deal at that speed, he spent his time standing at his desk, busy with bills of lading, while the little bottle of ink dangling from its nail jigged about incessantly. After any station where there was luggage to discharge, he had four or five minutes' writing to do. At Barentin two passengers had got out, so he had been putting his papers in order, when, stepping up into his look-out to sit on the stool there, he gave his usual glance behind and ahead. He always spent all his free time on the look-out like that. The tender hid the driver from him, but thanks to his elevated position, he often saw farther and more quickly than the driver could. So the train was still hurtling through the cutting when he sighted the obstacle ahead. He was so astonished that for a while he doubted his eyes, and was paralysed with fright. He thus lost a few seconds while the train rushed out of the cutting, when from the engine he already heard a piercing cry, and at the same time ordered himself to pull the alarm signal dangling just above his hand.

In this terrible moment, though his hand was on the control, Jacques saw and yet did not see, his whole mind for a moment distant, toying with hazy, far-off things, in which there was no longer any precise image of Severine. The mad clanging of the bell and Pecqueux yelling behind him awakened him. Dissatisfied with the way the fire was drawing, Pecqueux had just opened the grate, then leant out to check the speed, when, white as death, Jacques saw it all, understood it all – the waggon across the tracks, the engine at top speed, the imminent frightful crash, all with such sharp clarity that though the shock of the impact was already in his bones, he could even notice the detail of the grain of the two blocks of stone.

There was no avoiding it. He swung the regulator wildly, shut off steam, braked to the full, reversed Lison, clung automatically to the whistle cord, wild, all impotent determination both to warn and to clear the obstruction ahead. But Lison did not obey him, Lison still rushed on, her whistle a terrible cry of distress rending the air.

She was no longer as docile as she once had been, she had never made steam the same since that snow, her responsiveness had gone, she had become crotchety and cantankerous, like an elderly woman gone badly chesty from a winter chill. She wheezed, she buckled under the brake, but yet plunged on and on with all the stupefied stubbornness of her corpulence. Crazy with fear, Pecqueux now leapt out, but Jacques, one hand still on the regulator, the other automatically on the whistie cord, just waited, while, belching smoke, her breath hoarse and continuous with strident roar, Lison flung the enormous weight of the thirteen coaches she was pulling against the quarry-man's waggon. And in that instant, but twenty yards from where they stood aghast at the side of the track, Misard and Cabuche, arms in the air, and Flora, staring wide-eyed, witnessed the frightful result, saw the train rear up, seven coaches piling one on top of the other, to crash to earth with terrible din, in a shapeless tangle of debris. The first three were reduced to splinters, the other four became a small tangled mountain of stripped roofing, broken bogies, doors, chains, buffers, shattered glass. And over it all they heard the engine disrupt as it crashed into the stone, a vast dull thud ending in an agonizing screech of metal. Ripped open, Lison mounted the obstacle and tipped over to the left. The shattered stones meanwhile flew all ways, as if exploded by a mine. Of the five horses, four were killed outright, rolling over and over and dragged out of shape. But the tail of the train, six more coaches, remained quite intact, halted violently behind the piled-up disaster, without even leaving the rails.

Then the shrieks rose high, cries for help drowned by howling, incomprehensible like the howling of beasts.

'Here, help, help ... Please God, I am dying, help me, please God, help me!'

Next, all sound was lost and they saw nothing, for Lison, helpless on her back, her bowels ripped open, was hissing her steam away through broken pipes and cocks, a roar of tremendous breathing, like the death-throes of a giant woman, and up from her rose white vapour, endlessly in dense billowing clouds which thrust out along the ground, while from the furnace fell blazing coals, red as the bleeding entrails themselves, darkening the air with their smoke. So violent had been the shock that Lison's smoke-stack had ploughed deep into the ground. At the main body bearing the side members of the chassis had snapped and the stumps now crossed each other. Wheels thrust into the air, like a tall ungainly woman dismembered by the horns of a fabulous monster, Lison now showed all her twisted coupling rods, her shattered cylinders, her cams and her battered valve gear, the horrible tangle of her bowels gaping open in a wound

288

by which the life hissed and roared in despair as it drained from her. And there, quite close, lay the one horse which was not yet dead, its front legs broken off forwards, its entrails too slithering out through a gash which reached the length of its belly. They could see the animal's head reared stiffly back in a death agony, they could see the jaws gape in the animal's last terrible whinny, but not a sound of this could they hear, all was lost in the roar of the dying locomotive.

Shouts rose suddenly, suddenly to be broken off again and disappear.

'Help, here, here! Put an end to my misery! . . . I can't bear it, put an end to my misery, do please put an end to my misery!'

Amid this deafening noise and blinding smoke, the doors of the intact coaches began to open, and passengers poured from them in panic. They fell on to the track, they stumbled to their feet, they lashed out with fists and legs to get free, then, feeling solid earth beneath their feet and the open country before them, they fled, leaping the hedge, dashing across the fields, in the grip of blind instinct to get away from the danger, as far as they ever could. And women and men alike disappeared shouting into the woods.

At last, Severine was free of the mêlée. Her hair was tumbling down her shoulders, her gown torn. But she did not run away. Instead, she raced to that groaning engine. She came face to face with Pecqueux.

'Jacques?' she cried. 'Jacques? Is he all right?'

Pecqueux, who had miraculously not even sprained an ankle, ran forward with her, his heart cramped with remorse, at the thought that he was alive and his driver was underneath the wreck. They had done so many thousands of kilometres together, gone through so much as a team, constantly lashed by the elements. But there was their engine, their poor engine, faithful, fond old Lison, the third partner of their triangle, prostrate, breathing her last from ruptured lungs.

'I . . . I jumped,' he stammered, 'I don't know what's happened . . . to him . . . Quick! quick!'

Beside the crossing hut they came upon Flora. She stood there, stock still, watching their approach. She was stupefied by the thing she had accomplished, the massacre she was responsible for. All she knew was that it was now over and that was good. She knew for the moment only a sense of relief, knowledge of a need accomplished.

There was no sorrow in her for the misfortune of others. She did not even see them. Then suddenly she recognized Severine, and her eyes grew hideously large, her bloodless cheeks earthy with frightful pain. What, did this woman then yet live, with Jacques indubitably dead? And then, by reason of the piercing pain of the love she had murdered, like a knife-blow in her own heart she was aware of the whole vileness of her act. This killing of so many people, she had done. A terrible cry broke from her throat, she wrung her arms and ran madly away, crying:

'Jacques! Jacques! . . . He's there, behind, I saw him . . . Jacques! Jacques!'

Lison's death-throes were quieter now, only a hoarse and feeble wheezing, against which at last the cries of the injured gained strength and became audible. But the steam and smoke were still dense and the great heap of torn metal and wood from which came the cries of terror and agony was wrapped in black dust, a cloud which the sun did not move. What was to be done? Where start? How reach him?

'Jacques! Jacques!' Flora was still crying. 'I tell you, he saw me, he was thrown that way, under the tender . . . Hurry, hurry, for pity's sake, help me get him out!'

Cabuche and Misard had just rescued Dauvergne, who had jumped like Pecqueux, at the last moment. His ankle was sprained. They propped him up against the bank, whence with dazed eyes he stared in silence at the scene, but apparently in no pain.

'Cabuche,' Flora pleaded, 'come and help me. I tell you, Jacques is under there!'

But the quarry-man did not understand her. He ran to some other injured, carried out a young woman whose legs hung limp, with thigh fractures. And it was Severine who hurried to her cry.

'Jacques? But where? I will help.'

'That's right,' gasped Flora, 'you help me!'

The two women's hands met as they heaved together at a broken wheel, but the frail fingers of the one were without effect, while the other's powerful fists shifted one fragment of debris after another.

'Steady there!' cried Pecqueux, joining in the work.

Reaching out sharply, he halted Severine just as she was about to tread on an arm, still in its blue cloth sleeve, but cut off at the shoulder. She fell back, horrified. But it was not Jacques' arm, it was

290

the arm of a stranger which had been flung there, an arm belonging to a body which must be some distance away. But this first impression had so shaken her that she was now half paralysed, stood there with tears streaming, watching the others working, herself unable even to lift away the fragments of glass on which it was easy to get cut.

Now the work of saving the dying and getting out the dead became anxious and dangerous, for the engine coals had lighted fragments of matchboarding and the mass of debris nearly caught fire. Shovels had to be found, earth tossed on to the flames. While somebody raced to Barentin for assistance and a telegram was sent to Rouen, the work of clearing the line was got going as best they could manage, everybody helping with wonderful good will. Many of those who had run away had come back, ashamed of their panic. Nevertheless, the work called for the utmost caution. Every piece of debris they lifted had to be treated with care, from fear of giving the death blow to buried victims, if the remaining wreckage collapsed on them. There were injured whose head and shoulders only protruded from the mass. They were caught as if in a vice, howling with pain. It took a quarter of an hour to get out one man, who made no complaint, but was white as a sheet, assuring them he was all right, not hurt at all, but in fact was minus his legs, and died at once, suffering from such shock that he did not even observe his own horrible mutilation. From a third-class coach which had caught fire they extracted a whole family. The father and mother's knees were injured, the grandmother had a broken arm, but none of these felt their hurt. They were sobbing and crying for their little girl, fair-haired they said, just turned three, who had vanished under the wreckage. But they found this child safe and sound under a broken end of coach roofing, even amused, smiling. There was however another little girl smothered with blood, and her poor little hands were crushed. They took her away while they tried to find her parents. The lonely little stranger did not utter a word, but her face knit up in unspeakable fear if anyone approached her. The impact had twisted all the metal work, and they could not get the doors open, but had to clamber into compartments through broken windows.

Already four corpses lay side by side by the permanent-way. A dozen injured, stretched out near the dead, were waiting for medical aid, but there was no doctor to help them. The work was proceeding very slowly. Under each piece of wreckage they found a victim. Yet

291

the heap seemed no smaller. It seemed to be streaming, palpitating, from this butchery of men.

'But I tell you, Jacques is under there!' Flora repeated, for in this senseless, persistent cry, the cry of her own despair, she could ease her soul. 'I can hear him, quick, here, come!'

The tender was caught under the coaches, which had been flung into the air above it, then crashed down on it. And Flora seemed to be quite right. Now that the roar of the engine's death-throes had died down, the loud cries of a man trapped beneath it could be heard. As they drew closer to him, the voice grew more high pitched, so agonizing in its pain that the men clearing the debris found it unbearable and began to cry out themselves. But just as at last they reached him, got his legs free and drew him towards them, the cries of agony ceased, and the man was dead.

'No,' said Flora, 'that is not Jacques. Farther down, he's right underneath.'

And with her amazon arms she raised wheels, heaved them behind her, tore off the galvanized roofing of coaches, broke off doors, wrenched out broken chains, and whenever she unearthed a dead person or one of the injured, called furiously for help, to get him away and be able to go on with her frenzied search for Jacques.

At her back, Cabuche, Pecqueux and Misard laboured away, while Séverine, at collapsing point from standing in idle strain, had sat down on the torn-out seat of a compartment. Misard, however, had regained his usual impassivity. He seemed limp and indifferent, avoiding any great effort, and was principally helping to carry the dead away. Like Flora, he inspected each face, as if expecting to recognize it, out of the thousands and thousands who had passed this way at full speed in ten years, leaving in their trail only the confused notion of a crowd borne by in a flash of lightning. But for all that he looked, it was still only that flood of strangers whom he saw, the uneasy world of the restless, and each sudden brutal death remained as anonymous as that urgent living flood who passed that way, pressing forward each into his own future. They could put no name, no clear indication of identity of these faces. They were harrowed by the horror of all these unfortunate folk now broken on the ground, like soldiers whose corpses fill trenches over which new armies will come to make their mad charge. Nevertheless, Flora did seem to find one to whom she had actually once spoken, on that day when the train stuck in the snow. It was the American, whose features she had got to know quite well, but without a notion of his name or his connections. Misard put the man aside with the other dead of unknown provenance, halted there on their way to unknown destinations.

Then came another terrible sight. Caged in an upturned first-class compartment, they came upon a young couple, almost certainly a honeymoon couple. They had been thrown together so unfortunately that the woman had crushed her husband under her, without being able to move a finger to assist him. Suffocated, he was already in his death throes, while, being able to talk, she pleaded in desperation for them to hurry, and was broken hearted because she knew it was she herself who was his death. But when this couple had been liberated one from another, it was she who suddenly died, for a buffer had torn her loin open, and the husband, coming to his senses, knelt beside her, desperately staring at her eyes, in which the tears she had shed for him were still not dry.

There were now twelve dead and more than thirty injured. At last they were beginning to get the tender away. From time to time Flora thrust her head in between the splintered timbers and twisted iron, searching for Jacques – and suddenly cried out loudly:

'I can see him. He's under here . . . Look, that's his arm, in that blue wool jerkin . . . He is quite still. He is not breathing.'

She stood upright and swore like a man.

'God in Heaven!' she cried. 'For Christ's sake do get a move on, and get him out of there.'

With her naked hands she tried to tear away a floorboard of a coach, but other debris held it. She raced away, to come back with the axe the Misards used to split logs, and, legs straddled like a forester attacking an oak, she assailed the timber with blows, and others drew aside, to give her room, with warning cries to take care. She did not heed them, but carried on with superhuman urge, sure of herself, irresistible. She had hewn off the timber and now each new blow cut away a further obstacle. Her fair hair flying, her bodice loose, revealing her naked shoulders, she was like a menacing reaper as she cut a path through the destruction which she herself had caused. One last blow on an axle and the head of the axe split. With the assistance of others, she was now able to pull aside the wheels which in fact had protected Jacques from being utterly crushed. She was the first to get to him. Alone, she bore him out in her arms.

'Jacques, Jacques,' she was murmuring, and then cried: 'He's breathing, he's alive. God in Heaven, he's alive! I knew I had seen him fall, I knew he was there!'

Aghast, Severine followed. Together, they laid him gently on the ground under the hedge, near Dauvergne, who still did not seem to realize what had happened, but stared dully about him. Pecqueux came up and stood looking down on Jacques. He was shaken to the core, to see his beloved driver in such a miserable state. The two women, one on each side, were holding up Jacques' head, their eyes intent on the least quiver of his face muscles.

At last, Jacques opened his eyes, and without seeming to recognize anybody, dully examined first one, then the other. They meant nothing to him. Then his eyes caught sight of the dying engine, not far away, and into his glance at once came terror, and then an uneasy stare, as his sorrow welled up in him. Yes, Lison was something that he did recognize, and Lison recalled it all, the two blocks of stone barring his road, the terrible impact, the crushing and breaking he had felt simultaneously in her and himself, from which he had recovered but by which she was clearly condemned to die. She was not to blame, she had not got out of control, and if since that little disorder she contracted in the snow she had been less lively, that was not her fault. Besides, one had to forgive inevitable ageing, which makes all limbs more sluggish, all joints less flexible. Thus without hesitation he forgave her in his immense grief, seeing her prostrate there in her death throes, growing cold already, her fire fallen out in black cinders, the roar of steam from her shattered loins now but the plaint of a tiny babe. Even so, soiled with earth and spittle as she was, she was still shining and beautiful there on her back, prone in that pool of black ash, and her end was the tragic one of a thoroughbred struck down as she galloped by. For a space her ripped-up flanks had revealed the precise movements of her system, the twin heartbeat of her pistons, the blood flow of the steam through her circulating valves and then, like limbs convulsed in pain, her coupling rods had merely shuddered in the great gush of it which had given her life. And in the vast sigh which had emptied her lungs for ever, Lison's spirit had left her body. The immense feminine form sank in its evisceration deeper and

294

deeper into death till at last sweet sleep brought every member peace, and silence, and she was dead. And then the mountain of iron, steel and copper, her mortal remains, the shattered colossus of the frame, the trunk split open, the arms and legs broken away, the inner parts rendered shapeless, all assumed the grim melancholy of an immense human corpse, a world in itself which had known life and from which in pain the living essence had been wrested.

And when Jacques fully realized that Lison had ceased to be, he closed his eyes again, longing himself to die, moreover feeling so drained of life that he felt he might well be carried hence in the last frail gust of his engine's breath. From under his closed lids the slow tears trickled over his cheeks. It was more than Pecqueux could bear as he stood by his driver's side, and a choking seized the rough man's throat. Their dear old girl was dying, and Jacques, his chief, would gladly follow. This then was the end, was it, of their triangular life? The end of those trips when they rode her by the hundred miles and never a word between them, so well they all three understood one another, a mere nod sufficient. Poor dear Lison, so gentle in her strength, so lovely when she gleamed in the sunlight. And Pecqueux, as sober in this moment as ever a man was, broke into violent weeping, despite his will, each sob shaking his lanky frame.

Both Severine and Flora too were agonized, and when Jacques lost consciousness again they were very worried. Flora ran to the house to bring camphorated brandy with which she rubbed his forehead to try to bring him round. Their sense of misery was not made any the less by the endless death throes of the one surviving horse, minus its two front legs. It lay there close to them, continually whimpering with pain, the sound so terribly penetrating, almost human in its terrible woe that because of it two of the injured people had also begun to howl like animals. Never had death cries rent the air with such heart-wrenching, unforgettable, blood-curdling sound. The agony of it became unbearable, till there were voices raised, trembling with pity and anger, begging somebody to put this miserable horse whose throes were unending out of its pain. Now that the locomotive was stone dead, that sound of the horse's cries was the final lamentation of catastrophe. At last, still sobbing, Pecqueux took the broken axe and with one blow on the animal's head ended its life. Deathly silence covered the scene of the massacre.

Help now arrived, after two hours' waiting. The impact had pitched the coaches to the left, so that the other track was going to be clear in a very few hours. A train of three waggons, drawn by a pilot engine, brought out from Rouen a crowd of important people, all horror and urgency – the principal secretary of the prefecture, the public prosecutor, engineers, and doctors of the Western Company. By this time the Barentin station-master, M. Bessière, was also on the scene with a team of men who began work on the debris. This desolate corner of country, generally so silent, had suddenly become the scene of tremendous activity and tension.

After their first flush of panic, the passengers who were unhurt felt a feverish need to do something. Some of them wanted horsecarts. They were afraid to continue by train and wanted horse-transport. Others, seeing that out there not even a barrow was forthcoming, started worrying about where they were going to get a meal or a bed. They all wanted to send telegrams and some set out for Barentin for that purpose and took messages for others.

While the authorities and men of the railway management began their enquiry, the doctors hastened to give medical aid. Some of the injured had lost consciousness and lay in pools of blood. Others moaned as the surgeons got to work with probes and needles. The total casualties were fifteen dead and thirty-two seriously injured. Until their identity could be established, the dead were laid out on the ground, along the hedge, face upwards. A young assistant magistrate, fair-haired and pink-skinned, was dealing with them all by himself, fumbling in pockets to find documents, cards, letters, in the hope of indicating their names and addresses. Meanwhile, a gaping crowd formed around him, for though there were no houses here or within a mile or two, inquisitive folk soon enough turned up out of the blue, till there were about thirty men, women and children who offered no help, merely got in the way.

Now the black dust and veil of smoke and steam which had enveloped the scene, had cleared, and the radiant April day triumphantly flooded the scene with light and the soft rain of the morning sunlight bathed the features of the dead and the dying, lighted dismembered Lison and all the ugly pile of wreckage now being cleared back by the teams of railway workers, who were like so many insects busy repairing the ruin wrought by a casual clumsy boot in their city of earth.

Jacques was still without consciousness, and Severine caught the attention of a doctor passing near and begged him to look at him. The doctor found no trace of injury, but spoke of the possibility of internal injuries, for there were flecks of blood on Jacques' lips. Unable to state a definite opinion, he advised removing him as soon as possible and getting him to bed, avoiding any shocks. Under the touch of the doctor's hands, Jacques had again opened his eyes and he groaned faintly. This time, he recognized Severine, and he stammered vaguely:

'Take me away, take me away!'

Flora bent over him, and when he turned, he recognized her too. Then his eyes filled with the blank terror of a child, and, recoiling with hatred and terror, he turned back to Severine.

'Take me away, at once, at once!' he begged her.

Then, making no effort to conceal their intimacy – for Flora no longer counted – Severine whispered:

'The Maufras Cross house, yes? If you don't mind that, it's only a step away, and we shall be alone, there.'

He agreed, shivering again when he saw Flora.

'Anywhere you like, but at once.'

The expression of sheer horror and detestation in Jacques' eyes when he looked at her had turned Flora to a bloodless statue, for she saw that despite all this slaughter of strangers and innocent people whom she did not even know, she had not succeeded in killing either of these two lovers. The woman had emerged without a scratch and now he too might survive, and all she had done was to bring them closer together, flinging them into each other's arms, bringing them to the seclusion of Maufras Cross where nobody could stand between them. She could already imagine them living there, Jacques fully recovered, convalescent, his mistress waiting on him hand and foot, her hours of vigil rewarded by continual caresses, and here, far from the world, at absolute liberty, the lovers drawing out endlessly a new honeymoon created by the accident, and at this thought she felt cold to the marrow and stared blankly at the dead whom she had killed for nothing.

Suddenly, looking at the scene of death, Flora saw that Misard and

Cabuche were being interrogated, and guessed that the judicial enquiry had begun its work. Indeed, the public prosecutor and the prefecture secretary were already trying to find out how came that quarryman's load of stones on the track. Misard maintained that he had not left his post, but he could not say anything definite. He maintained that he knew absolutely nothing, he had been busy, watching his indicators. Cabuche, on the other hand, still in a very upset state, told a long, tangled story about having done wrong to leave his horses, because he wanted to see the dead woman, Madame Misard that was, and his horses had started without him and Flora Misard being able to stop them. He got mixed up again and again, going back to the beginning, without making his interrogators understand.

Then an untamed lust for freedom stirred Flora's blood again. She wanted to be free from herself, so she could think and make her own decisions, and never need assistance to get straight. Why wait till they pestered her with questions, even arrested her? For, quite apart from any criminal act, she had failed to do her service duty, they would make her responsible. But she found that so long as Jacques would be nearby, she could not leave that place.

Severine meanwhile had so pressed Pecqueux that he had procured a stretcher and got a work-mate to help him carry Jacques. The doctor had persuaded Severine to put up the guard as well – Dauvergne, though stupefied seemed to be suffering merely from brain concussion. One after the other, the two men were taken to Maufras Cross. Without caring who saw, Severine unfastened Jacques' collar and pressed her lips to his eyes, to give him courage while they transported him.

'Don't fear,' she whispered, 'we shall be happy.'

He smiled and kissed her in return, and that act was the final wrench for Flora, tearing Jacques from her for ever. She felt as if her own blood too were gushing out from a wound which would never heal. But when they picked him up to carry him, she followed. As she passed her own cottage, through the window she saw into her dead mother's room and perceived the pale light of the candle burning close to the corpse. All this time, the corpse had been alone, the head half turned round, the eyes staring, the lips twisted, as if Phasie had

298

been busy watching this shattering and slaughtering of strange human bodies.

Flora suddenly ran. She turned sharply where the Doinville road branched off and took a path to the left, through the undergrowth. She knew every corner of this country, and if they sent gendarmes to take her she could hold her own with them out here. Almost at once she stopped running, and with slow steps made her way to a hiding place where she was wont to go in her fits of melancholy. It was where a passageway had been cut into the hill above the tunnel.

Looking up, she saw by the sun that it was mid-day. Once in her hole, she stretched out full length on the hard rock and lay, hands behind her head, thinking it over. It was only then that she realized the gulf in herself, and now, with the feeling that she was already dead, her limbs too gradually grew numb. It was not remorse for having pointlessly killed so many people, for she had to make an effort to realize any horror or regret. But she was now convinced that Jacques had seen her holding back the horses, and from the way he had drawn back from her she grasped that from now on he had the revulsion from her that monsters inspire and he would never forget. But when one fails others, one must never fail oneself, and in a moment now she knew that she would kill herself. No other hope remained to her, and now that she had succeeded in finding peace in which to reason, she felt this was her absolute need. Only her exhaustion, the total cancellation of her whole person by momentary fatigue, now stood in the way of going to find the weapon and do it. But while she waited, from the overmastering drowsiness which had taken possession of her there once again arose a love of life, a need for happiness, a lingering dream of being happy herself, once she left those two their mutual joys. Why should she not wait till darkness fell and go to Ozil who worshipped her, and would know how to defend her? Her thoughts tangled in a new sweetness as she fell into a dead, dreamless sleep.

When Flora awakened, it was dead of night. In astonishment, she felt about her. And then, as she felt the naked rock, she recalled where she had come to sleep, and like a thunder-clap followed an ineluctable necessity: to die. That cowardly sweetness, that enfeeblement at thought of the possibility of resuming her life, had vanished with her fatigue. Now, only death was good, for in all this blood, with lacerated heart, abhorred by the only man she had ever desired, but who was now another's, she could not live. Now that she had the strength, she must die.

She rose and without hesitation left her hole in the rocks, for she had just realized where she would go. By the heavens again, for the stars were clear, she knew that it was nearly nine. Just as she reached the railway, a train flashed by at high speed on the down track, and this seemed to please her. It would be all right, they had obviously got that track clear, the other no doubt would still be obstructed, as nothing seemed to be passing. So she followed the hedge by the permanent-way in the vast silence of this wild region. There was no hurry, there would be no train before the Paris express, which would not be there till nine twenty-five, so she dawdled along by the hedgerow in the dark shadows, very much at peace, as if on one of her habitual strolls by lonely paths. But before she reached the tunnel she crossed the hedge and followed the track, still idling along, now going to meet the express. She had to be cunning, not to be seen by the night-watchman, and she managed this as she had always done whenever she went to see Ozil on the far side of the tunnel. In the tunnel she continued steadily on her way, following the track. But it was not like the last time she did this, now she was not afraid, if she turned, of losing her sense of where she was. There was no tunnel mania now to confuse her mind, nothing of that sort of madness in which things and time and space were all confused in the thunder of a train reverberating against the brickwork of the long vault. For did anything now matter, when she had ceased to argue, void even of thought, consisting but of the firm resolve to tread on and on until she saw that train ahead, then still on and on, straight at its head-light blazing in the night?

But in time Flora was puzzled, for it seemed that she had been walking thus for hours. How far away was that death she now desired. The thought that she would never find it, that the road would be miles and miles long and still she would not meet it, filled her with wild anxiety. Her legs failed her. Was she going to be forced to sit down and wait, or to lie across the rails? For to her that seemed humiliating, her virginal amazon instincts told her that she must march on to the very end, she must die upright, and that thought brought new energy, and she had thrust forward again, when at last, very far off, she perceived the headlight of the express, like a small star sparkling along in a sky of jet-black ink. The train was still outside the tunnel, and made no sound to tell her it was coming. There was only that cheerful, lively little light, now a trifle larger. She drew herself to her full height, her graceful body poised on her powerful limbs, and now trod forward with longer strides, though without running, trod on as if a girl who was her friend were coming to meet her, and she would go to her half way.

Now the train had entered the tunnel, the frightful clamour of it was drawing closer, it was shaking the very soil with its hurricane breath, while the star had been transformed to an enormous eye, ever bigger, which seemed to spring from the orbit of night. In the grip of a hazy impulse, as if to be entirely alone in her dying, she emptied her pockets as she strode on, throwing away key, string, two knives, even the scarf knotted about her throat, so that her bodice blew open, half slipping from her shoulders. The eye became a brazier, it became the mouth of a furnace vomiting hot ash.

The breath of the monster reached towards her, moist and warm now amid the rumble of thunder, and deafening her at last. But still she strode on, still trod straight at that fire, so as not to miss the engine, insect-like fascinated, drawn by the flame. And when the terrible impact came, when she too was in the grip of death, she reared herself higher still, as if, inspired by a final amazonian resistance, she would herself take the monster in her arms and in a wrestle of death bring its shoulders down to the ground. Her head struck the head-light full on, and extinguished it.

It was more than an hour before men came to recover Flora's body. The driver had clearly seen the tall, pale shape striding towards him. It had been a strange, ghost-like vision when the headlight picked her up, and when, the next instant, his head lamp was out and the train was thundering on in the darkness, he shuddered at the realization that the angel of death had already passed. As he emerged from the tunnel, he contrived to shout to the watchman at the entrance what had happened, but it was not till Barentin that he could report that he must have cut somebody down in the tunnel, and a woman, too, for with fragments of skull there were long hairs sticking to the broken head-lamp glass. When they went to search, and found her, they were astonished to find her so white. She was like brilliant marble, her

301

body lying on the up-track, where it had been flung by the frightful blow, the head pulped, but the limbs in their partial nakedness and the wonderful beauty and purity of her athletic form, without a scratch. They saw who it was, and silently they drew a covering over her. It was unquestionable to them that she had committed suicide to escape the terrible responsibility which lay at her door.

By midnight, Flora's corpse lay beside her mother's in the squat little cottage. A mattress had been put on the floor and there was a candle now burning between mother and daughter. Phasie's head was still cocked over, she still had that frightful grin on her twisted lips, and seemed to be examining her daughter with those large staring eyes of hers, and in the solitude and deep silence which had now come upon that house Misard could be heard breathing hard as he continued his search alone. At their scheduled intervals the trains swept by, in one direction and the other, for traffic was now completely restored. They swept by, inexorable in their over-riding mechanical might, indifferent and oblivious of tragedy and crime alike. What did those anonymous members of the crowd fallen on the way, crushed under the wreckage, matter? The dead had been removed, the blood washed away, and once again the flow of humankind went on, bound beyond this place and time, into time to be.

302

11

It was the big bedroom of the Maufras Cross house, that room with the red damask hangings, and two tall windows of which looked straight out on to the railway tracks, only a few yards away. From the bed, an old four-poster bang opposite the window, one could see the trains pass. For years not a piece of furniture had been moved, not a thing taken out of this room.

Severine had had them put Jacques in this upper room, the 'red room'. He was still unconscious from shock. Henri Dauvergne was kept downstairs, in a smaller room. For herself she selected the bedroom next to Jacques', with only the landing between them. In a couple of hours she and her patients were settled in with reasonable comfort, for the house had been left fully equipped, even with linen in the cupboards. Knotting an apron over her frock, Severine now transformed herself into sickroom nurse. She had merely wired Roubaud not to expect her, she would most likely stay there for some days, looking after 'some of the injured' whom she had taken into their house.

The very next day, however, the doctor was most reassuring about Jacques, saying that there was a good chance of his being on his feet in a week. He had had a miraculous escape, with only the minimum of internal bruising. However, the doctor did insist on the greatest care – above all, absolute immobility. So when her patient at last opened his eyes, Severine, who had been watching over him as if he were a babe, begged him to be such a good boy and do whatever he was told. Weak as he was, he could only nod that yes he would be a good boy.

His mind was now quite clear, and he had identified the room as the one which she had described to him that night when she unbosomed to him her past and her part in Grandmorin's murder. It was that same 'red room' in which, at sixteen and a half, she had first yielded to the perverse lusts of President of the Court Grandmorin. It had moreover all happened in this very bed in which he now lay, watching the trains whirl past, each in turn making the house vibrate for a few tumultuous seconds. But even when it was still, he could feel that house which now encased him, the whole of it, the house he had so often seen when he drove trains that way and Lison roared with him past it. He could picture it, so clearly as he lay there, its front placed cock-eyed to the railway, and all the grim gloom of its sealed shutters, and, rendered all the more distressing and eerie since it had been up for sale, by the huge board FOR SALE, bringing out all the desolation of the bramble-overgrown garden. He recalled too the frightful melancholy which it had always produced in him, every time he saw it, haunting him and filling him with strange uneasiness, as if it had reared itself there solely to menace him. Thus now, prostrate and enfeebled in this red room, it seemed to him that at last he could glimpse his own fate: here, without question, here he was to die. However, as soon as she found he was well enough to bear conversation, Severine hastened to put his mind at ease. Tucking the counterpane straight, she whispered into his ear.

'Don't worry, darling, I have emptied all your pockets, I have taken out the watch.'

Wide-eyed, he tried to follow the expression on her face, and strove to remember.

'The watch? . . . Oh, yes, of course, I know . . .'

'You see, darling, somebody might have gone through your pockets. I have hidden it among my things. So you've nothing to worry about.'

He gave her hand a feeble squeeze, to thank her. Turning his head, he then noticed another object which she had found in his pocket – that knife. But there was of course no need to hide the knife. It was just a knife, a knife like any other.

The following day Jacques had regained strength sufficiently to hope that after all he would not die there. Cabuche had been in to see him, and the sight of that clumsy giant gave him real pleasure. Poor Cabuche was all anxiety, too, trying his utmost not to clump his heavy boots noisily on the parquet. As a matter of fact, since the accident the quarry-man had not left Severine's side, as if he too felt a fierce devotion to her. He was neglecting his own work, coming round every morning to help about the house. He had become Severine's faithful hound, his eyes ever following hers. As he put it, he thought she was 'a regular tough'un for such a little'un'. She was worth helping she was, 'seeing as she did so much for others'. The two lovers even grew accustomed to him, talking to each other with complete intimacy and even kissing without the least embarrassment when, all discretion, Cabuche tiptoed through the room, making as little as ever he could of his bulky body.

Jacques, however, now began to be puzzled by Severine's frequent disappearances. The first day, because of the doctor's orders, she had hidden from him that Dauvergne was downstairs, for she felt sure that it would be all to the good if at first Jacques felt that he was absolutely alone there. For that was a thing he kept anxiously asking about.

'We are really alone here, aren't we, dearest one?'

'Of course, darling, we are all on our own, absolutely alone. . . . Now hushabye, my pet!'

But she was constantly flitting away, and the next day he caught the sound of walking about below him and whispers. The following morning, there was unmistakable jollification of some sort going on down below. The sound of bright bursts of laughter and two eager young voices going nineteen to the dozen, reached his ears.

'So we are not alone. What's that going on down there?' he wanted to know. 'Who is it down there?'

'Well, as a matter of fact, darling, we aren't quite alone. In the room underneath you there's somebody else who was hurt. I had to take him in.'

'I see . . . Who is it?'

'Henri! – You know, Henri Dauvergne. Your leading guard.'

'Henri Dauvergne? Oh, I see . . .'

'And it was his sisters came to see him this morning. That's who it was you've heard. Those two girls can never talk without a lot of laughing . . . But he's getting on so well that they're going back again this evening. Their father can't manage without them. But Henri's going to stay two or three days more, to get quite better. . . . Did I tell you, he jumped clear of the train before the crash, and not a bone broken. But at first he was quite out of his mind with the shock. He's all right, though, now again.'

As Jacques did not reply, merely looked steadily at her with unblinking eyes, she added:

'Well, you know, it's really rather a good thing he is here. Otherwise,

305

tongues might be wagging about you and me . . . So long as I am not alone with you, Roubuad can't complain, can he, I have every reason to stay on . . . See?'

'Yes, yes, of course, you're quite right.'

So all that long day, Jacques listened to the Dauvergne girls' laughter, the same laughter that he could remember having heard coming up from the floor below that room at the St Lazare Station in which, lying naked in his arms, Severine had confessed it all to him. Then came peace again, the only sound Severine's footsteps, when she went to visit her other patient. Suddenly, the downstairs room door closed. The house sank into profound silence. Lying there, Jacques began to feel thirsty. At last, he had to bang twice on the floor with the bedside chair, to bring Severine up again. And when she did come, she seemed to be in a great hurry. There was no end to it, she said, but with a radiant smile. She had to keep changing the ice-packs on Henri's head, she said.

On the fourth day, Jacques was able to get up and spend a couple of hours at the window in an armchair. By leaning forward a little, he could just see the narrow strip of garden, cut back by the railway. There was a low wall in front, and this was a mass of pale pink wild roses. And to his mind came that night when he had looked over that wall to examine the rather large area of land on the other side of the house, enclosed merely by a hedge, and how he had crept through the gap in that hedge, to come upon Flora, sitting on the threshold of the tumble-down little greenhouse, scissors in hand, untangling stolen string. What a revolting night that had been, a night full of the horror of his trouble. And once that memory had come back to him and insisted on becoming ever more vivid, that wretched girl Flora haunted his thoughts and he could never escape from her stalwart figure, lissom blonde amazon that she was, with those fiery eyes holding his own. At first he did not utter a single word about the accident, and for reasons of prudence everybody who came to see him also avoided it. Nonetheless, every single detail came to life, he reconstructed it all, he thought of nothing else, thought so persistently, so assiduously that now as he sat by the window he had nothing more to do than seek out any lingering traces of it, or catch sight of any who had played a part in the catastrophe. There was one thing which puzzled him very much: whyever could he never catch sight of her, flag in

306

hand, at her crossing-barrier post? He was afraid to ask, but the fact that he could not see her made him still more unhappy to be encased in this grim house, which seemed to be peopled with spectres.

At last, one morning, while Cabuche was in the room, helping Severine, he made up his mind to ask.

'I say, what's happened to Flora? Is she ill?'

The quarry-man misunderstood the signs Severine made to him. He thought they meant: 'Go on, tell him.'

'Poor Flora is dead,' he replied.

Jacques began to shiver inside, and his eyes flickered from one to the other. Now he had to hear the whole story. Together, they told him how Flora had committed suicide, knocked down and run over in the tunnel, how they had delayed burying the mother, to take the daughter in the same hearse. Mother and daughter were now at rest, side by side, in little Doinville churchyard, beside the first of the family to go, the youngest – sweet, unhappy Louisette, who had also died a violent, blood-stained, mud-bespattered death. Three unfortunates together, three women among so many, fallen by the wayside, trodden underfoot, three souls vanished from life as if the frightful hurricane of passing trains had swept them away.

'Flora dead. Dear God!' murmured Jacques, again. 'My poor aunt, and Flora, and Louisette, all dead.'

When he uttered the name of Louisette, Cabuche, who was helping Severine push the bed, looked sharply up at her. Good faithful doggie Cabuche, her faithful servant at the first pat on the head, soft-hearted and not too intelligent creature that he was, poor Cabuche now felt frightfully embarrassed, in the growing love for Severine which had taken possession of him, to be thus reminded of that earlier attachment of his. But Severine, who of course knew all about his tragic love, showed not a hint of what she might be thinking, merely turned towards him with a tender glance, which touched his simple heart. At the same instant as he passed her the pillows his hand touched hers, and he caught his breath, so that when in the same instant Jacques cried out and wanted to know if they had really charged Flora with being to blame, he could only stammer and answer:

'Oh, no . . . But . . . But you see . . . You must see . . . It was her fault, wasn't it?'

Brokenly, he told Jacques all he knew about it. He had seen

307

nothing himself, being inside the house when the horses started and pulled the waggon with the stone blocks on to the track. That was what he regretted so terribly. The magistrates had told him off about it, too. A man should never leave his horses. This terrible accident would never have taken place, had he remained with them. Thus the official enquiry had drawn the conclusion that on Flora's part there had been a mere act of negligence, and as she had meted out such an atrocious punishment to herself, that was as far as the matter was taken. The Company had not even dismissed Misard, who, for that matter, maintaining his usual humble, deferential attitude, had got out of the mess completely by laying the blame on poor Flora, saying she had always been a headstrong girl, he often had to leave his post to close the barrier. And the Company could find no fault with his service on that fateful morning, and to work the crossing barrier until such time as he might remarry they gave him permission to take on a middle-aged slut named Ducloux, who had once worked in a pub and now lived nearby on her past disreputable earnings.

When Cabuche had gone out, Jacques' questioning eyes sought Severine's. He was very pale.

'Surely you know the truth,' he said. 'Flora pulled those horses back on to the line, she deliberately got those blocks of stone in our way.'

Severine went very pale herself.

'Darling, what an awful thing to say! You must be feverish again. You ought to go back to bed at once.'

'But I assure you, no,' he said. 'I am not delirious . . . Don't you realize, I saw her. I saw her as plainly as I see you! She was holding those horses back, with all her strength, she simply prevented Cabuche getting the waggon off the line.'

Severine's legs would no longer bear her, and she sank down on to a chair.

'Dear God, darling, how you terrify me! But that is frightful! I shall never sleep again!'

'Good God!' he went on. 'It's surely obvious enough. She tried to kill us both, in that heap of destruction . . . She had had her knife in me for a long time, and she was jealous of you. Add to that being a bit cracked, with loony ideas in her head . . . What mass murder too, what a sea of human blood! What a bitch of hell she was!'

308

His eyes started from his head and his lips twitched irritably, but he said no more. While one could have counted a hundred they stared at each other. Then, wrenching himself free from the frightful visions which rose between them, he went on in a choking voice:

'So now she's dead ... That explains it, that's what it is. She is haunting me. Ever since I came to, I have had the impression she is in this house. Only this morning I turned round suddenly, because I thought she was right here, by my pillow ... She is dead, but we are still living. Now we've got to look out, or she'll have her revenge on us!'

Severine shuddered.

'Sh! Don't say such things!' she cried. 'You will drive me mad.'

She hurried away from him, and soon after Jacques heard her downstairs, tending Dauvergne. Still at the window, he sank deep into thought again, as he peered out at the tracks and the little crossing-keeper's cottage with its enormous well and the narrow timber railwayman's hut, where, at his never-ceasing, monotonous task, Misard seemed to be dozing. For hours at a time now Jacques would stare at this scene, as if searching for the solution to some insoluble problem to which he must find the answer if he was to be safe.

Misard, for instance, he was never tired of watching. A timid, gentle, so colourless little fellow with that persistent nagging cough, but a man who had poisoned his wife, so persistent that he in the end had mastered such a great lusty woman as she was. It was evident enough that for years now Misard could have had no other thought whether by day or by night throughout the whole twelve endless hours of his daily shift. Every time the electric bell tingled he had only to blow his horn and every time a train had passed and the route was closed he had only to press a button, to inform the next post along the line, then press another to open the road to the post on the other side. Those were purely mechanical little movements which in course of time had become mere reflexes in that vegetative life he lived. Illiterate and stupid, the man never read anything between trains. He just stood there, arms dangling, eyes vague and lifeless. He sat in his shelter almost all the day long, his only distraction being his midday meal, which he spun out as long as possible. After it he would relax back into his state of vacancy, his brain void, not a thought there, and limit all activity to fighting back those terrible fits of sleepiness, which at times did make him fall asleep with his eyes open. When it was dark, to keep off that frightful drowsiness he would have to get up and walk about, his legs as uncertain as if he were drunk. And that struggle with his wife, that hidden drawn-out battle for the hidden thousand francs, to decide who would outlive the other and get that money, must for months have been the sole preoccupation of that lonely creature's stupefied brain. When he blew his horn and worked his signals, watching like an automaton over so many lives, his thoughts were occupied with poison. And when, hands idle and limp and eyes swimming with sleep, he waited for another tinkle of the bell, he must still have been thinking only of that. And beyond that, nothing. Yes, he would do her in. He would seek her hidden money out, too. It was he who would get it!

Today, Jacques was astonished to find Misard so utterly unchanged. For this fact meant that there were thus men who could kill without any shock, whose lives just flowed on after. Indeed, after the frenzy of his first attempts to find the money, Misard had sunk back completely into his former phlegmatic state, that of a man with the sulky meekness of sheer physical frailty, apprehensive of any shock. When it came to the reckoning, he had done his wife in to no good purpose, she after all had won the day, for he was beaten, he had turned the whole house upside-down, without finding a brass farthing, and in the uneasy furtive glances of that ashen countenance one could see the man's dismay at his defeat. He never lost sight of those wide-open eyes of his dead wife, or that grim grin on the lips with their perpetual taunt of: 'Come on, find 'em then!' And he did search too, there was never a moment of rest for his brain, it worked incessantly day and night in the efforts to guess where she could have hidden her little bit. Time and again he ran through all the possible hiding places, rejecting those he had already searched, burning with fever if ever he conjured up a fresh likely spot, when he would at once drop whatever he was doing and hurry there, though always pointlessly. And in the end this had turned into unbearable torture for him, a torture which was Phasie's very real revenge. Misard now suffered from a sort of insomnia of the inner brain which kept him for ever awake, for ever therefore stupefied, for ever, against his very will, turning it over and over, living solely by endless tick-tocking of his one obsession. When he blew his horn, one blast for down trains, two for up, he was still seeking. When he responded to the electric bell or pressed the buttons of his instruments, he was still seeking, frantically seeking, somnolent by day because of the endless long waits which his work entailed, agonized by sleep at night, like a man exiled to the far end of the world in the silence of that inky-black countryside. And that woman Ducloux, who now looked after the crossing barrier and, being all out to get him to marry her, kept fussing about him, got quite worried by this fact that he never seemed to sleep any more.

One night, after he had begun to walk about in his room a little, and had just gone to the window, Jacques saw a lantern moving to and fro at Misard's cottage, and thought that the man must be at his searches again. But the following night, when he looked out again, Jacques was startled to recognize Cabuche in a tall dark shape standing in the roadway under the window of Severine's room. But instead of annoying Jacques, this filled him, in his understanding way, with feelings of real pity and sadness. Here was another luckless creature, this hulk of a man just standing out there, just like a stupid, faithful adoring hound. True, though no single feature of Severine Roubaud was beautiful in itself, and she was such a slight little thing, she was nevertheless a woman of immense charm, with those jet-black locks and those pale blue eyes, especially if sheer savages, stupid giants like Cabuche, could be so captivated as to spend long night hours under her window, just like sentimental schoolboys. Jacques now remembered a number of little things he had noticed, not to speak of the quarry-man's anxiety to be of assistance, and the slavish looks he gave her. Yes, it was plain as a pikestaff, Cabuche had fallen for Severine and lusted after her. Why, when the next day he kept an eye on the man, he caught him furtively picking up and hiding away on his person a hairpin which slipped out of her bun when she was making the bed! It reminded Jacques pointedly of his own tribulations, all the desire he too had suffered from, all the uneasy urges and terrifying thoughts which with the return of health were coming back to life in him.

Two more days passed, the suggested week was drawing to a close, and, as the doctor had foreseen, the injured men were more or less fit to resume work. One morning, when at the window, Jacques saw Pecqueux pass by on a totally new locomotive, and the fireman waved to him, as if calling him to the footplate. Nevertheless, Jacques was in no hurry. A recrudescence of the urges of love made him reluctant to leave. It was like a nervous expectation of what was destined to take place.

The very same day, down below him he again caught the sound of fresh young voices and laughter, the merry-making of over-grown girls, which lent that dismal house something of the atmosphere of a boarding-school at morning break. It was, he realized, again the Dauvergne girls. He did not mention them to Severine, for she, as a matter of fact, was absent most of the morning. Indeed, she seemed unable to spend five minutes with him. But when evening came the house was as silent as the grave. And when later she lingered in his room, he found her rather solemn and pale. He shot her a keen glance.

'So he's gone, has he?' he remarked. 'His sisters have taken him back?'

She answered briefly:

'Yes, he has gone.'

'So at last we really are alone, you and I?'

'Yes, we are quite alone . . . But we too shall have to part tomorrow. I will go back to Havre. It is the end of our sojourn in this waste land.'

He was still looking keenly at her, but still smiling, for all that he was rather troubled. Then he made up his mind to speak out.

'You wish he had not gone, don't you?' he said. And, seeing her start, as if about to protest, he stopped her. 'No, I am not trying to pick a quarrel with you. Surely you can see I am not jealous. Once you said I should kill you if you were untrue to me, but I surely don't look much like a lover about to kill his mistress, do I? All the same, you know, you have been spending a lot of time down there with Dauvergne. I hardly saw you all day. And I can't help recalling what Roubaud himself once told you, that one fine night you'd sleep with that fellow Dauvergne, not so much for pleasure, as to start up something new.'

She had ceased trying to fight this off, she was only murmuring after him: 'Start up something new, start up something new, eh?' Then, with a burst of irrepressible frankness, she cried: 'All right then, listen, Jacques, it's true . . . We can be frank with each other,

312

you and I, can't we? We have so many ties which bind us. . . . For months Henri has been after me. He knew I belonged to you, but he thought it wouldn't cost me anything to be his too. And when I went downstairs to look after him, he kept on and on, telling me he was dying of love for me, pleaded so sweetly, too, so gently, that I did really think for a moment that I might love him too and start up something new, as you put it – something better, something more gentle . . . Yes, perhaps without any excitement in it, but a tranquil little love which would have soothed me . . .'

She broke off, clearly wondering whether she should go on.

'After all, the road in front of us is barred, isn't it. We can't get any farther . . . Our dream of getting away, all our talk of being rich and happy away in America, all the happiness which depended on you – that's all out of the question, because you weren't capable. . . . No, don't think I want to reproach you, it's even a good thing it never happened, all I mean is that there's no future for you and me, is there? Tomorrow will be just the same as yesterday, the same worries and the same torments.'

He let her have her say and it was only because at last he saw that she meant to say no more that he questioned her.

'So that's why you've slept with him, is it?'

She had already gone half way out of the room. But now she swung round. She shrugged her shoulders.

'No, Jacques,' she said. 'I have not slept with Henri Dauvergne. I tell you straight, I haven't. And I am sure you will believe me. Because you and I need never lie to one another, need we? The fact is, I could not do it, no more than you yourself could do what we talked about. What, does it astonish you to hear of a woman being able to refuse a man when she already argues that it would be a good thing to let him have his way and a little affair with him would suit her book very well? It never took me long to make up my mind, did it? I was never mean about being nice to you. What I mean is, I was never niggardly, letting either Roubaud or you be with me when I could see you wanted it so much. But it just happens that this time I simply could not. I did let him kiss my hands, but he never even touched my lips. I swear it, he didn't. He thinks I will later on, in Paris. That was because I could see he was so unhappy. I did not want to make him so miserable.'

313

She was right and Jacques believed her. It was plain that she was telling the truth. But this only brought back to him his own agony and the frightful turmoil of his own desires grew enormous now that he knew he was alone in the house with her, far from everybody, with the fires of their love for each other again fanned to flame. In his longing to escape, he cried:

'But what about the other one, because there is another – Cabuche, I mean.'

Swiftly she came back close to him.

'Oh! So you've noticed that too, you know about it, do you? . . . Yes, you're quite right, Cabuche is another. It makes me wonder what is wrong with you all . . . But he has never uttered a word. All the same, I couldn't help noticing the contortions he goes into whenever he sees us kiss. He hears all the little things I say to you, and then he mopes about in corners. Another thing, he pinches anything he can of mine. Gloves, handkerchiefs, they all vanish, and he makes off with them like treasures to his cave . . . But you surely don't ever imagine I might give way to that wild creature! A great yokel of a fellow like that, why, I should be terrified. But then, he makes no demands . . . No, they're all right, big louts like that, when they are shy they just die of love without making any demands. You could leave me in Cabuche's hands for a month and he would never touch me, even with the tips of his fingers, just as he never touched Louisette, I can assure you of that today.'

Reminded of the story of Louisette and Grandmorin, their eyes met, and they were silent. All the past came back to them, that meeting at the Rouen examining magistrate's chambers, then their first trip to Paris, so quiet that had been, then their love-making at Havre and all the consequences of that, all the good and so much that was frightful too. She went up to him, so close that he could feel her breath.

'No, my dear,' she said, firmly. 'I assure you, him even less than Dauvergne. Nobody, don't you understand? I should be incapable of it . . . Shall I tell you why? Heavens, as if I did not feel it even now, as if I were not unmistakably sure: it is because you have absorbed every bit of me. There is no other way to put it. Yes, you have got the whole of me, just as you might take up a little thing in your two hands and carry it right away and use it whenever you wanted as if the thing were completely yours to use. Before you, I belonged to nobody. Now I am yours and I shall remain yours, even if you don't want it to be so, even if I do not want it myself . . . It is something I cannot explain. It is like that we came together. With others, it – it frightens me, it disgusts me. But with you it is different, you have made it the loveliest of all delights, you have made it heavenly happiness . . . My dearest one, I love you, and you are the only one I can love.'

She held out her arms to have him hers in close embrace, to lay her head on his shoulder, her mouth on his lips. But he had gripped her hands, to hold her back away from him, aghast, terrified, suddenly aware of that old urge pulsating through his limbs, borne by his blood, throbbing into his brain. His ears dinned as they used to din before, there were the same hammers smiting the same anvils in his skull, the same cry of the herd that he had known in his fits before he even knew her. For some time since he had indeed been unable to lie with her not only in broad daylight, but even by the light of a candle, for fear of going out of his mind if he but glimpsed her white body. And now there was a lamp nearby them, and it lit them vividly, and if he thus shuddered all through and felt the frenzy rise again in him, it must be because as she bent, all relaxed, against him, the loose yoke of her house-gown had suddenly revealed the white billows of her breasts.

Yielding in a conflagration of love desire, she continued:

'I tell you, I don't care if our lives are blocked. No matter if I can never expect anything fresh from you, no matter if I know that tomorrow will bring us the same old worries and the same torments, I don't care, I can do nothing else but drag on my life as it is and suffer together with you. We shall go back to Havre, and I don't care what happens, provided from time to time I can have an hour of you. I tell you, the last three nights I have not been able to sleep, I have been in agony in my room, with only the landing between us, because I have so wanted to come to you. But you were so poorly and you seemed so glum that I did not dare . . . But you will hold me in your arms this evening, won't you? You will see how lovely it will be, I shall be such a good little girl, I shall not be any trouble to you. Besides, dear heart, it is our last night here . . . We are at world's end, here, not a breath, not a soul to disturb us. Nobody can come to trouble us, we are alone, absolutely alone, nobody would even know if we died in each other's arms.'

Her caresses had fevered him and now in the frenzy of his desire to possess her, more absolutely than ever before, he had already, since he was without a weapon, begun to bring his fingers up to her throat, so he might strangle her. But in that awful instant, because of the habit which had grown between them, and without even a hint from him, she reached behind her and turned out the lamp. He then carried her to the bed and there they united. It was one of their most ardent nights of love, no, it was their finest night, it was the only night in which they felt negation of their own separateness which was absolute, and vanished utterly, one into the other. Shattered both by this supreme delight, sucked dry till body ceased to be for each, they still did not sink back into stealthy sleep, but remained luxuriously awake, knotted in their love embrace. And just as during that night of confession in 'Ma' Victoire's room in Paris he spoke not a word, only listened, as, her lips pressed to his ear, she whispered endlessly. Who knows but that this night she already sensed death's fingers draw close to her throat in that instant before she turned out the light, for hitherto, however dire the threat of death at his hand, she had always remained radiantly indifferent in her lover's arms. But now she did experience that swift chill shiver and it was by reason of the inexplicable new dismay which filled her heart that she clung so close to this man's breast, as if for protection there, and her faint breathing became the ultimate surrender of her being.

'Dearest soul,' she murmured, 'if only you could have done it, how happy we should have been out there! But no, no, dearest, I am not asking you to do what you cannot do, I am only sad, so very sad, about our dreams ... Something frightened me, sweetie-pie, just now ... I can't say why, but I felt something threatening me, as if there were a hand so near which might strike me down ... And I have only you, dearest heart, to be my protector. All my happiness depends on you, you are now the be-all of my life.'

He did not answer, merely crushed her more closely to him, hers, his grip of her body all his answer: his brimful heart, his genuine longing to be kind to her and also the fierce bodily love she still fired in him. But had he not just wanted to kill her? And, had she not turned and put out that lamp, would he not have strangled her? Now he knew there was no cure for him, that those attacks were certainly dependent on chance circumstance, beyond his power to discern or discuss. Indeed, why this evening, of all times, when he had just learned how true to him she was, how much greater and more trusting her love for him had become? Was it like this: that the more she loved him, the more he desired to possess her, even to the point in the frightful egoism of the male of destroying her? Would he not be satisfied till she was dead, like the earth inert?

'Tell me, dearest one, why am I so scary? Do you know anything which threatens me?'

'Of course I do not, sweet. Don't worry. Nothing threatens you.'

'But every now and then I tremble all through. I feel a constant danger at my back, something I cannot see, but which I feel . . . Why ever am I so afraid?'

'No, no, don't fear. I love you. I shall never let anyone do you any harm . . . See how good it is thus to lie together.'

A glorious silence followed.

'Oh, dearest soul,' she continued, breathing the very words at him as if caresses, 'more and more nights like these, endless nights for us to be like this, only one flesh . . . We could sell this house and run away with the money and find your friend in America. He still expects you . . . I never go to bed but I think of our life out there, where every night would be like tonight. You would take me, I'd be yours, till we fell asleep in each other's arms . . . But I know, you cannot do it. If I talk of it, I don't do so to hurt you, but because in spite of myself it wells out of my heart.'

And then a sudden decision came to him, one he had taken so often before: he would have to kill Roubaud, not to kill her. And this time, just like every other time, he thought his will was absolute and unshakeable.

And now he spoke, whispering in her ear.

'I could not before,' he said. 'But now I shall be able to. I promise. Can't you hear me?'

She protested weakly.

'No please, please do not promise . . . It is so horrible afterwards, when your courage fails you . . . Besides, it's so awful, we ought not! No, no, you must not!'

'But yes, you know very well, on the contrary, I must. And because

317

'I must, I shall find the strength . . . I was going to talk to you about it, and we shall. We are alone here and so quiet that we cannot even see the colour of our own words.'

She was already giving way, amid sighs, her heart full, pounding so hard that he could feel it against him.

'Oh, dear God! Though it should never be, I do want it so . . . But now that you really mean it, I shall not be able to contain myself.'

They were silent again, weighed down by their resolve. All round them they were aware of the empty countryside and the desolation of these wild parts. They were very warm, their intertwined limbs grown moist with sweat. They melted into each other. Then, as his lips began to fly everywhere about her neck and chin in butterfly kisses, she it was who began whispering again.

'Perhaps we ought to get him out here . . . I might be able to invent something, I don't know what . . . We'll see, later . . . Then you could wait for him, couldn't you, lie hidden, and it would be so easy, because we should be sure of not being disturbed here. Wouldn't we? Isn't that the way?'

Yielding to her will, his lips now fluttering down from her chin towards her bosom, all he murmured was: 'Yes, yes.'

But in her usual precise way she had to weigh every detail, and as she built up her scheme in her mind she discussed it and improved upon it.

'All the same, dearest one, it would be just too silly not to take precautions. If it meant getting ourselves in prison the next day, it would be far better to carry on as we are . . . Listen, somewhere, in a novel, I'm sure, I once read that the best thing is to make it look like suicide . . . He has been so queer for some time, morose, and not at all himself, it would not surprise anybody to hear that he had come here to commit suicide . . . But, you see, that's just it, we have to think how, we have to arrange it, so it looks like that. . . . Don't you agree?'

'I expect you're right.'

She went on speculating, a little breathless, for he had drawn her bosom up to meet his lips and kiss every inch of her.

'You know . . . something which would hide any trace . . . I say, Jacques! darling! I think I have it! . . . If, for example, you cut his throat, all we should have to do would be carry him down and lay him

318

across a rail, see? Then the first train to come along would cut off his head and however much they looked, it would all be for ever crushed out of shape, no single gash to show, not a hint. . . . Darling, do you think that would do?'

'Yes, that's all right, that would do.'

They both grew very excited. She was exultant, almost laughing, so proud of having the imagination. There followed a particularly fierce caress. A shiver ran through her.

'No, not just now, sweetie-pie,' she murmured. 'Wait a moment. . . . I am still thinking about our arrangements. I don't want it now, darling. I was thinking, that if you stay here with me, suicide would look a bit fishy. You will have to go away first. Hear? Tomorrow, but quite openly, in front of Cabuche and so Misard too sees, you go, and there's no doubt whatsoever about it. Take the train to Barentin, get off at Rouen, then, as soon as it's dark, find a way of getting back, and I will let you in the other door. It's only ten miles, you could be back in less than three hours. So now everything is fixed, it's certain – if you will do it.'

'Of course, I will, I agree.'

Now it was he who plunged into thought. He had stopped kissing her and lay inert. There was another spell of silence, while they remained thus motionless in each other's arms, as if the future act now established and for ever certain had destroyed them. But gradually their bodies' feeling returned and with mounting fury they crushed each other till breath was gone. Then again her arms suddenly fell away from him, and she spoke.

'Yes, but the excuse to bring him here . . . He won't be able to come before the eight o'clock, after the day's duty, and will not get here till ten. But that would be better . . . But I have it – the prospective purchaser of whom Misard told me just now, the man I am to go to see the day after tomorrow. That's it! I'll send Roubaud a wire as soon as I get up and tell him he simply must come out here at once, and he should be here tomorrow evening. You can leave after lunch, and somehow be back before he gets here. It will be dark, there's no moon, nothing to hinder us . . . Everything is in our favour.'

'It couldn't be better,' he said.

This time, their possession of each other swept them on to complete

319

unconsciousness. When at last they were asleep, amid the intense silence, still tightly in each other's arms, the break of day was just beginning to whiten the darkness which, wrapping them in its black cloak, had so far hidden them one from another.

He slept on till ten, with the dreamless sleep of a dead man, and when he opened his eyes, he was alone, she was dressing in her own room, on the other side of the landing. A flood of bright sunlight was pouring in at the window, lighting the red bed curtains and the red tapestry on the walls till the whole room blazed with its redness. As he wakened, the house was shivering, as a train swept by. This was no doubt what had wakened him. The brilliant sunshine and the universal redness were dazzling. Then it all flooded back into his mind: it was fixed now, he was to kill Roubaud that very evening which was coming, when this grand sunshine had gone.

Everything that day went off as they had planned. Before lunch, she asked Misard to take the telegram to her husband down to Doinville, and, when Cabuche was there, at about three, he made open preparations to go. Indeed, when he set out, to take the 4.14 at Barentin, the quarryman, having nothing to do, went with him, finding a sort of pleasure in being merely with the lover of the woman he desired. At Rouen, where Jacques arrived at 4.40, he put up in a pub near the station kept by a woman from his native village, and there he spoke of seeing one of his friends the next day, after which he was returning to Paris to resume duty. But he remarked that he was worn out. He had done too much at once. So at six he withdrew to the ground floor room which he had taken, to go to bed. And the room had a window opening on a little-used alleyway. Ten minutes later, having got out of the window unseen and taken care to close the shutter again, but so as to be able to get back in that way, secretly, he was on his way to Maufras Cross.

It was not till a quarter past nine that he found himself back at that lonely, deserted, dismal house, cock-eyed to the railway-lines. It was a very dark night and there was not a glimmer showing on the shuttered front. Once again he had a painful shock and was seized by terrible melancholy, a sort of presentiment of the evil deed to be performed. As he had agreed with Severine, he threw three pebbles, one after the other, at the red-room shutters, then slipped round to the back, where after a time the door silently opened for him. Closing

320

it behind him, he tiptoed up the stairs in the dark. But when he got up there, in the light of the large lamp, ablaze on the corner of the table, he saw the bed already opened, the young woman's clothes over the back of a chair, and Séverine herself, bare-legged, in nothing but an underslip, her mass of hair knotted on top of her head, ready for the night, and he was aghast.

'What, you're gone to bed?' he cried.

'Of course. Far better . . . You see, I thought like this: when he gets here, and I go down like this to undo the door, he will be less suspicious. And I shall tell him I have a headache. I've already told Misard I am not very well. That will make it all right when they find him down there on the track for me to say I never left this room.'

But Jacques got quite worked up. He was all nerves.

'No, no,' he cried. 'You must dress . . . You must be up! You can't stay like that!'

He surprised her. She began to smile.

'But, darling sweet, why ever not? You needn't worry, I assure you, I am not at all cold . . . Look, see how warm I am!'

With wheedling lissomness she was at his neck and had her arms round it. And as she hung there, her breasts stood firm, half revealed as the slip slithered off one shoulder. And when with increasing annoyance he stepped back, she pretended to be good.

'Darling, don't be angry with your little me, I'll pop back into bed, then you won't be afraid I'll take any harm.'

When she had drawn the sheets right up to her chin, he seemed easier, while without a hint of disturbance she babbled on, telling him all the little details she had thought of.

'The moment he knocks, I shall go down to open the door. First, I thought of letting him come right up, so you could be ready for him here. But that would have complicated it, as we should then have had to get him down again. Besides, there's this parquet floor. Whereas, with the stone flags downstairs, it will be easy to wash them, if there are any traces . . . But just now, as I was undressing, I thought of a story in which the author tells of a man stripping stark naked to kill another. You can see why, can't you? You wash down after, and there's not a fleck on your clothes . . . What do you say to it, undress yourself too, we could both of us strip to the skin.'

Horrified, he just stared. But she looked so gentle, with those

321

childlike, limpid eyes. She was merely concerned with doing it properly, to succeed. It was all working out in her mind. But at the mere thought of their two bodies, stark naked and splashed with Roubaud's blood, he had another violent attack of his trouble, and shuddered to the very bones.

'Oh no, no!' he cried. 'We should be like savages. We might as well turn cannibal and eat his heart. I say, you do hate him, don't you?'

Severine's countenance darkened swiftly. That one question brought her crashing down from her careful, housewifely planning to the horror of the actual deed, and her eyes flooded with tears.

'I have gone through too much in the past few months, you hardly expect me to like him, do you? I've told you a hundred times: anything rather than spend another week with that man! But, you are right, it is terrible to be reduced to this, we ought really only yearn to be happy together . . . Well, so shall we go down without any light? You will get behind the door, and when I've let him in, you do it! . . . If I do anything, it will only be to help you, so you don't have to worry about everything. I am arranging it all as best I can.'

On the table he caught sight of the knife, the very knife which Roubaud had used. It was obvious that she had put it out now for him in turn to use and strike. He froze, staring at it. It was open, and the blade gleamed in the lamplight. He picked it up and turned it over. She watched him, but said nothing. After all, he had taken it. What need for words? In fact, she said nothing, till he had put it back on the table.

'Darling, you don't think I am pressing you, do you? I am not. There is still time to go, if you are not capable.'

Stubbornness welled up in him. With a violent gesture, he cried:

'What? Do you think I am a coward? This time it is decided. Sworn.'

At that very instant the house shuddered, as a train thundered by, with the sudden crash of a storm breaking. It was so close to them that it seemed to roar through the very room. He added:

'That's it. His train. The Paris through. He will have got out at Barentin. He will be here in half an hour.'

Neither he nor she spoke another word. There was a long silence. They were picturing the man drawing near, through the inky darkness, by the narrow lanes. Jacques had begun mechanically pacing up and down the room, as if counting out the steps together with the other man, every step bringing him so much nearer. Another and another and another, and with the last one, Jacques would slip behind the hall door, to plunge the knife into Roubaud's throat, as he came in.

Severine lay motionless on her back, the sheet drawn up to her chin, her large eyes wide-open, watching him stride to and fro, the even beat of a lullaby, coming to her like an echo of the far-off steps of the victim. Ceaselessly. Another and another. Now there was nothing that would halt them. And when they reached full measure, she would leap from the bed and go down barefoot, without any light, to open the door to the man. 'Is it you, darling? Quick, I was already in bed.' And he would not even reply. He would just crumble to the ground in the darkness, his throat gashed, agape.

Another train passed, a down-train, the slow which crossed the through five minutes to the other side of Maufras Cross. And at that thought Jacques' heart again stopped beating: that was only five minutes. How long it made half an hour! Now he simply had to keep moving. He paced up and down the room. He was weak inside with anxiety, the sort of anxiety which might suddenly assail a vigorous man feeling doubts in his masculinity, smitten with some shock of the nervous system, so that he continually asks himself whether at the crucial moment he will or will not be able to perform the act. He was so familiar with these stages through which he went. He had been through it all a dozen times already. First, the certainty, the definite resolve to kill, then a feeling of fullness at the pit of the stomach and chilling of hands and feet. Next, all at once, the onset of feebleness, the impotence of mere will to stiffen sinews stubbornly inert. Trying to work himself up by reason, he ran through and through all he had so often told himself: how much it was in his own interests to liquidate Roubaud, the wealth awaiting him in America, the possession of the woman he loved. And the worst thing was that when just now he had seen her half-naked, he had immediately been sure that once again there would be failure, for the instant that chronic, deep-seated urge of his appeared, he immediately ceased to belong to himself. For a brief moment, faced by overpowering temptation, there had been the vision of her ready body, the vision of the ready knife, and he had shivered all through.

Now, however, he was firm again, screwed up to the effort. He was

323

going to be able to, the wait for his victim was resumed. He paced the room, from door to window, at every round brushing past the bed, but resolute not to see this.

In the bed, where for those inflamed tenebrous long hours the night before they had loved, Severine throughout lay motionless. Her head still on the pillow, she followed that coming and going with restless eyes. She too was strained, agonized by the apprehension that tonight too he was at the last going to lack courage. Put an end to it and start life again, that was all she wanted, the only desire in the unthinking heart-deeps of the woman of pure sex that she was, all compliance to the man she loved, all stone to the man she had never felt love for. They were getting rid of him because he was in their way. There was nothing more natural than that, and it was only if she thought hard that any sense of the abomination of the act could stir in her, and the moment the conception of seeing the blood, the moment all the loathsome petty details of it again receded, she sank back into her gentle radiance, her lovable countenance all innocent.

But while she watched, for all that she knew him so well, she gradually ceased to recognize her Jacques. He was a handsome boy, with his rounded cheeks, his wavy hair, his very dark moustaches and those gold-sparkling brown eyes. But now his lower jaw was jutting out so violently, just like a wild beast's snout, that it quite disfigured him. Just now, as he brushed by her, his eyes flashed over her, swiftly, and he suddenly drew his whole body violently backwards away from her, as if he wanted to avoid the sight of her, and she noticed then that the light in those eyes had been clouded by a reddish mist.

Whyever should he want to avoid her? Did this mean that once again his courage was petering out? For some time now, ignorant as she was of the constant danger of death through which she moved when with him, all she saw in the instinctive, apparently pointless fear which she felt was a presentiment of an early end to their liaison. And like a flash she conceived that if, in a few minutes, he was unable to strike, he intended to flee from her, never to return. She therefore now resolved firmly that he must kill, that if he needed it she would find the means to give him the strength.

A fresh train came by, an endless goods train, the trail of waggons breaking, so it seemed, without end against the immense silence of their room. She propped herself on one elbow and waited for this

324

new storm of rolling wheels to recede into the distance of the sleeping countryside.

'Another quarter of an hour,' said Jacques, loudly. 'He has got through Bécourt Woods, he is half way now. Oh, what a long time to wait!'

But as he came back again, towards the window, it was to find Severine standing in his path, naked in her thin shift.

'Supposing we go down a minute with the lamp. I was thinking,' she explained, 'you could have another look and see exactly where to put your feet and I could show you how I will open the door, and you see just what movements to make.'

Shuddering, he stepped away from her.

'Oh no!' he cried. 'Not with the lamp!'

'But, silly, listen, we shall put it out again, at once. We must get quite clear about positions.'

'Oh no!' he cried again. 'Do get back into bed!'

She refused. Instead, she went up to him, on her lips that unconquerable, despotic smile of a woman all aware of the absolute power with which her body's lust imbues her. All she needed to do was to hold him in her arms and he would yield to her flesh, he would do all her will. And, to master him, wheedling soft, her tongue murmured on:

'Dear sweet, tell me, what is the matter with you? Anyone would think you were afraid of me. As soon as I come close to you, you seem to avoid me. If only you knew what need I have, now more than ever, to feel your support, to sense you close to me, to know our oneness, for ever and ever, darling, can't you understand?'

She had driven him right back against the table. Now he could get no farther back. He stared wild-eyed at her, brilliantly lighted by the lamp. Never had he seen her thus before, the yoke-ribbon of her under-slip untied, letting her lovely breasts thrust out with all the white wonder of her bosom round them. He choked, struggling with himself. But already his foothold was crumbling beneath his feet. The onrush of blood stupefied him, the hateful tremor conquered him. And in that instant it came to his mind that only inches behind his back, there on the table, lay the knife. He sensed its waiting presence. He needed but reach out, to have it.

With a supreme effort he gasped his plea:

'Please! Please! Cover yourself again!'

But there was no deceiving her. She felt the quiver of his body and knew that it was his overwhelming desire for her that made him shudder so, and the sheer sense of it swelled her bosom with a sort of pride. Why should she cover herself, as he cried, when she too craved his equal possession of her, this evening above all others, possession such as they had never known before, to loss of reason. Instead, she pressed with infinite feline softness on to him, wrapping herself about him, murmuring:

'Sweetest, what is it? ... Kiss me! ... Kiss me hard, as you love me! That will give you courage ... For it is courage, dear heart, that we need. To do what we are going to do, we need to love differently from everybody else, more than everybody else! ... Kiss me then with all your heart and soul!'

Suffocating, he held his breath. There was the clamour of the horde in his skull, blotting out all else, while behind the ears fiery teeth penetrated his head, invaded limbs, drove him out of his own body as the wild beast whom he knew and feared galloped into his blood. Another moment, and his hands would no longer be his, so terrible the intoxication with the nakedness of this body of a woman. Her naked breasts were crushed against his clothing, the bare throat and bosom reached so white, so delicate, and the temptation was so hard to resist. Then there came the acrid warm smell of her, that mastering odour, and by that he suddenly lost all sense of balance, he swayed infinitely, over an abyss, down into which the will-power wrested from his own body fluttered lifeless away.

'But kiss me, dear heart! There is till a minute left us! ... You know he is coming. Already, if he has walked fast, he may be raising his hand to knock. But if you are so against going down first to see, don't forget: I shall open the door, you will be behind it, and don't wait, we shall be so happy. He is but a wicked man who has done me so much harm and he is the only obstacle to our fortune ... Kiss me, darling, oh, kiss me so hard, so hard! Kiss me as if you wanted to eat, devour me, kiss me so nothing of me remains outside yourself!'

Without turning round, Jacques reached out his right hand, felt and took up the knife. He remained like that for a few moments, just clutching it in his fist. Was this the old thirst returned to him, the thirst for vengeance of very ancient wrongs done, wrongs the exact nature of which was now forgotten, the hatred piled up through the generations of all males since the first deceptions in the depths of the caverns? He fixed his insane eyes on Severine, but the only desire which he had was to throw her on to her back, like prey torn from the others. And the door of horror opened wide on the blackest abyss of sex, love to the point of death, death but the more to possess . . .

'Kiss me, kiss me! . . .'

She let her head fall back, all yielding, pleading love, and the action lay bare her throat, all the voluptuous softness between neck and bosom, and when, as if in the flaring light of a burning house, he saw that white flesh, he raised his fist, armed with the knife – but not before she caught the flash of the steel and had flung herself back from him, gaping with terror and astonishment.

'Jacques, Jacques!' she cried. 'Me? Oh God, but why, why?'

His mouth grim, without a word, he pursued her. There was a brief struggle. It brought her near the bed. Aghast, she drew back, defenceless, her single garment torn from shoulder to loin.

'But why? Oh God, why?'

Then down came his hand and the knife dealt with the question, deep in her throat. As he struck, by a terrible, instructing, satisfying urge, his fingers twisted the blade, so he should strike in exactly the same way, in the same spot, with the same frenzy, as Judge Grandmorin was struck.

Did she utter any cry? He never knew. For in the same instant, the Paris express roared by, so violently, so swiftly, that the very ceiling shook. And there she lay dead, as if thunderstruck in that storm.

Jacques stood motionless now, staring at her, stretched beside the bed, at his feet. The train was vanishing in the distance.

He stared at her in the heavy silence of the red room. Centred against the red drapery and curtains, on the floor, she was bleeding copiously, a red stream flowing down between her breasts, spreading out over her belly, reaching one groin, then over the thigh, trickling at last in viscous drops to the floor. Her shift, torn half-way, was soaked. He could never have believed there could be so much blood in her. But what held him there was the mask of monstrous terror which the features of that woman, otherwise so gentle, so amenable, so pretty, now assumed. Her black hair, dark as the night, was standing on end, making a helmet of horror. The periwinkle eyes, gaping over-wide,

327

aghast, terrified by the incomprehensibility of it, were still questioning him. Why, whyever had he killed her thus? Thus, carried away by this fatality of murder, she had been slaughtered, even though she had never realized that life had already slithered down, first into mire, then from mire to blood. Gentle and innocent as ever she lay there, without having understood.

Jacques was utterly astounded. First he heard hoarse animal breathing, the growling of the beast of prey, the roar of a lion, then, calming down, discovered it was his own breath. So at last he had done it, at last he had satisfied himself, and killed. Yes, he had done it. His heart raced free with a strange delight, which buoyed him up in this absolute satisfaction of the longing he had known so long. The result was an unexpected gift of pride, a build-up of his male superiority. He had killed this woman, therefore he had possessed her as for so long now he had desired, with nothing held back, not even her absolute annihilation. She was no more and would never be for any other man. Only a poignant memory came back to him – that other victim, the corpse of Judge Grandmorin, which that awful night he had seen some five hundred yards from this house. This delicate body, of such whiteness, but now barred with red, was the same human debris, the same broken puppet, the same limp rag that a knife-blow could make of any living creature. Yes, this was it, he too had now killed, and there was this on the ground.

Like Grandmorin, she had slumped to the ground, though Severine was on her back, her legs spread wide, her left arm drawn up against her side, her right arm twisted back, dislocated. Indeed, had he not with thumping heart sworn to himself that winter night long since that he in his turn must dare this act? There, when first he saw an open throat and smoking blood, had begun the itch to kill, an itch which had grown ever greater, like the fiery lust of sex, to its pinnacle. Of course after that he could no longer be a coward, he too had to thrust home a knife and know the ultimate orgasm of it. The seed of the thing germinated thus long ago, not an hour, but a year away, surreptitiously growing and growing and yet ever persistently avoided, grim labour, even on this woman's bosom, under her kisses, had gone on within his heart and only now at last found culmination. Now the two murders had joined, each to each. Was not one but the logical sequel to the other?

A clatter and rattle of loose boards and windows plucked Jacques Lantier from the stupefied contemplation in which he was standing over the dead. Was it a clap of thunder rending the doors? Had men come to arrest him? He turned about him, to find nothing but unhearing silence. Of course, it was merely another train! But the man who would at any moment knock on the door, the man he had intended to kill? He had entirely forgotten Roubaud. Not exactly regret, but rather self-condemnation for being such an imbecile swept over him. What on earth was this which had been done? The woman he loved, who had loved him passionately in return, lay dead, her throat slit, on the floor, while the husband, who had been the one obstacle to their happiness, was still among the living, drawing nearer and nearer, too, step by step, in the darkness. He simply had not had the patience to wait so little time. For weeks the scruples and notions of humanity accumulated, inherited, bred and born into him, had made him spare Roubaud so that, against his own interests, he had been swept off his feet by inherited violence, by the need for blood which in primeval forests flung beast upon beast.

For does a man ever kill by reason? He kills solely under the impulse of blood and nerves, vestiges of primeval struggles, the ineluctable demands of life, the glory of a man's strength. There remained to him now the drouth of satisfaction. He began to lose his head, striving to find, in the depth of satiated passion of his heart of hearts, astonishment or bitter sorrow of the irreparable deed. The sight of the unfortunate woman, still staring up at him, terrified and questioning, became absolutely unbearable. He tried to look away, he had the sensation that another white shape rose by the foot of the bed, as if a double of dead Severine. Then he saw that it was Flora. She had come back. He still lay feverish, after Lison's crash, and now Flora triumphed in revenge.

He was seized with despairing horror. Whatever was he doing to tarry so in this house? He had killed her, he had gorged on blood, he was drunk with the frightful wine of crime. He nearly fell headlong, avoiding the knife that lay on the parquet as he fled tumbling down the stairs, flung open the large front door on to the front porch steps – as if the other was not wide enough to release him – and rushed out into the inky night, into which in frenzy he bounded, never once

329

looking back at that unholy house, cock-eyed to the permanent-way, wide open and void of life behind him, a desolation of death.

That night, just as he had done before, Cabuche had already crept through the gap in the hedge, to haunt Severine's window. He was well aware that Roubaud was expected and he found nothing strange in the light pouring through the gap between the shutters. But when a man came leaping down the front steps to gallop off into the open heath like a mad animal, he was transfixed in astonishment, so long that it was pointless to take up the pursuit. He just stood there, beside the wide-open door, bewildered, hesitant, gaping at the dark gash of the house's open hall. What on earth had happened? Should he go inside? And the intense silence, the absolute stillness, while the lamp upstairs burned on, clutched at his heart and filled him with growing anxiety.

At last, he found the courage and tiptoed up. At the half-open door of the room, he halted again. In the limpid light of the oil lamp he thought he distinguished a pile of petticoats beside the bed. Madame Roubaud must have undressed. Overcome with alarm, Cabuche called out, softly, the blood thumping through his temples. Then he saw the blood and understood. He rushed in, and a terrible cry tore from his broken heart. Dear Heaven, it was she who lay there, she murdered and thrown to the ground, pitiable in her nakedness. He thought he heard death-throes still coming from the throat and was overcome with such wretchedness, such agonizing shame, to see her end her life thus in nakedness, that with the love of a brother he thrust his hands under her, raised her, laid her on the bed, drew up the sheet to cover her. And, thus bearing her in his arms, unique act of love from him to her, he took her blood amply on himself, hands and chest covered till he was wet with it, and as he turned round, saw Roubaud and Misard together there, for they too had arrived and, finding the door wide-open, had come straight up. Roubaud was late because he had called first to see Misard, who had walked up with him, to discuss the business on the way, and the two men stared in astonishment at Cabuche, his hands as wet with blood as a butcher's slaughterer.

'That's just the same blow as killed Grandmorin,' said Misard, at last, when they had looked at the body.

Roubaud said nothing, merely nodded. He could not take his eyes

330

from Severine's mask of revolting horror, that black hair standing on end, and the straining blue eyes with their eternal question-mark.

12

One muggy, late June night, three months later, Jacques Lantier was driving the 6.30 Paris–Havre express. He had a completely new locomotive, No. 608 – married a virgin, as he put it – and was just getting to know her well, a rather troublesome, capricious, whimsical creature, one of those young nags only resigned to harness after a lot of hard riding. Many a time he cursed her and regretted Lison. He had to keep a close eye on 608, his hand constantly on the valve gear. But this particular night, the air was so deliciously soft and it was so lovely to breathe in deep lungfuls that he felt like being a little indulgent, gave milady her head for a while. He had never felt better in his life. He suffered no remorse. He was really happy, quite at peace, his mind at rest. Indeed, though usually most taciturn on the road, he suddenly began to jolly friend Pecqueux, whom he had managed to get back as his fireman.

'What's got you, man,' he cried, 'you're gaping like a gaffer on a water diet.'

It was quite true, Pecqueux did seem unusually abstemious and rather morose. Roughly, he snarled back.

'Want your eyes open, don't you, to see straight?'

Jacques shot his mate an uneasy glance. To tell the truth, his conscience was not quite clear, for, the week before, he had succumbed to the embraces of Pecqueux's mistress, that outrageous jane Philomène Sauvagnat, who had been rubbing round him for some time now, just like a female pussy on heat. True, Jacques slept with her merely in order to have a new experience. He was principally concerned to try himself out and discover if at long last, having assuaged his frightful need, he really was cured, if, in other words, he could possess another woman without sticking a knife into her throat too. And he had already slept with Philomène twice, without his old trouble, not even a hint of inward tremor. And, though he may not have been aware of it, his great contentment, that amiable, replete mood he was in, came from his delight at finding that he had now become merely a man like any other.

Pecqueux meanwhile had opened the fire-box door to stoke up. But Jacques halted him.

'N-No. Don't press her. She's doing all right.'

Pecqueux swore violently.

'All right, b—— it! . . . Bloody shame, I call it . . . Ruddy bit of ironmongery like this! When I think how you used to flog poor old Lison, and she was a decent bit of stuff . . . This bloody tart isn't worth my toe up her arse!'

Not to have to be angry at that, Jacques avoided making any response at all. But it was certainly beginning to be clear that the old triangular relationship they had once known was a thing of the past. The good comradeship between him and his mate and their engine had vanished when Lison was killed. Now they squabbled over the merest trifles, a nut drawn up too tight, a badly pitched shovelful of coal. And he told himself he had better lay off Philomène. The last thing he wanted was to end in open warfare on these few square feet of mobile steel plate, hurtling the two of them through the air. So long as Pecqueux, out of gratitude for never being hustled and having the chance of making a bit of money on the side, not to speak of regular dipping into his tommy-bag, had been his good doggie, and his loyal champion against all oncomers, they had lived together like a couple of brothers, but it was going to be hell if they no longer agreed and were constantly to be at each other's throats as they rode side by side on the footplate, shaken to the marrow of their bones. Why, it was only last week that the Company had had to separate the driver and fireman of the Cherbourg express, all because a woman stood between them and the driver had begun to bully his mate and the mate to be disobedient, till it came to blows, then to regular battles on the road, to complete oblivion of the passengers they were drawing at top speed behind them.

Twice more, Pecqueux opened the fire-box and tossed coal in, just to flaunt Jacques' instructions. He was clearly out to pick a quarrel. But Jacques pretended not to notice, concentrated on his controls and each time Pecqueux did this merely gave a half-turn to the injector wheel, to keep the pressure down. It was such soft air, and the breeze made by their motion through the hot night air was so good. At 11.5 P.M., however, when the express reached Havre, they cleaned their locomotive down together, apparently on the best of terms, just as before.

But when they were just leaving the station premises to go round to the François Mazeline Street lodging house, for the night, they heard a woman's voice hail them.

'We're in a nice hurry, aren't we? Come in for a minute, you two!'

It was Philomène, who had apparently sighted Jacques from her brother's doorstep, and he saw her quick gesture of annoyance, when she realized that Pecqueux was with him. But despite the presence of the old flame, she decided to call them both in, merely to give herself the pleasure of a few words with her new lover.

'You bloody well leave us alone!' growled Pecqueux. 'You're a pain in the neck, you are. We want a bit of sleep.'

'Isn't he polite!' cried Philomène, laughingly. 'But you needn't think M. Jacques is the same as you, I am sure he won't say no to a nice little drink . . . Will you, Monsieur Jacques?'

He was in fact about to decline, from sheer prudence, but Pecqueux at once said yes, he would take a drink. It had in fact occurred to Pecqueux that he might now have a chance to see if there really was anything in what he suspected. So they both went into the Sauvagnats' kitchen and sat down at the table, while Philomène got out glasses and a bottle of brandy.

'Better not make too much noise,' she said, in a lower tone of voice. 'My brother is upstairs, asleep, he doesn't like me having visitors.'

Then, filling their glasses, she added:

'I suppose you know that old biddy, Lebleu, pegged out this morning . . . Not surprised, either. I always did say: if they put her in that back flat it'd kill her, regular prison of a place. She held out four months, eating her heart out because all she could see was all that galvanized . . . But what finished her off, when she could no longer walk, there's no question, was no longer being able to spy on Mademoiselle Guichon and M. Dabadie, that was her regular occupation, you know. Too true. It made her simply mad, never being able to catch them at anything. That's what she died of.'

Pausing, she swallowed a tot of brandy, then, with a loud laugh, added:

'All the same, of course those two do sleep together. Only, they're spry, they are. Neither seen nor heard. That foxes you all right! But I reckon little Madame Moulin did see them one evening. But she's no worry, she's too simple to blab. Besides, her husband, being A.S.M. ... But, I say,' – she switched sharply to something else – 'Isn't it next week the Roubaud case is coming on, at Rouen?'

All this time, Jacques and Pecqueux had listened without getting a word in edgeways. Regular woman's blab, thought Pecqueux. She had never let herself go like that with him. And, seeing her get more and more worked up, all on account of Lantier, he could not take his eyes off her and smouldering jealousy began to burn fiercely in him.

'That's right,' said Jacques, completely unmoved. 'I've received my summons.'

Philomène drew nearer, for the mere pleasure of her elbow touching him.

'I've got to give evidence too,' she said. 'Yes, M. Jacques, when they interrogated me about you, because, you know, they wanted to know the truth about your relations with poor Madame Roubaud, yes, when they interrogated me, I said to the magistrate: "But he was terribly fond of her, you know, out of the question he could touch a hair of her head!" I'd seen you together, hadn't I, M. Jacques, I was in a good position to speak.'

'That's all right,' said Jacques, with a gesture of indifference. 'But I was not worried, I could tell them where I was, every minute of my time ... the fact that the Company has kept me on shows that they had nothing against me.'

Silence ensued, and all three of them sipped away.

'It gives me the shudders,' Philomene suddenly resumed. 'That savage brute, Cabuche, I mean, the man they arrested still with the poor lady's blood on him! But what an idiot a man can be! Murder a woman because you want her! As if that did any good, when you've killed her, you can't do anything, can you ... But what I shall never forget, I tell you, is when M. Cauche came right out on to the platform to arrest M. Roubaud. I was there. Remember, it was just a week, no more, after M. Roubaud came back to work, as calm as you please, after putting his wife to rest. That day, all M. Cauche did was give him a little tap on the shoulder and say he had orders to take him off to the lock-up. Just think! Bosom pals like those two, always

335

gambling together, day and night. But when a man's a police super, he's no choice, has he, he would take his own father or mother to the guillotine, that's his job, isn't it? A lot he cares, M. Cauche, either. I saw him at the Café du Commerce just now, shuffling the cards, no more worried about his friend than about the Great Turk.'

Grinding his teeth, Pecqueux suddenly brought his fist crashing down on the table. 'Bloody Hell! If that cuckold Roubaud were me!' – and he spat. 'You're the b—— slept with his missus, Jacques Lantier, aren't you? Then another b—— kills her. And to crown it, they put him in the dock! I tell you, it's enough to make a man go off his ruddy rocker!'

'But, you great silly,' cried Philomene. 'As if you didn't know, he's charged with getting Cabuche to get rid of his wife for him, and for money. Isn't that what it was? It seems that when they searched Cabuche they found old Grandmorin's watch. You remember Grandmorin, that judge who was killed on the train, eighteen months ago. Then they put that dirty job and this dirty job together and they got a nice kettle of fish. I can't tell you all there is in it. It was all in the paper. There were two whole columns of it.'

But Jacques seemed to be thinking of something else. Vaguely, he said:

'Why rack our brains about it, what is it to do with us? If the authorities don't know what they're about, it isn't our job, is it?'

Then, staring into the far distance, his cheeks rather pale, he murmured:

'The whole thing turns round that poor woman ... That poor, dear Severine ...'

'Ask me!' cried Pecqueux, fiercely. 'I've got a woman too, I have, and if any b—— dared lay his fingers on her, I'd start by wringing both their necks. After that, they could cut my head off, I wouldn't be fussy.'

Again there was a silence. Philomène filled the glasses up and rather pointedly shrugged her shoulders and grinned. However, this declaration had rather shaken her, and she was studying Pecqueux cautiously, out of the corner of her eye. Since 'Ma' Victoire was immobilized by her fracture, and had been obliged to give up her first-class ladies convenience job and enter a home, he had been letting himself go badly, his clothes ragged and very dirty. 'Ma' was

336

no longer at hand, tolerant, maternal wife to slip francs into his pocket and mend and darn for him, so that his auxiliary wife at Havre should not charge her with not looking after her hubby. So Philomène, whose heart was now full of the neat and natty appearance of Jacques, suddenly pretended to be shocked.

'You mean you would strangle your missus in Paris?' she demanded, over-boldly. 'Well, you needn't worry, there's not much chance of anybody wanting to seduce that one away from you!'

'I meant her,' he growled, 'or I meant somebody else.'

But she held out her glass to him to touch his.

'Come along, now,' she cried, tauntingly. 'Here's to yourself! You'd better bring that shirt and anything else you've got round to me to do for you. I must say, you're a disgrace to us both as you are . . . To your health too, M. Jacques!'

As if emerging from a dream, Jacques was shaken by a sudden shiver. Though he was completely lacking in remorse, he was so essentially kindly at heart that he could not at times prevent Severine coming back to his mind, and tears started to his eyes. But to hide how upset he was, he too held out his glass quickly and at the same time changed the conversation.

'There's going to be war, you know,' he said.

'You don't say!' cried Philomène. 'But whoever with?'

'With the Prussians, of course . . . Yes, all through that prince of theirs who wants to be King of Spain. The whole debate in the Chamber yesterday was about it.'

That definitely upset Philomène.

'That's fine goings on. They've messed us up enough already, haven't they, with their elections and their plebiscite and their Paris riots . . . But what will happen if it does come to war? Will all the men be taken?'

'Don't you worry, we folk are fixed all right, they can't put the railways out of action . . . Our only bother's going to be the way they'll push us round, because of troop transports and supply trains and all that. No matter, if it does come, have to do our duty, I suppose.'

As he said this, he rose to his feet, for at this moment Philomène had contrived to slip one of her legs under his and he could see that

337

Pecqueux had noticed it too. He was all red in the face at once, his fists clenched.

'Let's be getting to bed,' he said, 'it's high time.'

'Aye, 'twould be best,' stammered Pecqueux.

He had seized Philomène's arm, and was crushing it enough to break it. She all but cried out with the pain, but when Pecqueux took up his glass to drain the dregs she contrived to whisper into Jacques' ear:

'You'd better look out, he's a regular brute when he's been drinking.'

At that instant they heard heavy footsteps coming down the stairs. 'Quick! Run along, both of you,' she cried, in terror. 'That's my brother.'

The two men were not twenty paces away, when they heard slaps and then cries. Again, Philomène took a terrible beating, just like a little girl caught doing wrong, with her nose in a jam-pot. Jacques was on the point of going back, to her aid, but Pecqueux held him back.

'Here, what's it to do with you, eh? . . . The hot bitch she is, I wish her brother could slaughter her.'

At the lodging house, they went to bed together without another word between them. In the narrow room, their two beds almost touched, and they lay a long time awake, each listening to the breathing of the other.

The court proceedings of the Roubaud case were to come on at Rouen the following Monday. The trial constituted a triumph for the examining magistrate, M. Denizet, for the world of justice was not sparing in praise of the way he had conducted that most shady, tangled affair. It was a masterpiece of fine analysis, his colleagues averred, a logical tissue of reconstruction of the truth, indeed, a work of real creative power.

First, as soon as he was taken to the scene, at Maufras Cross, only a few hours after Severine had been murdered, M. Denizet had had Cabuche arrested. Everything frankly pointed to the man – the enormous quantity of blood on him, Roubaud and Misard's crushing depositions, and their account of how they had found him in a state of great stress, alone with the body. Interrogated and pressed to tell why and how he happened to be in the room, the quarry-man had stammered a yarn at which M. Denizet just shrugged his shoulders, it was such a stupidly hoary story of self-exculpation. He had in fact expected just such a yarn, all about an imaginary murderer, some other criminal, who was of course sheer invention, but who, so the real culprit always insisted, had been heard running away through the dark countryside. That classical savage killer must be a long way off indeed, if he was still running.

Further, when questioned as to what he was doing in the house at so late an hour, Cabuche grew confused, and refused to answer, finally saying that he was out for a walk. That was all too childish. How was one to believe in a mysterious stranger like that, who murdered and ran away, leaving the door wide open, but without touching a drawer or taking as much as a handkerchief? Where was he supposed to have sprung from? What had been his motive in killing?

Nevertheless, knowing of the liaison between the victim and Jacques, M. Denizet had from the outset been concerned about what Jacques had been doing at the time. But, apart from the accused himself admitting that he had gone to Barentin with Jacques and seen him catch the 4.14 train, there was a Rouen inn-keeper to swear to high Heaven that that young man had put up there and had gone to bed immediately after his supper and moreover had not gone out again till the following morning, a little before seven. Besides, a lover does not cut the throat of a much-beloved mistress without reason, especially when he has never had the shadow of a quarrel with her. That would be absurd. No, there could be but one feasible murderer, and that was the old lag found on the spot, his hands red with blood, the knife at his feet, that stupid brute of a fellow with his endless cock-a-doodle stories.

But, getting so far, despite his conviction and despite that flair of his which, so he said, always told him more than any clues, M. Denizet did come up against trouble. For, in a first search, made in the arrested man's hut, deep in Bécourt Woods, they had not found a thing. Since they had failed to establish any theft, they must find some other motive for the crime. Then, suddenly, a chance word which fell while M. Denizet was interrogating Misard, put him on the scent, for Misard said that one night he had seen Cabuche climb on to the wall in front of the Maufras Cross house and watch Madame Roubaud undressing to get into bed.

Interrogated next day, Jacques had calmly told what he knew, namely, the unspoken adoration which the quarry-worker had felt for Madame Roubaud and the fierce desire with which the man followed her about wherever she went, anxious to be of service to her. There was thus no more reason to doubt, it was animal lust which had been Cabuche's impulse, and after that it was all plain sailing – Cabuche getting back into the house by the front door, of which no doubt he had a key, Cabuche in his excited state leaving the door open, Cabuche going upstairs with intent to rape, then the struggle, leading to the murder, and finally, the arrival of the husband just as the mad creature was about to commit the act of rape on the dead body.

Nevertheless, even here there was one outstanding objection – it was strange that this man, who was aware of the husband being due home at any minute, should have chosen precisely this moment to do it, when the husband might so easily come on him red-handed. However, when one thought more about it, this really turned against Cabuche and was the final proof against him, for it went to show that he must have been acting in the grip of a culminating crisis of lustful desire and been out of his mind from the thought that if he did not profit by this last moment in which Severine was alone in this deserted house, he would never have her, for on the following day she was to leave. From this point the examining magistrate's conviction was complete and his case unshakeable.

Harrowed by interrogation and cross-interrogation, caught again and again in the cross-fire of questions, and insensitive though he was to the traps set for him, Cabuche stuck obstinately to his first account. He was passing by, taking a breath of fresh night air, when somebody brushed by him as he raced away from the house, running so fast in the darkness that he could not even be sure which way the man was running. Then, suddenly worried, he had glanced at the house and noticed that the front door had been left wide open. He had then thought he had better go up, and he found Madame Roubaud just dead, still warm, her large eyes looking at him so vividly that he had lifted her and put her on the bed despite the blood, because he had thought she was still alive. That was all he knew, and that was all he would say, every time, never varying by a single detail, and he said it all with the air of having thus fenced himself in by a story he had worked out in advance and was going to stick to. When attempts were made to jolt him out of it, he got frightened and subsided into the silence of a sub-normal intelligence which ceases to understand. The first time that M. Denizet questioned him about the love which he felt for Madame Roubaud, he turned very red, just like an adolescent teased about his first crush on a girl, but he denied it and swore that he had never had the slightest thought of sleeping with the lady, for to him that was a very nasty thing to suggest, sex was something one could never admit to, something which partook of mystery and great delicacy, deep buried in one's secret heart, something about which one would tell no man. No, no, he was not in love with Madame Roubaud, he had never desired her, they would never make him admit such a thing, which now that she was dead seemed to him a profanation of her memory.

However, this stubborn refusal of Cabuche's to admit a fact which was affirmed by more than one witness proved serious evidence against him. Obviously, the story of the prosecution made it self-evident that it was in his interests to hide the wild desires he had had for the unfortunate woman, whom he had been forced to slay, in order carnally to enjoy her. And when, bringing all the evidence together, the examining magistrate made his effort to wrest the truth from Cabuche by flinging in his face the culminating murder and rape, the man broke into a mad fury of protestation. He kill Madame Roubaud, he rape her? He, who respected that saintly little woman so? The gendarmes had to be called into the room to control him, for he suddenly declared he would wring the necks of the whole crowd of them.

In short, Cabuche was a very wild, dangerous type, a sullen monster whose very violence, breaking out at last, was in itself a confession of the crimes which he denied.

The enquiry had got so far, and the accused man had flown into a rage, shouting every time they returned to the murder that it was that other man, the mysterious man in flight, who had done it, when M. Denizet made a brilliant discovery which transformed the whole case and also revealed how important it was. As he always said, M. Denizet had a regular nose for things. Hence, guided by intuition, he decided a fresh search should be made of Cabuche's hut, and there, just behind a beam, what should he find but a hiding-place with some ladies' handkerchiefs and gloves, and under these a gold watch, which with a great surge of delight M. Denizet immediately recognized. It was Judge Grandmorin's watch, the watch he had previously searched for so diligently, a massive timepiece with two interlacing initials outside and inside the case the maker's number – 2516. M. Denizet was thunderstruck by his find. It illuminated the whole case. It tied up past and present, and when he pieced all the facts together, the logic of them was most fascinating. But the consequences threatened to be so far-reaching that first of all, without a word about the watch, he questioned Cabuche regarding the gloves and the handkerchiefs. For an instant, Cabuche had a full confession on the tip of his tongue, was about to admit that: yes, he idolized her, yes, he desired her too, yes, he loved to the point of kissing the garments she had worn, picking up or pinching behind her back little things she dropped, shoe-lace tags, safety-pins, ordinary pins. Then shame overcame him. He could not reveal his nakedness like that, and he was silent. And when the examining magistrate thought the moment had come to confront him with the watch, he merely stared at it in bewilderment. Of course he remembered the astonishment he had felt when he found that watch knotted into the corner of a handkerchief which he found under a bolster and thrust hastily into his pocket, to carry off as his booty, after which, there it stayed, while he racked his brains as to how to get it back to her. But whatever was the point of telling them all that? If he did, he would also have to confess to his other little thefts, such as that under-linen which smelt so wonderful, but of which he was ashamed.

Besides, they no longer believed anything he said. For that matter, he was himself beginning to lose his grasp of things. In his simple mind the whole world was now in an absolute tangle, turning into nightmare. He did not even get angry any more when they accused him of murdering her. In a permanent state of daze, he answered every question with: 'I don't know'. He knew nothing about the gloves or the handkerchiefs. He knew nothing about the watch. Why did they keep on pestering him? Why did they not let him be and guillotine him at once, without all this fuss?

The following day, M. Denizet ordered the arrest of Roubaud. He still lacked sufficient grounds against the A.S.M. but being as he was highly conscious of his absolute power in the matter, he issued the order for arrest in one of those inspired moments in which he was

342

convinced of his clairvoyant gifts. But despite the fact that there were still many things to clear up, he sensed that Roubaud was really the king-pin about which the two murders both turned, and he was indeed cock-a-hoop when he laid hands on a legal agreement which, only a week before acquiring Maufras Cross, Roubaud and Severine had made before the Havre notary public M. Colin, leaving the property 'to the survivor' of the two. From that instant, the whole story was automatically pieced together in M. Denizet's brain, and, moreover, with all the rigidity of logic, all the strength of the many pieces of evidence which lent the whole framework of the indictment such unshakeable solidity that the real truth must have seemed not merely less truthful beside it, but would even appear to be vitiated with all sorts of fantasy and illogicality. M. Denizet's story was that Roubaud was a coward who had twice lacked the courage himself to commit a murder, so had made use of that savage brute, Cabuche. The first time, aware of the clause in the will, he had been in a hurry to get Judge Grandmorin's legacy to his wife, and as he happened to be aware of the quarryman's hatred of the old man, he had put the knife into Cabuche's hand and at Rouen thrust him into Grandmorin's compartment. And, once the ten thousand francs had been shared out between them, no doubt the two accomplices would never have seen each other again, had it not been that the one murder inevitably led to the other. And it was here that the examining magistrate revealed that mastery of criminal psychology which was so much admired in him. Now he went so far as to maintain openly that he had of course kept his eye on Cabuche, being convinced that just as two added to two makes four, the first murder would lead to a second one.

Eighteen months had been all that were needed. The Roubaud household broke up, the husband spent his five thousand francs on gambling, while, being neglected, the wife went so far as to take a lover. No doubt she refused to sell Maufras Cross, from fear lest he squandered the money. In their continual quarrelling, she might even have threatened to denounce him to justice. But at least there was an ample sufficiency of witnesses to establish the complete break between the two, and that break had at long last led from the first crime to its sequel. Then Cabuche and his base lusts appeared on the scene, and in order to make quite sure of the ownership of that accursed house

343

which had already cost one human life, the husband, keeping well in the background, once again placed that knife in the other man's hand. And there you had the truth, the dazzling truth. Everything pointed that way – the watch found in the quarry-worker's hut, for instance, but most tellingly of all the fact that both the corpses revealed the same gash, wounds clearly made with the same knife – the one they found lying on the floor of the red room – wielded by the same hand, though it must be recorded that regarding this last little point the prosecution did express some doubt, for the gash in Grandmorin's throat would seem to have been made by a smaller and a sharper blade.

At first, Roubaud limited his answers to yes's and no's, uttered in that turgid, somnolent way in which he now invariably spoke. He had not seemed at all surprised to be arrested. By reason of the progressive decay of his very being, everything had become a matter of indifference to him. To get him to talk, he was given a cell companion, a stool pigeon with whom he played cards quite happily from morning to night. Of course, Roubaud was so far firmly convinced that Cabuche was the murderer, indeed, was the only man who could have been. Questioned about Jacques Lantier, he laughed and shrugged his shoulders, to make it quite clear that he knew all about the relations there had been between the engine-driver and his wife. But when, after having sounded him a little, M. Denizet at last came to unfolding the whole of his reconstruction of the crime, pressing him hard and finally charging him point blank with complicity, in the sudden shock of that accusation, seeing that they were very hot on his track, he became very wary. What stories were these they were telling him? He was not the man, it was of course that stone-worker who actually knifed the judge, just as he had knifed Severine, but yet he, Roubaud, was the real culprit, the other being merely his agent and instrument in both these deeds? This hypothetical tangle of crime staggered him and made him very suspicious indeed. It was suddenly plain to him that with this story they were merely setting a trap. They were putting forward this cock-and-bull yarn to provoke him into admitting his real part in the killing of Judge Grandmorin. Not for nothing had he from the outset been suspicious that all that was going to be raked over again.

Confronted with Cabuche, Roubaud declared that he did not know

344

the man at all. But when at this confrontation he added that this was the man whom he had found at the scene of the murder, red with blood, and on the point of violating his victim, the quarry-worker completely lost control of himself in his rage and there was a very violent scene, such a mix-up indeed that it complicated things still further. Three more days went by, while, convinced that these two men were accomplices and their mutual hatred no more than an act, M. Denizet cross-examined again and again. Wearying of it all, Roubaud for a time adopted the line of saying nothing at all to any question, and then, suddenly, his patience at last strained to the limit, he had to put an end to all this strain, so he yielded to the gnawing need which for months now had been working in him, and poured out the truth, nothing but the truth, the whole truth.

It so happened that on this particular day M. Denizet was fencing with his greatest subtlety. There he sat, at his desk, his eyes curtained by their heavy lids, his sensitive lips drawn to mere threads in his efforts to outwit. For a whole hour he had been treating that over-fleshed prisoner submerged in his sickly, sallow tissue to all the devices of his wily armoury of argument, for it was his conviction that beneath that cloak of superfluous fat he had to deal with a brain both wily and agile. And indeed, just as he thought he had sealed off every line of escape and at last got Roubaud in the bag, cornered, the man suddenly declared, with the gesture of a man who simply cannot stand any more, that he had had enough, he would rather make a clean breast than go on suffering that hell. Besides, he said, cunningly, if they were going to insist on making him guilty, he might at least be guilty of what he had really done. And then he told that endless story, his wife debauched by Grandmorin while still but a slip of a girl, how he had had a jealous brainstorm when he learned the filthy goings-on there had been, how he had then killed Grandmorin, and why he had taken the ten thousand francs. All this really did make M. Denizet begin to sit up. A frown of doubt puckered his forehead. M. Denizet's incredulity was irresistible, it was real professional incredulity, little by little, it twisted his lips into a sarcastic leer, till when Roubaud ended his version of what had happened M. Denizet was grinning openly. This rascal was certainly a tougher customer than he had estimated. This was certainly a bold stroke, taking the first murder on himself, but turning it into a pure *crime passionel*, thereby at one stroke absolving himself of premeditated robbery and above all of any complicity in the murder of his wife. It certainly did reveal both intelligence and a will quite above the ordinary. The only flaw, from Roubaud's standpoint, was the story would never hold water.

'Now, now, Roubaud,' said M. Denizet, 'you must not think we are babes in arms here. You want to make out that you were jealous, do you, and you committed the murder in a fit of jealousy?'

'Definitely.'

'So, if we accept your story, that would mean that you married your wife without any notion of the relations she had with the judge? Now, I ask you, is that really likely? On the contrary, in your circumstances everything would go to show that yours was a case of marriage by sheer calculation, you knew the whole story and you accepted everything. You got a girl brought up as a lady, she got her dowry, her protector became yours, you knew quite well too that he was leaving her a nice little house in the country, yet you would have us believe that you never suspected anything. No? Not a thing? Get away with you, Roubaud! Of course you knew all about it. That's the only possible explanation of your marriage. . . . Besides, there is one simple, obvious fact which alone is enough to dispose of your yarn. You are not at all a jealous man. Now, dare you maintain that you are?'

'I am telling the truth. I was in a frenzy of jealousy when I killed Grandmorin.'

'Very well. But perhaps after that you will explain how it was that, after killing the judge because of some vague liaison which was long past – and which in any case is sheer invention on your part – you were completely tolerant of your wife's having a paramour? I mean Jacques Lantier, of course. A tangible enough rascal, in all faith. I have been told about that liaison by everybody who knows you. Even you yourself have not concealed that you knew all about it. Yet you never once interfered in their goings-on. Now why?'

Pressed hard by this, Roubaud stared into space, with troubled eyes, and could find no answer. At last he stammered:

'I just don't know . . . I killed one, but I didn't kill the other.'

'Then don't tell me any more about being a jealous man having his revenge, nor do I advise you to tell the jury that story, they'll just

346

smile . . . Take my advice, Roubaud, change your tactics. Only the truth can help you.'

From that moment on, the more stubbornly Roubaud told his story, which did happen to be the truth, the more convinced was M. Denizet that it was a tissue of lies. And now everything turned against Roubaud, to such a point that the deposition he had made during the earlier investigation which should have supported his present one – since even in that he had denounced Cabuche – on the contrary turned into proof of the remarkably clever connivance between the two. With really professional enthusiasm, M. Denizet fined down the psychological interpretation of the case. Never, he maintained, had he probed deeper into the depths of human nature. There was more divination in all this than factual observation, but he prided himself on belonging to the school of dazzlingly clairvoyant investigators, who can see a man's inner workings at one glance. Besides, there was no lack of proofs. Indeed, there was a crushing assemblage of them. From now on, the preliminary enquiry rested on sure foundations. The certainty of it all was as dazzling as the sunlight.

What further added to M. Denizet's triumph was that when with such patience he had thus reconstituted it down to the most occult secrets of it, he presented the double case as one single tissue of indictment. After the brilliant success of the plebiscite, the country had been constantly racked by a fever suggestive of that lack of balance which precedes and heralds great catastrophes. In politics, and especially in the press, the French body politic in the last days of the Empire never knew a moment of calm. There was a constant state of high-tension in which even popular delight tended to assume an unhealthily savage form. Hence when it was learned that after the murder of a young woman in an isolated house at Maufras Cross the Rouen examining magistrate had drawn the earlier Grandmorin murder case out of the pigeon-hole in which it had been buried, and had connected it to the new crime, there was an outburst of triumph in the semi-official press. There had, it is true, all this time still been wisecracks from time to time in the opposition press about that legendary murderer whom the police could not discover, but who in reality was merely a dummy which they had invented to conceal the dirty dealings of 'certain highly-placed individuals' who were inculpated in the case. Now at last there was going to be a decisive answer to such allegations, for the murderer and his accomplice were under arrest and the memory of Judge Grandmorin was after all going to emerge unsullied. Fierce articles for and against once more filled the columns of the press, and as the days went by, tempers rose steadily, not only at Rouen, but in Paris too. Quite apart from the hold this frightful story of love and crime had on people's imaginations, men took sides fiercely as if when the truth were at last unshakeably revealed, this would consolidate the country. For a week the newspapers had been full of the details.

Then M. Denizet was summoned to Paris – to Ministry of Justice Secretary-General M. Camy-Lamotte's private residence, too. The Rouen examining magistrate found his superior standing erect in the centre of his sternly appointed study. M. Camy-Lamotte had grown thinner, was more fatigued. Indeed, he was on the downward grade, his sceptical mind the prey to depression, as if he sensed that this revelation of M. Denizet's was but a flash in the pan heralding the not far distant crash of the régime which he served. For the past two days he had been prey to an inner struggle. He still did not know what he was to do with Severine's letter, which he had kept, and which, by lending an irrefutable proof to Roubaud's story, would have ruined the whole structure of the indictment. Not a single person knew of the letter, and he could of course always destroy it. But only the day before, the Emperor had said that this time he insisted on justice pursuing its course, with no other influence interfering, even if that meant his Government suffering. This simple cry from the heart was perhaps only a superstitious notion that since the country had given him its support, a single miscarriage of justice might have a fateful influence on affairs. So although, having himself reduced the affairs of this world to a simple matter of mechanics, the Secretary-General was not encumbered in the same way by any twinges of conscience, he was nevertheless worried by the instructions given him, and wondered whether he really had any right to love his master to the point of disobeying him.

M. Denizet wasted no time, declaring his triumph.

'Well,' he cried, 'my nose did not deceive me after all, it was that fellow Cabuche who killed President Grandmorin . . . Though of course I do admit that there was something to be said for the other trail too, and I myself always felt there was certainly something fishy about the Roubaud business ... But now in the end we've nabbed them both.'

With colourless eyes, M. Camy-Lamotte stared hard at him.

'You mean, I take it, that all the facts outlined in the file you have sent me have their proofs, and your conviction is complete?'

'It is complete. There can be no doubt about it all ... Everything fits in. I cannot recall a case in which, despite certain surface complications, one crime followed more logical a course to its sequel, or one easier to anticipate.'

'But Roubaud won't have it, he takes the first murder on himself, but spins a yarn about his wife's virginity and himself mad with jealousy, killing in a blind frenzy – it's in all the opposition papers.'

'Agreed, they all of them carry that gossip, but not one dare go so far as believe in it. Jealous? This man Roubaud, who used to smooth the way for his wife's meetings with her paramour? Well, just let him tell a yarn like that to the jury, he'll never succeed in stirring up the sensation he wants ... It isn't as if he offered any proof. He hasn't got one. He certainly talks about a note which he says he made his wife write to Grandmorin, and says it ought to have been found among the judge's papers ... But you, sir, happen to be the man who has examined them, and you would surely have come upon any such note, would you not?'

M. Camy-Lamotte did not reply. The examining magistrate was right. With his version, the scandal about Grandmorin would at last really be given its quietus. Nobody would believe Roubaud, and the memory of Judge Grandmorin would be cleansed of disgusting suspicions. Such a much-publicized rehabilitation of one of its important figures would certainly serve the régime well. Further, seeing that in any case Roubaud confessed himself guilty of murder, what did it matter to ideal justice whether the man was condemned on the basis of this story or that? Of course, there did remain the case of Cabuche. But even if that defendant had not had a hand in the first murder, he certainly seemed to be the culprit of the second. And after all, good Heavens alive, what illusion more flimsy than that of justice? When the truth is overgrown with weeds and brambles, what self-deception it is to talk of absolute justice! Yes, it would be far

349

better for him to be sensible and bolster up this régime, so worn-out that at any minute it threatened to collapse altogether.

'Am I not right?' M. Denizet repeated. 'You have not come across the letter I mention, have you?'

Once again, M. Camy-Lamotte eyed M. Denizet keenly. Then, quite calmly, sole arbiter of the situation, he saddled his own conscience with the misgivings which had been worrying the Emperor and said:

'No, I have not. Not a trace of it.'

Then, smiling most amiably, he heaped praise on Rouen's examining magistrate, only the faintest of little twists at the corners of his mouth suggesting a sarcasm which he could not entirely suppress. Never, he said, had a judicial enquiry been conducted more penetratingly and – the matter had been decided at the very top – M. Denizet would be brought to Paris as Counsellor immediately after the forthcoming vacation. And with these words, the Secretary-General accompanied his visitor as far as the hall door.

'You are the only man who has seen through it all, and that is most praiseworthy . . . The moment the truth comes out, nothing can halt it, neither the interests of individuals nor any question of state expediency . . . Carry on, my dear sir, whatever be the consequences, let the matter follow its course.'

'You could not have expressed the duty of an examining magistrate more finely,' was M. Denizet's conclusion, as he took his leave, all smiles.

Alone, the first thing M. Camy-Lamotte did was to light a candle. Then from the drawer where he had tucked it away, he took Severine's note. The candle burned up brightly. He unfolded the little sheet of paper and could not help running through its two brief lines again. They brought back to his memory that dainty criminal, that little woman with periwinkle-blue eyes who had once stirred such warmth in his heart. Now, she was dead, and she seemed a tragic figure. Who knew what secret she had taken to the grave with her? Yes, there was no doubt, truth and justice were most illusory. All that remained for him of that delightful little woman whom he had never known was memory of the momentary desire to possess her which came to him in a moment in which her fingers touched his, a desire which he had never consummated. And as he brought the slip of paper into the candle-flame, and it flared up, he felt very, very sad, full of presentiments of misfortune, and wondered what good he was doing, destroying this proof and burdening his conscience with this act, if it was after all fated for the Empire to be swept away like the frail flutter of black ash which, an instant later, broke feebly from his fingers?

In less than a week, M. Denizet had completed the judicial enquiry. The Western Railway Company was most obliging, furnishing all the papers he needed and all the evidence. After all, it was in the Company's interest to see the matter ended, seeing that it involved this shocking life-story of one of its senior men, a story which, through the complex gearing of the Company's organism, had all but caused chaos in the Board of Directors itself. It behove them as rapidly as possible to cut off the gangrenous limb. Hence it was that once again all the staff of Havre station had filed through M. Denizet's chambers. M. Dabadie, Moulin and all the others had given their evidence and added to the disastrous details concerning Roubaud's ill conduct. Next came the Barentin station-master, M. Bessière, and a number of men of the Rouen station staff, whose evidence was of decisive importance regarding the first murder, then M. Vandorpe, the Paris station-master, Maufras Cross gate-keeper Misard and leading guard Henri Dauvergne, the last two being most positive regarding the accused man's complaisance regarding Lantier and his wife. Dauvergne indeed went so far as to assert that while Severine was looking after him at Maufras Cross he had one evening heard Roubaud and Cabuche plotting together under his window, a piece of evidence which explained a great deal and made hay of the assertion of the two defendants that they did not even know each other. Throughout the Company's staff the second murder had excited a cry of horror, together with touching expressions of regret regarding both unfortunate victims, that poor young woman whose peccadilloes had so much to excuse them and so grand an old man as M. Grandmorin, whose name was now completely washed clean of the ugly stories once told about him.

However, the new trial above all else revived the fierce feelings of Grandmorin's family, and though in one way M. Denizet found in them additional powerful allies, he also had to fight a stiff battle against them to keep his indictment together. The Lachesnayes were jubilant with victory. Outraged by the Maufras Cross legacy, in their vulgar greed, they had always maintained that Roubaud was guilty. Hence, when the Grandmorin murder came up again, they saw in it merely an opportunity for challenging the will, and as the only way of getting that quashed was to strike at Severine and demonstrate her unworthiness, they subscribed to part of Roubaud's story, and made her out to be his accomplice, assisting him in the murder, but not at all in order to avenge an imaginary injury, merely to rob him. Hence the examining magistrate found himself at loggerheads with them, particularly with Berthe, who was so vicious about the murdered woman who once had been her friend that she laid abominable charges at her door, whereas M. Denizet took Severine's part, and hotly too, quite indignantly, the moment anybody questioned his masterpiece, namely, this fabric of logic which, as he himself declared with an air of pride, was so well put together, that if you removed a single link, the rest of it fell to the ground.

There was one very lively meeting between the Lachesnayes and Madame Bonnehon about this in M. Denizet's chambers. Though once inclined towards the Roubauds, Madame Bonnehon had now been obliged to give up her support of the husband, but she continued to take Severine's part. This she did from a sort of sentimental complicity, for of course she had a constitutional weakness for charm and a great lover, and she was indeed genuinely upset by the tragic, blood-stained end of that romantic young woman. She was also most outspoken in her scorn for the Lachesnayes' money-grubbing. She could not understand how her niece had the face to raise that legacy question again. Besides, if Severine was to be made out guilty, why, that was to accept Roubaud's story in its entirety, and thereby sully Grandmorin's memory again. Had not M. Denizet's indictment established the truth so ingeniously, they would have been obliged to invent it, merely for the sake of honour of the family. And she went on to speak with some bitterness of Rouen society, where the case was making such a stir, for now that age was overtaking her and she was losing even that opulent blonde beauty of an elderly goddess, she no longer reigned supreme in Rouen's drawing rooms. Why, only yesterday again, at Madame Leboucq's – the salon of the Counsellor's wife, the tall, elegant brunette who had dethroned Madame Bonnehon – there had been a lot of whispering round of salacious anecdotes about the judge, everything that malicious tongues were inventing, including the case of Louisette. And when at this point M. Denizet intervened to inform Madame Bonnehon that M. Leboucq would be on the bench as assessor at the forthcoming assizes, the Lachesnayes said no more, but seemed to give way, though they were very worried. Madame Bonnehon however reassured them and said that justice would certainly be done, for the presiding judge would be her old friend, M. Desbazeilles, the man whose arthritis now limited him to mere memories of former love-making, while the other assessor was to be M. Chaumette, father of the young deputy prosecutor whom Madame Bonnehon had taken under her wing. So her mind was at rest, even though, when she mentioned the latter name, a sad smile tinged her lips, for latterly the son had been seen at Madame Leboucq's – indeed, she had insisted herself on his going, so as not to hamper his career.

When at last the notorious trial came on, the rumour of imminent war, which was shaking the whole of France, tended to muffle the publicity. Nonetheless, Rouen had three feverish days, with a tremendous crush at the entrance to the Law Courts, the reserved seats invaded by the city's society ladies. Never, since it was turned into the Law Courts, had the former palace of the dukes of Normandy seen such crowds. It was early in July, and the afternoons were sunshiny and warm, the brilliant rays setting fire to the stained glass of the ten big windows and flooding with brilliant light the carved oak benches, the alabaster crucifix standing out against the smocked red tapestry, the famous Louis XII ceiling with its divisions of gilded wood-carving, the gold of which was so old and soft to the eye. People were stifled even before proceedings began. Women reached up to peer at the exhibits on the table – Grandmorin's watch, Severine's blood-stained under-garment, and the knife which had been used in the two murders. Cabuche's defence counsel, a Paris barrister, was also the cynosure of many eyes. On the jury benches was the row of twelve burghers of Rouen, buttoned tight into their black frock coats, obese and solemn. And when the bench entered there was such a pressing forward throughout the standing general public that the Chairman of the Bench was at once obliged to threaten to have the court cleared.

At last, the trial began, the jurors took the oath, and waves of

353

curiosity ran through the general public as one by one the witnesses were called. At the names of Madame Bonnehon and M. de Lachesnaye, a wave fluttered the serried ranks of the onlookers' heads. It was, however, Jacques who excited the ladies the most. They simply could not take their eyes off him. Nor, since they first appeared, a gendarme on either side of each of them, had many people ceased staring at the two defendants and remarks were whispered one to another about them. The general opinion was that they were savage, sordid creatures. A couple of ruffians, in fact. Roubaud, in a dark waistcoat and a loosely-knotted neck scarf, in the style of a carefree gentleman, surprised everybody by looking so aged, his countenance bewildered and flabby with fat. Cabuche, on the other hand, was just as they had imagined him. He had on a lengthy workman's blue blouse, and was the classical murderer type, with massive fists and the jaws of a flesh-eater, in short, one of those rascally types whom one would prefer not to come upon in a lonely wood. Moreover, the cross-examination confirmed this bad impression, for some answers excited very lively comment. To all the questions put by the Chairman of the Bench, Cabuche replied that he did not know. Why had he let the real murderer escape? He did not know. Nevertheless, he stuck to that story of a mysterious unknown man, and said he had heard him bounding away through the darkness. Then, questioned regarding his bestial passion for the unfortunate victim, he began to stammer, and had such a sudden fit of violent anger that the gendarmes guarding him took him by the arms. No, no, he did not love her in the least, he did not desire her, that was all lies, he would have thought it was sullying her merely to want her, she being a lady and he a man who lived wild, all by himself, and had been to prison. Eventually he calmed down, but then fell into gloomy silence, his answers becoming mere monosyllables, showing him indifferent to the danger of the death sentence in which he stood.

Similarly, Roubaud stuck to what the prosecution called 'his elaboration'. He related how and why he had killed Grandmorin and denied any part in the murder of his wife, but all this in broken phrases which were scarcely coherent, with sudden losses of memory, his eyes so uneasy and his voice so thick that at times he seemed to be thinking out details and inventing them. And when the Chairman of the Bench pointed out to him the absurdities of his story, he ended

354

up by shrugging his shoulders and refusing to say anything at all. Why tell the truth when it was a fabrication which was logical?

It was this attitude of pugnacious scorn of the law which did Roubaud the most harm. Another thing which struck people was the profound lack of interest which the two defendants had in one another. That certainly looked like the proof of a previous understanding between them, a cunning scheme carried through with tremendous strength of will. They made out that they did not know one another at all, and if one charged the other, that was merely to confuse the court.

When the cross-examinations of the accused were complete, the case was a clear one, so skilfully had the Chairman of the Bench conducted it, so that, tumbling as they had done into the traps offered them, both Roubaud and Cabuche would seem to have condemned themselves. On this first day a few further witnesses of no importance were examined. The heat had become so unbearable that towards five o'clock two ladies fainted.

The following day, however, there was tremendous excitement about the examination of certain witnesses. Madame Bonnehon made a great hit with the nobility of her bearing and her tact. The Western Railway Company men, Vandorpe, Bessière, Dabadie and particularly Cauche, were heard with interest, the latter being quite verbose, relating how he had got to know Roubaud very well, since he had 'often had a game of piquet with him' at the Café du Commerce. Henri Dauvergne repeated his incriminating evidence, his almost complete certainty that while still drowsy with fever he had heard the two defendants making their arrangements, while, interrogated regarding Severine, he proved most discreet, indicating that he had certainly loved her, but, knowing her to be the lover of another, had loyally taken a back seat. Thus when that other man, Jacques Lantier, was called at last, there arose a great buzz of excitement in court, some standing up, to see him better. Even among the jury the eager interest was patent. Very calm, Jacques, with the occupational gesture of an engine-driver putting up his hands to drive his locomotive, rested his hands on the rail of the witness stand. This appearance at the trial as witness, which should have caused him considerable worry, left him entirely lucid, as if it was all nothing whatever to do with him. He gave his evidence like a stranger, a man innocent of anything. Since the murder he had known no return of his old trouble, never even gave a thought to such things. The memory of it was obliterated, he was in a state of perfect bodily and mental balance and health. Even here at the witness stand he was devoid of remorse or scruple, completely indifferent about it all. The moment he took his stand he gave Roubaud and Cabuche a clear-eyed glance. The first he knew to be guilty, but he gave him a little nod, a discreet little greeting, without giving a thought to the fact that today he was publicly branded as the lover of the man's dead wife. The other man, the innocent one, whose place he should be occupying, he gave a smile. For under Cabuche's ruffianly appearance the man was a decent brute, he had seen the rascal at work and had then shaken his hand. And so, utterly at his ease, he gave his evidence, replying in precise little phrases to the questions which the Chairman of the Bench put to him. After having interrogated him very extensively indeed on his relationship with the victim, the judge had him recount how he left Maufras Cross, a few hours before the murder, taking the train at Barentin and spending the night at Rouen. Cabuche and Roubaud listened and by their very attitude confirmed what he said, and in this moment an inexpressible melancholy hovered over all three men. There was a deathly silence in court, and an emotion of which they did not know the origin constricted the breathing of every juryman. To the question of the Chairman of the Bench as to what he thought of the unknown murderer, mentioned by the quarryman, who vanished in the darkness, Jacques, as if anxious not to incriminate the defendant, merely made a gesture expressive of an open mind.

There then occurred something which finally shattered everybody in court – tears appeared in Jacques' eyes. They brimmed over, and the tears trickled down his cheeks. Severine had just appeared before his mind's eye, just as she had done more than once already, pitiable little murdered woman whose image was for ever imprinted in his soul, with enormously staring blue eyes and black hair standing on end in absolute horror on her forehead. He still loved her desperately, and now he was suddenly engulfed in a tremendous wave of sorrow and wept copiously, oblivious of his crime, oblivious too of where he was, in the public court. A number of ladies were so moved by this scene that they too burst into sobs. They found this sorrow of the lover, while the husband remained so dry-eyed, most moving. The

356

Chairman of the Bench, having asked defending counsel if he had any question to put to the witness, these lawyers thanked him and said: no, and the stupefied defendants followed Jacques with their eyes while amid general sympathy he withdrew and found a seat in the body of the court.

The third day was entirely taken up by the speech of the State Prosecutor and the pleas of the lawyers. First, the Chairman of the Court summed up and under the guise of absolute impartiality underlined the charges of the indictment. Next came the State Prosecutor, who usually spoke with more conviction and a less hollow persuasiveness. This shortcoming was put down to the heat, which was really terrible. Cabuche's defending counsel, the Paris barrister, was on the contrary most satisfying, though not convincing. Roubaud's counsel, a distinguished member of the Rouen bar, also made the very utmost he could of a poor case. The Public Prosecutor, being tired, hardly said anything in reply. And when the jury retired to consider their verdict, it was only six o'clock, and broad daylight was pouring in through the ten windows, a last ray of direct sunlight lighting the arms of the towns of Normandy which decorate the transoms. A great hubbub of voices rose under the ancient gilded ceiling and the standing public began to press impatiently against the iron railings which separated them from the remainder of the court. The silence however became religious when the jury returned and the bench appeared. The verdict admitted attenuating circumstances and the bench condemned the two men to hard labour for life. This was a great *contretemps*. While the crowd bustled noisily out, a number of whistles of disapproval were to be heard, as if it were a theatre.

That same evening, all Rouen was talking about the sentence, and there were endless commentaries. The general opinion was that it was a rebuff for Madame Bonnehon and the Lachesnayes. Only the death sentence, surely, would have satisfied Grandmorin's relations, and it was clear that adverse influences had been at work. People were already whispering the name of Madame Leboucq, who had three or four trusties on the jury. No doubt the attitude of her husband, as assessor, was in no way incorrect, but at the same time people thought they had noticed that neither the other assessor, M. Chaumette, nor the Chairman of the Bench himself, M. Desbazeilles, had been masters of the trial to the extent that might have

357

been desirable. Or was it merely that the jury when it suggested attenuating circumstances had had genuine misgivings and had given way to the disturbing dubiety which certainly at one stage had swept through the court, a single silent flight of the dismal truth. In the upshot, however, the case as a whole remained the triumph of the examining magistrate, M. Denizet, whose masterpiece of reconstruction had proved unassailable. Besides, the Grandmorin relations lost much sympathy when the news got round that in an attempt to get Maufras Cross back M. de Lachesnaye, in flagrant contempt for the law, was actually talking of instituting an action for quashing the will, despite the death of the legator, all most surprising in a magistrate.

When he left the Law Courts, Jacques was joined by Philomène, who had been one of the witnesses called, and she simply would not let him go, being all desire to spend the night with him at Rouen. He was not due back on duty till the following day, and was quite ready to give her dinner in the inn near the station where he made out that he had spent the night of the crime, but he was certainly not going to spend the night there, he told her, he absolutely had to take the 0.25 A.M. train back to Paris.

'You didn't notice,' she said, as she went her way on his arm to the inn, 'but I could swear that just now I saw somebody we know. . . . Yes, Pecqueux, though only the other day he told me he wasn't going to make the effort to come here for this trial . . . I had just turned round and I saw a man's back vanishing in the crowd. . . .'

Jacques shrugged his shoulders.

'Pecqueux is in Paris,' he said, 'taking good advantage of the freedom my day off has given him, having a booze.'

'Perhaps you're right . . . All the same, we'd better be on our guard, because he's the roughest of brutes when he's wild.'

She pressed close to him, then she glanced back again.

'Do you know who that is, following us?'

'Yes, don't worry yourself. He may have something to ask me.'

It was Misard who had indeed been following them all the way from Jews Street. He too had given evidence, in his somnolent way, and afterwards had stayed behind, hovering round Jacques, hesitant about putting to him a question which was on the tip of his tongue. When Jacques and Philomène entered the inn, he followed, and ordered a glass of wine.

'Why, is that you, Misard?' cried Jacques. 'And how goes it, eh, with the new missus?'

'All right,' grunted the crossing watchman. 'The bitch, she certainly got me on the hook, I can tell you. I told you all about it last time we came, didn't I?'

The story had certainly amused Jacques greatly. Ducloux, the trollop of a former scivvy whom Misard had taken on to look after the crossing barrier, soon realized, from seeing him rooting about in every corner, that he must be searching for some hoarded money, so she had a brilliant idea for getting him to marry her – by the things she did not say and her sly laughs, she gave Misard the idea that she had actually found Phasie's thousand francs. Misard was at first almost on the point of strangling her, then, on reflection that that would not get him those thousand francs, he turned very nice and wheedling to her, but she still kept him at arm's length and would not even let him touch her – not, at least, till she was his wife, when he could have it all, she hinted, her body and the money too. So Misard did marry her, and after that she made a regular mock of him, telling him what an idiot he was to believe everything he was told. The best of it all, however, was that when she did learn all about the money she was infected with greed for it too and after that searched as much as Misard did and just as frantically. But someday they would find those francs, now there were two of them on it. And they worked hard at their search.

'Still no luck?' asked Jacques, tauntingly. 'Isn't the new missus much help?'

With a hard look, Misard at last said:

'You know where they are, tell me.'

Then the engine-driver got ratty.

'I know nothing whatsoever about it. Aunt Phasie never gave me anything. I hope you're not going to start saying I took the money.'

'Bah! I don't doubt that. Of course she didn't give you a penny. But you can see how it worries me! Look here, though, Jacques, if you do know where that money is, you might tell me.'

'You shut your trap! Look out I don't talk too much. You look in the salt-box, see if it's there.'

Pale, his eyes burning, Misard went on staring. Then his eyes flashed.

'The salt-box,' he cried. 'By God, what an idea! Under that drawer there's a snug little place I haven't tried.'

He quickly paid for his wine and hurried off to the station, to see if he could catch the 7.10 P.M. He was never tired of searching the little cottage.

Later, after dinner, waiting for the 0.25 A.M. train, Philomène tried to get Jacques to walk out with her through dark narrow alleys into the open country. It was a very sultry mid-July night, stuffy and moonless, which brought heavy sighs from him and seemed to cling to his neck. Twice Philomène thought she heard footsteps behind her, and turned round without seeing anybody in the darkness.

Jacques was finding this storm-charged air very troublesome. During dinner, despite the calm equilibrium he now felt, he had sensed a faint return of his old disorder, every time this woman's constantly fidgeting hands had touched his. No doubt it was only tiredness, or came from the electrified air. But all at once the stress of sexual longing flared up more vividly in him. As he thus held her close to his body, he became prey to a dull alarm. But yet he was so thoroughly cured, was he not? He had found out what killing womanflesh was like, and he had already possessed this woman too, sexually, just to find out what happened to him, but so far his flesh had remained under control. Yet now he became so worked up that fear of an attack of the murder impulse would have made him escape from her arms, had the night which enveloped her not been so pitch-dark. And suddenly, as they passed by a greensward in a deserted lane, and she drew him towards it, and stretched up against him, the monstrous longing all came back to him, his frenzy took charge of him and he groped wildly in the grass for any weapon, were it but a big stone, to crash down on her skull. Then, forcing himself free, he took to his heels in dismay. Suddenly, he caught the sound of a man shouting, and a squabble going on at his back.

'Ah, you tart! I waited to the last moment, I wanted just to be sure.'

'It's not true, let me go!'

'Oh, not true, is it? Let him run, I know who it was, I'll get him yet . . . Look here, you bloody tart, you dare tell me again it isn't true!'

Jacques raced through the night, but not in flight from Pecqueux, whom he had of course recognized, but, mad with grief, from himself.

He had reason to be so, too. One killing had not been sufficient,

Severine's blood had not satisfied him as he had still believed, so few hours since. It was to be another, then another, and yet another. First he would satiate himself, then would follow a few weeks' torpidity, after that the terrible hunger came back and he was for ever and ever to need the flesh of a woman to satisfy him. And now he did not even need to see the naked flesh to have the craving, it was enough to feel the woman warm in his arms, and he was swept into this heat of murder, the maddened, female-eviscerating male. It was the end for him. Before him there lay nothing but inky night, despair without light, and into this he fled.

The days passed. Jacques had resumed duty, but avoided his fellow drivers and firemen, sinking back into the strained, hermitlike life he had led before. After stormy sittings in the Chamber, war had just been declared and there had already been a small frontier skirmish, successful, so the news said. For a week now troop transports had been wearing down railway personnel with overwork. Regular services were all at sea and continual unscheduled trains made all others very late, not to speak of the mobilization of leading drivers to speed up the concentration of army units. It was thus that at Havre one evening, instead of his usual express, Jacques was detailed to drive a monster train of eighteen waggons, packed with soldiers.

That evening, Pecqueux turned up at the sheds very drunk. The day after the occasion when he caught Philomène and Jacques together, he had rejoined locomotive No. 608 with Jacques, but had never made the slightest reference to the incident, only went about very morose, as if afraid to look his chief in the face. Jacques became increasingly aware of a spirit of insubordination in Pecqueux, who now met any instruction with a surly grunt and was loth to obey. They had indeed completely stopped talking to each other. The footplate, that little deck which formerly had carried them as a united team of two, was now merely a narrow, dangerous piece of sheet iron on which their rivalry came to collision. Their mutual detestation increasing steadily, they were on the point of mutual destruction on those few square feet flying through the air at top speed, and from which the least jolt might send them flying. And this particular evening, seeing Pecqueux intoxicated, Jacques took great care of him, for though he knew Pecqueux to be too dour to lose his temper when he was sober, he knew equally well that alcohol set the brute in him free.

The train was to have left at six, but was held up. It was already dark when the soldiers were loaded like sheep into the cattle-trucks, in which rough planking had been roughly installed to provide seating for them. They were piled in as thickly as they could be squeezed, till they were packed one on top of the other, some seated, others on their feet, unable as much as to lift their arms. As soon as they got to Paris, another train was waiting, to take them to the Rhine. They were already worn out with fatigue and bewildered by this transport, but as there had been an issue of brandy and many of them had also paid calls to local wine and spirit merchants, they were all coarsely enlivened, red faced, eyes staring, and as soon as the train started off with a jolt, they began bawling songs.

Suddenly, Jacques cast a glance at the sky, and saw that a stormlike mass of cloud had hidden the stars. It was a very dark night and not a breath stirred the suffocating atmosphere. Even the air rushing past them, usually so fresh, seemed tepid. The only lights on the black skyline were the bright sparks of the signal lights. He built up pressure to climb the long up-gradient from Harfleur to Saint-Romain. Though he had been studying her for weeks now, he was still not quite master of locomotive 608. She was too new, and the whims and peculiarities of her youth frequently astonished him. This night in particular, he felt her crotchety, whimsical and ready to bolt the moment she had a little too much coal inside her. So he kept his hand on the speed regulator and at the same time watched the fire keenly, for the bearing of his fireman was worrying him more and more. The little light which lit the water level left the platform in half-darkness, which the red-hot fire-box door turned purplish. He could scarcely see Pecqueux, but twice he had thought he felt something brush by his legs, just as if somebody had tried to trip him up. But he put this down to merely a tipsy man's clumsiness. Above the din he could hear Pecqueux laughing raucously as he smashed his coal with savage blows of the hammer, then assailed it with the shovel. Every few minutes, the man flung open the fire-box door and pitched in foolishly large quantities of fuel.

'That'll do!' cried Jacques, at last.

Pecqueux pretended not to hear, and went on shovelling the fuel in, and when Jacques grabbed his arm, he swung round, threateningly, in the rising savagery of his drink, ready for the quarrel he wanted to pick.

'Hands off, or I'll fetch you one!' he cried. 'It suits me all right, going fast does!'

The train was at the moment bowling along at top speed over the level stretch between Bolbec and Motteville. It was scheduled to run straight to Paris without a stop, except where necessary to take in water. The enormous mass of it, eighteen trucks packed with human cattle, swept through the black countryside with a continuous roar, and these men thus being transported to massacre were singing at the top of their voices, so loudly that their bawling overpowered even the din of the wheels.

With his foot, Jacques swung the fire-box door to. Then adjusting the injector, and restraining himself, he said:

'She's over-fired already ... Sleep it off, man, if you're sozzled.'

In a flash, Pecqueux had the door open again and in a fury began shovelling in still more coal, as if out to blow locomotive No. 608 to smithereens. It was sheer rebellion, orders disregarded, a brainstorm with never a thought now about all the human lives at their mercy. Jacques bent down and lowered the grid control, to reduce the draught. In that instant, with sudden tackle, both arms about him, Pecqueux seized him and began trying to heave him right off the foot-plate, on to the track.

'So that's it, is it, you scoundrel? And you could say I fell out, you cunning bastard!'

He had managed to catch hold of the side of the tender. They both slithered on their constricted deck, the steel plates dancing dangerously under their feet as they wrestled silently, their teeth grinding, each trying to heave the other through the narrow cab doorway, which as only protection had a single bar across it. It was no easy task. Fed to the full, the locomotive rushed on and on. They swept through Barentin and plunged into Malaunay tunnel, still at death grips, backs straining against the coals, heads banging against the water-cistern, trying to avoid the red-hot fire-box door, which scorched their legs every time they stretched out.

For a moment, Jacques thought he might be able to raise himself up enough to shut off steam, to bring help and get free from this lunatic, out of his mind through drink and jealousy. For, being the

363

smaller man, he was beginning to lose strength, knew there was already no hope of throwing Pecqueux off. He was already beaten. He felt his hair rise on his head as the fear of falling swept through him. But as he made a supreme effort, and felt out with one hand, the other guessed what he was at and with iron grip on Jacques' haunches, suddenly lifted him off the ground as if he had been a little child.

'Ouf! Think you'll stop her, do you? . . . Take my woman, would you? . . . Come on, come on, now you're going to get it!'

The locomotive rushed on and on. The train burst noisily out of the tunnel and swept through the grim, bleak countryside. They dashed through Malaunay station at such speed that the A.S.M. on the platform there did not even see the two men destroying each other on the moving thunderbolt.

Then, with a final effort, Pecqueux flung Jacques out, but, just as Jacques felt space round him, in his desperation he succeeded in clutching at Pecqueux's neck, so convulsively that he dragged his murderer down with him. A double wild cry, voices of murderer and murdered confused in one, broke against the wind and was dispersed into nothingness. They fell together and as these two men, who so long had been like two brothers, went down, the draught of the train drew them in under the wheels, to be cut up, chopped into pieces, still laced together in a terrible embrace. Their bodies were afterwards found headless, legless, two bleeding trunks, with arms still enlaced one about the other, in suffocating grasp.

Devoid of control, the locomotive continued its wild rush through the night. At last this frisky, self-willed young thing, like a young, unbroken mare escaping from her rider, could indulge all the unchecked frenzy of her adolescence and gallop at will across the open land. The boiler was topped with water, the fire-box was roaring wildly, full of coal, and for the next half hour pressure rose madly and the speed became terrifying. The guard must have fallen asleep, worn out with fatigue, no doubt. And as being herded together body to body like that made the wine go to the soldiers' heads still more, this wild plunge of the train at reckless speed made them crazy with excitement and they yelled their songs at the top of their voices. They swept through Maromme at lightning speed, but their whistle no longer sounded as they came up to signals or rushed through stations. It was the all-out gallop of a maddened wild animal which rushes, head down, blindly at any obstacle. On and on rushed locomotive 608, as if the stridency of her own infuriated breathing made her yet madder still.

At Rouen they were supposed to halt to take in water, and the station hands were aghast when between the platforms they saw her flash through in a dizzy whirl of smoke, a train insane, a locomotive without either driver or fireman, and eighteen cattle-trucks cram-full of soldiers yelling patriotic ditties. They were going crazily to the war. This speed was merely to bring them more quickly to the shores of the Rhine. The men in the stations they passed through gaped and waved their arms. The general alarm went up. Out of all control, this runaway train would never get through Sotteville without meeting some obstacle. Sotteville was always in the throes of shunting, waggons and locomotives all over the place, for Sotteville was one of France's railway towns. And they rushed to the telegraph to warn Sotteville, just in time to have a goods train on the track shunted to a siding. Men were everywhere waiting for it, and, ears alert, caught its roar before it came near. Twice, outside Rouen, it plunged into tunnels, twice it emerged again, at wild gallop, a terrible, uncheckable force which nothing now could stop. Like wildfire it reached Sotteville, and without harm roared its path among obstacles to plunge again, a roar gradually receding, on into darkness.

By now the telegraph was busy all down the line. Hearts pounded with alarm when men heard the news of this ghost train seen flying through Rouen, through Sotteville, towards Paris. There was general fear. In front of it ran the regular express, into which this mad thing would crash. Like a wild boar through the forest it swept on its course, regardless of fog signals or red signal lights. At Oisel it all but crashed a shunting engine. Its speed apparently undiminished, it terrified Pont-de-l'Arche. And again it vanished into the night, rushing on and on, no man knew whither.

What matter the victims which that locomotive might crush in its tracks! Was it not itself plunging on into the future? So why care about blood spilt? Driverless in the darkness, blind, deaf beast let loose among death, on it rushed, packed to the full with cannonflesh, with soldiers now stupid with fatigue, in drunken song.

365

The world's greatest novelists now available in Triad/Panther Books

Aldous Huxley

Brave New World	£1.95	☐
Island	£1.95	☐
After Many a Summer	£1.95	☐
Brief Candles	£1.95	☐
The Devils of Loudun	£1.95	☐
Eyeless in Gaza	£2.50	☐
Antic Hay	£1.95	☐
Crome Yellow	£1.50	☐
Point Counter Point	£1.95	☐
Those Barren Leaves	£1.95	☐
The Genius and the Goddess	£1.95	☐
Time Must Have a Stop	£2.50	☐
The Doors of Perception/ Heaven and Hell (non-fiction)	£1.95	☐
The Human Situation (non-fiction)	£1.95	☐
Grey Eminence (non-fiction)	£1.95	☐
Brave New World Revisited (non-fiction)	£1.95	☐
The Gioconda Smile and other stories	£2.50	☐
Ape and Essence	£1.95	☐

Hermann Hesse

Stories of Five Decades	£2.50	☐
Journey to the East	£1.95	☐
Demian	£1.95	☐
Pictor's Metamorphoses	£1.95	☐
My Belief (non-fiction)	£1.25	☐
Reflections (non-fiction)	95p	☐
Hermann Hesse: A Pictorial Biography	£1.50	☐

To order direct from the publisher just tick the titles you want and fill in the order form.

TF181

All these books are available at your local bookshop or newsagent, or can be ordered direct from the publisher..

To order direct from the publisher just tick the titles you want and fill in the form below.

Name _____

Address _____

_____

Send to:
Panther Cash Sales
PO Box 11, Falmouth, Cornwall TR10 9EN.

Please enclose remittance to the value of the cover price plus:

UK 45p for the first book, 20p for the second book plus 14p per copy for each additional book ordered to a maximum charge of £1.63.

BFPO and Eire 45p for the first book, 20p for the second book plus 14p per copy for the next 7 books, thereafter 8p per book.

Overseas 75p for the first book and 21p for each additional book.

Panther Books reserve the right to show new retail prices on covers, which may differ from those previously advertised in the text or elsewhere.